W9-CAM-472

Praise for the *October Daye* Novels

"The brisk pacing, the effective mix of human and magical characters, and the PI ambience all make this an excellent choice for fans of Butcher's Harry Dresden series.... Toby's unusual heritage and her uneasy relationships with her mother's family will remind readers of Brigg's Mercy Thompson series, and Thompson fans will appreciate Toby's tough and self-reliant character. This outstanding first novel is a must for fans of genre-bending blends of crime and fantasy." —*Booklist* starred review

"McGuire successfully blends Robert B. Parker-like detective fiction with love and loss, faith and betrayal—and plenty of violence.... *Rosemary and Rue* will have readers clamoring for the next genre-bending installment."

—www.bookpage.com

"Well researched, sharply told, highly atmospheric and as brutal as any pulp detective tale ... sure to appeal to fans of Jim Butcher or Kim Harrison." —*Publishers Weekly*

"October Daye is as gritty and damaged a heroine as Kinsey Millhone or Kay Scarpetta ... an engaging narrator who promises to sustain as long a series as McGuire might wish to write.... Toby's nocturnal existence is full of the kind of shadows that keep the pages turning. Changelings, like all faerie folk, live long; may McGuire and these novels do the same."

—*The Onion A.V. Club*

"Second in an urban fantasy detective series featuring a resourceful female detective, this sequel to *Rosemary and Rue* should appeal to fans of Jim Butcher's *Dresden Files* as well as the novels of Charlaine Harris, Patricia Briggs, and similar authors." —*Library Journal*

"It's fun watching [Toby] stick doggedly to the case as the killer picks off more victims and the tension mounts."

—*Locus*

"A gripping, well-paced read. Toby continues to be an enjoyable, if complex and strong-willed protagonist who recognizes no authority but her own. McGuire has more than a few surprises up her sleeve for the reader."

—*Romantic Times Book Review* (4 Stars)

**DAW Books Presents Seanan McGuire's
October Daye Novels:**

ROSEMARY AND RUE

A LOCAL HABITATION

AN ARTIFICIAL NIGHT

LATE ECLIPSES

ONE SALT SEA
(September 2011)

SEANAN McGUIRE

LATE ECLIPSES

AN OCTOBER DAYE NOVEL

DAW BOOKS, INC.

DONALD A. WOLLHEIM, FOUNDER

375 Hudson Street, New York, NY 10014

ELIZABETH R. WOLLHEIM
SHEILA E. GILBERT
PUBLISHERS

http://www.dawbooks.com

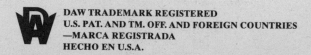

This book is for Amy.
Everyone should have a fiddler at the crossroads.

ACKNOWLEDGMENTS:

Late Eclipses is the fourth of Toby's adventures. You'd think it would be getting easier, right? I sure did. But the fact of the matter is, books remain a lot of work, no matter how many of them you write, and making them worth reading is the work of many hands. For me, those many hands begin with the faithful Machete Squad, a tireless team of heavily-armed and merciless editors who go through every chapter a dozen times before it becomes ready for prime time. Without them, I would be in a lot of trouble. Special thanks to Jennifer Midkiff, for scrupulous editorial attentions, and to Melissa Glasser, for being my "on-call vet" for weird questions about fae biology. Also, thanks to everyone at the Ohio Valley Filk Festival, who tolerantly allowed me to do copyedits during open filking.

On the publishing side of things, my agent, Diana Fox, saved my sanity and my sense of narrative on several occasions, all while continuing to rock like the superhero she is, and my editor, Sheila Gilbert, offered support, critique, and everything else a girl could possibly want. The rest of the team at DAW was just as fabulous, although special thanks go to Joshua Starr, who puts up with most of my random mid-week questions. Chris McGrath provided my fantastic cover, and Tara O'Shea provided my fantastic interior dingbat. I seriously could not have done this without them.

Here at home, my website was programmed and designed by Chris Mangum and Tara O'Shea, who gamely rose to every challenge I threw their way, even the insane ones. Kate Secor talked me through the big plot snarls, while her Tivo prevented me from destroying all mankind. Meanwhile, Michelle Dockrey and Brooke Lunderville helped me through everything else. Thanks to Tanya Huff, for San Diego, and to Jennifer Brozek, Jeanne Goldfein, and Cat Valente, for Melbourne. You guys made everything better. Finally, thanks to my cats, Lilly and Alice, for understanding that sometimes their monkey needs to stop petting them in order to type.

My personal soundtrack while writing *Late Eclipses* consisted mostly of *Promised Land*, by Dar Williams, *Little Voice*, by Sarah Bareilles, endless live concert recordings of the Counting Crows, and all of the soundtracks to *Glee*. Any errors in this book are entirely my own. The errors that aren't here are the ones that all these people helped me fix.

Thank you all so much for reading. It means the world to me.

PRONUNCIATION GUIDE:

All pronunciations are given strictly phonetically. This only covers races explicitly named in the first four books.

Bannick: *ban-nick*. Plural is Bannicks.
Banshee. *ban-shee*. Plural is Banshees.
Barghest: *bar-guy-st*. Plural is Barghests.
Barrow Wight: *bar-row white*. Plural is Barrow Wights.
Blodynbryd: *blow-din-brid* Plural is Blodynbryds.
Cait Sidhe: *kay-th shee*. Plural is Cait Sidhe.
Candela: *can-dee-la*. Plural is Candela.
Coblynau: *cob-lee-now*. Plural is Coblynau.
Cornish Pixie: *Corn-ish pix ee*. Plural is Cornish Pixies.
Daoine Sidhe: *doon-ya shee*. Plural is Daoine Sidhe, diminutive is Daoine.
Djinn: *jin*. Plural is Djinn.
Dóchas Sidhe: *doe-sh-as shee*. Plural is Dóchas Sidhe.
Ellyllon: *el-lee-lawn*. Plural is Ellyllons.
Gean-Cannah: *gee-ann can-na*. Plural is Gean-Cannah.
Glastig: *glass-tig*. Plural is Glastigs.
Gwragen: *guh-war-a-gen*. Plural is Gwragen.
Hamadryad: *ha-ma-dry-add*. Plural is Hamadryads.
Hippocampus: *hip-po-cam-pus*. Plural is Hippocampi.
Hob: *hob*. Plural is Hobs.

Kelpie: *kel-pee*. Plural is Kelpies.

Kitsune: *kit-soo-nay*. Plural is Kitsune.

Lamia: *lay-me-a*. Plural is Lamia.

The Luidaeg: *the lou-sha-k*. No plural exists.

Manticore: *man-tee-core*. Plural is Manticores.

Naiad: *nigh-add*. Plural is Naiads.

Nixie: *nix-ee*. Plural is Nixen.

Peri: *pear-ee*. Plural is Peri.

Piskie: *piss-key*. Plural is Piskies.

Pixie: *pix-ee*. Plural is Pixies.

Puca: *puh-ca*. Plural is Pucas.

Roane: *row-n*. Plural is Roane.

Satyr: *say-tur*. Plural is Satyrs.

Selkie: *sell-key*. Plural is Selkies.

Silene: *sigh-lean*. Plural is Silene.

Swanmay: *swan-may*. Plural is Swanmays.

Tuatha de Dannan. *tootha day danan*. Plural is Tuatha de Dannan, diminutive is Tuatha.

Tylwyth Teg: *till-with teeg*. Plural is Tylwyth Teg, diminutive is Tylwyth.

Undine: *un-deen*. Plural is Undine.

Urisk: *you-risk*. Plural is Urisk.

Will o' Wisps: *will-oh wisps*. Plural is Will o' Wisps.

ONE

April 30th, 2011

*These late eclipses in the sun and moon portend
No good to us: though the wisdom of nature can
Reason it thus and thus, yet nature finds itself
Scourged by the sequent effects: love cools,
Friendship falls off, brothers divide: in
Cities, mutinies; in countries, discord; in
Palaces, treason; and the bond cracked 'twixt son
And father . . .*

—William Shakespeare, *King Lear*

THE DOWNTOWN SAN FRANCISCO SAFEWAY was practically deserted. No surprise there, given that it was nearly one in the morning. May—my Fetch and current roommate—was in the produce department, tormenting the resident pixies. Their shrieks of irritation were almost enough to distract me from the task at hand. Almost; not quite. We had a mission, and I was, by Oberon, going to accomplish it.

Glancing along the row of cereals, I considered my options with exquisite care before reaching out and grabbing a box of Lucky Charms. The stuff's delicious when you combine it with enough coffee, even if it does mean putting up with that stupid cartoon leprechaun. I hesitated before taking a second box. It's not every night that I get to splurge.

My name's Toby Daye. I'm half-fae, half-human, and depressingly excited by the idea of being able to pay for name-brand cereal.

The empty Safeway was doing wonders for my mood. I hate shopping where I used to work, and the last thing I wanted to do after spending three days on stakeout was deal with my former coworkers. They seemed to share the sentiment, since they'd all vanished into the back as soon as they saw me. That was cool with me. I wasn't friendly when I worked at the store—"hostile" is a more accurate description—and I didn't "quit" so much as "walk out and never come back."

I wasn't meant to be a checkout girl. I probably wasn't meant to do anything that involves dealing with the public, which makes my career choice of "private investigator-slash-knight errant" all the more ironic. Still, when you live in the shady borderland between Fa-erie and the mortal world, neither beggars nor change-lings can be choosers.

The stakeout was for the first of my two vocations, the one that lets me pay the bills with a telephoto lens and a minimum of magic. My employer was a Silene who wanted to know where her husband was spending his spare time. Silene are horses from the waist down: sturdy, practical, and jealous as hell. She should never have married a Satyr if she didn't want him looking at other women, since that's basically what Satyrs are built to do. Her suspicions weren't unfounded: her goat-boy husband was getting a little extramarital action from the Hind two streets over, a doe-eyed lady if there ever was one. A couple of nights in the car, a few incriminating photos, and I was in the rare position of being able to pay for groceries.

The lack of clerks wasn't a problem, thanks to my shopping companions. May was racing through the store fast enough that she might as well have been on roller skates. Our mutual friend, Danny, was moving more sedately; it's just that he was doing it while being more than seven feet tall. He's not actually all that big, for a Bridge Troll, but he's good for getting things off of high shelves.

"Hey!" May jogged toward me with an armload of cantaloupes. She dumped them unceremoniously into the cart, without regard for what might be crushed in the process. "Did you know there were pixies in the produce section?"

"Yes, and so did you." I tapped my temple. No one's ever quite figured out what makes Fetches appear, but when they do, they come equipped with all the memories of the person they mirror. They're death omens; once a Fetch with your face shows up, your days are supposed to be numbered. Lucky for me, May has about as much innate interest in following rules as I do, and she's actually saved my life on at least one occasion. As far as I know, I'm the first person to live more than a month past the arrival of a Fetch—and I'm definitely the first person to ask their Fetch to move in.

May's store of borrowed memories includes my mind-numbing stint as a Safeway checkout girl. That's not a period of my life I like to dwell on, although the cynic in me insists on pointing out that fewer people were trying to kill me in those days. And yet, without all those attempts on my life, I wouldn't have needed a Fetch, and I'd have missed out on May's excellent vegetarian lasagna. There's a bright side to everything.

May pouted. Yet another expression never worn by my face until the universe decided to make a copy of it. "You take the fun out of everything."

"That's me," I agreed. "Toby Daye, assassin of fun."

"You should put that on your business cards," said

Danny, chuckling as he came around the corner. I promptly elbowed him. I just as promptly winced, making him chuckle even more. Bridge Trolls have skin like granite. Hitting them is a good way to break a knuckle.

I glowered. "Not funny."

"I disagree," said May amiably.

"Oh, go get the bread," I said.

"On it!" She saluted before zipping off again.

Danny gave me a sidelong look. "You okay? You seem tense."

"It's the store." I shook my head. "I know this is the best place to get groceries, but there's a reason I mostly live on things that come from drive-thru windows."

"Maybe that's why you got a Fetch. She's the nutrition fairy, here to punish you for all those double cheeseburgers."

"Well, that explains why she keeps trying to make me eat salad." I started dropping boxes of Pop-Tarts into the cart. Danny rolled his eyes and moved pointedly toward the granola bars.

I wasn't always a connoisseur of fast food hamburgers and microwave burritos. I've never been a very good cook—my ex-fiancé once compared my meatloaf to roadkill—but I used to make more of an effort. Then my liege lord asked me for a "little favor" and I wound up spending fourteen years as an enchanted fish. It was difficult to work up any enthusiasm about learning to make a casserole after that.

Curses and contradictions are the story of a changeling's life, mine maybe more than most. Changelings aren't stolen human children; we're crossbreeds, born to both worlds, belonging fully to neither. My mother was fae, and my father . . . well, wasn't. I was raised human until Mom's family found us and hauled us off to the Summerlands. Mom didn't want to go, and she mostly raised me through neglect after that. I ran away as soon as I thought I was old enough, and immediately fell in with a bad crowd. It's a sadly common story, but I got lucky. Good luck and good friends got me out of a bad situation, and I swore fealty to Sylvester Torquill, a man who didn't care how mixed-up my blood was. I met a human man, fell in love, and made my mother's mistakes all over again, even down to deserting my own little girl. Like mother, like daughter.

May eyed the Pop-Tarts as she returned with the bread. "Do we really need those?"

"They're part of a balanced breakfast."

"In what reality?"

"Mine." I grabbed another box of Pop-Tarts. "Danny, we got everything?"

"We do," he said, and lifted the three industrial-sized bags of cat litter from the floor, hoisting them with ease. "Let's get out of here."

"That assumes we can get somebody to ring us up." I started pushing the cart forward. "We could be reduced to shoplifting if my former coworkers stay in hiding."

"That's our girl." Danny patted my shoulder with one huge hand, nearly knocking me off my feet. "Making friends wherever she goes."

"Something like that," I muttered.

May can be as susceptible to colorful displays as any six-year-old; she tossed five candy bars into the cart while we waited in the checkout lane. I raised an eyebrow. "Do you need that much chocolate?"

"You get to criticize the amount of chocolate I eat when I get to criticize the amount of coffee you drink."

I wrinkled my nose. "Low blow."

"Yet so well aimed."

The door to the employee break room opened, and Pete—the night manager and my former boss—started toward us, expression suggesting that he'd just bitten into something sour. He usually looked like that when he had to interact with customers. That the customers included me was just a bonus.

"October," he said. He had the decency to try sounding surprised. He just lacked the acting skill to pull it off. He glanced at May and Danny, eyebrows rising in much more realistic confusion. Whoever warned the staff that I was in the store hadn't bothered to pass along the fact that I was traveling with my identical twin.

"Pete," I replied. "Busy night?"

His cheeks reddened. "Inventory."

Inventory would mean more staffers in the store, not fewer. I didn't call him on it. "Right. Well, this is my friend Danny," Danny nodded, his sheer size making the gesture intimidating, "and my sister, May."

"Hi!" May grinned, rocking back on her heels. "Nice to meet you. Thanks for being so awesome to Tobes when she worked here."

"Uh," said Pete. "Right."

I couldn't blame him. Meeting May has that effect on people, especially the ones who've known me for any length of time. She looks almost exactly like me, and people don't expect that level of pep to come out of my mouth. She's taken steps to distinguish herself from me, piercing her ears six times and getting a feathered bob before streaking her ashy brown hair with magenta and electric blue, but the underlying bone structure has stayed the same.

Pete rang up the groceries on a sort of swift autopilot, bagging them himself when no one came out to help him. He didn't try to make conversation. In a rare display of mercy, May didn't try to force him.

The total was over three hundred dollars: painful, but not unexpected, considering that we'd been down to ramen noodles and mystery cans from the back of the cupboard. I paid cash. Pete frowned but didn't comment. Sometimes it's better not to know.

"Nice to see you again, Pete," I said, starting to push

the cart forward. Danny and May followed, both keeping quiet for once.

We'd almost reached the door when Pete called, hesitantly, "Are things . . . you were pretty miserable when you were here. Are things better now?"

I looked back over my shoulder, breaking into a wide, honest smile as I said, "Things are wonderful."

Pete nodded. I nodded back, and we left the store without another word.

We were trying to fit everything into the car when May stiffened, eyes narrowing. "Someone's coming."

I blinked. "What?"

"Someone's coming," she repeated. "From . . ." She turned to scan the shadows edging the parking lot before raising an arm and jabbing her forefinger decisively toward the spot where the building gave way to the surrounding bushes. "Over there."

"Danny?" I put down the bag I was holding, reaching for the silver knife belted at my left hip. I keep the iron on the right, for emergencies that don't let me play nice. I have that sort of emergency way more often than I'd like.

"Got it." His human disguise crackled around him as he took a step forward, blurring to show the true slate color of his craggy skin. He curled his hands into fists. One punch from him would stand a good shot at stopping a freight train.

Neither of us questioned May's conviction that we were about to have a visitor. The normally transitory nature of Fetches means no one really knows what they're capable of. Every day with her is a whole new adventure.

The source of all that new adventure was shifting uneasily from foot to foot, eyeing the shadows she'd indicated. "I'm feeling a little unarmed here."

"Get in the car, May," I said.

"We sure this is somebody unfriendly?" Danny asked.

"If they were friendly, I wouldn't know they were there," May said.

Another bit of trivia for the growing compendium of Fetch abilities: she does laundry and she detects hostile guests. "Charming," I muttered, and inhaled deeply, the copper and cut grass smell of my magic rising around me.

My mother was the most skilled blood-worker in Faerie, before she went crazy. I'm not in her league, but I'm good enough to roll the air over my tongue and feel for the fae heritage of the people around me. May's magic tasted like cotton candy and ashes, and her blood was pure Fetch. Danny was the heavy stability of granite, Bridge Troll through and through. Fetch, Bridge Troll, and changeling. What else? I pressed further, feeling the first warning tinge of a migraine in my temples. Changelings have limits. Some of us more than others.

"Toby—" began Danny.

"Wait." I almost had it. The trace was slippery, probably because the person was invisible, but it was *there*. I grabbed for it, pushing as hard as I could . . . and caught it.

For a moment, I was too surprised to make sense of what I tasted. Part of me hadn't expected that little trick to work. Then I swallowed, focusing on the point where the blood seemed strongest, and said, "We know you're there. I didn't think the Daoine Sidhe were into sneaking up on people."

The taste of cardamom flared in my mouth, chasing my magic away and leaving a pulsing headache in its place. I winced, blinked, and missed the point where a man replaced the empty air.

He was tall, slender, and movie-star handsome, with dark hair and sharp-chiseled features that were about as natural as my own round-curved ears. The flicker of an illusion spell colored the air around him, hiding his fae nature from anyone who might glance out the Safeway window. And he didn't look happy about being caught. "October Daye?" he asked.

"Correct," I said. "You are?"

"The Queen of the Mists has sent me to inform you that your presence has been requested," he replied. His expression smoothed as he spoke, becoming the still, calm mask of a properly trained courtier. "You are to come at once."

"Still not answering my question." I dropped my hand from my knife, disgusted. I don't expect manners from the Queen of the Mists, or from anyone who works for her. That doesn't mean I wouldn't appreciate them. "Did she give a reason?"

"My name is Dugan Harrow. As for the other, Queens are not required to provide reasons to their subjects." His condescending smile barely concealed his irritation.

"Is this an order or a request?" I hadn't seen the Queen since I finished settling the affairs surrounding the death of Evening Winterrose, Countess of Goldengreen. I doubted she'd been any more broken up about my absence than I was.

He raised an eyebrow. "I was unaware the two differed. Your arrival is expected within the hour. I don't recommend disappointing Her Majesty." He left that dire proclamation hanging in the air as he turned on his heel and stalked away. The smell of cardamom rose again, now mixed with cinnamon, and he was gone.

Since Daoine Sidhe aren't teleporters, he was probably walking invisibly to whatever he was using to get home. The illusion was his way of making a big exit. That's the purebloods for you: always going for the special effects.

It was effective in this case, because we all just stood there, staring after him. May finally broke the silence, asking, "Do you think we have time to take the ice cream home and get it in the freezer before she gets really mad?"

Danny and I exchanged a look, and I groaned, pinching the bridge of my nose.

"Looks like we've got a date with royalty," I said.

"Well, crap," said Danny.

I lowered my hand. "My thoughts exactly."

TWO

WE REACHED A COMPROMISE and drove back to the apartment, where May and I shoved all the perishables into the refrigerator while Danny waited in the car with the engine running. There was no question of whether he'd be coming with us—Danny's been driving taxis in San Francisco for fifty years. If anyone could get us to the Queen's Court before she decided to get mortally offended, it was him. Of course, she could also decide his driving us meant he was officially "on my side," and include him in her long-standing grudge against me and mine. Danny was willing to take the risk. I was grateful. I don't go out of my way to endear myself to the Queen of the Mists, but I try not to antagonize her when I can help it.

I hung the belt that held my knives on the rack by the door while May stowed TV dinners. I don't always think things through, but I'm not stupid, and going into the Queen's presence armed might be the last thing I'd ever do. After a pause, I shrugged out of my leather jacket and hung it next to the knives. I love that jacket. It used to belong to Tybalt, the local King of Cats. I wear it almost every night, which meant wearing it to the Queen's Court would be a terrible idea. The woman has an unfortunate fondness for transmogrifying my clothes.

My fingers were oddly reluctant to let go of the jacket's collar. Wearing it would be a *terrible* idea, but this was a type of combat, and I hated the idea of going in without either my weapons or my customary armor.

"Toby?"

I jumped, twisting around to find May standing right behind me. She looked concerned.

"You ready to go?" she asked.

No. "Sure," I said, dropping my hand from the jacket and reaching for the door. "Let's hit the road."

Danny gunned the engine as we approached, and hit the gas before I finished buckling my seat belt, sending us rocketing out of the driveway at a speed that would have seemed unsafe with anyone else behind the wheel. Since it was Danny, it was almost soothing. I trusted him not to kill us, and if we were moving at these speeds, nobody was going to catch us in an ambush.

"Don't taxis have speed limits?" asked May, leaning her elbows on the back of my seat. She hadn't bothered with her seat belt. There was no point in nagging her about it, since the only way to hurt a Fetch is to hurt the person they're bound to. As long as I didn't get smashed up, she'd be fine.

"Mine doesn't," said Danny, and tapped the muslin bag that dangled from his rearview mirror. The brief, sharp smell of sea salt and mixed herbs wafted through the car. "Friend of mine runs an auto shop, makes these for her customers. I don't show up to the cops as long as I get it refreshed every few months."

I studied the bag with new interest. "Gremlin?"

"Yeah," he said. "Now I get to ask you a question."

"Why does that sentence always make me shiver?" I settled back in my seat, folding my arms over my chest. "Go ahead."

"What's the Queen got against you, anyways? Last I heard, you're the reason she's got a knowe. She should be grateful or some such shit, not treating you like trash."

I took a breath. Let it out. Took another breath, and said, carefully, "It's complicated."

"So un-complicate it."

"Toby wasn't supposed to take the credit," said May.

I shot her a withering look. She shrugged.

"It's the truth."

"I don't care. I still don't like talking about it." I looked back to Danny. "The Queen's knights were looking for the person who killed Evening's little sister, Dawn, and the Queen's seers and scouts were looking for a place to open a new knowe. I got lucky. I found both."

Sweet Oberon, that was an amazing moment. Everything came together for what seemed like the first time in my life. I'd been just one of Devin's kids before then, another changeling street rat fighting for survival. The search for Dawn's killer showed me I might be capable of something more important; something that didn't leave me going to bed every morning feeling like I'd traded in another little piece of my soul.

It was never supposed to get out, of course. The Queen made that clear. She called me to a private audience in her chambers, praised my ingenuity, flattered my mother's name, and even offered me a place in her household staff. All I had to do was keep my mouth shut and let her guards take the glory that would have been theirs to begin with, if I hadn't gotten lucky. Only it wasn't luck, damn her. It was hard work.

And I was going to let her take it away from me anyway, because growing up changeling in a pureblood world did an excellent job of teaching me my place. Sylvester was the one who insisted I take the credit I was due. The Queen never forgave me for listening to him ... and I never forgot that he was the one who was willing to speak up.

"Luck?" Danny eyed me dubiously, seeming to ignore the road he was blazing down at twenty miles above the speed limit. "Didn't think you traded much in luck."

"Oh, she's super-superstitious," said May. "She just mostly believes in the bad kind. How are the Barghests? Are they still chewing up the furniture?"

I know a conversational save when I'm offered one. I shot May a grateful look and settled back into the seat, trying to pay attention to Danny's cheerful stories of Barghest mayhem rather than dwelling on what the Queen could want me for. Danny runs a "rescue service" for Barghests—nasty, semi-canine beasts with horns, claws, fangs, scorpion stingers . . . basically everything but wings. Only a Bridge Troll could love something like that. Danny adores them.

All the Barghest mayhem in the world couldn't keep me from dwelling on what the Queen might have planned. But it was a nice try.

It was late enough that Danny was able to find a spot right at the edge of the parking lot, leaving us with only a short walk to the water. At least that meant we could get back to the car fast if we had to leave in a hurry. It wouldn't be the first time.

"Don't look so gloomy," said May, bouncing out of the car to open my door before I had the chance. "I think I'd know if you were going to be executed."

"That somehow doesn't make me feel better." I shoved my hands into my pockets, trudging across the pavement to the beach. Danny and May followed. Of the three of us, I'd navigated this particular path the most. Given my attempts to avoid the Queen, that was almost sad.

Knowes are the reality behind the old stories of faerie mounds and hollow hills: Summerlands estates connected to the mortal world by hidden, magically-maintained doors. The door to the Queen's knowe is tucked into a cave on a small stretch of the public beach that rings the San Francisco Bay. It's not the easiest place to reach, especially when the tide is in, and it seems like the Queen somehow always manages to call Court at high tide. Funny thing, that.

The sand made walking harder but provided plenty of traction, at least at first. It was replaced all too soon by wet, slime-covered rocks, forcing me to scramble if I didn't want to take a dunk in the Pacific. Danny and May navigated them more smoothly than I did, moving with the grace that comes so easily to the purebloods. Neither of them was going to wind up with a salt shampoo. It was hard not to resent them for it, especially when Danny grabbed my shoulder to keep me from falling and said apologetically, "I think maybe I should go first. It's sort of dark up there."

My night vision is incredible compared to a human's, but I'm running blind next to a pureblood. Not a desirable quality when you're basically nocturnal. I stopped to let Danny go ahead, trying not to show how annoyed I was, and almost certainly failing.

"It gets slipperier up here," Danny called.

"Oh, goody," I muttered, climbing over the last kelp-covered rocks between us and the door to the Queen's knowe. There was no sand here, just gravel, spindrift, and seaweed. "I can't believe we're doing this. I've got to be out of my mind."

"Answering a summons from the Queen ain't crazy, even if she is," said Danny.

"True enough." There was a splash behind us, and I turned to see May slogging out of the water, soaked to the hip. I raised an eyebrow.

May lifted her chin defensively. "The rocks are slippery."

They were slippery, but were they slippery enough to make a pureblood fall when I'd been able to make it to the other side? May's fall looked suspiciously like a sop to my pride. "I told you to be careful," I said, a smile tugging at the corner of my lips.

"I was careful. Gravity won." She grinned. "You need to lighten up before you worry yourself into an early grave."

"It's not worry that's going to put me in an early grave." I started for the cave, gesturing for her and Danny to follow. "Come on."

Wisely, Danny let me lead this time.

The entrance to the Queen's knowe is always dark, partly to dissuade human beachcombers, and partly, I think, because she likes watching changelings walk into walls. If there's a way to make it from the beach to the entry hall without wading through stagnant, ankle-deep water, no one's ever told me about it. I gritted my teeth and stepped into the muck, putting a hand against the wall to keep me on a straight line.

The dim light provided by the moon outside faded less than four feet into the cave, leaving me effectively blind. I kept going until a faint gray glow began coloring the air. The wall turned misty, my fingers dipping below the surface of what had been solid rock only inches before.

I closed my eyes and stepped into the light.

The more an entrance to the Summerlands is used, the more seamless the transition becomes. After two steps, I couldn't hear the ocean anymore. After three steps, the air stopped tasting like salt. The water around my ankles thinned out, first becoming mist, then fading entirely. The ground leveled out, and the wet jeans clinging to my ankles were replaced by heavy skirts swishing around my legs—the Queen was up to her old tricks again. When the last of the wall wisped away I stopped, opening my eyes, and looked around.

The cave was gone, replaced by a vast, white-walled hall. Ivory pillars filigreed with intricate carvings stretched up to meet a ceiling of faintly reflective ice-white marble. The floor was made from the same stone. People who spend a lot of time at the Queen's Court learn not to turn their heads too quickly, since an unexpected shift can cause a nasty case of vertigo.

"Hey, awesome!" said May, her reaction confirming that the Queen's sense of propriety extended to reclothing everyone, not just me. Steeling myself against the inevitable, I looked down.

My T-shirt and blue jeans were gone, replaced by a low-cut silk gown the color of dried blood. May's dress matched mine in everything but color; it was an odd shade of purple, complementing the streaks in her hair. Danny, meanwhile, was wearing a basic brown gentleman's suit of the sort that was fashionable in the early 1800s. He looked totally comfortable that way, like he'd always been a bouncer for the Fairy Tale Mafia in his spare time.

Their human disguises had vanished along with their street clothes. May didn't change much. Her eyes had bleached from blue to their natural shade of almost colorless gray, while her features acquired a more delicate cast and her ears became visibly pointed. Danny appeared to have gained a foot in both height and breadth. His skin was gray, with the rough, craggy texture of granite, and his hair looked more like moss. I raised a hand to tuck my hair back, feeling the point of my own ear. No illusions for anybody tonight.

"At least she has a sense of color," I said, and turned back to the ballroom.

The place was packed with fae from a hundred different races. They thronged around us, moving in slow eddies, like a living tide. Several of them stared shamelessly in our direction. I resisted the urge to flip them off.

The stares turned shocked as May stepped up beside me. She was gawking without a trace of shame, even going so far as to lean back on her heels and study the

chandeliers. She looked too much like me to be anything but my Fetch, and while bringing her to Court was
technically *allowed*—she was fae, and she lived in the
Kingdom of the Mists, at least until she blipped out of
existence—it wasn't what most people would consider
proper.

"I was never a big fan of propriety anyway," I said
reflectively.

May stopped gawking to blink at me, bemused.
"Huh?"

"Never mind." The crowd was turning away, buzzing
about the tackiness of May's presence. They didn't even
bother to pretend they hadn't been staring. Why should
purebloods—purebloods associated with the Queen's
Court, no less—care if they were rude to a changeling?

"Take a picture, it'll last longer," said Danny. The last
of the spectators sniffed and turned away, patently snubbing us. Danny ignored them, slanting a glance toward
me as he asked, "How long you think we've got before
she shows?"

"I don't know." The dais at the center of the room
was untenanted, the throne sitting empty. That wasn't
a surprise. The Queen knows the value of a dramatic
entrance. "Go ahead and mingle. We've probably got a
while to wait."

May frowned. "So why did we hurry?"

"When the Queen's late, it's fashionable. When we're
late, it's an insult. Now go on, go get on people's nerves
by existing."

May laughed and grabbed Danny's arm, tugging him
into the crowd. I smiled and shook my head, turning
to walk in the opposite direction. The courtiers whispered as I passed. Louder whispers in the distance told
me where May and Danny were. I let my smile become
a grin. My Fetch makes an excellent distraction, and I
have no problem using her as one. What's the point of

having a personal incarnation of death if you can't confuse the locals?

I found a clear patch of wall and settled against it, watching the Court return to its normal routine. Immortality makes *ennui* status quo, and not much is interesting enough to disrupt a gathering of purebloods for long. Apparently, traveling with your Fetch isn't in the right league. Good to know.

People moved in short arcs, shifting from group to group as they shared information, spread gossip, and looked for juicy bits of blackmail. Someone moved up next to me, waiting a few seconds before clearing his throat in a polite request for my attention. I turned and found myself looking into a pair of inhumanly green eyes set in a sharp-featured face.

I blinked, trying unsuccessfully to hide my surprise. "Tybalt."

"It's good to see all those blows to the head haven't impaired your ability to identify faces," he said, the hint of a smile crossing his lips. His pupils contracted against the light, taking on a feline cast. "They haven't improved your manners, either. In case you weren't aware, 'hello' is typically what comes next."

"I—what are you doing here?" The Cait Sidhe are the only race in Faerie with their own independent aristocratic hierarchy. Tybalt has been San Francisco's King of Cats for years. He's not exactly forbidden to visit the Queen's Court, but he definitely isn't someone I'd expected to see there.

His smile became real. "Picking wallflowers."

I felt my cheeks go red.

Growing up around the Daoine Sidhe left me severely desensitized to "pretty." Pretty is cheap in Faerie. Beauty is even cheaper. Tybalt has more than beauty. He has . . . presence. He can catch and hold a room without even seeming to try.

I'd have an easier time ignoring him if he'd stopped at pretty.

Ironically, the things about him that appeal to me are the ones that make most non-Cait Sidhe purebloods view him as "common" or "savage." His face is eye-catching but too strong for most fae tastes; his hair is brown with tabby-streaks of black, cut practically short to display the subtle points of his ears. His canines are a bit too sharp, more cat than man no matter what shape he's in.

Qualifiers aside, Tybalt's one of those people who'd look good in a burlap sack. He could probably make burlap the hot new thing, and what he was wearing that night was a long way from burlap. Skintight brown suede pants and a crisply-cut white linen shirt made him look like a modern interpretation of a Victorian gentleman. His boots and vest were darker brown leather and fit just as tightly. I wasn't sure he could breathe in that outfit. A tiny, traitorous corner of my mind whispered that the effect was worth losing a little oxygen.

I batted the thought forcibly away. "Seriously, why are you here?"

"Tonight's festivities sounded like fun," he said. "I like fun." Something in his eyes conflicted with his smile, cautioning me not to dismiss him.

"Fun," I echoed.

"Indeed." Eyes locked on mine, he added, "For someone, anyway."

I wasn't sure what to say to that.

Tybalt and I have always had what's politely called a "strange" relationship. He used to hate me on general principles: I was half-human, and I annoyed him, and that was enough. Hate somehow gave way to grudging respect . . . and then things got really strange. Lingering-looks-and-cold-showers strange, at least on my side. Not that it can ever go anywhere. Tybalt's a King of Cats, and I'm, well, me.

Our current pattern looked a lot like our old one, from the outside. He smiled more than he used to; I smiled back more than was necessarily wise. There was just one problem: Tybalt kept insisting someone was lying to me about something major enough that I wouldn't believe it unless I figured it out for myself. And he was refusing to get any closer until I knew what it was.

The man can be insufferable when he wants to. Just like every other cat I've ever met.

He offered his arm with perfect courtly grace. "The Lady of the Mists will be calling Court soon." He wouldn't call her "Queen," but he was smart enough to be polite inside her domain. "May I stand as your escort?"

I glanced sharply at him, looking for any trace of mockery. It wasn't there. Just the smile, and the guarded caution.

"I guess so," I said, and slipped my hand into the crook of his elbow.

His smile grew, briefly chasing the caution from his eyes. "I know you object to others choosing your attire, but the gown suits you. You should wear red more often." My cheeks burned. He laughed. "Not quite what I meant, but the compliment stands." Standing straight and proper, like the gentleman his clothes proclaimed he was, he turned to lead me to the front of the room. I watched him as we walked, trying to figure out what he was up to. His expression didn't offer any clues.

Tybalt pulled his arm away when we reached the edge of the crowd, and the bow he offered wasn't mocking in the least. I offered a curtsy in automatic response, my blush rising once more. He glanced to the side while I was straightening from my curtsy, and for a moment, I thought his cheeks were as red as mine. Just a trick of the light; when he turned back toward me, he was as composed as ever.

"You'll have a better view from here," he said.

"Uh, right." I frowned. "Tybalt, what are you up to?"

"Oh, no," he said, waving a finger as he stepped closer. "Don't question your betters. It's not attractive."

That was the Tybalt I knew. "Right," I said. "You're here to piss me off."

"You seem to view it as one of my strengths, and I like playing to my strengths." Suddenly serious, he stepped toward me again, stopping well within what I considered my personal space. Dropping his voice to a near-whisper, he said, "The Lady of the Mists is planning something. Take care, little fish; she has no love for you."

"Tybalt—"

"I need to leave you with anger on both sides. I'd rather she had no cause to think us friends." His smile dimmed, turning wry and sincere at the same time. "You'll do better if you keep me in reserve."

I blinked. The Queen was plotting against me? It wasn't totally surprising—I couldn't stay off her radar forever. Lacking better instructions from my brain, my mouth seized on the point that seemed the strangest, asking, "We're friends?"

Tybalt's laughter was so soft it would have been inaudible if I hadn't been close enough to feel the heat coming off his skin and smell the faint pennyroyal undertones of his magic. "When I can bear your company. And in the interests of friendship, I hope you'll forgive me what I'm about to do."

"Forgive you wha—"

My sentence was cut off as he clamped his mouth over mine, kissing me deeply.

Well. That was new.

THREE

TYBALT'S HAND SOMEHOW FOUND ITS WAY to my hip, giving me something to brace myself against. That was considerate of him, since my knees were shaking so hard I could barely stay upright. Every nerve I had was on fire. The fact that we were standing in the middle of the Queen's Court seemed utterly inconsequential. So did the fact that we were surrounded by courtiers, even though part of me was sure I'd regret that later. Most of me was busy kissing Tybalt, and as long as he was kissing me back, I was going by majority rule.

On the few occasions when I'd considered what it might be like to kiss Tybalt, I always assumed he'd be pushy, the kind of man who makes it clear that he's entirely in charge and you'd better just go along with things. This kiss wasn't anything like I'd imagined. It was firm, yes, and he was definitely making a case for its continuation . . . but it was also soft, and a lot more considerate than I would have expected. I'm not sure what that says about me.

Tybalt's free hand skated up my back to the bare skin between my shoulders. I leaned into him, deepening the kiss. His lips tasted like pennyroyal. His hand slid still farther up, finally pausing on my shoulder.

Then he shoved me away.

I staggered back, my shocked stare meeting his icy, familiar sneer. In a tightly controlled voice pitched loud enough for everyone around us to hear, he said, "There. Our accounts are settled. Good evening, *Sir* Daye." He turned on his heel and stalked off into the crowd before I could recover enough to ask what the hell he was talking about.

The courtiers parted to let him pass, closing the gap behind him. The less considerate ones smirked in my direction, their expressions telegraphing the belief that I was getting just what I deserved.

My instincts said to stay put until my knees stopped shaking, while the lessons on courtly behavior Devin and Sylvester worked so hard to drill through my thick skull told me that was the worst thing I could do. I straightened my shoulders, trying to emulate my mother's default expression of superior unconcern as I beat a decorous but hasty retreat to the safety of the nearest pillar. Seeing that I wasn't going to provide further entertainment, the crowd turned away, leaving me free to fade into the shadows. I sagged against the wall, rubbing my forehead as I waited for my heart to stop pounding. Life was a lot simpler when Tybalt just sniped at me all the time.

"Guy troubles?" asked May, walking up and leaning next to me.

I eyed her. "Did you miss what just happened?"

"Nope, and it's about time," she said, with disturbing relish. "I caught the whole thing. Is he a good kisser? I know you've wondered."

"May!"

"What? I'm just asking. I mean, sure, maybe it's not important that Tybalt kissed you. And I'm sure it doesn't matter that he's leaving, and you look like someone stole your puppy." She paused. "Maybe 'stole your kitten' would be a better comparison."

"Can we *not* have this conversation?"

"Okay," said May, amiably. "It's no skin off my nose if you want to ignore the hottie making 'pick me up and take me home' eyes at you."

"It was just a ploy." A ploy that felt an awful lot like a kiss. There was no way he'd ever kiss me like that and mean it, but for a moment, it felt like . . .

"You're not that dense. You have to know he digs you."

"You've got to be kidding."

"Would I lie to you?" She grinned. "Watching the two of you is fun, in a sick, sad, voyeuristic sort of way."

"Get a life."

"I've got yours. Now come on. Don't you want to get snuggly with him?"

I didn't have to find a way to answer that. The scent of rowan sliced through the air, washing away all traces of lesser magic and casting an anticipatory hush over the Court. My shoulders locked with a whole new type of tension.

"Whoa," said May.

I turned toward the dais at the head of the room, and stared.

The Queen had made some changes to her image. When I brought her the hope chest Evening Winterrose died to protect, the Queen was an ethereal siren, as elegant and regal as a Tolkien wet dream. Now she looked like the bastard daughter of Titania and Alice Cooper. Kohl ringed her eyes, blue lipstick coated her lips, and her formerly floor-length ivory hair was chopped in a ragged bob, streaked with black and vivid blue. She was wearing fishnet stockings, a ripped white top, and a black leather miniskirt too short to be decent. But it was her. There was no mistaking the moonstruck madness in her sea-foam eyes.

She studied the room before dropping onto the throne, bracing her elbow on the armrest and propping her chin on her knuckles. She looked as casual as a teenager getting ready to settle in for an evening of mindless television. Only this "teenager" was the most powerful Faerie monarch in Northern California. She waved a hand, still casual, and said, "The Court of the Mists is now in session."

That seemed to be all the fanfare we were going to get. Courtiers stepped forward and started reading from scrolls as they made proclamations, clarified prior judgments, and generally made a lot of noise about nothing. The Queen didn't say a word. She just sat there, studying her black-enameled fingernails.

This went on for about an hour, long enough for Danny to find us, May to start sniping in a whisper about the Queen's fashion sense, and me to start relaxing. The Queen looked up, almost as if she'd sensed my guard beginning to drop, and said, "Will Sir October Daye of the Kingdom of the Mists, Knight of Lost Words, daughter of Amandine of Faerie, oath-sworn to Duke Sylvester Torquill, please stand forth?"

She was using my full title, something that has never, in my experience, been a good sign. I schooled my face into a neutral expression as I stepped away from the pillar and walked through the silent crowd, finally stopping in front of the dais.

The Queen's gaze stayed on me throughout my approach, her own expression cool and calculating. I dropped into a deep curtsy, holding the position until she said, "You may rise."

I straightened, keeping my eyes focused on the floor. I never look at the Queen when I can help it. I have enough mortal blood in me to make her type of inhuman beauty dangerous.

"We have summoned you to discuss your recent actions." Each word was cold and precise as cut crystal. "Raise your head, if you please."

I winced, looking up. The sight of her face was just shy of physically painful. "My actions, Highness?"

"Yes, October." She sat up and crossed her legs languidly. "Do you remember the last time you stood before me in this Court?"

That would be the time she'd thrown me out for daring to tell her that Evening was dead. Oh, yeah. I remembered. "Yes, Highness."

"You returned the hope chest which had been in the keeping of the Lady Goldengreen before her ... departure." She pursed her lips. Most purebloods consider it a *faux pas* to admit that they can actually die. "You haven't been to see me since then. I must wonder why."

"I've been busy, Highness."

"So you have. The Countess O'Leary tells me you spent some time in her lands, and brought the efforts of—" again the moue of disapproval "—a dissident to an end, preventing a possible war."

"Yes, Highness," I said. The Countess O'Leary in question was April, not January; that was one more murder the Queen wasn't mentioning. I wasn't sure where she was going with all of this, but it wasn't helping my nerves.

"It pleases me to know your memory remains excellent," she said dryly. A nervous giggle rose from the crowd, stopping when her gaze flicked in its direction. Looking back to me, she said, "I am informed you are the reason Blind Michael's Hunt has vanished. Is this true?"

"Yes, Highness."

"Excellent." She leaned back in her throne. "There have been many requests for the custodianship of Goldengreen since the departure of the Countess Winterrose. Some of the petitioners were quite compelling in their arguments."

I frowned, not sure I liked where this was going. "Highness?"

"The decision was complicated by the fact that the Countess left no heir, placing the burden of choosing a proper custodian on my shoulders." Her smile was as triumphant as it was bitter. "By my power as Queen of the Mists, Regent of these Western Lands, I name you Countess of Goldengreen. Welcome to the peerage, *Lady* Daye."

The Court erupted in excited whispers. I stared at her, too stunned to speak. Changelings don't inherit titles, not even from their parents. What was she trying to pull?

The Queen uncrossed her legs and stood, still smiling. "This Court is closed. If any still have petitions, they will be heard next week."

"Highness, wait—" I began.

"Good night, Lady Daye. Your mother must be *so* proud." The smell of rowan filled the air as a thick mist rose around her. When it cleared again, she was gone.

Great. Just great.

The Court kept whispering as I walked back to May and Danny. More than a few hostile looks were shot in my direction. Just what I needed: more enemies. At least May and Danny didn't look angry. Surprised and confused, yes, but not angry. I slumped against the pillar between them, putting a hand over my face. "Oberon's hairy balls."

"Damn," said May.

"Yeah," I said. "Damn."

"I mean *damn*."

"I think she gets the point, May," said Danny. One huge hand settled gently on my shoulder. "You okay?"

"I have no idea," I said, resisting the urge to break into hysterical laughter. It seemed like the only suitable response to the situation. "She set me up."

"Can't you get out of it?" demanded May.

"I don't think so."

"That sucks."

I sighed. "Tell me about it."

"October!" Tybalt came shoving through the crowd toward us. There was no amusement or false mockery in his voice now. His face was composed, but his pupils were narrowed to hairline slits that telegraphed his agitation. "A word, if I may."

"Tybalt? What's wrong?" I stepped forward before remembering the way he'd kissed me. Danny and May clearly hadn't forgotten, because they moved to flank me, both watching him carefully. "I thought your little show was so people wouldn't think we were willing to be seen together in public. Or did I miss something?"

"Things have changed. We have to talk." He grabbed my wrist, starting to pull me toward him. "Come with me as quietly as you can. I don't think you fully understand what's just happened."

I froze, looking at his hand. "You might want to let go of me now."

"Toby, you don't—"

"See, if you don't, I'm going to feel compelled to try breaking your fingers." My voice was calm, belying the fact that my heart was beating way too fast. "I didn't give you permission to touch me, especially not after your little 'ploy' earlier."

"Please." He squeezed my wrist before releasing it. He didn't step back. Neither did I. "You need to come with me. This is a trap. You have to trust—"

A commotion spread through the crowd to our left, distracting us both at practically the same time. Tybalt stepped forward, half-shielding me from whatever was coming. "What's going on?" asked May, sounding more interested than concerned.

Danny and Tybalt exchanged a glance, briefly united by dismay. My Fetch got my memories, but she didn't get the instinct for trouble to go with them, and I didn't know how far her newly-demonstrated ability to sense danger extended. Tybalt moved again, this time putting himself between May and the commotion. I shot him a grateful look, which he answered with a nod.

"Any idea what this is?" asked Danny.

"Not yet, but I'm really wishing I wasn't unarmed right now," I muttered. I was giving serious thought to grabbing May and heading for the door when Marcia— the quarter-blood changeling who served as a handmaid in the Tea Gardens—shoved her way through, followed by a Tylwyth Teg man in conservative, incongruously modern clothes. He looked exhausted.

"Toby!" Marcia wailed, almost knocking Tybalt over as she lunged to grab my arm. Her eyes were wide and glassy within their rings of faerie ointment. A necessary cosmetic, at least for Marcia; her blood's too thin to let her see most of Faerie without it.

"Marcia?" I put my hand over hers. "What's wrong?"

"You have to come," she babbled. "You have to come *right now*, please—"

"What is it? Calm down and tell me."

She froze, eyes filling with tears, and whispered, "It's Lily. She's sick, Toby, she's really sick, and we don't know what to do."

The world came to a sudden crashing halt. "Lily's sick?"

Lily was Marcia's liege, the Lady of the Tea Gardens— and an Undine. The Undine are biologically weird, even for Faerie, since their bodies are made entirely of water. Water doesn't understand illness. It can get polluted, but it can't get sick. Which meant that if Marcia was right, something was terribly wrong.

"She's sick, really sick. She didn't know who I was, so I ..." Her voice dropped until it was barely audible. "Please come."

"Of course I'll come." I hesitated, looking at the crowd around us. Many were staring openly, and those that weren't were probably listening in. Dropping my voice, I asked, "Tybalt? What's the Queen going to do if there's a sudden exodus out of here?"

His eyes narrowed as he caught my meaning. "Nothing we, or the Tea Gardens, would be likely to enjoy."

"Right," I said. Fae don't have paparazzi, but my elevation to the peerage was the news of the hour. If I left now, my destination might draw an unhealthy amount of attention, and the Tea Gardens were an independent fiefdom. The last thing they needed was the full focus of the Queen. With Lily out of commission, they'd have no way to stop the "proper nobility" from taking over. We needed a distraction. I glanced around our little group.

May provided a distraction just by existing, and Tybalt was more than capable of causing a public disturbance if he was given the right motivation. I dropped my voice even lower. "Danny, can you get May home?" He nodded curtly. "Okay. When things calm down, I'm going to need you to do that. In the meantime, you're going to make sure nobody thinks to follow us to the Tea Gardens. Marcia, how did you get here?"

Our conspiratorial little knot must have looked odd from the outside, but the Tylwyth Teg who'd accompanied Marcia seemed to be taking it in stride. He answered for her, holding up what looked like a stubby handmade broom as he said, "We took the yarrow broom express."

"Does it seat three?"

"What?" said May and Danny, almost in unison. Tybalt didn't say anything. He just nodded, understanding spreading across his features. He didn't look like he approved, but at least he understood. That would have to be good enough, for now.

"I think so," said the Tylwyth Teg, looking bemused. "This may not be the best time for an introduction, but it seems polite. I'm Walther Davies."

"Toby Daye, hi," I said, and turned to Tybalt. "Ready to make a scene?"

He raised an eyebrow. "Do I have a choice?"

"Not really. To quote something someone said to me recently, in the interests of friendship, I hope you'll forgive what I'm about to do." I drew back my hand and slapped him across the face. The smack of flesh striking flesh echoed through the hall. Conversations stopped as people whipped around to stare at us. Raising my voice to something just below a shout, I snarled, "You asshole!"

Tybalt snarled back, almost quickly enough to conceal the amusement in his eyes. "I only offered the respect that you have earned, *Lady* Daye."

May was quick to grab her cue. She rounded on Tybalt, interposing herself between us and jabbing a finger at his chest as she started yelling. I didn't catch what she was saying; it was too difficult to make out the words under the muttering of the crowd and Danny's shouts for them to cut it out and act like adults. I turned to Marcia and Walther.

"Let's go."

I started for the exit at a fast trot, with the two of them close behind. As I'd expected, the sight of a Fetch and the local King of Cats getting into it was fascinating enough that no one seemed to remember what actually started the scene. No one stopped us as we made our way out of the Queen's knowe and into the chilly mortal night.

FOUR

THE SPELL THE QUEEN CAST ON MY CLOTHES was transformation, not illusion; it didn't break when we left her knowe. I made the trip from the beach to Golden Gate Park in the ball gown, clinging for dear life to the back of Walther's makeshift "broom." Marcia rode sandwiched between us, arms locked around Walther's waist and eyes squeezed resolutely shut. I didn't blame her. Tylwyth Teg can fly, but they aren't good illusionists—in order to keep us from being spotted, Walther had to stay six stories up for the entire flight.

Spring in the Bay Area starts around the end of February, but San Francisco is a coastal city. It gets cold fast once the sun goes down, and most dresses aren't built to combat extreme wind chill. I was shivering uncontrollably by the time Walther brought us in for a landing inside the Tea Garden walls. So was Marcia, whose trendy jeans and lace tank top gave her almost no protection against the elements.

"Sorry about that." Walther stepped off the broom, turning to help Marcia dismount. "Are you both okay?"

"Are Tylwyth Teg self-defrosting or something?" I

climbed down, shaking my skirt back into a semblance of order. "I'm fine. Where's Lily?"

"Lily's in the knowe." Marcia paused, swallowing hard before she added, "None of us know what to do. That's why I came to find you."

I looked around the darkened garden before returning my attention to Marcia. She had moved to lean against Walther. "Did Lily tell you to do that?"

"No." She shook her head. "We just . . ."

"We didn't have any other options," said Walther.

The statement hung between us, utterly true, and utterly tragic. Independent Courts like Lily's enjoy a lot of freedom . . . at a price. There's no one to help them when things go wrong, and someone's always watching them, waiting for signs of weakness. Most of them hold their land through a mixture of inertia and looking like it would be too much trouble to take them down. That's why we had to deflect the Queen's Court onto something more scandalously interesting. If the Queen took an interest . . .

"Well." I took a breath. "Does she know I'm here?"

"I don't know," said Marcia.

"Okay." I took the lead as we walked toward the moon bridge that served as the entry to Lily's knowe. "Can I ask a few questions before we go in?"

"Anything," said Walther.

"Well, for starters, who the hell are you? I've never seen you before, and now you're one of the people coming to tell me there's an emergency. It seems a little—" I stopped as I realized where that statement wanted to go.

"Fishy?" finished Walther, not seeming to notice Marcia's wince.

I shot him a sharp look. His expression was entirely innocent. "Yeah," I said. "That."

Walther shrugged. "I moved to the Bay Area last semester, for work. I didn't want to jump right into working for any of the local nobles, and Lily agreed to let me hang around if I'd do some odd jobs for her while I get settled. You can check my references, if you want."

"I may do that. For right now, when did this start? Was it tonight, or earlier?"

"We don't know," said Marcia miserably. "She didn't say anything about being sick, but she's been really quiet for the last few days."

"Pieria hurt her wing. I went to get Lily, and I found her passed out on the pavilion floor." Walther looked away. "I managed to wake her, but she didn't remember who I was. I got worried after that, and took some of her water for testing. It's clean. I don't know what's going on."

"I really don't know what you expect from me." I started up the moon bridge, pulling myself higher one step at a time. The branches began snarling together overhead, weaving the roof of Lily's knowe and shutting out the mortal world.

"I didn't know where else to go," whispered Marcia. I wouldn't have heard her if she hadn't been right behind me. "You weren't home, so I called Sylvester, and he said you'd been called to Court."

Meaning she'd technically been sent by my liege. This just got better—although I was going to have to ask Sylvester how he knew I'd be at the Queen's knowe. "I'll do what I can," I said.

The last of the branches slithered into place above us, marking the final point of transition between the mortal world and Lily's corner of the Summerlands. I stepped off the bridge, stopped, and stared, feeling the bottom drop out of my stomach.

Pixies clung to the woven ceiling, casting a faint glow over a landscape that seemed less complicated than it should have been. We were surrounded by an endless array of ponds, streams, and tiny islands—but where were the elegant bridges, the pavilions, the decoratively twisted Japanese maple trees? It looked like half the knowe was missing. The only concrete landmark was the stand of willows to our left. I started in that direction, Walther and Marcia following close behind.

Two women stood in front of the willows, leaning against each other for support. One had scales peppering her face; the other had a Gwragen's gray-white skin and deep-set eyes. The scaled woman raised her head as we approached, prodding her companion into doing the same. They were standing a bit apart by the time we reached them.

The Gwragen moved to grab my hands as I drew close, and then shied back, looking startled by her own boldness. "Our Lady is in the grove," she said, slanting a glance past me to Marcia. Her eyes were an almost human shade of brown, marking her as a half-blood.

I nodded. "Is she awake?"

"She was," said the scaled woman. "Wakefulness comes and goes. Please don't stay too long. She isn't strong."

"I won't." I turned to look at Walther and Marcia.

They shook their heads, a few beats out of unison. Walther gestured me forward, saying, "It's better if . . . it's just better if we don't."

". . . Right," I said, and swallowed hard. I've faced down killers, crazy Firstborn, and the Queen of the Mists. None of those could compare to the fear I felt as I stepped forward to push the dangling curtain of willow boughs aside, squared my shoulders, and stepped through.

The inside of the grove was filled with a hot, thick mist, practically turning it into a sauna. Sweat beaded on my skin almost instantly, and the moisture soaked into the fabric of my gown, making it hard to move. It wasn't entirely dark inside the trees; pixies clung to the branches overhead, their pale glow barely providing enough light to navigate. I started forward, moving slowly as my eyes adjusted.

"Lily?"

Like so many things in Lily's knowe, the grove seemed to be bigger on the inside than the outside. I walked a good twenty feet before a shallow pool came into view, filled with shadows that resolved, between one blink and the next, into Lily. I stopped dead, clapping a hand over my mouth as I tried to make myself believe what I was seeing. It wasn't easy, because what I was seeing was impossible.

Walther and Marcia said Lily was sick, but they hadn't been able to make me really understand what they meant. I understood it now. And I didn't want to.

"Lily?" I whispered, taking another hesitant step forward.

"Ah." It was more a sigh than a fully shaped word, accompanied by a slight slumping of already half-submerged shoulders. Her head was propped up on a cushion of moss; the rest of her was under the water, cloaked by the thin black shroud of her unbound hair. "My October. I wondered when you'd find your way here." Her accent was stronger than I'd ever heard it, all traces of San Francisco shed in favor of a Japan that died centuries ago. "Come here, my dear one."

"I'm here." I stumbled through the last steps to the pond's edge, where I dropped to my knees in the damp moss.

Lily didn't look any better viewed up close. Her skin was waxen, and the scales around her eyes were dull, all their shine leeched away. She was too thin, and too faded. "I'm sorry if I've worried you. Who brought you?"

"Marcia and Walther. I would've worried even more if I'd found out later than this."

"Really? That might have been a taste of your own medicine." She turned toward me, eyes opening. I bit my lip to stop the words that threatened to escape. The green had run out of her irises, leaving them the dark, undefined shade of deep water. "They brought you for nothing, because nothing's wrong. I'm just tired."

"You don't look tired. You look—" I let the sentence trail off, unsure how to finish. She looked like she was dying.

"I know how I look." Lily sighed again, eyes drifting gradually shut. "I thought it was something in the water, some new weed killer being washed in from the park. The world isn't as clean as it was when I was young, and I thought it would pass. It didn't."

"How long ago did this start?"

"Sometime last week. I asked Walther—dear Walther, you should get to know him better. He's Tylwyth Teg; your mother would approve. He works at one of the mortal universities. I asked him to take my water for testing." The skin at the base of her jaw split as she shook her head. Brackish water trickled from the wound. "He found nothing. But something's wrong."

"You're going to be fine."

"Am I? I wonder. What will happen to my children when I'm gone? They'll have no one to care for them without me."

"You don't need to worry about that," I said fiercely. "You're going to be *fine*."

"Oh, October. If repetition were healing, you'd have me saved in an instant." She smiled, sending water cascading down her throat. "You were always so fierce, even when you were just a tributary of Amandine's greater river. But her river is dry now, while you run toward the sea."

"Lily, please." I put a hand on her shoulder. Her skin was like ice.

"What?" Her smile died, replaced by confusion. "I'm sorry. It's hard to find the words. You'll try to save me, because that's your nature; it's what you are. But please, if you do anything, make sure my children are cared for. They need you more than I do."

It took me a moment to compose myself. Finally, I said, "I promise."

"Good." She sank lower in the water. "I'm sorry, but I'm so tired . . ."

"It's all right," I said, pulling my hand away. "Get some rest. I'll see you soon."

I stood carefully, backing out the way I'd come in. If Lily was aware that I was leaving, she didn't give any sign. She didn't give any sign of being aware of anything at all. She just stayed in her pool, silent and unmoving, and let me walk away.

FIVE

LILY'S HANDMAIDENS STEPPED ASIDE AS I made my way out of the willows. They didn't need to ask what I'd seen; they knew. My feet carried me to the moon bridge without any orders from my brain, which was entirely occupied with reviewing Lily's condition. Oak and ash, how was this happening? Lily's illness was an impossibility. Faerie thrives on the impossible, but some rules aren't intended to be broken. Undine don't get sick. Lily was sick.

I was missing something.

The passage from Lily's knowe to the mortal world was still smooth; she might be sick, but she hadn't completely lost her grip on her domain. That was probably a good thing. I stepped off the bridge, my feet carrying me toward the gate.

"Toby?" said Marcia. I hadn't realized she was there until she spoke. That wasn't good. I was worried about Lily, but that didn't mean I could zone out completely.

Stopping where I was, I turned to face the moon bridge. Marcia and Walther were standing at the base, watching me. Tears ran freely down Marcia's cheeks. I didn't say a word. I didn't know where to begin.

"Is . . ." Marcia hesitated, biting her lip before continuing, "Is Lily going to . . . ?"

"I don't know." As reassurances go, it wasn't my best. I couldn't get the image of Lily's water-dark eyes out of my head. "I wish I did."

She looked stricken. I couldn't blame her. Faerie isn't kind to changelings. We carve out places for ourselves on the borders of fae society, but they're never stable and rarely safe. People like Devin, who saw changeling kids as a resource to exploit, are a lot more common than people like Lily, who opened her doors to the weakest among us and never asked for anything but loyalty. She offered protection, kindness, and a place to belong. Some of her subjects never had any of those things before.

Walther put an arm around Marcia's shoulders, asking, "What's going to happen if she doesn't get better?"

"I don't know," I repeated. That wasn't true. I had some idea of what would happen. An entire fiefdom of unaligned, unprotected changelings? At best, they'd find predators like Devin. At worst . . .

"Most of us don't have anywhere else to go." Marcia leaned into Walther's arm. "My family doesn't even acknowledge me."

That wasn't surprising. I still winced. "Lily won't die, Marcia. I won't let her."

Marcia bit her lip again. "Do you promise?"

"I can't do that until I know what's going on, but I promise to try." I hesitated. "Is there a phone around here?"

"Use mine," said Walther, digging a hand into his pocket long enough to pull out a cellular phone smaller than a deck of cards. He tossed it to me.

"May keeps trying to make me get one of these

things," I said, wrinkling my nose and flipping the phone open. "It's like nobody believes in privacy anymore."

"Convenience wins," said Walther. "Who are you calling?"

"Hopefully? Help." I studied the display before dialing backward from zero to one, hitting the pound key three times, and pressing "talk." The phone hissed dully. That was a good sign. I raised it to my ear, chanting, "Red Rover, Red Rover, send the cranky sea witch who's probably gonna kill me one day on over."

Marcia gasped. Walther just looked perplexed. Everyone's heard of the Luidaeg, but almost no one knows her, and most people definitely don't have her home phone number. Walther hadn't been in town long enough to hear about my "special" relationship with a woman any sane person would stay the hell away from. He'd learn.

My magic responded to the request by rising around me, filling my mouth with the taste of copper and fresh-cut grass. The hissing cut out, replaced by the sound of distant static. I sighed, letting my shoulders relax. The Luidaeg doesn't technically have phone service, and that can make it hard to get a connection. The special effects were a sign that things were going right.

The static stopped abruptly. The spell I'd been trying to cast shattered around me as the Luidaeg snarled, "Who is it?"

She sounded pissed. Nothing new there; the Luidaeg usually sounds pissed. Before she could hang up, I said quickly, "Luidaeg, it's me."

"Toby?" There was a faint edge of hysteria in her voice. That worried me. Anything that could actually upset the Luidaeg was something I wanted to avoid. "What the hell do you want?"

"I need your help."

"Do you, now? Well, how about you deal with your own shit for once?"

Arguing with the Luidaeg is stupid bordering on suicidal, but I didn't have time to try diplomacy. "I need *you*. Lily's sick."

She paused. "Sick, how? Is that the only reason you're calling, or is the world ending, too?"

"Nobody's told me if it is," I said. "She can't focus, she's forgetting things, and she doesn't look right. It's like she can't remember what shape she's supposed to be."

"If she's sick, she *can't* remember. Undine are only material because they concentrate." Something in the background shattered. "Have you checked her waters?"

I looked toward Walther and said, "They've been checked magically and mundanely. They're clean."

"What about her pearl?"

I hesitated. "Her what?"

"Oh, for fuck's sake." The Luidaeg sounded more tired than annoyed. "Undine have pearls that serve them as physical anchors. If they're damaged, the Undine is damaged. Do you know where Lily's pearl is hidden? Have you checked it?"

"No, I—"

"Ask her, and get those waters tested again. That's all I can give you." She sighed. "There are things you can't fix, Toby. Maybe it's time you learned that."

"Luidaeg, please. This is serious."

"It's always serious to heroes, but they can't save everyone. Just ask my father." She laughed bitterly. "There's nothing else I can do for you, or for her. I'm in the middle of something." There was another crash, and the sound of splintering wood.

I hesitated. "Is everything okay?"

That seemed to be the wrong thing to say. "There's nothing here that needs a hero," she snapped. "I wish I were the answer to all your problems, but I'm not. Now leave me alone. I have work to do." She slammed the receiver down. I heard plastic crack before the connection went dead.

I lowered Walther's phone, vaguely aware that my fingers were clenched tight enough that my knuckles had gone white. "She hung up on me."

"The sea witch hung up on you?" asked Marcia, sounding awed.

"Wait—are you saying that was—?" Walther gaped at me.

I tossed him back his phone, starting to massage my aching fingers. "Yes, it was, and yes, she did. I guess she's not having a good night. Do either of you know where Lily keeps her pearl?"

"Her what?" asked Marcia.

Walther kept gaping. "Why does the sea witch want to know where Lily keeps her pearl?"

"Can we just accept that I know the Luidaeg and move on?" I asked. "She says Lily's pearl being damaged might explain why she's so sick. She also says we need to test the water again."

"I'll get right on that," said Walther slowly, "but I don't know where Lily keeps her pearl."

"Neither do I," said Marcia.

"Right." I pinched the bridge of my nose, reviewing our options. Finally, straightening, I said, "Screw it. Let's ask Lily."

Marcia's eyes widened. "Do you think she'll answer?"

"I think we're playing with her life if we don't try." I started for the moon bridge. "Come on."

They came.

The temperature in Lily's knowe had dropped several degrees while we were outside, and the pathways were even harder to find. Her illness was definitely affecting the place, and that couldn't be good. The three of us wandered lost for almost a quarter of an hour, seeing no one, before we found our way back to the willows. The handmaids were still there, waiting for Lily to need them. I asked if they knew where she kept her pearl. They shook their heads. So much for the easy way.

Marcia stopped a few feet from the entrance to the willow grove. "I can't. I'm sorry. I just can't."

"It's okay." I glanced to Walther. "Stay with her?" He nodded. "Good. You two wait here. I'll be out as soon as I can, and we'll figure out what comes next."

I walked into the hot shadows under the trees alone. "Lily?" There was no reply. I kept walking. "Lily?"

She came into view ahead of me, her skin impossibly pale against the black water around her. I dropped to my knees next to the pool, leaning in to put a hand on her arm.

"Lily?" I whispered. She didn't react. She would have looked peaceful if she hadn't been so bloodlessly white, and so cold. I risked giving her a small shake. "Please, I need you to wake up and tell me where you hid your pearl. We need it to save you."

"She won't wake up," said a voice behind me.

"I had to try." I twisted to look over my shoulder, not moving otherwise. "How did things go at the Queen's Court?"

"I was politely asked to leave." A flicker of amusement crossed Tybalt's face. "Your Lady Fetch has a true talent for being insulting. I don't think I've ever been called some of those names before, and I've been called a great many names. I believe your large friend was taking her home. I came to see if you needed any aid." He walked over to offer his hand. I took it, letting him tug me to my feet.

"Not unless you know where Lily keeps her pearl." Keeping my voice as level as I could, I repeated what the Luidaeg had said. He didn't let go of my hand. "Oak and ash, Tybalt, I don't know what to do."

"You'll do whatever needs to be done. You always do."

"And if it doesn't work?" I wanted to get angry. I wanted something to hit. But anger wasn't going to help, and no targets were presenting themselves. "What then?"

"Then I suppose we'll have a problem."

I glared at him before letting out a heavy breath and tugging my fingers free. "I should head home. Will you—"

"I'll watch them until Lily can tell me my services aren't required." He offered a small smile before he turned away, walking out of the willows without another word. There was nothing else I could do in the grove, and so I followed.

Marcia and Walther were standing on a patch of green a few yards from the trees. She was leaning against him and shivering, although it looked more like exhaustion than cold. Walther looked up when he heard us coming, and blinked at the sight of Tybalt, but didn't say anything. The Court of Cats has been loosely affiliated with the fiefdoms of Golden Gate Park for a long, long time. Everyone who lives in the Park gets accustomed to the Cait Sidhe coming and going as they please.

"Lily isn't waking up," I said, without preamble. "I need you to ask around the knowe and see if anyone knows where her pearl is hidden. If she wakes up, ask her directly. All right?"

"Y-yes," said Marcia. Walther just nodded.

"Good. Call me if you need anything, or if you find anything. I'll check in tomorrow." I hesitated before adding, "If Lily gets worse . . ."

"We'll call," said Walther.

"Good," I said. That seemed insufficient, so I repeated, lamely, "Good."

Marcia took a deep breath, and said, "The rules won't let us thank you, but we're grateful you came. We know you don't like us. So it was good of you to come."

"What?" I frowned at her. "I don't understand what you mean."

"We wouldn't have blamed you if you never wanted to have anything to do with the Tea Gardens, or us, ever again. Simon hurt you here, and we didn't stop him."

"Marcia . . ." I groaned. "Oh, root and *branch*."

Sixteen years ago, Simon Torquill turned me into a fish and abandoned me in the Tea Gardens. I'm pretty sure he expected me to choke to death on the air. Subtlety isn't a lost art in Faerie, and neither is screwing up. I couldn't turn myself back, but when a tourist scooped me into the water, I could sure as hell swim for freedom. Furious, Simon wrapped the Tea Gardens in a shroud of forgetfulness, hiding them from the rest of Faerie. I don't know how: he shouldn't have had that kind of power. He did it anyway, and for fourteen years the people I loved thought I was dead, while the people who loved Lily forgot she'd ever existed.

As for Lily's subjects . . . they couldn't see her, couldn't touch her, couldn't even remember why they were there. They scattered, and not all of them made it back when the spell hiding the Tea Gardens from fae eyes was finally broken. As for exactly where they'd been and what they'd been doing . . . they'd never tried to tell me, and I never asked. I knew too well how hard Faerie can be on the weak when there's no one to protect them. When the walls came down, they came home, and I'd let that be enough.

Some of the purebloods in the Tea Gardens had lived there longer than I'd been alive, and they'd just gotten their home back. Could they survive losing it again? "Lily matters to me," I said finally. "I won't abandon her because of what Simon did. I won't abandon any of you."

Marcia pulled away from Walther and flung her arms around me before I had a chance to react. She was sobbing in earnest now. I winced, beginning to stroke her hair with one hand. "Shhh, Marcia. It's gonna be okay."

"Promise?" she whispered.

I didn't argue this time. "I promise. If there's a way to make this better, I will. It's my job. But I have to go now."

"Okay, Toby," she said, and let go of me, stepping back. "Okay."

Several more of Lily's subjects had wandered over while we spoke. They almost surrounded us, standing at a respectful distance and watching with hungry eyes. They were hoping I'd fix things. There was just one problem: I didn't think I could.

"Come on," said Tybalt, putting a hand on my shoulder and steering me toward the moon bridge. Walther followed, tugging Marcia gently along by one hand.

The garden exits were locked for the night. That might not have been an issue if Lily were awake, but with her incapacitated, we had to deal with certain limitations. Tybalt looked measuringly at the shadows, finally shaking his head. "Not after running here from the Queen's knowe," he said. "I'm already stretched too thin to carry anyone else along."

"That's okay." It was almost reassuring to hear that he had limits. "Walther, is there another way out of here?"

"Yes," he said, and led us to a door in the bushes. It was being held open by another of Lily's courtiers. I didn't recognize him, and he didn't meet my eyes as we approached. I gave Marcia a quick hug, murmuring a last, "Call me," before stepping through the opening. Tybalt followed. The door closed behind us, disappearing. They don't call us "the hidden folk" for nothing—we're not seen when we don't want to be.

Tybalt walked me to the parking lot. When we reached the end of the grass, he said, abruptly, "I'm not sure how to say this so you'll listen."

"How about you just say it, and we'll see what happens?" I turned toward him. His eyes were very green in the streetlight glow. "Is this about what happened at the Queen's Court? I'm sorry I slapped you. It seemed like the best way to cause a diversion."

"That's nothing," he said, waving it off. "The Queen

didn't give you Goldengreen out of the kindness of her heart, Toby. You should know that."

"I do." I flashed a tight, sardonic smile. "My mama didn't raise no fools."

"Your mother didn't raise you at all." His expression was grave, eyes searching my face. I just didn't know what he was looking for. "I don't know what she's trying, but it's a trap of some sort. I've been a King too long not to know that much."

I nodded, feeling a new layer of stress adding itself to the mountain I was already carrying. "There was no way to say I wouldn't take it. Not unless I wanted to get myself exiled for insolence."

"Even so." He reached out and brushed his fingers along the side of my jaw. "October . . ."

"Why did you kiss me?" The question was asked almost before I realized it was forming. I felt myself go red.

Tybalt jerked back like I'd slapped him again, hand dropping. "My reasons were the same as yours. I needed to cast the eyes of the gossips on something concrete, rather than risk them gossiping about our acquaintance."

"You could have stayed away. There wouldn't have been any gossip then."

"No, I couldn't. The Lady of the Mists was planning something."

"Tybalt—"

"It was a means to an end; that's all. I'm sorry if I offended. I'll set my people to watch the Tea Gardens; call if you need me." He stepped backward into the shadows. "Take care, little fish. These waters are deeper than you're accustomed to." The shadows closed around him, and he was gone.

I looked at the place he'd been for a long moment before I sighed and turned toward the parking lot . . . where my car wasn't, thanks to my having taken the yarrow broom express from the Queen's Court.

"Damn," I said. This didn't make my car appear, but it made me feel a little bit better. I considered turning around, walking back to the Tea Gardens, and asking if anyone could give me a ride. The urge passed as fast as it came. Lily's subjects were upset enough without their erstwhile protector stomping in and admitting that she forgot she didn't drive there.

Most of the world's payphones have vanished in the last twenty years, but there are survivors, if you know where to look. I made my way through Golden Gate Park to the phone near the oh-so-touristy "picnic meadow," swearing under my breath as I realized that the Queen's transformation of my clothes hadn't left me with pockets, much less pocket change. Calling a taxi was out; I've been developing moral objections to hexing taxi drivers since I started hanging out with Danny, and he was busy taking care of May. It was the bus or nothing.

If the bus driver thought there was something strange about a bedraggled woman in a ball gown getting on in the wee hours of the morning, he didn't say anything. The odds were good I wasn't the worst thing he'd seen that night. I held up a hand, palm cupped to make it look like I was holding something, and used the last of the magic I'd called up for my makeshift human disguise to make the driver see a monthly pass. He grunted acknowledgment, and I slumped into the seat nearest the door.

At that moment, I would have given almost anything for a way to find my mother and tell her what was happening. She was the strongest blood-worker in Faerie before she went crazy. She could probably follow Lily's waters back to their source and give us the key to everything. Or she could have, once. Unfortunately, while I might have been able to find Amandine's body, there's no detective in the world good enough to find her mind. The lights are on, but nobody's home, and the electric bill is getting high.

The ride to my apartment took twenty minutes, mostly because several of the late-night passengers were drunk, and insisted on trying to talk to the driver before they'd take their seats. I left the bus with a hearty respect for bus drivers, and a renewed desire to never take public transit again.

The living room lights were on as I walked toward the door, and the wards had been dissolved, not broken. That's a crucial difference: broken wards mean something's in your house that shouldn't be there. Open wards mean somebody's home. I let myself inside.

May was asleep on the couch with Spike in her lap. The television was on but muted. I turned it off before walking down the hall to my bedroom, careful not to disturb May. It was better if she took the chance to get some rest. We'd know more soon, and in the meanwhile, I needed to close my eyes for a few minutes before I called Shadowed Hills and brought Sylvester up to speed.

Once I was in my room, I kicked off my shoes and sat down on the bed, still wearing my ball gown. I needed to call Sylvester. I needed to change my clothes. I needed to get moving.

I vaguely remember hearing the cats jump onto the foot of the bed. After that, there was nothing.

SIX

IOPENED MY EYES TO A WORLD made entirely of flowers. Entirely of white flowers, no less, morning glories and white roses and the delicate brocade of Queen Anne's Lace. I blinked. The flowers remained.

"Okay, this is officially weird," I murmured. The flowers overhead shook in the breeze, sending loose petals showering down over me. There was no perfume. Even when the wind was blowing, there was no perfume. I relaxed, suddenly understanding the reason for the bizarre change of scene. "Right. I'm dreaming."

"That was *fast*, Auntie Birdie," said an approving voice to my left.

I sat up, shaking petals out of my hair as I turned. "Given how often you people throw me into whacked-out dream sequences these days, it's becoming a survival skill. Why are you in my dreams, Karen? I'm assuming it's not just boredom." I paused. "Crap. I'm asleep. I can't be asleep now. I have things to do."

My adopted niece looked at me gravely. She was kneeling in the grass, petals speckling her white-blonde hair. Her blue flannel pajamas made her look out of place, like she'd been dropped into the wrong movie. Karen is the second daughter of my best friend, Stacy Brown, and oh, yes—she's an oneiromancer, an unexpected talent that decided to manifest when she was captured by Blind Michael. She sees the future in dreams. She can also use dreams to tell people things she thinks they need to know. Lucky me, I'm a common target.

Good thing I like the kid, or I might get cranky about having my dreams invaded by a twelve year old on a semiregular basis.

"You can't be awake now, either. There's something you need to see," she said, and stood, walking away into the flowers. Lacking any other real options, I stood, brushed the flower petals off my jeans, and followed.

She had an easier time making it out of the impromptu bower than I did; she was lower to the ground, and could duck under branches that slapped me straight across the face. I was swearing under my breath by the time I pushed the last spray of gauzy white irises aside, stepped into the open, and froze, the profanity dying on my lips. I knew this place. Oh, sweet Titania, I knew it.

Amandine's tower stood tall and proud ahead of us, white stone glowing faintly against the twilit Summerlands sky. It always glowed like that, a lighthouse that never needed to be lit. Stone walls that matched the tower circled the gardens, delineating the borders without doing a thing to defend the place. Amandine never seemed to feel she needed defending, and when I was living with her, I was still too young to realize what a strange attitude that was in Faerie.

"Karen," I said, slowly, forcing myself to breathe, "what are we doing here?"

"Just watch," she said.

So I watched.

Dream time isn't like real time. I don't know how

long we stood in my mother's garden, but being there, even in a dream, made my chest ache. I spent half my childhood in that garden, trying to be something I wasn't. It's grown wild since Amandine abandoned her tower, and I'm glad. It's the only reason I can bear to go there at all.

"There," Karen whispered, taking my hand. "Look."

The eastern gate opened; someone was making her way down the garden path. I narrowed my eyes, squinting at the woman walking toward us. Black hair, golden skin, pointed ears, and eyes the bruised shade of the sky between stars. Oleander de Merelands. I stiffened, trying to push Karen behind me. "Damn," I hissed. "Karen, get down."

"This is a dream, Auntie Birdie," she said calmly. "Just watch."

Thrumming with tension, I stayed where I was, watching Oleander like a mouse watches a snake. Not a bad comparison. Oleander de Merelands was half-Peri, half-Tuatha de Dannan, and all hazardous to your health. She was there when Simon Torquill turned me into a fish; she laughed. Even knowing the things they say about her—the rumors of assassinations, the fondness for poisons, the trafficking in dark magic and darker services—that's the thing I can never seem to forget. She laughed.

Fae never get old, but most grown purebloods look like adults. Oleander barely looked sixteen, with a dancer's build and straight black hair that fell unchecked to her narrow hips. It was easy to see why no one took her seriously . . . at least until the stories about her started getting around. A velvet scarf with weighted edges circled her waist: barbs glittered in the fringe. Anything's a weapon if you know how to use it.

She walked straight past us. I relaxed slightly. This was a dream; she couldn't see what wasn't really there. She stopped at the tower door, where she raised her hand and knocked, calmly as you please. A minute or so later, the door opened, and my mother stepped out onto the tower steps.

My breath caught again, this time for an entirely different reason. I haven't seen my mother in years—not really. The real Amandine slipped away while I was in the pond. I wasn't prepared for the sight of her in her prime. It was easy to forget how beautiful she was, to assume I was romanticizing her, making her into some impossible ideal. I wasn't.

Karen's hair was white-blonde and looked faintly bleached. Amandine's hair was white gold, the simple, natural color of some unknown precious metal. She wore it twisted into an elegant braid that trailed down the back of her wine-colored gown to her waist. Her eyes were the same smoky gray-blue as morning fog. They widened when she saw Oleander, before narrowing in outrage.

"What are you doing here?" she demanded. "You are not welcome. I grant you no hospitalities, nor the warmth of my hearth."

"Why, Amy, aren't you the high-nosed bitch these days." Oleander's own voice was thick with loathing. "*He* sent me. Someone thought he should know you'd come home again, and now he's wondering after your welfare."

Amandine pursed her lips. Finally, dismissively, she asked, "Is this what you're reduced to? Playing messenger girl for the Daoine Sidhe? I thought you held yourself better than this."

"At least I didn't whore myself to the mortal world for a replacement," Oleander spat. "Has he even seen your little imitation, Amy? I can take her to see him, if you still think you're too good for social calls. Or are you afraid she'll realize what she is? Are you afraid—"

I winced even before Amandine started to move. Oleander didn't know her like I did, and didn't recognize the tension in her posture until it was too late. Amandine lunged, wrapping one hand around Oleander's throat and the other around her wrist before the other woman had a chance to react.

I shouldn't have been able to hear what came next. We were too far away, and she was speaking too softly. But this was a dream, and I was going to hear what Karen wanted me to hear.

"If you come near my daughter, if you touch her, if you *look* at her, I will know, and I will make you pay." Amandine's tone was light. She would have sounded almost reasonable, if not for the fury in her expression . . . and the fear in Oleander's. Oak and ash, one of the scariest women in Faerie was looking at my mother like she was the monster in the closet. "Do you understand me, Oleander? I will make you pay in ways you can barely comprehend. I will make it *hurt*, and the pain won't stop just because I do. Do you understand?"

"Bitch," hissed Oleander.

Amandine narrowed her eyes. The smell of her magic—blood and roses—suddenly filled the formerly scentless garden, and Oleander screamed. Her own magic rose in response, acid and oleanders, and was almost immediately buried under Mother's blood and roses. Amandine didn't move, but she must have been doing *something*, because Oleander kept screaming, a high, keening sound that wasn't meant to come from any human-shaped throat.

The smell of blood and roses faded. Oleander slumped in Amandine's hands. My mother looked down at her dispassionately, not letting go.

"How much of who you are is what you are?" Amandine asked. Her voice was still soft. That was possibly the worst part. "How much do you think it would change? Would you like to find out?"

"No," whispered Oleander.

"I'm afraid I can't hear you. What was that you said?"

Oleander licked her lips. "I said I wouldn't go near your daughter. I'll leave. I'll say you don't want to be disturbed."

"Ah, good." Amandine released her, looking satisfied. Oleander dropped to her knees, gasping, as Amandine stepped back to her original position. "That's what I hoped you said. Your visit has been most enlightening, Oleander. I trust it won't be repeated."

Oleander staggered to her feet, glaring daggers at my mother as she stumbled backward, out of reach. "It won't. I won't come here again."

"Not even if he sends you?"

"There are some things I won't risk for anyone." Oleander took another step back, keeping her eyes on Amandine the whole time. "Keep your little half-breed bitch. The two of you can rot for all I care."

"I'll take that under advisement," said Amandine. Turning her back on Oleander, she walked back into the tower and closed the door.

Oleander stayed where she was for a brief second, glaring daggers at my mother's wake. Then she turned, storming down the path and out the gate, into the fields beyond the tower grounds.

I turned to Karen. "Why did you show me that?"

"I don't know." She shrugged helplessly. "I'm still not very good at this. I just sort of do what the dreams tell me I have to. But I didn't show it to you."

"What?" I frowned. "Of course you did. I just saw it."

"No." She looked past me, into the bower of white-on-white flowers where the dream began. "I didn't show you. I just reminded you that you knew it."

It took me a moment to realize what she was saying. Slowly, I turned, and saw myself—my much smaller, much younger self, still new to the Summerlands, still so dazed by the wonders of Faerie that I hadn't started looking for the dangers—crawling out from underneath the branches.

"See?" said Karen. "You already knew."

"I . . . I don't remember this."

"You do now." I felt her hand on my arm, as light as the flower petals still drifting in the air around us. "It's time to wake up, Auntie Birdie."

So I did.

SEVEN

LATE AFTERNOON SUN STREAMED through the bedroom window, hitting me full in the face. I opened my eyes, trying to blink and squint against the glare at the same time. Not a good combination. Sunlight. I was only supposed to sit down for a few minutes before calling Sylvester. But then I'd fallen into Karen's dreamscape, and that meant I'd been asleep. And it hadn't even been dawn yet when I got home.

"Crap!" I sat bolt upright. The cat that had been curled in the middle of my chest went tumbling to the bed, her purr turning into an irritated yowl.

"Afternoon, Sleeping Beauty," said May. I turned to see her standing in the doorway, a coffee mug in one hand. "Welcome back to the land of the living."

"What time is it?" I demanded, raking my hair back with both hands. It was tangled into hopeless knots, matted stiff with sea salt. Crossing the city on a yarrow broom probably hadn't helped. The cat—Cagney—stalked stiff-legged to the foot of the bed where she settled, her back to me. "Why didn't you wake me sooner?"

"You didn't tell me to," she replied matter-of-factly.

Expression turning solemn, she continued, "Also, you didn't twitch when I opened your curtains half an hour ago, so I figured you needed the sleep. It's almost sunset. Marcia's been calling every two hours; there's been no change in Lily's condition."

"She filled you in?" I let my hands drop to my lap.

May nodded. "Yeah. Now get up, get something into your stomach, and get dressed before we're late."

"Late? For what?" Cagney stood again, arching her back into a furry mirror of the moon bridge, before strolling across the bed and smacking her sister awake. Lacey responded by biting her. I sympathized.

"I repeat, it's almost sunset. On the first of May. That means what?"

"Oh, *no*." I groaned, falling backward on the bed. "May, I can't. Karen was in my head last night. She showed me this screwed-up . . . I don't know if it was a memory or what, but it had Mom in it, and Oleander. I need to call and find out what the hell she was getting at."

"Cry me a river. The Torquills expect you to attend the Beltane Ball, and you're attending. You can explain the situation when we get there."

"I hate you sometimes."

"That's fine. We're still going."

The Beltane Ball at Shadowed Hills is one of the Duchy's biggest social events, and has been for centuries. It's a night of dancing, drinking, and welcoming the summer. In short, May's sort of party. My sort of party involves less of a crowd, and a lot more physical violence. "I don't think this is a good idea."

"It's not," she agreed. "But you can't become Countess of Goldengreen, run out of the Queen's Court like your ass is on fire, and then miss the big party. Not if you want to keep the Queen from figuring something's up."

"Crap," I said, staring up at the ceiling.

"Basically." I heard her sip her coffee. "You okay?"

I laughed bitterly. "I'm peachy."

"There's the manic-depressive sweetheart we all know and love. Get up. You'll feel better after you've had a shower."

"Look, can't you just call Sylvester and tell him I'm not coming?" I threw an arm over my face to block the light. "Tell him I'm busy saving the world. Better yet, how about you just be me for the night? You look the part."

"Uh, one, no way. Two, I might *look* like you, but the jig would be up the minute I opened my mouth." She walked over and kicked the bed. "Get up before I get the ice water. You're trying to wallow in your misery, and I'm not putting up with it."

I moved my arm to glare at her. "I hate you."

"I know. Now come on. We'll go to the Ball, and you can meet my date."

That was news. I sat up, blinking. "You have a date?"

"I do. See, unlike some people, I know a good thing when I see it."

"I'm going to leave that alone," I said, scooting to the edge of the bed. My skirt snarled around me, hampering my movement. "I'm up. See? I'm up."

"Good girl. Just for that, you can have a *hot* shower."

"Don't make me kick your ass."

"You can try. Now come on: breakfast, coffee, shower, clothes." She stepped out into the hall, whistling. I flung a pillow after her. It bounced off the doorframe.

May was in her room with the door shut when I emerged, clearly having chosen retreat as the better part of valor. Smart girl. I made a beeline for the phone in the hall, only to find a cup of coffee sitting next to it. I had to smile a little at that. It's weirdly reassuring to live with someone who knows me better than anyone else does, even if she *is* the living portent of my inevitable, probably messy, demise.

I leaned against the wall, dialing the number for the

Tea Gardens. The phone rang enough times that I was giving serious thought to panic when Marcia picked up, saying, "Japanese Tea Gardens. How may I help you?"

"It's me, Marcia. How is she?"

"Toby!" Her voice was naked with relief. "I'm so glad you called."

"I would have called earlier, but I just woke up." I sipped my coffee, scalding my lip. The pain wasn't enough to stop me from sipping again. "May gave me a status report. Has anything changed?"

"No. Lily isn't any worse. That's good, right?"

I wanted to reassure her. I couldn't do it. "I don't know. Has there been any progress in finding her pearl?"

"Not yet. Everybody's looking."

"Keep looking, and make sure that whoever you have watching Lily knows to ask about it if she wakes up. I have to go to Shadowed Hills and make an appearance at the Beltane Ball before I can come. Call there if you need anything."

"Okay." She sniffled. "I will."

There was nothing to say after that. We exchanged a few vague reassurances before I hung up, still unsettled. Attending a Ball while Lily was sick felt too much like Nero fiddling while Rome burned, but May was right; I didn't have much of a choice, especially not the day after I'd been elevated to Countess. Playing by the political rules was suddenly a lot more important.

I took another large gulp of coffee before dialing Mitch and Stacy's. "Almost sunset" meant everyone would be up; fae kids may be nocturnal, but that doesn't make them immune to the allure of afternoon TV.

"Brown residence," said the solemn, almost too-mature voice of Anthony, the older of the two Brown boys. He was ten on his last birthday.

"Hey, kiddo," I said, relaxing a bit against the wall. "Is your sister up yet?"

"Auntie Birdie!" he crowed, sounding delighted. Then

he sobered, the moment of exuberance fading as he said, "Karen went back to bed, but she told everybody that if you called, we should say you know everything she knows, and she doesn't know why it's important. Did she dream with you last night?"

"Yeah, she did," I said, resisting the urge to start swearing. "Look, when she wakes up, tell her to call if she thinks of *anything*, okay? And tell your mom I'll try to come over soon."

"Promise?"

"Double-promise. I miss you guys." The Browns are some of my favorite people in the world. It just seems like there's never time for the good parts of life these days, like hanging out with my old friends and their kids. It's been one emergency after the other, practically since I got out of the pond.

"We miss you, too, Auntie Birdie," said Anthony gravely.

Much as I wanted to stay on the line and ask him to tell me what he was studying, what his brother and sisters were doing, all the things a good aunt would ask, there wasn't time. I repeated my promise to visit soon and hung up, realizing as I did that I was hungry. Apparently the coffee had been enough to wake up my stomach.

I went to the kitchen and filled a bowl with Lucky Charms and coffee. Cliff used to make gagging noises and pretend to choke when I did that, but it's how I've always liked my cereal. I paused with the spoon halfway to my mouth as I realized that, for the first time in a long time, the thought of Cliff didn't hurt. It made me sad, sure—he wasn't just my lover and the father of my child; he was one of my best friends, and losing friends is never fun—but it was only sadness. No pain. No longing.

Maybe I was starting to move on.

I did feel better after eating, and a shower would probably make me feel almost normal. I left my empty bowl on the counter, fighting with my dress all the way to the bathroom. I've worn enough formal gowns to know how to move in them, but they were almost all illusionary, making changing out of them nothing more than a matter of dropping the spell. This dress was heavy, dirty, and all too real. Getting it off felt almost like a moral victory.

The apartment has excellent water pressure. I turned the taps all the way up before stepping into the shower, letting the spray sting my arms and face. I stayed there long after I was clean, breathing in the steam. There's something reassuring about standing in the shower; as long as you're there, you can't get dirty.

May was waiting on the couch when I came out of the bathroom. She looked me up and down before asking, "Feel better?"

"Actually, yes."

"Told you so. Now get dressed."

I flipped her off amiably. Her laughter followed me down the hall to my bedroom, where Cagney and Lacey curled up on the bed in the remains of the sunbeam. Lacey lifted her head, eyeing me.

"Don't worry," I said. "You're the lucky ones. You get to stay home." I started for the dresser, pausing with one hand stretched toward the top drawer.

The Queen's habit of transforming my clothes is incredibly irritating, especially since I lack the magical oomph to change them *back*. There are only a few bloodlines in Faerie talented at transforming the inanimate; the Daoine Sidhe aren't among them, which is why we depend on illusions and chicanery to enhance our wardrobes. But if I happened to have a dress formal enough for the occasion . . .

I grabbed the crumpled gown off the floor, holding it up. If I could figure out how to get the grass stains out of the skirt . . . I stuck my head out of the room. "Hey, May, you know anything about cleaning silk?"

She leaned over the back of the couch, eyes widening when she saw what I was holding. "Are you seriously thinking about wearing that?"

"I don't think I should be throwing magic around if I can help it, do you? It's not like I have that much to spare." Every changeling has a different amount of power, and pushing past your limits is a good way to mess yourself up. If I was going to stay at the top of my game, I needed to avoid magic-burn for as long as possible.

May hesitated before getting off the couch and walking toward my room. She bit her index finger, looking torn, and finally said, "I can help. Go get your knife."

I blinked. She met my eyes, nodding marginally. Something in that gesture told me to listen. I stepped past her, heading for the rack by the front door, where my knives still hung. I unsnapped the loop holding my silver knife in place and glanced back to May. "I assume I can use the silver, and not the iron?"

"Yeah," she said, with another nod. "Now cut yourself, and bleed on the dress."

I raised an eyebrow. "What?"

"Just trust me." She offered a wan smile. "It's a funky Fetch thing."

"Right," I said, slowly. I didn't have any better ideas, and so I nicked the back of my left hand, my stomach doing a lazy flip as the blood welled up. I hate the sight of my own blood. I glanced at May before wiping my hand on the bodice.

The already red fabric darkened, drinking the blood like dry earth drinks the rain. May grabbed my wrist, pressing my hand into the dress. I hadn't even realized she was moving up behind me. "May, what—"

"Trust me," she said, and snapped her fingers.

My magic flared in response to the sound, rising with an eagerness that was almost scary, even discounting the fact that I wasn't the one raising it. May was pulling less than a quarter of the power I'd need for an illusion. Her magic rose to join mine, adding ashes and cotton candy to the mingled scents of copper, fresh-cut grass, and blood.

And then the Queen's magic snapped into place around us, filling my mouth with the taste of rowan and damp sand. I stared at May as she let go of me, holding up the dress like a fresh canvas in a children's art class.

"The spell's fresh enough to argue with," she said. "Now tell it what to be."

I stared for a moment more before reaching out with my still-bleeding hand, grabbing for the Queen's spell the way I'd grab for mists or shadows when shaping an illusion. I hit a brief resistance, like the air was pushing back. Then my fingers caught, my magic surging to obscure everything else, and I understood what to do. The Queen taught my clothes to become a gown. I couldn't break her spell—not even blood gives me that kind of power—but as long as I wasn't trying to break anything, I could change the definition of "gown."

Visualization is important when you're assembling an illusion, and this was close enough that the same principles applied. I fixed the image of a simpler, *clean* dress in my mind and muttered, "Cinderella dressed in yellow went upstairs to kiss a fellow. Made a mistake, kissed a snake, how many doctors did it take?"

The magic pulled tight before bursting, leaving me with the gritty feeling of sand coating my tongue. My head didn't hurt. May's magic had fueled the spell, not mine; my magic only directed it. May offered me the dress.

"Done," she said.

"I didn't know you could do that," I said faintly, and took it.

The Queen designed a gown too fragile for heavy use and too impractical for anyone expecting to do something more strenuous than a waltz. It wasn't that gown anymore. The fabric was still the color of dried blood, but it was velvet now, not silk, and the material was slashed to reveal a dark rose under-skirt. The slashes were designed to look decorative, while allowing me to both conceal and draw my knives.

"Well, I can. Now go get ready."

I slung the dress over one arm before sheathing my knife and taking the belt off the rack. "Seriously, do you want to tell me how we did that?"

"Radical transformations stay malleable for a day or so; her spell was fresh enough to transmute. And you bled on it for me." She shrugged. "I'm your Fetch. I know when things are possible. Just go with it."

I eyed her, trying to figure out what she wasn't telling me. She smiled guilelessly. I finally sighed. "Be right back."

"I'll be waiting."

I managed to resist the urge to slam the bedroom door, but only because it would have bothered the cats.

Getting into the transmuted gown was a hell of a lot easier than getting out of it had been. Most of the hooks and ties were gone, replaced by buttons; my knife belt went over the interior skirt, the slight bulge it made hidden by the gold brocade band that rode easy on my hips. Maybe it's tacky to go to a formal party armed, but these days, I try not to go anywhere without a way to defend myself. Sylvester would understand. He always did.

I raked a brush through my hair, scowling at my reflection. It scowled obligingly back. One good thing about having hair with no real body: if I brush it out and clip it back, it stays clipped. "The things I do for Faerie, I swear," I muttered, before dropping the brush and calling it good.

Spike jumped onto the couch when I came back into the living room, rattling its thorns encouragingly in my direction. It chirped happily as I walked over and started stroking it. There's an art to petting a rose goblin without injuring yourself. They're basically animate, vaguely cat-shaped rosebushes, and you have to make sure not to move against the grain of the thorns.

"Let's go!" May gestured at the door.

I only flinched a little as Spike jumped up onto my shoulder. "Are you coming?" I asked. It chirped, rubbing a prickly cheek against mine. "Of course you are." Spike likes riding in the car a bit too much. I've had to fetch it from Stacy's twice, after she left without checking for hitchhikers.

"Think of it as a fashion statement," said May. "Ladies used to wear parrots and little monkeys. You wear a rose goblin. It's very chic." She waved her hands. The smell of cotton candy and ashes rose, fading to leave us both looking entirely human. I also appeared to be wearing an outfit identical to hers.

I raised an eyebrow.

"What? You *said* you needed to save your magic for later, and you can't go out looking like you just escaped from a Renaissance Fair." May grinned. "I'm not on the super-saver plan. I'll make myself something when we get there, after I see what my date's wearing."

"Show-off." I grabbed my jacket, shrugging it on over my illusionary sweatshirt and too-real ball gown. It was going to look funny either way, but I wanted it with me.

May waited for me on the walkway, trying to look huffy, and spoiling her own efforts by giggling as I locked the door and reset the wards. "Are you ready *now?*" she demanded, with a playful stomp for emphasis.

"As ready as I'm going to get," I replied. "Come on."

Still giggling, May grabbed my elbow and steered me toward the car. One way or another, I was going to the Ball.

EIGHT

THE DUCAL SEAT OF SHADOWED HILLS is anchored to the mortal world through Paso Nogal Park, located in the small, sleepy suburb of Pleasant Hill. It's the sort of town where kids play in the streets, men mow lawns, and women walk dogs, content and happy. A nice place. I could never live there. I'd go nuts and start shooting people inside of a month, driven over the edge by picket fences.

The parking lot was packed when we arrived, holding everything from a small bus to a pair of motorcycles held together with duct tape and ropes of enchanted ivy. Fae magic doesn't work on iron, but newer vehicles don't have much iron in them. That can save a lot on repair bills, if you know the right sort of mechanic.

Spike jumped out of the car as soon as I opened the door, vanishing into the bushes. I sighed. "I'm starting to feel like a taxi."

"Does that mean we should start tipping?" May asked. I glared. She laughed, putting up her hands in mock-surrender. "Kidding!"

"Liar. Now come on. I want to get in, see Sylvester

and Luna, and get out. This is going to be a long night." I paused. "Can you find your own way home?"

"Don't worry about it." She climbed out of the car, starting up the hill. I double-checked the locks, and followed.

May dropped our illusions as soon as we were out of view of the street. They might make me look and even feel like I was wearing jeans, but brambles without any senses to confuse would still tear my skirt if I didn't keep it out of the way. Getting into Shadowed Hills through the front door requires executing an ornate series of maneuvers that wouldn't look out of place in a gymnastics competition. May scrambled through them three yards ahead of me, pureblood grace combining with sensible clothes to let her beat me to the top by almost a minute.

The door into the knowe was open and May was gone when I finally got there. Quentin was standing in the doorway. "Took you long enough," he said, and grinned.

I paused, studying him as I caught my breath. He was wearing a dark blue tunic over yellow linen trousers—the Ducal colors are blue and gold—and the crest of Shadowed Hills was embroidered above his heart. He'd grown over the summer. The dandelion-fluff of his hair was starting to darken, going from childhood's blond to an almost metallic bronze. That happens with pureblood Daoine Sidhe kids. They're born pale, and they darken into their adult coloring as they move through puberty. Quentin was growing up.

"Yeah, well, I'm old and slow," I said. "You look spiffy. Something going on?"

"You mean besides the Beltane Ball?"

"Oh, right. I knew I was forgetting something."

"Because you'd so be dressed that way if you didn't have to be." He rolled his eyes. "Get in here."

"Your wish, my command." I stepped past him into the knowe. The walls of the entry hall were draped with floral garlands, and the floor was polished to a mirror shine. "Aren't you going to say something about my dress?"

"The fact that you're wearing one without Her Grace needing to slap you is too weird to think about." Quentin closed the door. It dissolved into the wall.

"Way to insult my fashion sense." I've known Quentin almost two years, and I've never heard him call Sylvester or Luna by their proper names. "You on duty?"

Quentin nodded. "Care for an escort?"

"If you insist." I hooked my arm through his, letting him lead me down the hall.

Shadowed Hills pays little attention to silly concepts like "linear floor plans." The archway at the end of the hall showed a peaceful-looking library. Lies. Bracing myself, I closed my eyes and let Quentin tug me through. The world did a sickening dip-and-weave around us. I opened my eyes when the floor stopped moving, and found that we were standing in a vast ballroom, the walls decked with ropes of flowers and ribbons.

The band at one end of the room played a waltz with more enthusiasm than skill. Dancers of every shape and size packed the floor, ranging from a Centaur in a farthingale trying to tango with a Urisk to a Hob foxtrotting with a Glastig in widow's weeds, while a pair of Cornish Pixies danced an aerial polka above them. Dancers shouted across the crowd, dignity and propriety abandoned for the duration of the party. Those were things for other nights. Tonight was for welcoming the summer home. It was a cross-section of Faerie, standing in perfect contrast to the cold perfection of the Queen's Court.

"Can you find Sylvester for me?" I asked, letting go of Quentin's hand before shrugging out of my leather jacket and handing it to him. He took it without comment or complaint. As a working courtier, taking my coat was part of his job. He'd have been a lot more likely to object if I'd tried to walk into the dance with the jacket still on.

Quentin nodded. "I should be able to."

"Good. I'll be over there." I indicated a relatively clear stretch of wall, suitable for leaning against and waiting. Quentin nodded again and turned, vanishing into the crowd with admirable speed. I moved more cautiously, skirting the edge of the dance floor until I reached the wall. A Brownie passed with a tray of drinks. I snagged a glass of wine and settled in to watch the room.

Beltane is one of the fixed points of the fae year, when the Unseelie Court steps down in favor of the Seelie and everything starts over. It used to be celebrated only by Titania's descendants, but it's become more general since the King and Queens disappeared. Now even Maeve's lines come to join in the fun. The fae equivalent of going secular, I suppose.

"Toby!" shouted May. I turned to see her bearing down on me, tugging a dark-haired woman along with her. "There you are!"

"Here I am," I agreed.

My Fetch wore a subdued smoke-gray dress that complemented our mutual skin tone, accented with opal jewelry in tarnished silver settings. She looked fabulous. She also looked almost shy as she stopped in front of me, the dark-haired woman stopping next to her. "Toby, I want you to meet my date, Jasmine."

I nearly choked on my wine. "Your *what*?"

"My date. Remember, I told you I had one?" She leaned over to pluck the glass from my hand. "Jasmine, this is my roommate, Toby Daye."

"Most people call me Jazz," said Jasmine, with a semi-avian bob of her head. "May's told me so much about you. It's great to finally meet you."

Still coughing from the wine I'd inhaled, I gave Jazz a quick once-over without even trying to be subtle. She was barefoot under her brown velvet gown, and barely topped five feet. Her skin was a rich medium-brown, and her hair was glossy black, filled with green-and-blue highlights. Her eyes were amber, rimmed with brown. Bird's eyes. They confirmed her bloodline; Raven-dancer, skinshifter cousins of the Swanmays, probably from one of the flocks that originated in India.

Raven-dancers used to be considered death omens. Just like Fetches.

Catching my appraisal, Jasmine said, "I promise my intentions are good."

May laughed. "Don't mind Toby. She's my parent and original."

It takes more than an unexpected girlfriend to get me too flustered for Shakespeare. "Fairy, skip hence," I replied. "I have forsworn your bed and company."

"Haven't," she countered. "The rent would be awful, and you'd have no one to do the dishes."

"Fair enough." I turned to Jazz, offering her a smile. "Nice to meet you."

"I know, right?" She grinned. I decided to like her. "I was starting to feel like May was hiding one of us away."

"Toby's been too busy inheriting a County to talk to us peons," May said.

I groaned. "Oh, don't start."

Jazz cocked her head to the side. "You didn't want it?"

"What gives you that idea?"

"The way you wrinkle your nose when May says 'County.'" She laughed. "She wasn't kidding when she said you looked alike."

"There are reasons for that." I gave May a sidelong look.

She shook her head. "It's cool. She knows I'm your Fetch."

"You do?" I looked back to Jazz, surprised. A lot of people won't even talk to a Fetch. What sort of person dates one?

"I'm a raven." She shrugged. "We're psychopomps. If

she wants to be an omen of death when we're not hanging out, that's cool."

"So you're saying you don't mind if your girlfriend has a job?"

"Pretty much."

"Congratulations, May," I said, reclaiming my glass. "You found someone weirder than you are."

"It took work, but it was worth it." She winked at me. "And now we're off."

"To do what?"

"Dance!" She grabbed Jasmine's hand, hauling her back into the crowd. I returned to my spot against the wall. That's yet another thing we don't have in common: I hate dancing.

So May was dating a girl. Huh. Faerie isn't hung up on sexual orientation—experimentation is normal when you have forever—but I'm straight, and I expected May to be the same way. I kept telling people not to assume we were the same. Maybe it was time to start taking my own advice.

A petite Hob with pale eyes and honey-colored hair paused, offering her tray. "Fancy a drink, ma'am?" I didn't recognize her, but that wasn't unusual; the big knowes often borrow servers from one another for the big parties, just to take up the slack.

"Got one." I raised my glass. "Are you new, or just guesting?"

"New, ma'am," she said, and bobbed a curtsy. The contents of her tray remained miraculously unspilled. "Just hired from Wild Strawberries, ma'am."

"Ah. Cool." Wild Strawberries is the Tylwyth Teg Duchy up by Sacramento, which probably explained why she'd moved on. The Tylwyth are nice folks, but they're hard on the staff. Hobs don't usually settle long in their holdings. "Well, welcome. I'm one of Sylvester's knights; my name's—"

"Oh, I know *you!*" she said. "We all know *you*, ma'am. You're Toby Daye, the Duke's favorite."

"Uh . . . if you say so." I blinked. His favorite? That was news to me.

"Don't mind me, ma'am, I ramble." She winked, moving the tray to her other hand. "My name's Nerium, call me Neri, everyone does. I'd love to chat, but it's my first party here; I need to make a good showing if I want them to keep me on."

Her cheer was infectious. I smiled. "You'll do fine."

"I hope so, ma'am. If I see the Duke before he sees you, I'll tell him you've arrived." She curtsied again before vanishing into the crowd.

I settled against the wall, taking slow sips of my wine. The tempo of the music changed, sliding into a slower, statelier pattern. I felt a hand on my shoulder, accompanied by the faint scent of dogwood flowers. I turned, my instinctive smile tempering to something more solemn than the norm. "Your Grace."

Sylvester nodded, his own smile as tempered as mine. "You made it."

"I did. May wouldn't let me skip out."

"Remind me to give that girl a Barony. May I have this dance?"

If there's anyone who can get me onto the dance floor, it's him. I put my glass on the table. "We need to talk," I said. "It's about Lily."

"That's why we're dancing," he said, and took my hands, pulling me along. "Don't look at your feet. Just trust me."

I don't take that sort of suggestion from most people. Sylvester's special. I kept my chin up, letting him guide me into the dance. His steps were steady enough to make up for how unsure mine were. He was doing what a good liege is supposed to do: he was making me better than I would be on my own.

"Sylvester, I—"

"In a moment," he said, and bore me along.

We circled twice before he spun me out, fingers circling my wrist, and pulled me back to the stability of his arms. I looked around. We had somehow managed to move to the center of the crowd, where the sheer volume of the bodies around us would keep even the most experienced eavesdropper from making sense of our conversation.

"Now," said Sylvester, leaning toward me so that his words fell into the hollow space between our bodies. "Is Lily as bad as her handmaid seemed to fear?"

I nodded. "As bad, if not worse. She's really, really sick." I gave a quick run-down of her symptoms.

The muscles around his eyes tightened. "If the Queen—"

"She won't. But I'm sure you understand why I can't stay long."

"I do. If there's anything we can do, you need only ask. You know that."

It was a shot in the dark, but it was one I needed to take. "Did Lily ever tell you where she hid her pearl?"

"No." There was honest regret in his voice. "Your mother might have known, but I never did. Lily and I . . . respected each other for the shared elements of our past. That didn't make us friends."

"Damn," I muttered. I looked past him, trying to figure out what else to ask, and caught a flash of gold from the other side of the crowd. I frowned. "Who's that?"

Sylvester didn't turn. "That would be Raysel." His voice was flat and impassive.

"Raysel?" I looked closer. He was right; it was her. I guess a conveniently timed summer cold was just a little bit too much to ask.

Rayseline Torquill looked superficially like her father, but where he was understated and elegant, she was gaudy and overdone. The blue rosettes on her gold silk gown clashed with her hair. The bodice was cut too low and the skirt was cut too high, but no one was going to question the Duke's daughter at her own family's Beltane Ball. She looked like a tacky costume party rendition of a fairy-tale princess.

Her partner . . . wasn't her husband. I stared. He was dressed entirely in blue, and the formal cut of his clothes echoed Quentin's—but Quentin looked comfortable in his court clothes, and this boy looked like he was longing for jeans. His hair was a rich gold a few shades darker than Raysel's gown. A pale track of pixie-sweat glimmered in the air behind them as he spun her around the dance floor, expression dour.

"Manuel." I looked back to Sylvester. "How is he?"

"Doing better. Quentin tells me he was even seen smiling the other night."

"Good."

I was a petty criminal in the service of a man named Devin before I was a knight of Shadowed Hills. I went to Devin when Evening was murdered, and the help he gave me included two of the kids who'd replaced me in his entourage: Manuel and his sister Dare. Devin was always a bastard, but I thought he loved me, and I never dreamed he'd betray me. Even after I knew how wrong I'd been, I didn't know the kids were involved. Not until Manuel pulled a gun.

Devin and Dare both died that night. I lived, and Manuel blamed me. That was okay; I blamed me, too. I should've seen the truth sooner, or reacted faster, or . . .

You can live your life in "should" and never change anything. What's done is done. We buried our dead. I went home. Manuel went to Shadowed Hills to hate me in peace. We'd been avoiding each other since then, a practice Sylvester was wise enough not to object to. Some wounds only heal with time.

The dance was ending. Sylvester spun me one last time before leading me back to the wall, where he let go of my hands and bowed. I curtsied in return, putting every ounce of courtly courtesy I had into the gesture.

"I would stay," he said, as he straightened. "But a

host's duties demand I go. Will you consult with Luna before you leave?"

"Absolutely. I'm hoping she might know . . . something."

"No rest for the wicked, is there?" He smiled sadly before he turned, slipping into the crowd. The band was striking up a fresh waltz. The dancers swirled around him, and he was gone, leaving me to return to my original position alone.

Someone had shifted my wine to the side to make room for a tray of canapés. I gave it a dubious look, considering the wisdom of drinking something I'd left unattended, and settled for picking it up and putting it on the nearest tray of dishes to be returned to the kitchen. Better safe than really, really sorry. The stem of the glass was coated with powdered sugar from a stack of tea cakes. It came off on my fingers, leaving them gritty. I slipped my hand through one of the slits in my dress and wiped it surreptitiously against my underskirt as I returned my attention to the crowd, scanning for Luna.

May and Jazz flashed past, a streak of black and silver amidst the riot of color, and I smiled. My smile grew as I saw Connor O'Dell—the husband Raysel hadn't been dancing with—moving toward me, skirting the edge of the crowd with exaggerated care. Selkies tend to be awkward on dry land, and Connor was no exception. He saw me watching, and flashed me a grin that made my knees go weak.

"Hey," he said, once he was close enough to be heard without shouting. He didn't bother concealing the worry in his seal-dark eyes. "Is there any news?"

"No," I said. "I'm heading for the Tea Gardens as soon as I'm finished here. Have you seen Luna?"

"She was with the delegation from Roan Rathad a little while ago." He grimaced, shoulders dipping upward in an involuntary semi-shrug. I understood the reaction. Roan Rathad was his original home, a mostly Selkie fief-

dom that swears fealty to the Undersea Duchy of Saltmist. It was Saltmist that decided he was expendable
enough to be sold into marriage to a madwoman for political reasons, and Roan Rathad didn't fight them. I've
never asked whether it was our relationship that made
them see him that way. After all, a man who was willing
to sully himself by getting involved with a changeling
would probably never marry expediently on his own.

If that's why they did it, I genuinely don't want to
know.

"That explains the clothes." I gave him a sympathetic
once-over. He was wearing white linen trousers with a
smoky blue tunic trimmed in silver; the colors of his particular Selkie clan. He looked like a ghost next to the vibrant colors of the rest of Shadowed Hills. The contrast
was a visual reminder of his status in the Court: always
an outsider, whether he was technically part of the rul-
ing family or not.

It was also, if I was being entirely honest with myself, a damn good look for him, contrasting with his dark
coloring and making him look like a movie star from a
1940s film noir mystery. Very few men can pull off white
linen without looking like they're about to hit the beach,
but on Connor, it made him look like he was about to hit
the dance floor at some nightclub in Monaco.

"Yeah, well." He shrugged for real this time. "I like
your dress."

"May helped me pick it out." A new song was starting. "Can you point me in Luna's general direction?"

"I can do you one better." He offered his hand, cou-
pling it with a slightly lopsided smile. "May I have this
dance?"

I raised an eyebrow. "Fastest route across the floor?"

"You got it."

"And so do you." I slid my hand into his. Rayscline
was perpetually jealous of my nonrelationship with
Connor, but for once, I didn't feel compelled to refuse

the invitation. Turning down a dance on Beltane is an insult almost beyond measure, as is snubbing an old friend. Connor and I could waltz the night away if we wanted to, and Raysel couldn't say a damn thing about it.

He tugged me onto the floor, still cautious. People parted around us, making room for us to move without knocking into anyone. It helped that he was recognizably a Selkie, with fingers webbed to the first knuckle and short brown hair stippled with gray like the blotches on a seal's coat—even people who didn't know that he was the husband of the current Ducal heir would move aside, out of politeness. No one wants to be responsible for causing one of the polite, slightly-awkward sea fae to go sprawling.

I was standing close enough to see the edge-to-edge darkness of his eyes, irises blending seamlessly into pupils. They were the color of the sea at midnight, and just as easy to drown in. I've been drowning in those eyes for years. Every time I thought I might be learning to swim, he just smiled at me, and I went under again.

"I know you hate to dance," Connor murmured, beginning to waltz me in an almost straight line across the floor. "At least you might get the pleasure of seeing me fall on my ass."

"Oh, right. I guess *that's* a fair exchange."

"Why else would they call us the Fair Folk?"

"Because we steal their kids and cows if they call us fairies?"

"I mean besides that," he said, and smiled. The expression died quickly. "How bad is Lily really? Don't lie to me. Please."

"Bad." I took a shaky breath, forcing my back to stay straight as I followed him mechanically through the motions of the dance. I could see flashes of night sky through the open doors on the far wall. We'd have a much easier time finding Luna once we reached the terrace outside. "Really bad."

"Did you ask . . ." He glanced around, lowering his voice before he asked, "The Luidaeg?"

"Yeah. She said she couldn't help me. We're on our own this time."

He took an unsteady breath. "Root and branch."

"My thought exactly. So I'm going to talk to Luna, see if she has any—" I stopped mid-sentence as the scent of familiar magic cut through the air, sharp enough to make my sinuses ache. It was a mix of sulfuric acid and crushed oleanders, as out of place among the delicate perfumes of the dancers as a fox in a henhouse.

Connor blinked as our unsteady waltz came stumbling to a halt. "Toby?"

"Hush," I hissed, putting all my concentration into trying to follow the scent back to its source. I hadn't smelled that combination in years, but I would've known it even without the immediate, visceral reminder of the dream Karen sent me. I'll never forget Oleander de Merelands' magic.

Especially not when it's coming in with the wind off the terrace.

"What's going—"

"Call the guards," I said. "Call Sylvester. *Now*." I pulled away without waiting for his reply, gathering my skirts and bolting for the door like Cinderella leaving the ball for the battlefield. Connor shouted something, the exclamations from the dancers I shoved out of my path rendering his words unintelligible. I didn't stop. Oleander stole my life from me once already. I'd be damned before I let her do it to anyone else.

NINE

THE TERRACE OUTSIDE THE BALLROOM doors extended in both directions and around the corners, out of sight. I knew from experience that it made a complete circuit of the building, regardless of what shape the hall happened to be at any given moment. The architecture of Shadowed Hills may shift, but some things don't change, and the place is always riddled with towers, nooks, and crannies. That meant more doors than we could possibly cover, even if Connor found every guard in the knowe. When I factored in the general chaos of the Ball, I had to assume it would take him several minutes to convince anyone he found that there was a problem and get them heading in my direction. Possibly longer, since I hadn't told him exactly what the problem *was*.

A soft breeze wafted up riotous perfume from the gardens below, burying any trace of Oleander's magic. I wouldn't be able to track her that way, and the stone floor of the terrace showed no footprints. I hesitated, trying to decide how to proceed. I could wait until the guards came, losing any advantage I might have gained by spotting her quickly, but getting myself some backup. Or I could follow blind and hope to get lucky.

It couldn't be a coincidence that Karen made me dream about Oleander the night before I picked up traces of the bitch's magic in a crowded room. There were no good reasons for Oleander to be at Shadowed Hills, but there were a hell of a lot of bad ones, and I wasn't willing to take the chance she'd get away while I was playing it safe.

I started down the terrace. The light filtering through the curtained double doors into the ballroom made navigation easy, as long as I stayed close to the side of the building. Silver stars sparkled in the sky overhead, throwing down rays of frosted light that managed to be brighter and gentler than mortal moonlight.

I paused at the first corner, listening for footsteps, but all I heard was the muted sound of the Ball coming from the windows. I started forward again, walking along the stretch of terrace above the main rose garden. Something rustled to one side, and I whirled, hands going to my knives.

One of the climbing roses that crawled up the side of the hall had pulled loose from its trellis and was slapping against the rail. I took a deep breath, counted to ten, and started walking again. Jumpy? Me? Damn right. I spent fourteen years wearing fins the last time I got near Oleander de Merelands. That's not the sort of thing you forget. That's the sort of thing that—

I stopped in my tracks. That's the sort of thing that should make you too smart to go wandering around alone, in the dark, with no real guarantee of backup.

"What the hell am I doing?" I muttered.

The light from the ballroom didn't quite extend to the rail surrounding the terrace. The figure standing there was almost obscured by the shadows, right up until she turned to face me. For a single heart-stopping moment, it looked like Oleander: long dark hair, slim hands, and a smile full of poison. I snapped into a fighting stance, all hesitation forgotten . . . and the woman laughed, stepping forward.

The light shifted, revealing her smile to be sweet, if weary, and her hair to be a deep, true brown. "Am I that fearsome, or did Sylvester send you to put me out of my misery after dealing with those meddlesome 'guests' from Roan Rathad?" asked Luna. "I've dodged them for now, thank Titania."

"Luna?" I dropped my hands away from my knives, reeling at the enormity of my own mistake. If I hadn't realized who she was before I drew . . . "I—I'm sorry. I didn't see you there."

"That was my intent, given the delegation I was just meeting with. Have you seen them? Please tell me they didn't follow you."

"Not that I noticed," I said, still trying to swallow my dismay. My conviction of Oleander's presence was fading, replaced by confusion and a pounding headache. "Has anyone passed you in the last few minutes?"

"No, no one." She turned to pluck a goblet from the rail behind her before flashing me a concerned look. "There were people here when I first came out, but they've gone back inside. October, what's wrong? You look like you've seen a ghost."

"I'm starting to think I have." My headache was getting worse. Where the hell were the guards? Connor was the husband of the presumptive Ducal heir. Even if they thought he was being crazy, they should have humored him and come looking for me.

"What are you talking about?" Luna's question dragged my attention back to her. She was frowning, her silver-furred tails beginning to twitch. She wasn't born Kitsune, but she'd picked up a lot of the body language after wearing a Kitsune skin for over a hundred years. I never would have suspected her of being something else if I hadn't met her parents.

"I thought I was following someone," I said lamely.

"And this phantom would be . . . ?"

There was no point in lying. If nothing else, I'd have to explain when the guards showed up—*if* the guards showed up. "Oleander de Merelands."

Luna's eyes widened in justified dismay. "That's impossible. She'd never . . . she'd never dare!"

Sixteen years ago, Luna and Rayseline Torquill vanished into thin air. Our only leads pointed to Sylvester's brother; that was why Sylvester sent me to find him. I learned a lot of things from that little errand, including what it's like to be a fish . . . but I didn't find the missing Torquills. They beat me home by almost three years, and I still don't know how. Sylvester normally tells me everything. He won't tell me that. All I knew for sure was that they made it home before I did, and that Raysel came home broken.

"It was her," I said, trying to sound confident. Oak and ash, could I be wrong? Did I *want* to be right?

"It's not possible. The roses would tell me." Luna meant that literally. Her mother was the Dryad Firstborn, and Luna was essentially a Dryad of roses before she hid herself inside a Kitsune skin.

"I just—"

"We all make mistakes." Luna nodded like she was trying to convince herself. "This must have been one of them. You've had a hard few days."

"Yeah," I agreed, uneasily. "I was meaning to find you anyway."

She glanced away. "I thought you might. Sylvester sent a messenger to the Tea Gardens to ask if there was anything we could do to help, but we haven't heard back."

"Lily's subjects are a little distracted right now," I said. That was the understatement of the night. "Have you ever heard of anything like this? I mean, Undine aren't supposed to get sick, are they?"

"No. They're not." She took an abrupt gulp from her

goblet and grimaced like she'd tasted something bitter. "Maeve's teeth, I have no idea what convinced our steward to stock this vintage . . . Undine are born of water, they live by water, and they don't get sick. I've never heard of such a thing."

"Right." I pinched the bridge of my nose. Medicine gets a lot more complicated when half the people involved aren't technically "alive" by any normal standard of measurement. "Would your mom know anything?"

"No, October." Luna actually sounded amused. "Her children are plants. We *drink* water, we're not *made* of water."

I lowered my hand. "I had to ask."

"I know. I'll send word to Mother, see if she might have encountered this sometime in the past. It's a long shot, but since we can't ask my grandmother . . ."

"Yeah." I laughed sourly. "There's a quest for some other idiot: looking for Maeve so they can get medical details for all her descendants." Our King and Queens have been missing for hundreds of years. Someone's eventually going to have to go and find them. Personally, I have other problems to deal with.

"I suppose that's true," Luna agreed, rubbing her forehead. "It's a very warm night. The summers were never this warm when I was younger."

"If you say so," I said. California has a reputation for strange weather patterns, but the Summerlands are in a league of their own. I've seen snowstorms in July and heat waves in December. "I'm going to be at the Tea Gardens for a while, and then . . . well, I don't know where I'll be after that. Check with May. If she doesn't know where to find me, check with—check with Tybalt. He usually seems to know where I am."

Luna's smile was brief and knowing. "Yes, he *does* go out of his way to keep tabs on you, doesn't he? One might think he cared."

I groaned. "Don't you start, too."

"You should be flattered. He's a sweet man, in his way." She paused before adding, "My daughter's mad, you know."

I stared at her.

Unheeding, Luna continued, "People think I don't see it because I'm mad, too, in a quieter way, but madness isn't blindness. I lived with my father. I know what she is. I can't blame her. I still can't help feeling she had as much choice in her madness as I had in mine, and chose the wrong path."

"Luna, what are you—"

"I was afraid for her. That's why we found her a husband. Saltmist was begging for a treaty, what with that madwoman Riordan sniffing at the borders of Roan Rathad and them so restricted from intervention, and Raysel needed an anchor." Her eyes were far away; she wasn't talking to me anymore. "We were trying to save her the way my parents never saved me."

"Luna?" I put a hand on her shoulder, jerking it away almost immediately. "You're burning up!"

"I don't feel well." She wiped her forehead again, giving me a pleading look. "Can you tell Sylvester to turn the summer down?"

"You're shaking." I caught her hand. Her fingers were so hot that they felt like they might blister my skin. "Come on. We need to go inside."

"I'm fine," she said, trying to tug away. "It's just warm."

"You have a fever. That's not fine." Purebloods almost never get sick. When they do, it's either a laughable thing, over in a matter of hours, or serious enough to be incredibly scary. Luna's parents were Firstborn, making her blood purer than most. If she was sick, it wasn't going to be the easy kind of illness.

"It's not?" she asked. The color was draining from her cheeks, leaving her pale—too pale. Whatever was happening to her couldn't be entirely natural.

"No. Come on, now. We need to find Sylvester."

"If you say so," she said, and reeled, knocking her goblet to the terrace as she slumped toward me. The heat from her skin was intense. "Is there time for me to faint?"

I slid an arm around her, propping her up. She turned wide, haunted eyes toward me. Threads of pink and yellow were lacing through her irises, eroding their familiar brown. "Oh, oak and *ash*," I whispered.

"Has my father heard us? Is he coming?"

"Luna—" Luna couldn't escape her father in the shape she was born in, and so she stole the skin of a dying Kitsune and fled to the Summerlands. I'd seen the colors bleed into her eyes twice, and both times she was under such stress that she almost reverted back to her original form.

"I forgot my candle," she said, in a voice as thin and strained as wind through the trees. Then she went limp, eyes closing. I staggered, trying not to drop what was suddenly a dead weight.

"Luna?" There was no reply. I lowered her to the terrace, fumbling for a pulse. "No. No, not you, too. Don't die. Please don't die." I slid her head into my lap in the vague hope that it might help her breathe, and looked frantically up and down the terrace. There was no one in either direction.

Taking a deep breath, I tilted back my head and screamed for help.

TEN

I'D BEEN SHOUTING FOR A GOOD FIVE MI-
nutes when a tipsy Hind staggered out of the ballroom.
She had a champagne flute dangling precariously from
one hand, and was already starting to scold me for making too much noise when she realized what was happening in front of her. Her cloven hooves clattered as she
staggered to a stop.

The sound barely registered; it was her champagne
flute shattering against the terrace floor that snapped
me out of my panic, like the breaking glass somehow
flipped a switch inside my brain. I sat up straight, ordering, "Go inside and send the first person you can find
wearing the Duke's livery to me," in my best "I am a
Knight of this Duchy, do not fuck with me" tone.

I turned my attention back to Luna as the Hind turned
and fled. She was still breathing, but her fever seemed to
be getting worse, and that couldn't possibly be good. I
reached for her goblet, intending to use whatever was
left of its contents to cool her down, and paused.

Purebloods almost never get sick. Oleander's weapon

of choice was poison. The two weren't necessarily connected, but did I really want to take that chance?

I was staring at the goblet like I expected it to turn into a snake and bite me when a wonderfully familiar voice demanded, "Tree and thorn, October, what in the name of Oberon's honor is going on out here!"

There's just one man in Shadowed Hills—maybe just one man in all of Faerie—who can say things like "in the name of Oberon's honor" and sound like he believes what he's saying. Not even Luna's condition was enough to quash my relief as I twisted around to face him. "Etienne. Root and branch, I'm glad you're here."

Etienne stopped and stared.

I had to admit that the scene was strange; not even the weird training exercises he put me through when I was new to my knighthood approached finding me on the ground in a ball gown with an unconscious Duchess in my lap. Rendering Etienne speechless has been a goal of mine for years, and under any other circumstances, I might have savored the moment. Sadly, this was neither the time nor the place to enjoy my little sideways victory.

"Luna has a fever. She won't wake up." I was trying to be as clear and concise as possible. Maybe that way, I wouldn't start crying. "We need to get her inside."

"Sweet Maeve," he breathed. "What happened?"

"Not yet. Explanation time comes after getting-Luna-inside time. Please." I couldn't keep my voice from cracking on the final word.

That was enough to galvanize him into action. "Stay where you are," he snapped, before wheeling to run back into the ballroom.

I stayed where I was.

I didn't have to wait long; it seemed like only seconds before he returned with three people in tow. I knew two of them—Tavis, a Bridge Troll who entered Sylvester's service about six months after I did, and Grianne, a thin-faced Candela who rarely spoke without prompting. The third was unfamiliar: a tall, thin man with grayish skin and moon-white eyes. I took note of them and dismissed them in the same breath, turning back to Etienne.

"We need to—"

"I know what we need," he said, cutting me off. "Tavis, take her."

"Yes, sir," Tavis rumbled. All Bridge Trolls are big, but Tavis is a veritable mountain, nearly ten feet tall. His shoulders don't fit through most human doorframes. He shambled toward me, offering a genial, worried nod as he lifted Luna from my lap. "Evenin', Toby."

"Hey, Tavis." I caught his elbow as he straightened, letting him lift me to my feet. I stepped back and pulled my silver knife in the same motion.

Etienne raised an eyebrow. Grianne frowned. Tavis didn't even blink. It was the one I didn't know who stiffened and started forward, stopping when Etienne placed a hand on his shoulder.

"Peace, Garm. I'm sure Sir Daye wouldn't have called for help if she merely wanted witnesses to assault."

"Got that right." I bent, starting to hack off my skirts just above the knee. A moment's work left me with an armload of velvet and a "dress" that was more like a tunic with delusions of grandeur.

"Then what is she doing?" demanded Garm.

"Hopefully? Being paranoid." I knelt to wrap my severed skirt around Luna's goblet before standing again. "Where are we taking her?"

"Jin is meeting us at the Ducal chambers." Etienne gave the bundle in my hands a sidelong look. "Will you accompany us? I'm certain the Duke will have questions."

I nodded. "Does he know?"

"My Dancers are retrieving him," said Grianne. Her voice was soft as wind rattling through tree branches, and just about as human.

Each Candela is accompanied by two or more balls

of self-aware light called Merry Dancers. They can be sent on simple errands—like fetching a Duke—but if someone extinguishes a Candela's Dancers, the Candela dies. Not exactly what I'd call a fair trade for never needing to call a page.

At least Grianne's Dancers meant we didn't need to wait around. We gave the area one last glance before starting down the terrace, Luna in Tavis' arms, the possibly poisoned goblet in mine.

Etienne dropped back to walk next to me as we climbed a narrow stairway to the battlements, where we could cut across to the Ducal quarters. Garm stuck to him like a second shadow. I stayed quiet, waiting for one of them to start the conversation. My throat hurt, my head hurt, and I wasn't in the mood for small talk.

Fortunately, Etienne's *never* been in the mood for small talk. "I need your report, Sir Daye. What happened?"

"One of two things," I said. "Either the Duchess has come down with a sudden cold, or she's been poisoned. I'm voting the latter, in case you wondered. Why the hell didn't you come sooner? I told Connor to call the guards."

Etienne eyed me. "No one called for the guards. The first I heard of the situation was when I was summoned to the terrace."

My throat went tight. "Etienne, has anyone seen Connor?"

"Not in some time." He paused, eyes widening as he caught my meaning. "Grianne, has the Duke been summoned?"

Grianne cocked her head, like she was listening to something the rest of us couldn't hear. Then she nodded. "Yes, sir. He plans to meet us at the Ducal chambers."

"Good. I have a new task for you."

"Sir?"

"Master O'Dell is missing. Find him."

"Yes, sir," said Grianne, and bowed before turning and flinging herself off the edge of the walkway. There was a flare of greenish-white light, and she was gone.

"Never get used to that," muttered Tavis.

"Try hanging out with the Cait Sidhe," I said. "They do something similar, but they skip the fireworks and just sort of show up."

Tavis grimaced. "Charming."

"Yeah." I looked to Etienne. "I told Connor to call the guards because I thought we had an intruder. Now that Luna's sick, I'm sure of it."

His eyes narrowed. "Who?"

"Oleander. She's back."

Silence greeted my announcement, finally broken when Tavis asked, "Can someone get the door? My hands are full."

"I have it," said Garm, pushing forward in an obvious hurry to put some distance between us. He opened the door in the battlement wall, holding it open for Tavis and Luna to pass through. Etienne nodded for him to follow. Lips drawn into a disapproving line, Garm went.

I took a deep breath, turned to face Etienne, and waited.

"Support your claim, Daye."

"I smelled her magic in the ballroom."

"While no one else caught any trace of her?"

"You know that doesn't matter. I've always had a good nose for spells." Mother used to say having a nose for spells was connected to having a nose for blood.

"Fair." Etienne continued to study me, eyes grave. "October . . ."

I didn't want to hear what he had to say until I'd seen Sylvester. "Let's go catch up with the others," I said briskly, and stepped through the tower door. Reality did another dip-and-weave as I crossed the threshold, this time disorienting enough that I had to catch myself against the wall and duck my head, waiting to see if I was going to vomit. My stomach seemed determined to join my head in its rebellion against the tyranny of not being in pain. Gritting my teeth, I forced the nausea down one sickening inch at a time.

"October?" asked Etienne, from beside me.

"It's not normally that bad," I managed. Understatement of the night. Travel through the knowes hasn't been that bad for me since I was a kid. "Where are we?"

"We're here," Etienne replied.

I nodded, barely, and raised my head.

We were in a large, simply decorated room, with varnished oak walls and plain curtains draping the windows. Sylvester's tastes have always been simpler than the rest of the knowe implies, and Luna didn't challenge those tastes in the Ducal quarters. Looking around, I could see what the knowe would have been like without her. It was a very different world.

Luna herself was stretched out on the king-sized bed, looking small and fragile in her ornate gown. A woman sat on the edge of the bed, one hand resting on Luna's forehead, gauzy mayfly wings vibrating so fast they were barely a blur. The motion cast a haze of sparkling dust through the air around her. I didn't know her face, but that didn't matter; the dust told me who she was.

"Jin," I said. "How is she?"

"Her pulse is too high, she's severely dehydrated, and her fever isn't responding." Jin glanced up, her pale, sharp features framed by a pageboy bob of glossy black hair. A gallows-humor smile ghosted over her lips. "Nice dress."

"Nice face." I put the swaddled cup on a shelf before moving toward the bed. Garm glared. I ignored him. "How fresh is the molt? Could it be interfering?"

"Wow, Toby, I didn't think of that!" she snapped.

Then she sighed. "I'm sorry, that wasn't fair. I came out of molt a week ago; my magic isn't compromised. She's just ... not responding."

I winced. Ellyllon are healers and hedonists. It's not such a strange combination; both focus on the flesh. Ellyllon use their bodies hard, and Faerie's eternally creative biology compensates for their self-destructive instincts by giving them an entirely new body every decade or so. They crack open their skins and shrug them off, like insects. A recent molt could have interfered with Jin's powers. If that wasn't the problem ...

"Can you check for poisons?" I asked, half desperately. "She was drinking something right before she collapsed."

"That's part of a standard health-charm. If she's been poisoned, it's with something I don't know how to counter."

"Then ... then can you call for her mother? Maybe Acacia—"

"Luna's the only one who can access the Rose Roads, and she's not opening any doors right now."

"Oh."

Silence fell. It held the room for several minutes, until it was broken by the sound of a door opening. We all turned to see Sylvester step into the room, white-faced and shaking. Quentin slipped in behind him, apparently without attracting his notice. Sylvester's eyes were focused on the bed.

"Luna?" he whispered. "Luna, please. This isn't funny. Please, don't do this."

If Faerie was like the fairy tales say it is, his words alone would have been enough to break whatever spell Luna was under. This wasn't a fairy tale. She didn't move.

Jin stood. "Your Grace—"

Sylvester motioned her to silence. He was crying, tears running unchecked down his face. It felt like the room held its breath, waiting for him to move. Finally, expression bleak, he turned and looked at me. That was all. He just looked at me.

Etienne stepped forward. "Your Grace, there was a disturbance—"

"I was already looking for her." Sylvester sounded dazed. "The roses screamed loud enough to make the sky bleed when she fell."

"I . . ." Etienne looked at me, clearly at a loss for words. I shook my head. Daoine Sidhe aren't known for speaking the language of flowers, but Sylvester and Luna have been married for a long time. If anyone could teach him, it was her. "Your Grace, the Duchess collapsed without warning, and—"

"Yes. I know." Sylvester smiled. It was just a reflex. I could see the screaming in his eyes. "Toby, what happened?"

I took a breath. "I was dancing with Connor when I caught a trace of magic that shouldn't have been there. I told him to call the guards and followed the trace to the terrace, where I found Luna." Quentin crossed the room while I was talking, falling into position behind me like a squire falling in behind his knight. "She seemed fine at first. Then she collapsed."

"Oh, she'll be fine again. She always is." He moved closer to Luna, bending to smooth her hair with one shaking hand. "What did you follow?"

"The smell of sulfuric acid and oleanders." Sylvester's head snapped up. Jin stiffened. Only Quentin stayed where he was, looking puzzled. I made myself meet Sylvester's eyes. "It was Oleander, Sylvester. She was here. I'm sure of it."

"But you went after her alone? After everything she did to you? To *us?* How sure is sure, October?"

"Sure enough that I told Connor to call the guards." I shook my head, letting the frustration creep into my voice as I said, "I don't know why I didn't wait. I *should* have waited. I just . . . I couldn't."

"My wife was outside."

"I didn't know. Sylvester—"

"How could you go *alone?!*" He straightened, striding around the bed before I could react. Grabbing my shoulders, he jerked me toward him, fingers digging in hard enough to bruise. "How could you risk yourself—how could you risk my *wife?*"

"I thought I could catch her!" The smell of daffodils and dogwood flowers was rising around him as his magic surged, responding to his anger. My own magic tried to rise in self-defense. I forced it down. Sylvester had never hurt me.

He'd never grabbed me before, either.

Bringing his face to within an inch of mine, he hissed, "You were wrong."

Etienne started to step toward us. Sylvester stopped him with a glare before swinging his attention back to me. Suddenly, all those stories from my absence—the ones about "the mad Duke of Shadowed Hills"—didn't seem so farfetched. I could see the threat of madness in his eyes so clearly it burned.

"Will I lose her every time you're wrong?" he asked. "Is that all your family is good for? Must you destroy everything you touch?"

"Sylvester?" I whispered.

Jin stepped up behind him, the top of her head not even clearing his shoulder. Wings vibrating more rapidly than ever, she placed a hand against his arm. "Rest, my liege," she said, words carrying the weight of a command.

His eyes widened. The madness drained out of them, replaced first by confusion and then by a deep resignation. Then his knees buckled and he toppled forward, almost knocking me over. Etienne and Quentin moved to help hold him up.

Jin stepped back. "Tavis, Etienne, get the Duke onto the bed. Try to leave me room to work. Toby . . ." She hesitated. "I heard that Lily's sick. Is it true?"

I nodded.

"What do we know?"

"Not much. The Luidaeg says it could be her pearl. I checked with the Tea Gardens before I came here; Lily hasn't been cogent enough to tell them anything." I paused, and added, "The Luidaeg says she won't help me."

"I don't know if she could," said Jin wonderingly. "I've never even *heard* of a sick Undine. Illness in someone with Luna's . . . constitution . . . is almost as strange."

The pause before "constitution" was reassuring; it meant she knew Luna wasn't Kitsune. I took a deep breath. "I should get back to the terrace. There may be something that can help me figure out what's going on." Basic investigative procedures are all but foreign in Faerie, where people are used to counting on magic to solve their problems. That makes me damn useful. It also makes *them* lousy at preserving evidence.

"Not alone," said Garm, sounding horrified.

I raised an eyebrow. "Did you not know that was your outside voice?"

"He's right." Etienne shook his head. "You have to realize that I can't let you go alone. Given the situation—"

"You mean the part where I'm the one who thinks she spotted Oleander, I was with Luna when she collapsed, and you only have my word that I asked Connor to call the guards?" I sighed. "I get it. Can we leave Tavis to stand watch? I don't want the Duke and Duchess unguarded."

"I'm not much use in a fight, but I can do you one better," said Jin. "Garm?"

"Ma'am?" he responded.

"Can you please conceal the room when you leave?"

"It would be my pleasure." Garm turned and stalked

to the door, casting a final mistrustful glance my way before he exited.

"I guess that's our cue," I said.

Jin nodded. "I'll call for you if anything changes."

That would have to be enough. I offered Tavis a shallow bow, collected the cloth-wrapped cup, and turned to lead Etienne and Quentin out the door.

Garm was waiting outside, hands raised. Etienne pulled the door closed before stepping to the side, leaving Garm room to work. I moved to stand beside him, and Quentin moved to stand beside me. Finally, Garm gave a faint nod, and lowered his hands. The air went cold, filling with the scent of moss and still, stagnant water as his illusion began to come together.

The Gwragen are reclusive people who like their privacy even more than the Coblynau. It makes sense that they're some of the best illusionists in Faerie; a Gwragen-spun illusion can supposedly fool even the Firstborn. I'm certainly not going to argue. The door in the wall grew faint as Garm's spell took hold, finally vanishing into the stone. The smell of moss and water faded, and Garm turned to face us.

"There are no other entrances," he said.

"Good," said Etienne. "Let's go."

ELEVEN

WE WALKED IN AN UNEASY FORMATION, Etienne beside me, Quentin slightly behind, and Garm a few feet ahead, occasionally casting glances back at us. I did my best not to glare at him. It wasn't easy.

Etienne cleared his throat to catch my attention before nodding toward the bundle under my arm. "You said you were being paranoid. About what, precisely?"

"Luna was drinking from this before she fell. If Oleander *is* involved, she probably poisoned Luna's drink, and I don't want to risk anyone coming in contact with the residue. Besides, this may protect the fingerprints." The fabric would blur some of the prints, but hopefully not all of them; I just had to hope a few would be preserved to a reasonable degree. There's no database of fae fingerprints, but some investigative techniques have become second nature after years of mortal-world cases.

"Mortal methods," he said, amused respect tinged with unavoidable worry.

"They've worked pretty well for me so far," I said, and shrugged. Mortal methods let me find the Queen's knowe. That got me knighted. It also got her started on hating me. The jury's still out on whether that was a fair exchange.

"I don't understand why we can't do this without her," said Garm, not turning. "This all seems a little too convenient."

"Garm," said Etienne, sharply. "My apologies, October. I'll have words with him later."

I was starting to put two and two together. "How long ago did he graduate from being your squire?"

"Just after the turn of the year," Etienne replied. Raising his voice a bit, he added, "Sometimes I wonder about the wisdom of it."

Garm hunched his shoulders and said nothing.

The fact that Etienne had graduated his squire might mean he was getting ready to take a new one. I glanced at Quentin. He was staring resolutely ahead as he walked, trying to look like he wasn't listening to our conversation. He was almost succeeding.

Then we reached the place where Luna fell, and all thoughts of squires and knighthoods dropped away.

Grianne was sitting on the railing, with her Merry Dancers spinning around her. Her face was serene as ever, but her skin was glowing a pale green only slightly dimmer than her Merry Dancers, betraying her displeasure. Candela only light up under stress. Several more guards stood along the terrace, protecting the scene from intruders while hopelessly contaminating any evidence. Sometimes the fae ignorance of basic crime scene protocol makes me want to cry.

That wasn't what made my stomach clench; that honor was reserved for the doors standing open, revealing an empty ballroom, and for Connor, who sat on a chair just outside them with blood covering the front of his tunic.

"What happened?" I asked, voice tight with the strain of keeping myself from running to Connor. I couldn't lose it. Not now. Later, maybe, but not now.

Grianne gave me an uncomprehending look. One of

the other guards said, "With the Duchess indisposed, we ordered the Ball be ended."

I wheeled on him. "You let people *leave*?!"

"Er." He glanced toward Etienne, looking for support. Etienne shook his head, saying nothing. "Why should they have stayed?"

"I don't know. Maybe because there's a good chance one of them tried to kill your Duchess?" I turned away in disgust, focusing on Connor. He was watching me with pained amusement, rubbing the back of his head with one hand. I walked over and crouched in front of him. "Connor, what happened?"

He managed a weak smile. "I'm not sure. I went looking for the guards, and somebody hit me from behind. I think I hit my nose against the floor."

"My Dancers found him in a changing room," said Grianne.

"Oh, for the love of Maeve," I muttered, casting a glance toward Garm. "Now do you believe I had nothing to do with this?"

"Helpers are not restricted to serving the virtuous," he replied, standing at attention next to Etienne. "You've killed before."

My eyes widened. "You don't trust me because I killed Blind Michael?" He didn't answer. I turned, scanning the assembled guards. "Does anybody else think I might be behind this because I killed a child-stealing monster? Please. Let's get it all out in the open now, so I can be allowed to do my job."

No one said anything. But half of them wouldn't meet my eyes.

I shoved the cup into Connor's arms, snapping, "Don't let anyone touch that," before I straightened and stalked over to the spot where Luna and I were standing before she fell. There were no visible clues. I could smell the sticky-sweet residue of Luna's wine, but I had no way of knowing whether or not it had been poisoned.

The fact that I could smell the wine at all meant the smell of the roses below wasn't as strong as it was earlier. I don't know much about flowers beyond what can be used in simple charms, but I knew Shadowed Hills, and I knew Luna was tied to her roses. If she was sick, they'd be sick, too, out of sympathy.

One thing hadn't changed; there was no trace of Oleander's magic. "There's nothing here," I said, disgusted. "She didn't leave a damn thing behind."

"She who?" asked the knight who'd admitted to clearing the ballroom.

I started back toward Connor, replying, "Oleander de Merelands."

The guards—except Etienne and Garm, who'd heard it before—erupted into protests. Watching their reactions, I saw a glimmer of logic in sending everyone home. While there was a good chance their actions allowed Oleander to escape, there was a better chance that they had accidentally prevented a riot. Blind Michael might have been a child's terror, but Oleander was a terror for adults. The record of her crimes goes back centuries. Sure, it's never been proved that she assassinated King Gilad's parents, or King Gilad himself; in both cases, other explanations conveniently presented themselves. Too conveniently.

I ignored the arguing guards as I knelt in front of Connor, putting a hand on his knee before I could consider the ramifications of the action. Screw it. If Raysel wanted to start shit with me over touching her husband, she'd just be giving me a target. "Did you see who hit you?"

Connor put his hand over mine. "No. Before you ask, I didn't hear anything, either." He shook his head, and winced. "That was dumb. Don't let me do that again."

"Gotcha; no head-banging. What happened?"

"I went out to the receiving hall to look for someone I could grab without attracting too much attention. Everything after that is black."

"Jin's with Luna and Sylvester now, but you need to have her take a look at you. You could have a concussion."

"Just what I always wanted," said Connor dryly. Touching the back of his head, he winced again. "It hurts like hell. Do you really think you saw Oleander?"

My own head was still pounding, and I didn't even have a concussion to blame it on. "I didn't see her. I thought I sensed her magic, and with Luna in something close to a coma, I'm not ready to write the idea off." I paused, twisting to face Etienne. "Oh, oak and ash. Etienne? Has anyone seen Rayseline? The last time Oleander was here—"

"Sweet Titania," said Etienne, catching my meaning. Pointing to three of the guards, he snapped, "You! Locate Rayseline, *now*!" The guards stopped arguing, gave him a uniformly horrified look, and ran.

I turned back to Connor, whose face had frozen in the pained expression of a man who didn't know how he was supposed to feel. "Hey," I said, squeezing his knee before pulling my hand away. "It'll be okay."

"Liar," he said softly, and let me go.

I straightened, realizing as I did that the way my dress was hacked off meant I'd been giving anyone behind me a free peepshow. "Where's May? She can't have gone home. She doesn't have the car keys." What she did have was access to my memories leading up to her "birth," including Devin teaching me to hotwire damn near anything with wheels. It was better not to think about that too hard.

"She refused to go with the others. She's in the western antechamber," said Grianne, cocking her head. "She has sandwiches."

"Sandwiches." Grianne nodded. I resisted the urge to yell at her. "Oleander may be in the knowe, and you left May alone with a plate of sandwiches." If our unknown assailant could get to Lily and Luna, who was to say she or he couldn't get to a Fetch? Fetches are supposed to be invulnerable. I didn't want to test it. "Etienne, can you take me to my Fetch?"

"Of course," said Etienne.

Connor stood shakily, tucking the cup under one arm. "I'm coming with you." He must have recognized my impending protest, because he added, "Come on, Daye. Do you really think you'll feel better about my survival chances if you leave me?"

"Sometimes I hate how well you know me," I muttered. More loudly, I asked, "Is anyone *else* planning to play tagalong?"

Quentin stepped forward.

I sighed. "I should've known. Grianne, can you make sure no one walks barefoot on this section of terrace until *after* the Hobs have a chance to scrub it down?" That was technically destruction of evidence, but any poison on the cobblestones would also be in the cup. I wouldn't be losing anything, and the last thing I wanted was for somebody else to get hurt because of something as stupid as an unwashed terrace.

True to form, Grianne didn't answer out loud. She just nodded, the constant spinning of her Merry Danc ers throwing green-and-white shadows across her face.

"Good," I said, skirting dangerously close to the forbidden thanks. "Guys, come on." I started into the ballroom, where I could cut across to the receiving hall, and walk from there to the western antechamber, as long as the knowe hadn't rearranged itself again. Quentin and Connor followed close behind me; Etienne and Garm followed them. Between the five of us, we had two knives and two ceremonial swords. At least one of the knives was iron, and even so, I have never felt so unarmed inside the walls of Shadowed Hills.

Connor was walking even more slowly than normal, probably due to the head injury. I dropped back a bit to walk between him and Quentin, glancing from one to the other. "You guys doing okay?"

"Fine," said Quentin.

"My head hurts, but I think I'll live," Connor said.

"You're *going* to see Jin when this is done," I said. "No one gets to ignore a concussion on my watch."

Connor frowned. "Are you going to see her, too?"

"Huh?" I realized I'd been rubbing my temple as we walked. Suddenly scowling, I leaned over to pluck the cup from his unresisting hands. "It's just a headache. Changeling, remember? I gave myself a bad case of magic-burn."

"I thought that was a real dress," said Connor, frown fading into bafflement. "What did you do? Try to cast a don't-look-here on the entire ballroom or something?"

I hesitated. *Had* I used any magic since we reached the Ball? I didn't remember doing anything since resetting the apartment wards, and that was a small enough spell that it shouldn't have been an issue, even for me.

I didn't have time to answer; we'd reached the antechamber door. I reached for the latch, pausing as I realized we hadn't passed a single person during the walk from the terrace. The knowe might as well have been deserted. "Now there's a pleasant thought," I muttered, and opened the door.

May looked up, mouth half-full of cucumber salad, and mumbled something through the gooey mass of mashed-up bread, cream cheese, and vegetable matter. My leather jacket was on the bench next to her. Swallowing, she tried again: "Did you find out who pulled the fire alarm?"

Raising an eyebrow, I looked at Etienne.

"We couldn't precisely evacuate the knowe on account of attempted regicide," he said. He at least had the grace to look embarrassed.

"So you pulled a fire drill?" I shook my head. "Oberon's ass, this place gets weirder all the time. May, Luna's been attacked. I need you to go down the hill and call Danny to come give you a ride home."

She stared at me, sandwich dangling forgotten in her hand. "Luna's been *what*? Is she going to be okay?"

"We don't know yet, but she—"

"Will do far, far better when she knows that you're far, far away," replied a familiar voice behind me. I stiffened. "Not that she knows much of anything right now, since she's basically a corpse that happens to be breathing. Nasty business all the way around."

I squared my shoulders, taking a breath before I turned to face the next unpleasant challenge of the night.

"Hello, Rayseline," I said.

What do you get when you cross a Daoine Sidhe with a Blodynbryd pretending to be a Kitsune? Something that scrambles my capacity to read bloodlines. I used to wonder where Raysel got her height. Sylvester's about average for a Daoine Sidhe, and since I didn't know about Luna's stolen skin, I always thought it was weird for such a short woman to have such a tall daughter. Having seen Luna's true form, the fact that Raysel was almost six feet tall was less strange. That didn't make needing to tilt my head back to meet her eyes any less annoying.

"October," she said, with acid sweetness. "I'd expected you to flee the scene by now."

I shrugged. "I've never been good at fleeing."

"You'll learn." Her smile was vulpine, baring the tips of the blunted fangs she somehow inherited from her mother. That's about the only thing she got from the Luna I grew up knowing. Raysel has her father's fox-red hair and Torquill gold eyes. Those eyes were filled with a malicious glee I've never seen from any other member of the Torquill family—not even Simon. "This would be an excellent time to start."

"I have nothing to flee from. I didn't hurt your mother."

"Didn't you?" Raysel's eyes flicked to Etienne and Garm, who stood like silent statues to my left. "How many people in this knowe will believe you? How many in this Duchy? In this Kingdom? You killed my grandfather, and everyone knows he had a way of breaking his toys. You were his. Your word is suspect here."

A wave of coldness washed over me, bringing the phantom taste of candle wax to my lips. Blind Michael had me long enough to do a lot of damage. I sometimes think he'll always have me, in my dreams. "What Blind Michael may or may not have done hasn't changed my loyalty to this Duchy. I serve your father. I'd never hurt Luna."

"Do you truly think my father is going to be capable of such distinctions when she dies?" Raysel infused the question with almost believable curiosity. "They tell me he was less than reasonable when we were missing."

Connor paled. I reached over to give his shoulder a reassuring squeeze, keeping my attention focused on Raysel. "She's not going to die."

Raysel's eyes narrowed when she saw my hand on Connor's shoulder, but her smile grew, spreading to fully display her fangs. "No, she won't, because you won't be here to hurt her. You're banished until my father says you can return, and right now, he's not saying much of anything."

"On whose authority?" demanded Etienne. I glanced over, startled. I'd almost forgotten he was there. "You forget yourself."

"Do I?" Raysel smiled. "My father has no named heir. That means I speak in his place, unless and until someone of higher rank says otherwise. Do you want to dispute my authority? Do you *really?*"

Etienne met her eyes for a long moment before he looked away, shoulders drooping. Raysel's smile returned, as serene as if she were issuing an invitation to tea.

"I'll see you tried under Oberon's Law once she's gone. You'll pay for everything you've done to us." There was no sorrow in her eyes; just the petulance of a child whose wishes haven't been granted. She was waiting for her mother to die and her father to go mad, and she was impatient because it wasn't happening fast enough.

If I ever really hated her, it was then.

"I'd like to see you try," I said tightly.

"You can take your trash and go, before I decide you're better kept confined." Raysel made a shooing motion with one hand. Glancing at Quentin, she added, "Best you don't forget who holds your fealty, boy."

"I know where my loyalties lie," said Quentin.

His tone made me wince. Making an enemy of Rayseline Torquill might seem like the "noble" thing to do, but it sure as hell wasn't smart. Quickly, before Raysel's attention could fix on him, I said, "You know I didn't hurt her."

"You killed my grandfather. Some would say that's enough."

"She deserves a medal for that," said Quentin. I blinked, surprised at the venom in his tone. "Any parent in this Kingdom would agree. *My* parents would agree."

Almost sweetly, Raysel said, "Your parents have no power here." Smirking, she turned on her heel and stalked away. The echoes of her footsteps filled the hall until she turned the corner, and was gone.

May stared, openmouthed. "What a—"

"That's enough, May." I turned to look at Connor. "Are you okay?"

"No." He met my eyes without hesitation, shoulders falling into a resigned slump. "I don't think 'okay' is really an option. But I'll keep an eye on things. Let you know if I see anything suspicious."

"Good. Keep an eye on Quentin." If anyone was going to be "keeping an eye" on someone, it would probably be Quentin keeping an eye on Connor. Still, arguing over who was watching out for whom might keep them both occupied, at least for now.

"What?" protested Quentin. "I'm going with you!"

"No. You're staying here." He started to speak. I raised my hand, cutting him off. "If you follow me, Raysel won't let you come back, and you need a way to contact me if she gets out of control." Her tenuous sanity was clearly slipping, and I was getting worried about the people I was leaving in harm's way. Especially Connor. Selkies aren't built for combat on land, and she could break him if she really tried.

Quentin frowned, studying me before he said, "I'll stay because you told me to. But I don't like it."

"You don't have to." I turned to Etienne. "You know I didn't do this."

"I'd kill you where you stand if I thought you had," he said calmly.

"That's fair." I'd have done the same thing in his place. "Raysel . . ."

"I know." He glanced at the others. "We all do."

"She might be dangerous." It was a gamble, but I couldn't walk away without warning them.

To my relief, he nodded, Garm mirroring the motion. "I know."

"You'd best find out who did this," Etienne said. "If you don't—"

"I'm not stupid. I know what the risks are."

"No," he said, stepping back, "you've never been stupid, have you?"

"Only on occasion. Good night, Etienne, Garm, Connor. Quentin."

" 'Bye, Toby," said Quentin. Connor didn't say anything at all. He just stepped shakily over and hugged me. I returned his embrace as tightly as I could with the possibly poisoned cup tucked under my arm, closing my eyes for a split second. Then I straightened, pulling away, and reached for May's hand.

"Good night, October," said Etienne. He bowed awkwardly to May, obviously unsure of the etiquette involved in addressing a Fetch. "Ma'am."

She managed an unsteady smile, grabbing my jacket as she stood. "See you later."

Leaving them standing where they were, I led May down the hall and out the door, into the warm dark of the mortal night. We were halfway to the parking lot before she asked, "Toby? What just happened?"

"Luna was attacked, and Raysel's telling people I did it." I kept pulling her along, my shoes slipping on the damp crabgrass. "So now we have to find a way to fix things."

"What if there's not a way?"

"We'll burn that bridge when we come to it." We were approaching the car. Spike was curled in a ball on the hood. "Tired, guy?" I asked, picking it up and slinging it over my shoulder. It made a vague, sleepy sound as I unlocked the car.

"Don't you mean 'cross'?"

"What?"

"You said 'we'll burn that bridge when we come to it.' Don't you mean 'cross'?"

I turned to look back up the hill. Somewhere up there, in a different world, a killer was on the loose, a Duke was mourning his wife before she was even dead, and that same Duke's crazy daughter was already trying to take control.

"No," I said, "I don't."

TWELVE

MAY WAITED UNTIL WE WERE IN THE CAR before turning to me and saying, "You're going to tell me *everything*. Got that? *Everything*."

"You're right, but first you're going to cast a don't-look-here on us." Her expression turned quizzical. I explained: "My head's killing me, and I'd rather not risk getting followed home." The statement "it's not paranoia if they're really out to get you" may be a cliché, but it's a cliché I think I've earned the right to use.

Her eyes widened as my words sunk in. Nodding, she pressed her hands against the dashboard, and chanted, singsong, "A-tisket, a-tasket, a green and yellow basket, I wrote a letter to my love, and on the way I lost it." Her magic gathered, rose, and slammed down on the car in a wave of cotton candy and ashes. We weren't wearing human disguises, but we didn't need them; no one would see us. Hopefully "no one" included Oleander.

I pulled the car out of the parking lot, grateful for the familiarity of the route as I began my terse review of the situation. It helped that May shared enough of my

memories to understand why the situation felt so wrong.
She'd never seen Luna's true form—she was "born" before that particular revelation—but she didn't seem to
have any trouble seeing how deep the shit would have
to be before Luna's grip on her Kitsune skin started slipping. I laid it all out, every bit of it, and went quiet, waiting for her response.

May stroked Spike, staring off into the distance before she asked, "Are you sure?"

My hands clenched the wheel as a sharp, sudden anger hit me. How *dare* she question what I'd told her? She
knew what Oleander did to me better than anyone else
ever could. She *knew*. Typical Fetch, just looking for an
excuse to send me off to die—

"Whoa." The car swerved as I shook off the unexpected veil of rage. May wasn't doing anything wrong.
More importantly, May was the last person who would
send me off to die. If I went, she went with me.

"Toby?" May looked at me with open concern. "What
just happened?"

"I must be more on edge than I thought." I forced
the last of the anger down. "Yes, I'm sure. There weren't
any oleanders in the floral arrangements at the Ball, and
I don't know anybody else in this Kingdom who smells
like sulfuric acid. Either I was having the world's worst-
timed drug flashback, or it was her." We zipped through
the tollgate on the heels of a little red sedan, barely
making it before the gate came down.

"Wow." May resumed her thoughtful stare. Finally,
she said, "You have to take me home."

"What?" Taking your eyes off the road when you're
driving under a don't-look-here is never a good idea, but
I couldn't keep from glancing in her direction.

May shook her head. "If it's Oleander, she's going
to be watching for you. You're under a don't-look-here
that doesn't feel like your work, and I was made to look
like you. Let me do my job. Let me go back to the apart-

ment and play decoy." She chuckled darkly. "What's she gonna do? Kill me?"

"If you're sure—"

"I'm sure."

We drove on in silence, both lost in our own thoughts. Raysel was right when she said she could have me executed; Oberon's law forbids the killing of purebloods for any reason other than royal command. My life was forfeit under the law the moment I killed Blind Michael, if anyone cared enough to claim it. I've done a lot for this Kingdom, but people have died on my watch. The purebloods don't like death. It makes them uncomfortable. My former mentor turned out to be a psychopath, and changelings go crazy all the time. How many people would believe Raysel if she said I'd finally snapped?

Too many. That was the problem.

I pulled up in front of the apartment, keeping the engine running. "Take Spike with you? I don't want it vanishing into the park."

"I don't think it's in the mood—poor thing's still asleep." May snapped her fingers, the smell of cotton candy rising as a version of my normal human disguise locked into place around her. She cradled Spike to her chest as she opened the door. "Be careful out there. I've got a bad feeling about all this."

"Funky Fetch powers?"

"I've met you."

"Jerk."

I managed to keep smiling until the door was closed and May was walking up the sidewalk toward our apartment. Letting the expression die, I leaned over to rummage through the glove compartment and pull out the Tylenol. I popped the bottle open with my thumb and dry-swallowed three pills. They wouldn't kill my headache, but they'd keep me functional a little longer, and I was ready to take whatever I could get.

Midnight had come and gone in the chaos surrounding Luna's collapse. I returned the bottle to the glove compartment as I pulled away from the curb, too aware of the time. The last thing I needed was to cap my evening by getting caught out at dawn.

Searching the Tea Gardens was a long shot, but it was the best idea I had. If anyone knew how to poison an Undine, it was Oleander—and she'd have needed to get inside the Tea Gardens to do it. Her willingness to mix fae and mortal methods was part of what made her so effective, and if she'd done anything with mortal components, something would've been left behind. I just had to find it.

The entrances to Golden Gate Park are never locked, even though the park supposedly closes at sunset. The police make periodic sweeps, unaware of how pointless it is. They may catch the human homeless, but they'll never catch the fae who make up most of the park's nighttime population. I parked across from the Tea Gardens, leaving the cup in the passenger-side footwell as I twisted around to dig my emergency sneakers out of the back. I might not be able to change the fact that I was about to go wandering around Golden Gate Park after midnight in a hacked-off ball gown, but I could at least do it in sensible shoes.

Donning sneakers and my leather jacket made me feel considerably more capable of handling what was ahead. I hesitated, finally tucking my hair over my ears before getting out of the car. They were the only thing that really gave me away as anything but human, and I wasn't kidding when I told May I needed to conserve my strength; magic-burn is nothing to sneeze at.

Neither is murder.

The ghostly outline of the car was visible until my fingers broke contact with the door. Then it vanished, leaving the parking space apparently empty. The spell would keep anyone from parking on top of me. It would also keep me from getting busted by the cops for being in Golden Gate Park after "closing."

"Hope I can remember where I parked," I said, and started walking.

A narrow strip of grass separated the Tea Gardens from the parking lot. I knelt to study it, but saw nothing more telling than some half-chewed bubblegum. Countless tourists visit the park every day. If Oleander had been there, her tracks were long gone.

Sometimes I regret my choice of careers. I like my work. I enjoy finding out where people have hidden their secrets, and I like knowing nothing's ever as secure as people think, even if it means knowing that none of my secrets are safe, either. Still, there are times when something a little stronger than my own knowledge of human behavior would be nice. A full forensics lab, for example.

"Devin was right," I muttered. "I should've joined the police."

I turned as I stood, and found myself nose-to-nose with a male pixie. He was about four inches tall, glowing with a warm amber light that almost distracted from the fact that his short toga-style garment was made from a Snickers wrapper.

"Uh, hi," I said. "Can I help you with something?"

It's hard for pixies to hold still for more than ten seconds—their wings aren't built for it, and a light breeze has a longer attention span—but he was just hovering there, expression giving every indication that he was waiting for something. I squinted. He was holding something behind his back.

"What've you got there?" I asked, and held out my hand.

The question seemed to delight him. Laughing, he darted forward and dropped something into my palm before vanishing into the underbrush. I looked down, just in time to see the oleander flower in my hand burst into pale flames. They burned without heat. The flower was gone in a matter of seconds, leaving an ashy smear behind.

Feeling suddenly exposed, I turned in a slow circle, rubbing my hand against my hacked-off skirt as I studied the area. Something moved behind the fountain on the far side of the parking lot. I took a cautious step forward.

Black hair flashed through blue water as Oleander turned and ran.

There wasn't time to think, and so I didn't; I just bolted for the fountain. Everything was suddenly clear, like I'd fallen into a dream where the course of events couldn't be changed. She ran, and I chased. That was the only way it could go.

She was ten yards ahead of me when she came into view. My legs were longer, and I was gaining when she ducked into the botanical gardens. I didn't remember drawing my knives, but I must have, because they were in my hands. That was fine. If I caught her, we'd be done. Killing her would violate Oberon's law. I didn't care, just like I hadn't cared when I killed Blind Michael. He was a monster, and so was she.

Trees choked the path, cutting off most of the ambient light. I would have paused to get my bearings, but I didn't need to; the bitter tang of acid hung in the air, marking her trail so clearly that I didn't need eyes to follow her. I just ran.

The path opened into a clearing. Oleander stood at the center, silhouetted by moonlight. She looked over her shoulder as I ran into the open, and smiled. The smell of sulfuric acid and oleander flowers was suddenly overwhelming. I gathered the last scraps of my endurance and dove, intending to tackle her—only to slam headfirst into a young elm tree, the illusion shattering around me.

The pain broke through the haze that had fallen over me, leaving me suddenly aware of my own actions. What in Maeve's name was I *doing*? I was chasing a known killer through a manmade forest, alone, when no one knew where I was. That wasn't even stupid. That was *suicidal*.

Behind me, Oleander laughed. I turned in time to see the bottom of one bare foot vanish between two rose bushes, and the dream slammed back down, too strong to be denied. I ran after her, close enough now to hear her feet hitting the ground.

She was always just a few steps ahead and a few feet out of reach, almost in sight but never quite there. My lungs were burning. I promised myself that if I lived, I'd start working out. Better cranky and alive than cheerful and dead. That thought probably contained some vast truth, but I had better things to worry about, like what would happen if Oleander exhausted me before I caught her. I picked up the pace and was rewarded with a fresh glimpse of her hair. I was gaining. The smell of acid was so heavy it burned my throat. That didn't matter. Nothing mattered but the chase.

I flung myself around corner after corner, running ever faster. She wouldn't get away. The path twisted, and I swerved to follow; as long as Oleander stayed on the path, so would I. Her silhouette was framed by the dark mirror of the lake ahead of us, and the sight of water gave me the strength for one last burst of speed. Peri are desert creatures, and Oleander was part Peri; the lake would stop her. I could catch her and force her to tell me what she'd done. And once I was sure she'd told me everything . . .

I put the thought aside and concentrated on running. I killed Blind Michael in self-defense. If I ran Oleander down and killed her, it would be murder. She deserved it, but it would still be murder. Had I fallen that far? It was time to find out. I skidded around the last corner, knives raised . . . and found myself alone.

Moonlight bathed the water in white, chasing away the shadows. I came skidding to a stop, feet sinking into the mud as I frantically scanned the lakeshore. There was no one there. I looked down, and my breath caught in my throat, making my already oxygen-deprived lungs stutter. A single trail of footprints led from my feet back to the path. If you judged by the ground, I'd made the run alone.

I stayed where I was for several minutes, panting, before I heard a twig snap behind me. I stiffened. Maybe I'd come alone—somehow—but one thing was clear.

I wasn't alone anymore.

THIRTEEN

I RAISED MY KNIVES, HOLDING THEM at waist-level as I turned. It was a good defensive position, and it wasn't offensive enough that the person behind me would automatically realize they were about to be attacked.

Tybalt stood on the hard-packed earth of the path, well out of reach of the mud. He raised an eyebrow as he saw my posture. It rose further as he got a good look at what I was wearing. Clearing his throat, he said, "Fascinating as I find your choices of couture and activity, what in the world is going on out here?"

"Tybalt?" I lowered my knives. He was draped in a human illusion, features blunted and smoothed into a semblance of mortality. I opened my mouth slightly, breathing in the solid Cait Sidhe of his heritage before letting my shoulders relax. It was really him. "What are you doing here?"

"Now you're answering questions with questions. You've been spending too much time with the sea witch." He walked primly forward, stopping where the mud began. "The Dryads called me. They said you were tearing through the park like a madwoman, and given the situation in the Tea Gardens, they were concerned."

"I . . . wait, what? I was following someone."

Tybalt's eyebrow arched upward again. "Not according to the Dryads."

I hesitated, covering my confusion by sheathing my knives. *Had* I seen Oleander, or was I chasing a lure-me spell? Both were possible. The Peri aren't illusionists on the level of the Gwragen, but they're close.

Tybalt was watching with concern when I looked back up, a frown creasing his unnervingly human features. I wasn't accustomed to seeing him like that. It seemed wrong, somehow, like it was more of a deception than the illusions I wore. It didn't help that he'd changed out of his Court clothes and into something much more reasonable: weathered denim jeans, a linen shirt, and unornamented boots. It was more appealing than the finery, even if it was less openly attractive. He looked . . . normal.

"Toby, what's going on?"

"I don't know." My voice sounded small and frightened. I raked my hair away from my face and squelched my way out of the mud, trying to ignore the obscene sucking noises that followed every step. "Root and branch, I need a cup of coffee. Have you heard the news from Shadowed Hills?"

"What?" He shot me a startled glance. "No. I've been here all night. What's going on?"

". . . Right." I pinched the bridge of my nose. "Luna collapsed outside the Beltane Ball. I think she was poisoned."

"She sent you to your death once, in case you've forgotten," he said, a sudden chill dropping into his voice. "Why should her collapse concern me?"

I paused. Tybalt was a cat before he was anything else. If something didn't affect him personally, he was unlikely to give a damn. Slowly, I said, "Because Rayseline is blaming me, and if Luna dies—"

"The little bitch will push for your execution under Oberon's law," he snarled. I blinked. I'd expected a reaction, but nothing that strong. "She'll want your head. Titania's bones, Toby, what *happened?*"

"I'm not sure anymore. Remember Karen?" He nodded. "Well, she sent me a dream about Oleander, and then I thought I caught a trace of Oleander's magic at the Ball. People keep saying Oleander wouldn't come back here, but I can't think of any other way to explain what I felt."

"I believe you."

The words were so simple and so calmly said that it took me a moment to find my voice. Finally, I managed, "Why?"

"If you were killing people, you wouldn't start with Luna." His smile didn't reach his eyes. "Besides, you're smarter than that. You wouldn't get caught."

"What, are you waiting for me to snap?"

Tybalt shrugged. "I'm waiting for everyone to snap."

I decided to let that slide. There wasn't time to think about what it really meant. "If it's Oleander—if I'm right—then she's also the one responsible for whatever's happening to Lily. She has to be stopped."

"Why would she attack the Lady of the Tea Gardens?"

"Lily kept Oleander from killing me once, and she's a nutcase. Does she need more of a motive than that?"

"I suppose not, especially since attacking that particular pair implicates you nicely. They're very . . . unique women. It would take an intimate knowledge of the both of them to accomplish something like this."

I stopped, suddenly wary. "What do you mean?"

He sighed. "Please don't treat me like a kitten. I know what Luna Torquill is, and I'll grant that Oleander has motive. Still, why would she risk coming back here? Being caught in this Kingdom would mean her life."

"I don't know. People say she kills for money. Maybe she's here on a job and just having a little fun on the side."

I rubbed my forehead, longing for aspirin. "There's no one else who works with poisons the way she does *and* has a grudge against me. I came to look for signs that she was behind the attack on Lily, and I saw her across the parking lot. I chased her into the botanical gardens, but she vanished, and—" Tybalt was looking at me oddly. I frowned. "What?"

"No one but the two of us has been here in hours. I don't smell her, or anything like her magic, anywhere around us."

"Somehow, I'm not surprised." Weariness washed over me. "I'm too tired for this shit."

"Liar." Tybalt glared at me. "Forgive me for calling you on it, but you're lying. You aren't tired. You're exhausted. You keep squinting like you have a migraine, your voice is raspy, and you look like you haven't slept in a week. You're going to run yourself to death."

"It's been a long night," I snapped.

He snorted. "Maybe it'll be a relief to bury you. You'll be quieter. Now what?"

"I need to check in with the Tea Gardens," I said. "After that . . . I need to find Oleander. I don't know what I was chasing, but if it wasn't her, I need to know what it was."

"A tall order."

"Yeah, well, thinking small hasn't been working out too well so far, now, has it?"

The briefest flicker of a smile crossed his lips. "Fair enough, and I suppose it's a start." He turned to start down the path toward the parking lot. Lacking any other options, I followed. "I'll tell my people to watch for her, and I'll send Raj if we find anything. If she hurts you . . . my eyes are everywhere. She'll find no peace and no rest until I have my vengeance."

I blinked. "Tybalt—"

"You're more fun alive than dead." He gave my hacked-off dress a once-over before adding, "You look like an idiot. Although I must say I approve of the jacket."

"Asshole."

Tybalt's smirk was short-lived, quickly replaced by something less familiar: concern. "I do have to wonder what it is you were chasing. If Oleander is involved . . ."

"She hasn't gotten to me, if that's what you're wondering. She hasn't had a chance." I didn't drink anything I couldn't identify after getting to the Ball, and Sylvester's staff was well-screened enough that I wasn't worried about my single glass of wine.

Tybalt looked at me dubiously, and kept walking. Much as I hated to admit it, his presence was reassuring; if Oleander wanted to come back, she wouldn't catch me alone.

I stopped when we reached the Tea Garden gates, squinting as I tried to work out the best way of getting inside. Shouting would just attract the police, and that was a complication we didn't need. "Care for a little trip through the shadows?"

"Always amusing, but not necessary tonight." Tybalt pointed off to my left.

I turned.

Marcia was standing a few feet away, arms wrapped around herself, crying. She'd been crying for a while. Her mascara was running in patchy streaks, and her fairy ointment was all but washed away.

My stomach sank, but I held to hope, asking, "Marcia? Honey, what's wrong?"

"I called the apartment, and May said you were here. I knew if I waited long enough, you'd come. I just had to wait until . . ."

Tybalt's hand was on my shoulder, steadying me. "Marcia, what's going on?"

"It's Lily." Those two words held all the things I didn't want to hear. "She's been asking for you."

I took a deep breath, shrugging Tybalt's hand from my shoulder, and nodded. "Well, here I am. Let's go."

It only took a few moments for Marcia to get us into the Tea Gardens. She never stopped trembling. Her dread went beyond grief and made a sad, terrible sense, highlighting one of the ugly truths about Faerie. Lily might have been the only person in Faerie who'd ever shown Marcia any kindness. I was afraid of losing a friend. Marcia was afraid of losing her entire world. I complain about being a changeling, but things could have been a lot worse. If my blood were any thinner or my mother less highly thought of—Amandine isn't titled, but everyone knows her—I could have been Marcia. There's always something worse than what you have.

We climbed the moon bridge in silence. Lily's knowe resolved around us as an almost featureless expanse of half-frozen marsh. It seemed like the only solid ground was the spot where we were standing, and the patch of green surrounding the willow grove a few yards in front of us.

Marcia made a small, strained sound when she saw the trees. I squeezed her fingers, trying to offer what comfort I could. It wasn't much. There was no way it could have been. Lily's subjects were gathered on that tiny patch of land, clustered tight to keep from falling into the surrounding swamp. They spanned the gamut from purebloods to changelings, with a few even I couldn't identify somewhere in the middle. A Hamadryad leaned against a woman with blue feathers instead of hair; a half-blood Urisk sat in the grass with the head of his Glastig companion in his lap.

Walther was standing at the edge of the crowd. I started toward him, dragging Marcia along. Tybalt followed a few feet behind. The faces I knew were a minority. I should have known more of them. I should have been there more. I should . . .

I broke that train of thought as firmly as I could. It was too late for "should." I'd been there as much as I could. That would have to be enough.

Walther straightened when he saw us. "You found her," he said, relieved. Tears were running down his face, but his unnaturally blue eyes weren't puffy or bloodshot. Purebloods get all the breaks.

"I'm sorry I made you wait," I said.

"She's resting," said Walther, ignoring my lame attempt at an apology. "I thought we should leave her alone until you got here." The words "because it's almost over" hung unspoken between us.

"That was good of you." I tugged my hand free of Marcia's. "Can I see her?"

"She's waiting for you."

Marcia sobbed, knocking me aside as she rushed into Walther's arms. He stroked her hair one-handed, cradling her with his free arm. I looked away.

"Maybe I should go in now."

"Yes," Walther agreed. "Maybe you should."

Something in his tone made me hesitate. "Walther, how much worse . . . ?"

"Just go," he said. That seemed to be all the answer I was going to get. I took a deep breath as I turned and walked into the grove. Tybalt followed me, and Lily's subjects followed him. They didn't have permission to come, and they came anyway. That, more than anything, told me how bad things were; they'd never have broken protocol like that if they expected her to recover. I was moving quickly, anxious to reach her before it was . . . just before.

Then she came into view and I froze, rational thought shutting down as my eyes refused to process what they saw. That's when I realized that whatever happened wasn't going to be fixed or forgiven; it was going to be Evening Winterrose all over again, one more person I loved and couldn't save.

Then the shock passed—shock always passes when you don't want it to—and time started moving mercilessly forward.

Lily's head was propped against the edge of the pool, hair cascading around her. It didn't just obscure the lines of her body; it wiped them out, erasing the point where she ended and the water began. Her skin was translucent, strengthening the illusion that she and the water were the same—if it even was an illusion, anymore.

"Lily?" I whispered.

She opened colorless eyes, offering me a heartbreaking smile. New gashes opened in her throat as she moved, "bleeding" water. "You came. I knew you would. You were always stronger than she thought you'd be."

"Oh, Lily." I knelt next to the pool. Her hand sought mine, and I clasped it tightly, not letting myself flinch from the cold.

"Thank you," she said. Looking past me to Tybalt, she added, "Thank you both."

Some of her subjects gasped. I sighed, the last of the fight slipping out of me.

"There isn't much time," she said. "It's all slipping away, like water running downhill. This will be done with soon."

"You're going to be fine," I said, trying to sound comforting. "Just tell me where your pearl is. We'll find out what's wrong, and we'll fix it."

"The tide may turn that way, but I think not. Only time heals a heart of pearl, and my time is over." Catching my expression, she added, "I'd tell you if I could, truly."

"There's no reason left to hide it."

"I don't know where it is, child." Her voice was calm. "It passed from my knowledge as I sickened, and now I can't say if it's safe or stolen. It's done."

"I don't believe that."

"What you believe doesn't matter." Tilting her head,

she asked, "Did I ever tell you what came between your mother's heart and mine?"

"I don't think this is the time—"

"Your friend would disagree," she said, almost playfully, her attention darting to Tybalt. Focusing on me again, she said, "He all but burns with what he doesn't say to you, and this time is mine to spend. Do you know what happened?"

I sighed. "No."

"It was you." Her laughter was a heavy, watery sound that turned into a cough. I winced, tightening my grip on her hand until the coughing passed.

"You don't have to tell me this," I said. A small, traitorous voice in my head said, *No, and you don't want her to, because if she does, you'll know.*

"It's all right," she said, with surprising strength. "I have time for one more story. It was you, October, you and your father. She loved him, you know, not just for what he represented, but for who he was. My foolish little princess. She dared too much, given what she was, what she was refusing to be."

"I don't understand."

"She thought he'd save her, and when he didn't, she thought you would. Oh, my dear, what she did to you, what you didn't know she was doing, and how you fought! Like a lion you fought, never knowing the battle." Lily sighed. "You were the last of her protections against roses and crossroads and all they meant, and when you failed her, she didn't know what to do. My foolish princess who thought she'd be a shepherdess, if only she could make you a sheep. I loved her because she brought me to this wonderful land where I found such friends—I even loved her when she left me for you."

I frowned. "She didn't leave you."

"You both left me. But you came back, and you brought her shadow with you, to sit at my table. I was so grateful when you brought her back to me. It was never your fault; you carry the sins of your mother as she carries the sins of hers. Try not to blame her. She didn't mean to lay those sins on you. She tried to take them back, when she thought she could." She closed her eyes, shivering. "I'm cold. Why am I cold?"

I lifted her icy hand, pressing it to my cheek. "I don't know, Lily. I'm sorry."

"No sorrow. There was so much your mother never let me say. *Anata wa jibun no koto wa shiranakatta wa . . .* you never knew yourself. So much like my Ama-dear, trying to prove she didn't need me when she needed me more than ever . . . do you remember where the Undine began?"

"I do." My mother and I used to walk in Lily's gardens, back when she never let me out of her sight. I lived my life at arm's reach, and thought that was love. Childhood is a game of concessions, and everyone pretends to understand the rules, even though the only constant is that no one wants to be alone. Back then, we were content with our mutual captivity, before she started shoving me away; before I started running.

We were in Lily's gardens when Amandine taught me about the Undine. "Even new Undine are older than the rest of us," she said. "They remember when the ocean ruled the world."

"Where do they come from?" In those days, her every word was gospel truth, and I would have asked anything to keep her talking to me.

"Tears. The first time Oberon left Maeve for her pretty sister, she didn't understand, and she nearly died of sorrow."

"She cried?" I pictured Maeve as looking like my mother, beautiful and alien and broken, and I would've done anything to keep her from crying.

"She did. Her tears were the first Undine. They're hers alone, and because of that, they can't mate with humans." Her smile was bitter. I knew she was thinking of my father. "There are no changelings among the Undine."

Then she took me back to the Summerlands—home for her, and never for me—and put me to bed. I dreamed all day of children who'd never break their mother's heart, because they were born from nothing but tears.

Lily's cold fingers pulled me back to the present. I shivered. Lily was a constant, like the Torquills; someone who'd always be part of my life. I'm fae enough not to take kindly to change, and she was dying. "Please don't go. I'm not ready." I was begging. I didn't care.

"Don't worry, love." Cracks were opening around her eyes; water glimmered in their depths, where bone should have been. "It doesn't hurt. You silly ones with your blood and your bones, always so concerned about dying."

Tears ran down my cheeks. I wiped them away, but they kept coming. "Please."

"Don't cry." Lily pressed her free hand against my neck. I was numb enough not to flinch from the cold. "I'm sorry to go, but it's all right. Rivers dry up; tides ebb; the sea goes on."

"We don't."

"Are you sure? Immortality isn't flesh. You know that." She took a bubbling breath. Soon those breaths would stop, and she'd be gone. I was holding as tightly as I could, and she was slipping away. What's the point of holding on if I can't save the ones I can't afford to lose?

The whispering of Lily's subjects was like a roar behind me. Who would look after them now? I wanted to care, but I couldn't find the strength. I'm the changeling. I'm the one with the impure blood. I should have been the first to go. Not Lily, not Evening—not any of them. I'm the mortal one, and the world has no right to make me watch them die.

"I'll live forever," she said, hand slipping from mine.

"In the rise of rivers in spring, in winter's snows, in rain running down autumn's forests. It's not the immortality of men, but it's immortality. I know it's not something you can understand. I wish I could put it in words to comfort you, but the shape of your world and the shape of mine have always been different. Here, more than anywhere, we're alien to each other. Just believe me when I say this isn't the end . . . and I am not afraid."

"Don't leave me," I whispered. "I can't lose anyone else. I *can't.*"

"I won't leave you. That's the glory of it; don't you see? The night haunts won't come for me, because there won't be anything to come for. What I am, what I've been, it's all part of the water." Lily smiled, eyes closing as the outline of her face faded into the ripples around her. "Look to the water." Her voice changed, becoming distant; she wasn't talking to me anymore. She was done talking to me. "Oh . . . oh, look, Ama-chan, look. *Konya no sakura wa totemo kirei da na* . . . the cherry blossoms . . . so beautiful . . ."

And she was gone, body melting into the pool, hair becoming nothing but a shadow. I pitched forward, arms driving into the water up to the elbows. For a moment, there was silence. Then someone made a single, sobbing sound of protest, and it was like a dam breaking. A keening wail rose on all sides as Lily's subjects realized that it was over, it was finished. She was gone.

Tybalt pulled me to my feet, drawing me into an embrace. I didn't fight. For the moment, I belonged there. And when I didn't belong in the Tea Gardens anymore, someone was going to die. Oberon's law be damned.

FOURTEEN

I STEPPED FROM THE MOON BRIDGE into the darkness of the Tea Gardens, shoving my hands into my jacket pockets in a vain attempt to warm them. It felt like the cold had crept all the way into my bones; between that and the pounding in my head, it was a miracle I was upright at all. Tybalt walked beside me, not saying anything. That was good. I wasn't sure there was anything *to* say.

Lily's subjects followed us, watching with wide, terrified eyes as they waited to be told what to do. I didn't hold their neediness against them; if following made them feel better, let them follow. I didn't care. Lily was gone. The knowledge was sinking in by inches, becoming part of the way the world was. Fire burned, iron killed, and Lily was dead. Lily was dead, and it was time for me to go.

"Toby?" Marcia's tone demanded attention.

I turned to face her. "What?" I asked, struggling to keep my own voice neutral. I was exhausted, and anger was starting to win out over my grief. I wanted to get out of the Tea Gardens before I said or did something I'd regret.

"What's going to happen to us now?" She asked the question so softly that it took me a moment to realize what she'd said.

I stiffened, cursing inwardly as I scanned Lily's gathered subjects. There was an almost uniform despair in their eyes; they clearly expected us to walk away. With no one to take care of them and Lily's knowe collapsing, they had nowhere to go. The other denizens of Golden Gate Park respected Lily, and that would protect her subjects for a while, but not forever. With no one to hold the knowe, greed would overcome respect, and the Tea Gardens would fall.

Lily wouldn't have wanted that. I wasn't going to let it happen.

"Don't worry." I put a hand on Marcia's shoulder. "I'll take care of you."

"Really?"

"Really."

Walther stepped up next to her, saying, "Not to sound like a doubting Thomas, but how are you planning to do that?"

"In the long run, I don't know. For now . . ." I turned to Tybalt. "You were watching the Tea Gardens before. Will you keep watching them long enough for me to find out what's going on?"

From the look on his face, Tybalt expected the question. He took my hand, studying me gravely as he asked, "Why me, and not one of your more accepted allies?"

"Right now, there's nobody I trust more than I trust you."

"Ah. The truth." He smiled, looking almost tired as he released my hand. "Go, then; I'm sure you have promises to keep. My cats and I will guard your flotsam until you return."

"I appreciate that," I said, skirting the forbidden thanks.

"I know you do. You always do." Tybalt sighed. "She was my friend, too. Find whoever killed her. If you need me, call."

"If I can." I wasn't making any promises, but I meant it.

He paused before reaching out to brush my hair back with a surprisingly gentle hand. "Don't run yourself to death until you know you have no choice."

"I have to go." I pulled away, turning back to Walther and Marcia. "Can you do me a favor?"

"What?" asked Marcia, sniffling.

"Keep everyone here until we know what's going on." I wasn't *sure* Luna and Lily were targeted because of their connection to me, but the odds were too high to ignore. "I'll be back as soon as I can."

Marcia nodded, whispering, "I promise."

"I can't stay here," Walther said. "I have class."

Lily mentioned him testing her water; I hazarded a guess. "You teach forensics?"

"Chemistry."

"Close enough. If I bring you something, can you test it for poison?"

Walther nodded. "Sure." He dug a business card out of his pocket. "My class schedule and office hours are on the back."

"Great." I took the card and flipped it over, checking to be sure I could read his writing before tucking it into the pocket of my jacket. "I'll see you soon."

That was that. There were no more excuses to stay and too many reasons to go. Walking out of that garden alone was still one of the hardest things I've ever done. Lamentations filled the air behind me. I was almost to the gate when a new voice joined in, adding its own harsh, deep sobs. I didn't look back.

Tybalt would never have forgiven me for seeing him cry.

I had to walk in circles with my hands stretched out in front of me for several minutes before my palms bumped into my still-invisible car. When May casts a don't-look-here, she *really* casts a don't-look-here. Unlocking the door took several more minutes. I was swearing steadily by the time I got inside.

There was no traffic so close to dawn, and having an invisible car meant there were no speed limits, either. I drove home fast enough to be a danger to myself and others, so focused on the road that I didn't notice I was crying until I reached my apartment complex, parked the car, and realized my cheeks were damp. I frowned, trying to figure out why. That's when it wore through the shock and hit me all the way: Lily was dead, and Luna was dying, and nothing I did seemed to be making things any better. I was failing them. "Oh, Lily," I whispered, wiping my cheeks. "How *could* you?"

I left the car in a daze, pausing only to retrieve Luna's cup. I should have given it to Walther while we were both in the same place . . . or not. I'd feel safer if I could be there while he ran the tests, and that needed to wait until his office hours. My head was pounding, and tears were running unchecked down my cheeks, but that didn't matter. Even I'm allowed to grieve.

The living room was dark. I shoved Luna's cup into the front closet without turning on the light, then paused, frowning. Spike was compacted into a ball on the corner of the couch, and the cats were pacing in front of May's door, yowling. May never locks the cats out. She's more tolerant than I am, and she doesn't mind being woken at seven in the morning because the girls want to be fed.

Cagney gave me an indignant look, clearly expecting me to open the door. I moved her aside with my foot, knocking instead. "May? You in there?"

"Go away!"

That wasn't good. "Are you okay? Is something wrong?"

Something hit the inside of the door. She was throwing things. "I said *go away!*"

I frowned, putting my hand on the doorknob. My Fetch is normally good-tempered in the extreme, unless you've done something to piss her off. She might have heard about Lily, somehow; she'd know what the Undine's death meant, for both of us.

"I'm coming in," I said. She wasn't ready to deal with this, and she definitely wasn't ready to deal with it on her own.

There was no answer. I opened the door.

May's room amazes me. I'm not tidy—I tend toward "congenial clutter"—but I'm not a pack rat, whereas May would happily keep a souvenir for every moment of her life. Her room reflects that. One wall is lined with mismatched bookshelves holding her "collections;" the other wall is occupied by two dressers and an oak vanity that I helped her carry home from a garage sale. No one needs as much makeup as was spread across the top of her vanity, or that much costume jewelry.

May herself was huddled in the middle of the bed with her legs drawn up to her chest and her forehead pressed to her knees. There was something wrong with the shape of her. I just couldn't tell quite what it was, and that scared me.

"May?"

"Lily's dead, isn't she?" she asked, not moving.

I stepped the rest of the way inside, closing the door behind me. "Yeah."

"Thought so." May raised her head, looking at me through the washed-out brown curtain of her hair. I froze, realizing what was wrong as she offered me a bitter smile. "It grew out about an hour ago. Look." She pulled back her skirt, displaying a circular scar on her upper thigh. "That's where Blind Michael's men shot you, isn't it?"

"May—"

"Don't. You know what this means. We match because the universe thinks you're going to die soon. And that means I'm going with you."

"We can cut your hair." I didn't think we could fool reality that easily, but it was worth trying. Anything was worth trying.

"I already did." She waved a hand at the floor. A small heap of hacked-off hair lay near the foot of the bed. Some of it was streaked in magenta and blue; the remains of her dye job. "It grew back. You can't cheat fate, October. We were stupid to try."

"No, we weren't." I sat down next to her on the bed. "I'm not sorry."

May sighed. "I guess I'm not, either. It's been fun, y'know? This whole thing, it's been fun." She shook her head. "I'll miss the farmer's market at the Ferry Building. And Telegraph Avenue. And Danny's crazy Barghest rescue service." More quietly, she added, "And Jazz. I'll miss her."

"Hey. We can still win." I stroked her hair back from her face. "Tell me more about Jasmine. Where did you meet her?"

"On Telegraph." May sniffled, offering a wan smile. "She runs a junk store. I was buying costume jewelry, and she asked if I wanted to join her in the office for coffee. She was pretty obviously flirting, so I started flirting back. I said sure. I didn't want her to think I was . . . you know . . ." She waved a hand, indicating me.

Since I'd never met Jazz before the Ball, it seemed unlikely that she would have mistaken May for me. I ventured, "Daoine Sidhe?"

"Yeah." May's smile grew. "Full disclosure, y'know?

So as soon as we got out of the public shop, I dropped my illusions and told her what I was. I figured she'd throw me out as soon as I said 'Fetch.'"

"But she didn't."

"She didn't," May agreed, putting her head down against my shoulder. "She said she'd been in relationships with way bigger problems than one of us being a transitory manifestation of impending doom. Like this one girl who liked her computer more than she liked her girlfriend, and another one who smoked."

"She sounds sweet."

"She is." May sighed again, the sound seeming to come up all the way from the soles of her feet. "I think I could've loved her."

"Hey. Don't talk like that. It's not over yet."

"It may as well be." She closed her eyes. "I tried to be different from you. I tried so hard. I guess I just wasn't good enough."

"Hush," I said. "It's not your fault. It never was."

May wasn't to blame. She didn't choose what she was. She did her best with what she had, and that's all any of us can do. We're handed the balance of our blood and the shape of our lives and told to do something with them. May started with nothing but a copy of my past, and became someone I couldn't have been. The universe made her to show that I was going to die, but she developed a life of her own. She became real.

We all have our roles to play. Even wayward Fetches with no fashion sense.

We sat that way for a long time before she asked, "Will it hurt?"

I hate the hard questions. "I don't know," I said. "Maybe you can tell me."

"I don't know, either." She pulled away. "I think it will. I can almost remember that it will, but it's not there yet. I can't know how you're going to die in time to stop it."

"It's okay," I said, and I meant it. "I didn't expect you to know."

"Good." May settled against me, putting her head on my shoulder. "I'm scared."

"So am I." I was starting to cry again, and my head was killing me. I wanted to stay with her and hold her forever, where nothing would ever find or hurt us. I wanted us both to live forever. I just didn't see any way to make that happen.

FIFTEEN

EXHAUSTION CAUGHT UP WITH ME while I was sitting with May; serial killers and sleep deprivation are practically part of my daily life. I woke to the sound of a ringing phone. We'd slept through the dawn, me slumping forward until my elbows rested against my knees, May falling backward to sprawl across the mattress. She looked so damn fragile, one arm thrown over her eyes to block the light.

"I'll fix this," I said, and kissed her forehead before I left the room. I propped the door with a pillow to keep the cats from complaining and still managed to reach the kitchen before the machine picked up. Snatching the receiver from its cradle, I tucked it under my ear and walked toward the kitchen. "It's Toby."

"It's Connor," replied the voice on the other end, sounding even wearier than I felt. My breath caught in my chest. I hadn't realized I was worried about him until I heard his voice. "Are you okay?"

Connor's known me longer than almost anybody else. There wasn't any point in lying to him. "No," I said. The coffeepot was still half-full. I grabbed a mug and

filled it before shoving it into the microwave. Hot coffee.
I was not going to survive the day without hot coffee.
"You've heard?"

"About Lily? I've heard. Luna's no better, Sylvester's
not talking to anyone, and Rayseline . . ." He hesitated,
taking a breath before he continued, saying, "She's
stalking the battlements looking for victims. It's like the
haunted halls of Elsinore around here."

"Did you just make a *Hamlet* reference?" The microwave beeped, and I pulled out my mug, moving to get
the milk from the refrigerator. The clock on the wall told
me it was almost noon. "I guess I really am a bad influence on you."

"Yeah, I guess you are."

A brief silence fell while I prepared my coffee, broken only by the sound of our breathing. Finally, quietly,
I asked, "Is Raysel a danger? Do we need to start thinking about getting you and Quentin out of there?"

Connor smothered a bitter chuckle. "Has Raysel ever
not been a danger? But no, I don't think she's more dangerous than usual. She's focusing on things other than
the two of us."

"Like pinning the attack on Luna on me," I con-
cluded, before taking a gulp of scalding coffee. "I'm serious. She starts looking like she's going to hurt one of
you, you get the hell out of there."

"Why, Toby. I didn't know you cared."

"I never stopped caring."

Silence fell between us again, lasting an impossibly
long-seeming time before Connor said, "Toby . . ."

"I know. We need to talk about it. Can it wait until
things are a little less hectic, maybe?"

"So, fifty years?" Connor laughed again, this time
without the undercurrent of bitterness. "It sounds like a
plan. I'll call again if anything changes."

"Okay. Stay safe. Please. For me."

"I will." There was a pause where it seemed like he

was about to say something else. Then he whispered, "Open roads," and the connection went dead, leaving the dial tone buzzing in my ear.

I sipped my coffee as I walked the phone back to its cradle in the hall. That was an interesting way to start the day. At least everyone at Shadowed Hills was still alive. Lily was gone, but Luna still had a chance.

The phone rang again as soon as I put it down. I snagged it, asking, "What now?"

"It's good to see you've been taking telephone etiquette lessons from the Luidaeg," said Tybalt. He sounded exhausted. "Have I called at a bad time?"

My stomach twisted into a knot as his tone registered. "I don't think there are any good times left," I said, walking back toward the kitchen. "Is everything okay?"

"Intrigued as I am by the fact that you apparently think I'd call when everything was 'okay,' I'm afraid I have to answer that in the negative. No. Everything is most assuredly not 'okay.' How quickly can you come to the park?"

"I can be there in half an hour." I grabbed a thermos from the dish drainer next to the sink, tipping my coffee hastily into it. "Can you hold out that long?"

Tybalt chuckled humorlessly. "I don't suppose I have a choice. Hurry, October." He hesitated before adding, "Please." The line went dead.

I stared at the phone before dropping the receiver on the counter and bolting for my bedroom. It only took me a few minutes to get ready. I detoured by the kitchen on my way to the door, grabbing my thermos and a box of Pop-Tarts. I wasn't hungry. That didn't mean my body didn't need to eat. At least spending several hours dozing with May had helped my headache—I could think again, even if I wasn't happy about the things I had to think about.

Spike was still huddled on the couch. I paused to run a hand along its back, hoping it would wake up and come with me. The company would have been nice. It made a faint snuffling noise and didn't move.

"Okay, buddy" I said, and moved away from my sleeping rose goblin.

There was an empty duffel bag at the bottom of the closet. I shoved the velvet-swaddled cup into it and tucked it under my arm before pulling the baseball bat from the umbrella stand. My knives were belted at my waist, but there's something to be said for street-legal weapons and blunt trauma.

There was a knock at the door.

I frowned. "Who is it?" Better safe than sorry-you're-dead.

"Manuel."

"Manuel?" I dropped the duffel next to the umbrella stand and switched the bat to my left hand before opening the door. Manuel Lorimer was on the porch with his hands shoved into his pockets and his startlingly golden hair almost hidden under a baseball cap. It looked like he was trying to be inconspicuous. It wasn't working. "Look, Manny, this isn't a good time—"

He looked at me challengingly. "Can I come in?"

I blinked. He'd probably been sent on official business. I thought of human process servers tracking people to their homes, but dismissed the idea. I didn't think they'd send an untitled half-blood to arrest me.

Of course, I've been wrong before. "Sure." I stepped out of the way. "Can I get you some coffee or something?"

Manuel glared as he stepped inside. "Don't play nice."

I closed the door, "I didn't think I was playing anything. What do you need? I was on my way out." I thought of telling him where I was going, and just as quickly thought better of it.

"The body count isn't high enough for you?" He looked at me with genuine loathing. "You should've stayed in the pond. People die when you're around."

"That's not fair."

"My sister's blood is on your hands, and you say I'm the one who's not fair?"

"How can you say that? Dare died because—" I stopped, forcing myself to take a deep breath before my temper could run away with me. I've had the argument with myself a thousand times. I endangered her, I shouldn't have let her interfere, I should have known better. I always cycle back to Devin. He'd changed while I was away, and I had no way of knowing how deep those changes went until it was too late. "I didn't kill her. Devin did. He was sick."

"He was our *guardian*!" Manuel shouted, the pretense of rationality dissolving in the face of an anger that had been allowed to fester for far too long.

That made it strangely easier to stay calm. I don't like anger, but I understand it. "He used you the way he used everybody else. Dare got in his way. Now please, can we discuss this like adults? My roommate is asleep, and I'd like her to stay that way."

"No, I'm not," said May. I turned to see her leaning against the hallway wall, holding her robe closed with one hand. "Hey, boss. Hey, Manny."

"Filth," Manuel spat. "You're so in love with death you even let it *live* with you. You're disgusting."

"I think it's time for you to leave," I said, quietly. "I'm not going to let you talk about her that way."

He thrust his open hand toward me. "Give me my sister's knife, and I'll go."

"What?" I stared at him. This conversation was a bit too full of bombshells for my tastes. "You're kidding."

"It was hers. I want it back." He glared, still holding out his hand. "It was a loan. As her brother, I'm telling you the loan is over. Give it back."

"It was a gift," said May. The conviction in her voice was enough to make us both turn. She shrugged, looking Manuel in the eyes as she said, "Ask the night-haunts if you disagree. Toby can call them for you."

His eyes widened, and he looked briefly lost. Then he shifted his attention away from May, focusing on me. I stifled a sigh, seeing where this was about to go. Manuel was on the streets for years before he went to Shadowed Hills, and all Devin's kids learned how to fight.

Trouble is, most of them only learned to fight well enough to make it from one day to the next. I was Devin's favorite for a long time, and I got better lessons than most. I braced myself when I saw Manuel tense, letting the objects I'd been holding fall as he started to charge. He wasn't expecting my hands to be free; his approach left him no defense against a grapple. I caught his arm, using his own momentum to spin him around and pin him against the wall.

It was over in seconds. Planting my knee against his back, I said, "I don't have time to fight you. Do you get that? I refuse to do this when people are dying."

He made a thin choking noise. For a moment, I was afraid I was even more out of practice than I thought, and that I'd hit him hard enough to hurt him. It was somehow even worse when I realized he was crying.

I dropped my foot to the floor and let go of his elbow, stepping back. He stumbled away from me, fumbling for the doorknob.

"You'll be sorry you ever touched me," he said.

"Go back to Shadowed Hills, Manuel. It's over."

"It's not over!" He wrenched the door open. "It's not. You'll pay."

"Whatever." I closed the door behind him and started retrieving my things. The thermos had rolled halfway under the couch. Thank Maeve for locking lids; if I'd been forced to leave the house without coffee, someone would have died. "May? You okay?"

"Yeah." She tossed something at me. I caught it automatically with my free hand, and almost laughed when I saw what I was holding.

A bottle of Tylenol.

May smiled when I looked up. "I'm getting your headaches now, too. Try keeping it to a dull roar until you dodge certain death, okay?"

"Okay," I said, solemnly. "May—"

"I know." Manuel danced with Raysel at the Ball; if she really wanted me blamed for the attack on her mother, having my knife to plant in a convenient place wouldn't be the worst approach. "Just get moving."

"All right," I said, opened the door, and left.

My headache was bad enough to make spinning an illusion a bad idea. I scurried to the car with my hair pulled over my ears, wishing like hell that I didn't feel like there was something shameful in being myself. I've spent my whole life being ashamed of what I am. There's no place in the human world for fae, and no place in the fae world for humans. I just wish they'd stop trying to meet in the middle. It's too hard on the kids.

I opened the Pop-Tarts after tucking the baseball bat and duffel bag behind the seat. The smell of powdery sugar and fake fruit filled the car. I took a massive bite from the first pseudo-pastry, stuck the key into the ignition, and drove.

Distance was making it easier to think about what was going on. Lily was an untitled landholder; her death was tragic, but it wouldn't inspire the nobility to lead a manhunt. Luna was a Duchess. If she died, the game would change completely. Poison doesn't break Oberon's law unless somebody dies. There are circles where putting your enemies to sleep for a thousand years is perfectly normal.

"What the hell kind of game is Oleander trying to play?" I muttered, washing down my Pop-Tart with a swig of coffee. Did she just want to hurt me, or did she have a bigger plan? It couldn't be coincidence that both people who'd been attacked were ones I loved but could easily have hated. If you didn't know me, you'd almost expect me to hate them. If Oleander was targeting me, she was doing it the right way. She was keeping me off-balance and had a good shot at getting me executed. Bully for her.

If anyone would know how to poison an Undine, it was Oleander. Poisons have always been her trademark. The question was really "what did she expect to gain?" The entire Torquill family had good reason to hate her. She stole Raysel's childhood, and stole her sanity in the process. There was no way—

My hands tightened on the steering wheel as a chilling thought struck me. Raysel was insane, and she wasn't surprised to hear that her mother was sick. Was she that crazy? Or was she the one who let Oleander into the knowe? It was a horrible idea, but I couldn't afford to dismiss it out of hand. Raysel wanted the Duchy; this might be the fastest way to get it, if she was crazy enough to work with Oleander. If.

Was I paranoid enough to imagine a conspiracy between my liege-lord's daughter and the woman who tried to kill me sixteen years ago? More importantly, could I afford *not* to be that paranoid?

Some idiot in an SUV pulled out in front of me. I swerved, swearing, and managed to dump the rest of my coffee on the seat, where it immediately soaked into the upholstery. "This day had better not get any worse," I snarled, resolving to swing through the first drive-through I passed and buy an entire gallon of coffee. Without it, I doubted I'd survive to see the sun go down.

Still swearing, surrounded by the taunting smell of the spilled coffee, I drove on

SIXTEEN

IT TOOK LONGER TO REACH GOLDEN GATE park than it should have, largely because the tourists were out in force. I wasn't sure whether they were more annoying in their cars, where they missed lights and tried to drive the wrong way down one-way streets, or out of their cars, where they jaywalked with suicidal abandon. I settled for "yes." More and more, I've come to appreciate the fact that the fae are naturally nocturnal. It lets me live in San Francisco and still avoid all the damn tourists. Most of the time.

I managed to get to the park without having an accident or giving in to the siren song of road rage. My headache actually helped, since it required me to focus on the road, keeping me too distracted to get really pissed. The pounding was back at full force, and had lasted *way* too long to be magic-burn—not that I'd cast any large spells recently. It was the sort of thing that would normally send me running for Lily. As it was . . .

I shivered, and pushed the thought away.

The parking lot nearest the Tea Gardens was packed with tourists, some of whom had managed to take up two or more spaces with their outsized SUVs. I indulged in some good, old-fashioned swearing as I drove around the pavilion to park in the shadows next to the snack bar dumpsters. The smell of cooking oil and decaying vegetation assaulted my nostrils as soon as I stopped the engine. Swell. Just *swell*.

The pain in my head was bad enough to make me unsure of my ability to cast an illusion without some sort of help. Thankfully, Devin was firm that all his kids would understand how to use hedge magic and "cheap tricks"—just in case.

"You always did know best, you old bastard," I muttered, digging the bottle of marsh water and crushed mint leaves out of the glove compartment. I always keep one in the car. Just in case.

I squirted water around the inside of my car until I was nearly gagging on the smell of mint. My magic rose with sullen sluggishness, sending a warning bolt of pain through my temples. I did my best to ignore it, closing my eyes and chanting, rapidly, "Pussy-cat, pussy-cat, where have you been? I've been to London, to visit the Queen. Pussy-cat, pussy-cat, what did you there—

The spell burst without my telling it to, leaving me sticky with marsh water and mint. My head hurt worse than ever. "I frightened a little mouse under her chair," I said, half-gasping, and dropped the bottle, reaching up with one shaking hand to feel the curvature of my ear. Round. Whether it was a good idea or not, the spell was cast. Now I just needed to get to Tybalt and find out what the hell was going on.

I was faintly dizzy from pain, which didn't make it any easier to get out of the car. I staggered the few feet between my bumper and the back of the snack bar, barely catching myself against the wall before I was enthusiastically and messily sick. So much for actually eating something.

"Dammit," I mumbled, wiping my mouth with the

back of my hand. That didn't do anything about the taste. Well, I knew how to deal with that.

I was waiting for my coffee at the snack bar's pick-up window when the familiar scent of pennyroyal rose behind me, which could only mean one thing: Tybalt in a recently-crafted human disguise.

"I was on my way to meet you," I said.

"Did I sound overly relaxed on the phone, or did you simply choose to ignore the fact that I was requesting your help?" His voice was tight with anger, making him sound cold and distant. It took a moment to realize why that was so familiar.

That's how he used to talk to me all the time.

When given a choice between confusion and irritation, I'll almost always go with irritation. It's easier to deal with. "Neither," I said, stepping up to claim my coffee from the teenage attendant. He gave me an uneasy look. My strained smile didn't make him look any calmer.

"So what possible motive can I assign to this little detour?" asked Tybalt.

"How about 'Toby was just vilely ill, and didn't want to have puke-breath when she showed up at your place'?" I asked, turning to face him. "Call it a matter of etiquette, and let it go, okay?"

Tybalt glared at me, arms folded over his chest. His human disguise was a good one, smoothing away the black streaks in his hair and adding an overlay of hazel to his overly-green eyes. It wouldn't have fooled me for a second. He could look like a man, but he'd always move like a cat.

"Your opinions of proper behavior are always fascinating," he said finally, shaking his head. "It's no matter. Come along."

"What?"

"You're not that dense. Now come." He turned and stalked away, forcing me to scramble after him. I don't usually have trouble keeping up with Tybalt, but I had to pace him at a jog, making it impossible to drink my coffee.

We crossed the parking lot to the botanical gardens. Tybalt stopped at the hawthorn bushes. I did the same, taking the opportunity to down half my coffee, and didn't see him reaching for me until he grabbed my arm. "Hey, what are you—" I managed. Then the world went black and freezing cold.

I swore inwardly, fighting to keep from breathing. Maybe Cait Sidhe are comfortable on the Shadow Roads, but I'm not, and I don't appreciate being pulled onto them without my consent. We fell through darkness for some unmeasured time—long enough for me to realize this wasn't the road I'd walked with him before, this was something new—before we tumbled into the light.

Tybalt caught me before I hit the ground. My coffee wasn't so lucky; it fell from my hand, landing with a "thud" that meant the contents were no longer liquid. "Are you all right?" Tybalt asked.

I staggered away from him, glaring. "Why did you do that?"

"I needed to get you to my Court."

"There wasn't an easier way? Like a *door?*"

"Not to get you this deep." He sounded more like the Tybalt I'd grown used to now that we were in his Court. I wasn't sure how reassuring that really was. "I'm sorry, but the other roads would all have taken too long."

"This deep?" I echoed. Abandoning my glare, I looked slowly around.

The hall was wider than it was tall; I could have reached up and touched the ceiling. Tattered lengths of silk and velvet hung from the walls. Muddy foot- and paw-prints marred the gray marble floor. This wasn't the Court of Cats I knew. This was something else. "Tybalt?" I glanced back to him. "Where *are* we?"

"When Faerie was divided, Oberon gave the lost places of the world to the Cait Sidhe," Tybalt said, falling into the strange half-cadence almost all purebloods use for reciting history. It couldn't overcome the weariness increasingly coloring his voice. "The hidden halls and shadowed corners are ours. We hold Court in alleys and groves, plain to all eyes, but we live in the places that have been forgotten."

My gut clenched as I realized what he was saying. "This isn't the Court of Cats. This is your Kingdom."

"Yes," he said, with a tiny smile. "It is."

"Why are you telling me this? Why am I *here?*"

"I'm telling you because you need to know, and because you're the first child of Oberon to walk here since I claimed my throne." He shook his head. "There was a mortal woman here once. But that was years ago, and there have been none of any fae line but the Cait Sidhe. Bringing you here would be treason if I weren't King."

"But you *are* King."

"I suppose that means it's just foolish. Now come." He grabbed my hand, pulling me down the hall. My footsteps echoed on the marble. His made no sound.

We passed through an arched doorway into a hall with walls of golden wood. Tall windows were spaced every few feet. I glanced through one into a ballroom full of broken, mismatched furniture. The angle of the view was somehow wrong, like the rooms had been shoved together through a bend in space. Tybalt pulled me through another door and into a massive room with a domed ceiling. It looked like a church. A pile of wooden benches was heaped against one wall, adding credence to the theory.

I pulled my hand free and stopped, staring. "Oh, sweet rowan . . ."

The floor was obscured by dozens of makeshift pallets, each one holding an unmoving Cait Sidhe. Some of the Cait Sidhe were in human form. Others were cats, and more were caught between shapes, blending human and feline features in ways that were simply wrong. The only sounds were groans and muffled whimpers, and the air was filled with the stench of sickness.

My life has left me far too familiar with death. I know what it looks like, what it smells like; the flat, tinny taste of it. And there was death in the air all around us.

"This is what I wanted you to see," Tybalt said. "Now do you understand why I'm willing to break my own laws?"

I gave him a startled look. He looked back, some desperate, unexpressed hope in his eyes. I didn't know what he wanted from me. I just had to try to give it to him.

I crossed to the nearest prone Cait Sidhe and knelt, pressing my fingers against his throat. His skin was hot, and his pulse was irregular enough to feel like it might stop at any moment. I studied his face, noting the tabby pattern on his cheeks and forehead. His features were rough-hewn, lacking the beauty of the Cait Sidhe nobles: he was a back-alley scrapper, not a show cat. My breath caught. "Gabriel?"

"And Louis, and half the rest of my guard," Tybalt said. "This is just one room. We've filled three."

"Oh, oak and ash." I straightened, looking around. I could see at least twenty Cait Sidhe, from men Gabriel's size to kittens no bigger than my fist. Three rooms like this? That made at least sixty—and that was just the sick ones. I hadn't realized there were so many Cait Sidhe in the Bay Area. The fae cats guard their numbers carefully, but still. How big *was* Tybalt's kingdom?

I crossed to a pallet occupied by a white cat and two tiny tabby kittens. She roused herself enough to hiss when I reached for the smaller kitten. I stopped, hand outstretched, and said, "I'm not going to hurt your babies."

The cat looked at me before turning to Tybalt.

"It's all right, Opal," he said. "I trust her."

She flattened her ears at that, but didn't stop me as I scooped the kitten into my hand and stroked it with one finger, noting the unsteadiness of its breath. It panted, tiny legs making swimming motions against my palm. It was fighting to hold on, but I didn't know how much longer it could last.

"What happened?" I asked, looking up.

Tybalt reached over and took the kitten, cradling it against his chest. It relaxed, nuzzling his sleeve. "Someone poisoned the food supply," he said. "The nobility hunts; our subjects are fed, either from our kills or from supplemental food we purchase from local shops. They eat better and with more dignity when they hunt for themselves, but no one goes hungry. It's part of my duty as King."

"Who eats the food that you provide?"

"My guards, when they're on duty; they don't have time to hunt. Nursing mothers, the young, the injured. All the weakest and most vulnerable of my subjects."

"And someone poisoned them."

"Yes." His expression was pained. "The nursing children collapsed first. We didn't know why. By the time we understood, even the strongest had succumbed."

"The children . . ." My breath caught again. "Is Raj all right? Is he *here?*"

He shook his head. "Raj will be King someday. He hunts for himself."

I nodded, not bothering to conceal my relief as I reached down and ran a hand over Opal's side. She stayed limp, not reacting. I reached for the second kitten, and froze, hand still outstretched. "Tybalt?"

"What is it?" He crouched, putting the first kitten next to its mother. I indicated its sibling. His face went blank. "Oh. I see."

I bit my lip. "Is it . . . ?"

Opal raised her head, eyes half-open and pleading. Tybalt shook his head and rose, folding his hands around the kitten as he lifted it away from her. "Opal, I . . . I'm sorry. I regret your loss." Opal moaned and closed her eyes, putting her head down.

I rose, putting my hand on Tybalt's shoulder. Not looking at me, he said, "She and Gabriel married two hundred years ago; this was their first litter. They may never have another, even if they both survive. Two hundred years to produce four kittens, all born alive and perfect."

"I'm so sorry," I whispered.

"I've lost six of my people since last night. I don't know how many will follow. How can I tell Gabriel his children are gone? How can I claim to be a good King to Opal when I provided the meat that killed her family?" He raised his head, pupils narrowed to thin slits. "I don't know how to stop this. I don't know what to *do*."

I didn't think before I acted; I just put my arms around his shoulders, squeezing before I said, "I don't know, either. That doesn't matter. We're going to stop this. I can't bring back the dead, but I can help you avenge them."

He stared at me, hands still cupping the kitten. I reddened and let go, stepping away. Voice soft, he said, "If you do this, I'll owe you a debt I can never repay."

"You won't owe me a thing. I refuse to believe there's more than one person targeting the people I care about. This is my fight." I looked around the room again, resisting the urge to comfort him. "Six dead. Two more rooms like this. Is any of the meat left? I was getting ready to go have Walther analyze some samples when you called. I can ask him to do a little more."

"What's left of the meat is in the alley. The children collapsed halfway through the meal; Gabriel and Louis called me before they succumbed."

"Good." I paused. "Where's Julie? She should've attacked me by now."

"Julie?" Tybalt sighed. "She's not nobility, Toby. She eats with the Court."

"Oh, Maeve." I closed my eyes. "Dammit, Julie."

"Come on." Tybalt put his hand on my shoulder. When I opened my eyes, he nodded toward the door. "I'll get you out of here. Raj will bring you the meat."

"What about the baby?" I asked. The kitten was still cradled against his chest.

"I'll leave him for the night-haunts." He started walking. "He was one of us. Even if it was only for a little while."

I trailed behind him, breathing shallowly as I tried to get the taste of death out of my mouth. Tybalt didn't speak, and so neither did I; we walked through the patchwork halls in silence, both trying not to look at the kitten lying limply in his hand. There were tears on his cheeks. I tried not to look at them, either.

And then he took my hand, and we stepped into the shadows, leaving the Kingdom of the Cats behind us.

SEVENTEEN

I SAT ON A BENCH NEAR THE LAKE, drinking a fresh cup of coffee as I waited for Raj. The sun glittering off the water made it seem transparent and impossibly blue at the same time. Most of California gets too hot in May, but not San Francisco; the "perfect summers" they talk about in movies really happen here. I wished I'd thought to bring bread for the ducks. It was a stupid, escapist idea, but it was a beautiful day, and my head hurt, and I was so tired of running.

A fat gray goose waddled over, webbed feet slapping the ground, and gave me an inquisitive look. "Sorry, no bread," I said. It flapped its wings, spraying water in my eyes. It stung. I wiped my face dry, laughing. "I guess I deserved that, huh?"

Something in the bushes rustled. The goose hissed, neck snaking out, before waddling away. I stiffened, forcing myself not to turn around. Humans notice beautiful days, too, and the park was full of tourists. Stabbing one of them wouldn't help.

"Hello," I said. "I'm in a pretty rotten mood, so you

might want to move along. And I don't have any spare change."

"I . . ." The speaker paused, clearing his throat. "I don't want any spare change."

I knew that voice. I turned, flashing a small, tired smile. "Hi, Raj."

"Hi." Raj stepped out of the bushes, clutching a package wrapped in white butcher paper against his chest. His human disguise was flickering, barely covering the points of his ears. He hadn't bothered to hide the circles around his eyes or the tearstains on his cheeks. With half the Court down for the count, Tybalt had to have been working him pretty hard. Just another consequence of being a prince, but one I was glad I didn't have to bear.

"Is that the meat that got everyone sick?" I asked.

"Yeah." He held out the package, eyes wide and vacant. I'd seen that look on his face before, when he thought we were going to die in Blind Michael's lands. "He said to let us know if you need more. There isn't much, but he won't get rid of it until you say you don't need it."

"Good." I took the package, putting it down on the bench. "Are you all right?"

He glanced away. "I'm fine."

"You don't sound fine." I studied his face. "Is Tybalt working you too hard? Do you need me to talk to him?"

"It's my duty as Prince to follow my King's commands." He should have sounded proud when he said that. He didn't. He just sounded numb.

"Hey, if Tybalt's being a dick, tell your parents you need him to lay off and let you get some sleep. They'll talk to him." He froze, and I realized what the missing piece had to be. "Raj, are your parents . . ."

He stared at me before crumpling to the bench, al-

ready sobbing. I put my arms around him, and he clung
to them like they were the only anchor he had, crying
even harder. I started stroking his hair. I know what
it's like to lose someone; the last thing you need when
you're grieving is some well-meaning moron telling you
it's going to be all right. It's *not* going to be all right. It's
never going to be all right again.

Raj cried for a good fifteen minutes before he pulled
away, stiffening. I shook my head, leaning over to brush
his bangs out of his eyes. "You don't have to do that," I
said. "I don't mind."

"I'm not supposed to cry," he said, in a dull, wounded
voice. "Princes don't cry."

"Did Tybalt tell you that?" There was a time when I
wouldn't have asked. I was learning I didn't understand
Tybalt as well as I'd always assumed I did.

He shook his head. "It was my father."

"Your father?" I echoed, irrationally pleased to hear
that it *hadn't* been Tybalt.

"He says I'll never be King if I'm weak enough to
cry."

I frowned. "Crying isn't weak. It's good sense. It
means you know it's all right to mourn the dead and let
them go."

"I guess," he said, looking down. "If you say so. But
he said I shouldn't."

"I do say so." I paused. "If your father's alive—"

"My mother." He wiped his eyes with the back of his
hand. "Her blood was weak. She was a pureblood, but
she wasn't strong. That's why I was such a surprise. She
couldn't even be human when she was pregnant with
me, because she was so weak."

"I've known some people like that," I said. "Being
a pureblood doesn't always mean you'll have strong
magic." Usually, but not always.

"You have to have strong magic to be noble, and she

didn't," he said, huddling against me again. "She almost always hunted, because she was proud. But she got hit by a car a week ago, and her leg was broken, and so . . ." He stopped.

"So she ate the tainted meat with the others," I finished softly.

"Yeah. She fell down, and she wouldn't open her eyes, and we called Uncle Tybalt, but he . . . he . . ."

"He couldn't wake her, either."

Sniffling, Raj nodded. "Dad was holding her, and she just stopped. She wasn't supposed to stop. We're supposed to live forever. Aren't we?"

"We're supposed to, but sometimes it doesn't work that way." Not for Raj's mother, or for Lily, or Evening. Maybe not for any of us.

"Will I live forever?"

I paused, looking at him. His eyes were wide, earnest, and glossy with tears. He'd believe whatever I told him. He was offering me the chance to soothe away his fears, if I'd just lie to him. And I couldn't do it. Sometimes I hate my sense of honor.

"You might not," I said. "The only way to be sure you'd live forever would be to stay in the Summerlands and lock the doors so nothing could ever touch you. But I don't think that's living. Do you?"

He frowned, considering. "No. I don't think it is."

"I'm sorry," I said. There are some truths you shouldn't be forced to learn, and that's one of them. But he asked, and I couldn't lie to him.

"It's okay. Truth is better." He managed a wan smile, fangs showing through his fading human disguise. "I should go. I'm helping Uncle Tybalt with everyone."

"Right." His dignity was already wounded; he needed to go and soothe it before it died. "You'd better go. Call the apartment if you need anything. May will be there even if I'm not."

"Okay." He stood, melting into the shadows before I

could say good-bye. That was fine with me; I wasn't up for many more good-byes.

I finished my coffee and tossed the empty cup into the nearest trashcan before tucking the tainted meat under my arm and walking back to the snack bar. I was trying to review what had happened without dwelling on it. It wasn't working. I kept picturing Opal and her kittens, or Raj and his parents. The worst was the thought of Tybalt, somehow sick like the rest. The image sent shivers down my spine.

The crowd at the snack bar had scattered, dispersing to do whatever it is tourists do when they're not getting in my way. A breeze caressed the back of my neck as I circled the building to reach my car. The scents the wind carried were enough to make my nose itch. It smelled of roses, violets, fresh grass, and oleanders, all undercut with the distinct, deadly tang of sulfuric acid.

I stiffened. The car doors were unlocked—I'd been in such a hurry to get out and puke that I hadn't been as careful as usual. That was actually a good thing, just now. I dropped the meat on the passenger seat and pulled my baseball bat out of the back, every movement deliberate. My headache was fading, and my mind was clear; I didn't want to kill her if I had a choice. The last of my mercy died with Opal's kittens. I wanted to see Oleander stand trial and face the immortal, unforgiving judgment of the fae.

A footstep scuffed the asphalt behind me. I whirled, falling into a defensive posture. I was ready for anything she could throw at me.

There was no one there.

"What the—" I could still smell the distinctive taint of her magic on the wind. So where the hell *was* she?

Someone started to clap. I turned, holding the bat in front of me, to see Oleander standing in front of my car. She was totally relaxed, resting her elbows on the hood as she applauded. "Well done, October," she said. "You still react without stopping to think."

"I'll work on that," I said, eyes narrowing. It was probably too much to hope that she'd stay where she was long enough for me to get behind the wheel and run her over.

"See that you do." She smiled. "You're no challenge like this."

"Playing with your food?"

"Are you surprised?"

"I suppose not."

"Of course not. There's no free will in Faerie—isn't that what you children of Oberon say?" Her smile widened. "Blood will tell, isn't it?"

She was right about that: blood will tell, and Oleander told the story of the Peri in every snake-supple gesture and poisoned-sugar smile. Peri live in the high deserts, keeping their distance from the rest of Faerie, and Faerie doesn't mind. They're instinctively cruel, geared toward a type of sadism even monsters find hard to bear. By all rights, we should've cut off contact with them centuries ago.

There's just one problem: Peri are evil, but they're also beautiful. The fae are as easily distracted as everyone else, and sometimes we only see the beauty, not what's lurking underneath it. A Tuatha de Dannan got distracted by that beauty once, and Oleander was the result.

"I'm not sure I want to know the story your blood's telling." There was no way I could get around the car fast enough to catch her. I needed her to come out into the open.

"But it's a lovely tale, all death and treachery." She dropped her chin into her cupped hand. "Did you think I was an illusion, little girl?"

"I was starting to." I still wasn't sure either way. If I'd chased an illusion through the botanical gardens, I could easily be talking to another one.

"How do you know I'm not?" she asked, and vanished.

"I don't." I circled the car. There was no sign that she'd been there at all. "Why are you doing this?"

"Such petulance doesn't suit a woman of your rank, *Countess*." I turned toward the sound of her voice. She was standing behind me, arms folded across her chest. "What's it like to wear a dead woman's title? Do you finally feel like one of us?"

"Leave Evening out of this." I wasn't sure I was talking to a real person, but I was becoming more convinced that the illusionist was Oleander. That was reassuring, in its way. I wasn't losing my mind. Just my friends.

"You're not one of us. You'll be mongrel scum until you die. Thank your mother for that, if you see her again before you go." She was casting a shadow. Illusions don't cast shadows unless the caster is smart enough to create one, and they don't move naturally. Her shadow moved like any other.

"Why did you kill Lily?" I asked, trying not to look at that telltale shadow.

"So you're sure of your villain, are you? Why would *I* kill your little Undine, I wonder?" Her tone was almost playful. "Did you know 'Lily' wasn't her real name? She used that so the Americans could pronounce it. Her name was Katai Suiyou—'honorable willow.' Did you call her by name before she died?"

The truth is sometimes the most effective weapon. I *hadn't* known that, and I'd never tried to find out. I squared my shoulders, drawing myself to my full height. She barely came up to my chin. It wasn't much of an advantage, but it was what I had. "Don't talk about Lily."

"Or you'll do what? Cry? Beg for mercy? Murder another one of your friends? Really, I can't wait to see what you'll do next."

That was all I could take. I lunged—

—and grabbed empty air. I whirled, already searching for her as I tried to figure out what was going on. She'd been casting a shadow! The Tuatha can teleport, but

I'd never heard of Oleander possessing that particular talent. Faerie magic matures as people get older, but it usually stops after the first century or two; adults rarely develop new gifts. So if she wasn't an illusion, what did her disappearances mean?

Oberon help me, I was afraid to find out.

"Surely you've figured it out by now." She was ten feet away, smirking. Her clothes had become skintight and a decade and a half out of fashion—the outfit she wore the day I caught her in the Tea Gardens. "You're not that stupid."

"Figured what out?" I asked, resisting the urge to charge her again.

Her smile faded. "You have to know I'm not here, October. Do you think I'd endanger myself to get back at *you*?"

"What are you saying?" I asked, around the sinking numbness in my stomach. My head was starting to pound again. I knew what she was trying to tell me.

I didn't want to hear it.

"Do I need to spell it out? Fine, then. I'm. Not. Real." She vanished. She cast a shadow. But when April O'Leary—the only teleporter I knew who didn't open some sort of visible door—moved like that, there was a flare of ozone and a rush of displaced air. When Oleander did it, there was nothing but emptiness. She wasn't there.

Her voice came from behind me: "You're a changeling. You knew this would come."

"I'm not crazy," I said. I wasn't sure which of us was lying, and that was the worst part: the uncertainty. Because her words didn't sound false to me.

"So why am 'I' only targeting your friends? Why would 'I' do such a thing? You did it, all of it. It's happened. You've gone over the edge." She giggled. "Devin did it. Gordan did it. Even your mother did it—she's as crazy as any changeling. It comes of confusion in the blood, and she was always confused. Falling doesn't hurt *you*. Just the people you care about, and once you've fallen far enough, they won't matter."

"You're *lying!*" I whirled. I was half-blind with tears, but I knew where she was standing. I could grab her before she had a chance to run.

There was no one there.

EIGHTEEN

THE BASEBALL BAT SLIPPED FROM MY nerveless fingers, clattering against the ground. The noise was enough to break the haze and let me start moving. It was also enough to let me start thinking again. Taken together, those two things weren't much of a mercy.

I dropped to my knees, barely noticing the gravel biting through the thin denim of my jeans. I was alone, just like I'd been in the botanical gardens, just like I'd been on the terrace with Luna. I was alone, and Oleander . . . she had to be lying. If I was losing my mind—if I was the one doing these terrible things—I'd know. Wouldn't I?

Footsteps approached from behind me. I stood, slamming my back against the side of the car. The man who'd been jogging toward me stopped, expression concerned. "Miss? Are you all right?"

"I—what?" I couldn't see an illusion-haze around him; that was good. It meant he was probably human, and mankind's instinctive tendency to ignore the fae would protect me if I could get him to stop focusing on me. Unfortunately, the words to reassure him wouldn't come. I've always been good with words, and they'd deserted me. "I'm fine."

"I'm Paul," he said, holding his hands out in the palms-upward gesture men always seem to use with distressed women they don't know. I tentatively filed him under the mental category of "harmless." My panic was fading, replaced by numb focus distorted by the pounding in my head. "Did something happen? Should I go for help?"

"I'm fine," I repeated. People need to be reassured; he'd leave when he was sure I wasn't hurt. He'd probably be glad his good deed had been so easy. "It was the heat."

That was an answer he could understand. He offered a relieved smile. "It's getting warmer. You shouldn't be wearing that coat, especially if you're going to park your car back here near the vents. Be more careful, okay?"

I forced myself to smile. The numbness made it easier. "Sure thing. I'll head straight home and change."

"Good." Turning, he jogged on toward the parking lot. I waited until he was out of sight before bolting for the botanical gardens, heading for the hawthorns where the shadows would be deepest.

Oleander was a liar. I *knew* that . . . but suppose, just suppose that "she" was a figment of my imagination, a little part of me trying to tell myself the truth. If I was going crazy—if I was losing time—I didn't know it. But that didn't make it impossible.

Luck was with me in at least one regard: I didn't see any tourists as I ran to my destination. The day was bright enough that even the shadows around the hawthorns were shallow, and they didn't part at my approach. I had no key to the Cait Sidhe kingdom. I didn't know how to get their attention, but I had nowhere else to go, and nothing else to try. I flung myself at the bushes, beating my fists against the thorns.

"Tybalt!" Maybe I was going crazy and maybe I wasn't, but there was a killer on the loose and I didn't know what to *do*. Worse, I didn't know whether that killer was *me*. I needed Tybalt, and I needed him now, because I trusted him enough to let him be the one to decide whether he couldn't trust me anymore.

I called his name until the words were gone and there was nothing left but sobbing, and still I kept beating my hands against the thorns. My head was killing me, and I couldn't *think*, and I was so *scared* . . .

Tybalt's hands gripped my shoulders, pulling me away from the hawthorns. I didn't question how he'd managed to get behind me; I just huddled against him and cried, cradling my bloody hands in my lap. He plucked the twigs out of my hair, one by one, before putting a hand under my chin and turning my face toward him.

And then he slapped me.

I clapped a hand over my cheek and stared at him, ignoring the blood covering my fingers. Blood's something I can always understand, even if I hate the sight of my own. Tybalt gave me an impassive look. "Are you done, or should I come back later?"

"What . . ."

More gently, he said, "We don't have time for you to fall apart. Raj said he spoke to you; you helped him feel better. Why are you like this now? What happened?"

"I—" I licked my lips. They tasted like blood. That steadied me a little. Blood generally does. "I saw Oleander."

"What?" His eyes narrowed. For a moment he was the Tybalt I'd always known—cold and predatory. It was oddly reassuring. "Where?"

I pointed to the dumpsters, and he took off at a run. I levered myself off the ground and followed, more slowly. He was crouching next to my car when I caught up with him, letting a handful of gravel and broken glass trickle through his fingers. "Are you sure this is where she was?" he asked. His tone was soft and distracted.

"I'm sure."

"I see." He stood. "Toby . . ."

"Stop, please." I held up my hand, looking away. "Don't say it."

"If she'd been here, I'd smell her. I can smell you—I can smell how scared you were—but not her." He paused. "Oleander hasn't been anywhere near here."

"She was here," I said, balling my hands into fists. "I *saw* her."

"Look at me. She wasn't here." I turned back to him, flinching at the look in his eyes. He was scared. I could see it in his face. Did he know that I was going crazy? Worse, did he know I was already too far gone to save?

"Then she was right. I'm crazy." I started laughing helplessly.

"Please." He sounded like he was on the verge of panic. I was right there with him. "You're not making sense."

"She wasn't here, and that means I'm crazy, and I killed them. I killed them all." My hands were starting to shake. I realized the rest of me was shaking, too. "You can't trust me. She wasn't here. I did it all."

"Toby—"

"Will you kill me, Tybalt? May said I'd die soon. I didn't think it would be now, but that's okay." Laughter overwhelmed me, threatening to turn into sobs.

"October, *listen!*" He grabbed my wrists, forcing my hands open. "You can't break down on me. My people need you. Raj needs you. *I* need you."

"But how do you know you can trust me? How do you know I—"

"I know because I know." His claws dug into my wrists, not quite hard enough to break the skin. "Maybe she wasn't here physically, but there are other ways of being places. Oleander is half-Peri. She has more tricks up her sleeves than just the standard parlor games and illusions." He shook me slightly. Somehow, that stopped my own shaking. "I know because I *know*."

"I . . . you're right. If I'm going crazy, why see Oleander, not Devin or Gordan? Even Simon would make more sense. This is too real. It *can't* be entirely me."

"You're a lot of things, Toby, but I promise, you're not crazy."

"She has to have *been* here, somehow. Are her illusions that strong?" Maybe I wasn't crazy. Maybe I just needed to kick Oleander's ass. "The Peri do a lot with illusions, but she was casting a shadow."

"We don't know what she's capable of."

"You're right." I nodded, and then yanked my hands out of his as the pressure of his fingers finally registered. "Ow! That hurts!"

"I'm sure it does," he said, smiling. The panic in his eyes was gone; he was looking at *me* again, not some possible, dreaded future.

"I guess that means I'm still alive." And being alive meant having options.

"What are you going to do?"

"Do?" I looked up at him. He was still smiling, and somehow, that made me feel better. The world was falling apart, but Tybalt could find something to smile about, even if I wasn't sure what it was. "I'm going to finish this."

"How?"

It was a good question. "Remember Walther, the chemistry teacher from—" I swallowed "from Lily's Court" before I quite said it, substituting, "—from the Tea Gardens?" Tybalt nodded, and I continued, "I'm going to take him your meat, and the cup Luna drank from just before she collapsed. He can check for traces of poison and try to devise some possible treatments."

"What then?"

"When we have the results, I'll contact you and Sylvester to let you know. Will you make me a promise?"

He froze, mouth tightening as he realized what I was

about to ask. Slowly, he nodded. "Yes. But I don't want to."

"I know. I still need you to promise."

"Tell me what you want me to promise."

"I think you know."

"So say it, and let me be sure." His shoulders were hunched, braced against my request. It was almost funny. There was a time when I'd have expected him to celebrate what I was about to ask, not turn away from it.

People change. "If it turns out it's not Oleander—she's just a hallucination, and it really *was* me who did all these horrible things—I need you to kill me, because I think we've reached the point where I can't be trusted to do it myself. Will you do it? If I've snapped, will you kill me?"

He raised a hand, pressing it against my cheek. Something told me if I spoke before he did, he'd refuse me and walk away. I didn't want that. So I stood there, and I watched him, and I waited.

Finally, his voice pitched so low I'd have missed it if I were any farther away, Tybalt said, "Yes. If you've lost your mind, I'll kill you. Just me, and no one else. I'll take you to the place that no one leaves, and I'll take you there alone."

I frowned, studying his expression. There was something there that I didn't quite understand. Still . . . "I owe you for this."

"You owe me for allowing you to ask." He pulled his hand away and shook himself, like he was trying to get water off his skin.

"Tybalt . . ."

"We're wasting time. We need to get your hands taken care of before you go." He turned and stalked toward the Tea Gardens. I hesitated before following. I owed him. If I wanted him to kill me, I was going to need to wash my hands.

NINETEEN

NOT EVEN MARCIA'S BEST EFFORTS had done more than dull the pain in my hands. That was another complication for the denizens of the Tea Gardens—Undine can't teach their natural skills, and without Lily, they didn't have a healer. The Court of Cats wasn't in a position to be much help. Cait Sidhe are better at hurting than they are at healing.

Marcia didn't ask how I'd hurt myself. She probably didn't want to know. She just produced a first aid kit from the admissions booth and ordered me to go sit down in the pavilion, where underpaid teenagers in "traditional" Japanese robes sold overpriced tea to tourists. Those same tourists stared as Marcia slathered my hands with antibiotic cream before wrapping them in gauze and athletic tape.

We must have looked strange to human eyes: a rumpled brunette receiving elementary first aid from a gaunt-eyed blonde, with a glowering man looming off to the side. It made sense if you knew the situation. Like most things, my life looks stranger when viewed from a distance. I was Marcia's temporary liege, and it was rea-

sonable for Tybalt to bring me to her for medical care
after I impaled myself on a hawthorn bush fleeing from
what might have been a figment of my imagination . . .

Okay, my life makes even less sense when you understand it. Whose doesn't?

Once Marcia was done taking care of my hands,
I hugged her and reminded her to go to Tybalt if she
needed anything. She agreed, but she wouldn't meet my
eyes; I think we both expected this to be our last good-
bye. She'd seen me bleeding, and she knew things were
moving toward a conclusion. Encouraging her to hope
I'd still be standing when everything was done would
have been unbelievably cruel, so I didn't try.

Tybalt walked me to the car without saying a word.
I almost asked what he was thinking, but I stopped myself. I was confused enough, and I had too much left to
do. Tybalt could wait. Still, the fact that he didn't even
say good-bye flustered me enough that I didn't realize
until later that I'd managed to drive away without my
baseball bat.

Finding UC Berkeley is easy once you're off the
freeway. Berkeley is a college town, and practically all
roads lead to the campus—a vast, central sprawl of open
space and green growing things. A creek cuts through
the middle, blocked by fences designed to keep drunken
co-eds from taking accidental dips. I was too busy trying
to survive my time in Devin's service to go to college,
but I've lived in the Bay Area for most of my life, and
I've cut through the university on my way to Telegraph
Avenue more than once.

I bought a parking slip from a machine at the edge
of the student parking lot. The students the lot was intended for passed as I got out of the car, chatting with
one another and ignoring me. Apparently, rumpled
women with gauze-wrapped hands wearing leather jack-
ets in May showed up at their school all the time. Considering the air of genial weirdness that surrounds the

people of Berkeley—fae and mortals alike—that wasn't surprising. I shoved the meat from the Cat's Court into the duffel bag alongside Luna's cup and started to walk.

Berkeley is a neutral city, belonging to no fiefdom and answering to no liege but the Queen. That's always attracted the more outré fae elements, and they, in turn, surround themselves with the weirdest that the human world has to offer. It's the chicken and the egg all over again—which comes first, the crazy or the strange?

I looked around with unabashed curiosity as I entered the campus, hoping to find a map. Given the size of the school, I didn't know which way I was supposed to go to find the chemistry labs. I waved at the nearest student. "Excuse me?" He kept walking. I turned to the next available person, repeating, "Excuse me?" She didn't stop either.

"Great," I muttered. "Now I'm invisible." Humanity's tendency to ignore the fae is sometimes annoying, but this was a bit much. I sighed and sat on the nearest bench, putting my packages to the side and resting my aching head in my hands.

"It's not you," said a voice. I looked up. A thin young man with deeply tanned skin and untidy black hair was standing nearby. He was grinning. I didn't grin back, but I didn't scowl, either. "They're like that to everyone this time of year. Too close to finals for common courtesy to apply, y'know?"

"So why are you talking to me?"

"Chemistry major," he said, like that explained it. I looked at him blankly. He laughed. "I've been awake and cramming for the last three days, and I figure if I can't pass my finals now, it's too late. No reason to be rude just because I'm failing."

"Right." I finally smiled. "If you're a chemistry major, can you tell me where to find the chemistry *classrooms?* I'm here to meet one of the instructors."

"I figured," he said blithely, dropping himself onto

the bench next to me. "My psychic powers tell me you're looking for a blond guy with spooky blue eyes."

I blinked. "Your psychic powers?"

"Yeah, the ones that kick in when my adviser tells me he'll give me extra credit if I'm willing to lurk around the parking lots watching for lost-looking brunettes. He left off the 'cute' part, but I figured that out for myself from the way he was cleaning his desk." He offered his hand. "Jack Redpath. I'm Professor Davies' grad student."

"Toby Daye." Shaking his hand put pressure on my bandaged fingers. I tried not to wince. "Nice to meet you. What do you mean, spooky?"

"Spooky." He reclaimed his hand, making circles in front of his eyes with thumbs and forefingers. "You're sitting in class, innocently drawing naked chicks on your syllabus, when suddenly wham, Mr. Spooky-Blue-Eyes is looking right through you. Anyway, the chemistry classrooms are over there." He indicated a building on the other side of the walkway. "Be sure to tell him I get my fifteen points, okay?"

"Deal," I said, and stood.

Jack did the same, still grinning. "Nice to meet you. Have fun with the Professor." He turned and strolled away, whistling.

"Okay, that was weird but productive." I scanned the quad one last time before walking over to the building he'd indicated. The doors were unlocked. I hesitated, shrugged, and went in.

The air inside was cool, with the antiseptic tang I've always associated with hospitals and large institutions. The floor was linoleum, easy to wash and maintain, and the fluorescent lights were refreshingly dim after the glaring sunlight outside. I peered at the classrooms as I walked down the hall. The fifth door was standing open, and Walther was inside, erasing something from the whiteboard. Tucking the duffel under my arm, I knocked on the doorframe. His head jerked up, expression startled. "Hey," I said. "How long have you had that guy out there waiting for me?"

"Oh, a while now," said Walther, starting to smile. "I figured you might have trouble finding the place." He was dressed to fit the professorial stereotype, in tan slacks and a brown sweater. I could see what Jack meant about the "spooky" eyes; they were a piercing, slightly eerie shade of blue even through the filter of Walther's human disguise. He was wearing a pair of black-framed glasses to blunt the effect, but they weren't working entirely.

"I did. So it was a good plan."

"I try to think ahead." He hesitated, smile fading as he saw the bandages on my hands. "What happened?"

"I had a little run-in with some hawthorn bushes." I stepped into the classroom. "I brought the cup, and some meat I need to have tested. Do you have the facilities to check for fingerprints?"

"I don't, but the forensic science class might." He reached for the duffel. "What's the meat for?"

"The inhabitants of the Cat's Court have been poisoned. Whoever did it used this meat. Everyone who ate it has collapsed."

That stopped him. "What? Is everyone okay?"

"No. There have been several deaths so far, and there are going to be more if we don't do something. I need to know what's in that meat."

He paled. "Deaths?"

"Yeah." I looked down, trying to put the image of Opal and her children out of my head. "There are a lot of sick Cait Sidhe in Tybalt's Court right now."

"I have a lab down the hall; we can go there." He crossed back to the desk, putting the duffel down on top of a large stack of papers, and then picking up the whole thing. "Did you come straight from the Cat's Court?"

"I checked in at the Tea Gardens first; everyone's as well as can be expected." I didn't mention that I'd only stopped by long enough for Marcia to bandage my hands. She'd tell him herself, soon enough.

"Right." Walther walked into the hall, staggering as he tried to balance all the things he was carrying. "I'll ring for a fingerprinting kit when we get to the lab. Get the lights, would you?"

I followed, flicking off the light as I passed it. "Can I take some of that?"

"Nope. Wouldn't be right to let a lady carry her own deadly toxins." He stopped at an unmarked door. "The keys are in my pocket. If you'd do the honors?"

"I—oh, right." I dug the keys out of his coat, only slightly embarrassed about rummaging in the clothes of a man I barely knew, and unlocked the door.

The lab was about half the size of Walther's classroom, with messy heaps of paper and equipment I didn't recognize serving to make the space seem even smaller. I hadn't seen a room that cluttered since January O'Leary's office, otherwise known as "the place where paper goes to die." I fumbled until I found the light switch and clicked on the overheads.

Walther dropped his armload of papers and potential murder weapons onto the counter before reaching for the phone. "I assume you know how to use a fingerprinting kit, and I don't need to try to lie to a lab tech?" he asked, glancing in my direction. I nodded. "Good."

"I have many useful skills," I deadpanned.

"I'm sure you do." He dialed, waiting a moment before saying, "This is Professor Davies from organic chemistry. Can I get a fingerprinting kit sent to lab four? No, no one broke in. I just need to do a demo." He laughed. It was a broad, amiable laugh, and didn't sound forced, even though I could tell from his expression that it was. "Great."

Walther hung up, removing his glasses and setting them off to one side. "It'll be here in twenty minutes. What are we looking for, exactly?"

"Anything." I leaned over to unzip the duffel bag, pulling out the bundle of meat and offering it to him. "Look for floral toxins first. Poisonous flowers."

"Right." He pulled on a pair of latex gloves before taking the meat and putting it down on a clean section of the counter. Removing the blood-spotted butcher paper released a musky, rancid smell. He wrinkled his nose. "Well, whether this is poisoned or not, it's started to go off. At least we shouldn't need to keep it around long in order to find out what we need to know."

"What are you going to do?" I dropped his keys on the pile of papers next to the duffel bag before moving to perch on a relatively stable-looking stool.

"Do you know anything about chemistry, alchemy, or hedge-magic divination?"

"Not really."

"In that case, I'm going to put pieces of meat in jars full of chemicals and herbal tinctures, and see what happens." He picked up a scalpel, starting to slice off slivers of meat. "Are we looking for floral toxins on the cup, too?"

"I think so."

"Got it."

After that, I might as well not have been in the room. Walther produced a startling assortment of jars and beakers from the cupboards and dropped a sliver of meat into each one before producing an even wider assortment of strange-smelling, brightly-colored liquids. He poured them over the slivers of meat, frowning as they fizzed, changed colors, or did nothing at all. I didn't interrupt. He was right when he assumed I wouldn't understand what he was doing.

He'd been working for about fifteen minutes when someone knocked. Walther didn't seem to notice. I stood and moved to answer the door, preparing to lie. I didn't have to: a bored-looking student pressed a fingerprinting kit into my hands and walked away, not bothering to ask who I was or whether he'd brought us the thing we needed.

I blinked, several times. Then I closed the door and moved to another clean section of counter, pausing on the way to remove the velvet-swaddled cup from the duffel bag. Walther was still off in chemistry la la land, so I pulled on a pair of latex gloves and started the laborious process of checking for prints.

His voice broke the silence ten minutes later: "That's not right."

"What?" I turned, the fingerprint kit's dusting brush in one hand, to find him scowling at a jar full of purple liquid.

"Just a second." He waved his free hand over the jar, muttering in Welsh. His magic rose, filling the air with the taste of ice and yarrow, and the ghostly image of a branch of oleander flowers appeared in front of him. He lowered his hand, even as the brush fell from my suddenly nerveless fingers and clattered to the counter. "Well. That's an unpleasant piece of work."

"Oleander," I whispered, not taking my eyes off the flowers.

"Exactly," said Walther, clearly missing the importance of the word. "Someone spiked the meat with oleander extract. I've never seen the stuff so refined. It's practically pure—" He stopped, catching the look on my face. "What's wrong? I can cure oleander poisoning."

"That's Oleander," I said. My head was pounding again. I was too relieved to care. Oleander's always had a preference for using her namesake—call it hubris or plain old evil—but I don't know how to distill the stuff. I wouldn't know where to start; with Devin gone, I wouldn't even know who to buy it from. She was real, and I wasn't crazy.

"Yes, oleanders." I could tell he didn't have any clue Oleander de Merelands might be involved. She was ancient history for most people, just another boogeyman beneath our racial bed. I'd been starting to think I was the only one who couldn't let her go. "They're poisonous."

"I know." I picked up the brush and turned back to the cup, resuming my dusting. "I've seen them before."

"I'm not surprised. They're stupidly common in Californian landscaping. What did you say happened to your hands?"

"Hawthorn bush."

"Uh-huh," he said. "When you finish with that, I want a blood sample."

"What?" I glanced back over my shoulder, eyeing him. "You didn't say what I think you just said."

"Do you think what I said was 'can I have a blood sample?'"

"Does it have to be from me?" I've always hated the sight of my own blood. The thought of sharing it didn't appeal, especially not with my hands already beaten raw.

"Since you're the only other person here for me to ask, yes, it does."

"Take it from yourself." I squinted at the cup. "The only prints here are Luna's."

"You know what Duchess Torquill's fingerprints look like?" Walther removed his gloves and tossed them into the trash can.

"I can be pretty persistent when I want to be."

"Really," he said, dryly. He picked up a lancet, walking over to me.

I decided to ignore both his sarcasm and the sharp object he was carrying. "I went through a forensics phase, so I hassled her into letting me take her prints. They're unique enough that I remembered them—see?" I indicated the scalloped flower-petal whorls of one print. "Never seen anything else like it." I gave him a sidelong look. "I'd rather not give blood today. I feel fine."

Walther sighed. "Toby, your pupils are dilated, your pulse is up, and you keep staring at your hands—which, by the way, you've managed to hurt in some way that makes no sense to me. You've brought me meat spiked with enough refined oleander to kill dragons, and a cup covered in Duchess Torquill's fingerprints. Please excuse me if I don't believe you 'feel fine.'"

"Dragons?" I echoed, momentarily distracted from the lancet. "This stuff could kill dragons?"

"Tybalt's lucky any of his subjects ate this and survived."

"It's a little early to say they survived," I said. "Can you make some sort of antitoxin for the ones that are still alive?"

"Cait Sidhe are odd, biologically speaking, but I should be able to come up with something."

"We don't have much time."

"I know. That's why I need you to let me take a blood sample before you drop dead and force me to explain your corpse to the administration." His voice stayed level and soothing. "Chemistry professors who wind up with dead women in their labs don't get tenure, and I don't want to change jobs for at least another thirty years."

"How do you know my pulse is up?" I felt my wrist. He was right—my pulse was racing like I'd been running a marathon. I frowned. Finding Walther's office wasn't that stressful, and watching him play with the chemicals had been almost soothing.

"Trade secret." He paused. "You're breathing too fast. You've been practically panting since you got here, and that forces your pulse up. That can't be good, especially since you may have been exposed to some sort of toxin."

"I've barely eaten today," I protested. "I've been running in circles since last night."

"Food and drink aren't the only ways to poison someone. You can use inhalants, contact poisons—want the list? Unless you can prove you've managed to go without breathing all day, you're at risk, and since you're not a Gnome, you've been breathing."

"Fine." I offered my less-battered hand and turned my face away, squeezing my eyes shut. "Just make it quick."

"I only need a little—it won't even hurt. Tell me, are all Daoine Sidhe as squeamish as you?" He took my hand. "Not that you look like any of the Daoine Sidhe I've known, but I thought your people specialized in blood."

"I don't mind *most* blood, just mine." Something pricked my finger. It wasn't any worse than being clawed by one of the cats or stroking Spike the wrong way. I still winced.

"That's it," said Walther.

I looked back to see him wiping my fingertip with a cotton ball. I blinked. "Really?"

He smiled, holding up a test tube with a few drops of blood at the bottom. "This is all I'll need."

"Good." I shuddered.

"You must've been hell as a kid," he said, turning to drop the test tube into a rack. "I'd have hated being your family doctor. Imagine trying to give you a shot!"

"I mostly grew up in the Summerlands."

"That explains a few things." He added some clear liquid to the test tube, flicking it gently with his forefinger. "What and where have you eaten today?"

"A few Pop-Tarts and some coffee, in the car. May made the coffee. Oh, and some coffee from the snack bar in Golden Gate Park, but I didn't get to drink much of that before Tybalt froze it solid." I paused. "Long story."

Walther looked up. "I'll take your word for that. You said May made the first batch of coffee—you mean your Fetch?" I nodded. He frowned. "She lives with you?"

"Why not? She pays half the rent, and she does dishes."

"But isn't she supposed to, well, kill you?"

I almost laughed. "If anyone's interested in keeping me alive, it's May. She's the one who ceases to exist when I die."

"I see." Walther held up the test tube. Somehow my blood and the clear liquid had combined to make something bright purple. He shook it, and the contents turned green. He frowned. "That's strange."

I moved to stand behind him. "Is that supposed to happen?"

"No." He dropped the test tube back into the rack, starting to chant in Welsh. The liquid flared incandescent white before dimming to a dark gray.

"What does it mean?"

"It means you were poisoned more than twenty-four hours ago, with a recent 'booster.'" The liquid kept getting paler. "If you didn't eat anything questionable, did you drink? Touch anything unusual? Get something in your eye?"

"No—wait. Yes. A goose splashed water in my eyes. How can you tell I've been poisoned?" I'd almost been expecting him to say it, but it was still jarring.

"Are you sure it was a goose?" He looked at me levelly until I shook my head. I *couldn't* be sure. Life in Faerie doesn't work that way. "What I'm doing isn't exactly chemistry; it's a sort of cheater's alchemy, a mix of science and magic. I get faster results, and science can't handle most Faerie things, anyway."

"You should meet my friend Stacy's eldest daughter," I said. Cassandra would love this guy. "But how do you know I've been poisoned? Or when?"

"The colors tell me." The stuff in the test tube was almost white now. "I don't know everything they used, but there's absinthe and gentians in here, and maybe some lavender. This wasn't supposed to kill you, just confuse you. Probably also give you one mother of a headache."

"You're doing a pretty good job of confusing me right now," I said. "Aren't gentians for protection?"

"In magic, yes; when you ingest them, no. Everything I can identify here acts as a mild hallucinogen to the fae. This should make you more susceptible to suggestion and less likely to understand what's going on around you. Have you been seeing things?"

"I think so." Oleander laughing; my headache; the scent of sulfuric acid and oleanders on the wind; hallucinogenic poison in my blood. Things were making sense. Bad sense, but sense. "Does this stuff make it easier for me to get caught in a glamour?"

"Definitely. Anybody with halfway decent illusions could ensnare you. Hell, *I* might be able to do it." Walther turned, squinting into my eyes before I could move away. "How long have you had the headache?"

"Since the Beltane Ball at Shadowed Hills," I answered. "How—?"

"That's probably when you were first dosed. As for how I know you have a headache, you wince every time I raise my voice. I can make an antitoxin for this, but it's going to take longer than the cure for Tybalt's people. Hell, if I were working with a mortal lab, I wouldn't be able to make you an antitoxin at all. Without magic . . ."

"Am I in immediate danger?"

"It's not going to kill you, if that's what you mean. You should take some Tylenol and try to avoid getting poisoned again."

"Good." I stepped back, raking my hair away from my face with both hands. "The Cat's Court comes first. No deaths because you were busy trying to cure me."

"I knew you'd say that." He sighed. "I'll take care of the Cait Sidhe first, but you shouldn't make major decisions or operate motor vehicles while you're like this."

"I'll take that under advisement," I said. "How long will the antitoxins take?"

"A few hours for the Cat's Court; longer for yours. I have to figure out exactly what I'm countering. And I'm going to need more blood."

"Do whatever it takes." I held out my hand, not looking away this time.

"Toby . . ." Walther took my hand, reaching for a clean lancet. "Whoever did this didn't want you dead, just confused."

"I figured that part out for myself."

"They could be . . ." He paused, slow horror creeping across his face. "They could be planning to frame you for Lily's murder."

"They're probably going to frame me for more than Lily; there's also Luna and the Cat's Court." I managed not to wince as he pricked my index finger and pressed it against the side of a jar. "I figure they plan to set me up and have me executed."

"How can you be so calm?" he asked. "This is dangerous!"

"That's why I have to get back to Shadowed Hills. Sylvester needs to know what's going on." Assuming he'd understand what I was trying to say; assuming Luna was still alive. Those were some pretty big assumptions, but they were what I had.

"What?" Walther frowned. "You're not driving *anywhere*. You could kill yourself if you got behind the wheel of a car. Doesn't Shadowed Hills have telephones? Just call them. And don't argue with me. You're not safe to drive, and I don't want to be forced to shake my finger at you in a threatening manner."

"Walther, Rayseline has decided I'm trying to kill her mother. What makes you think Sylvester will get any message I try to give him?" He was still holding the hand he'd pricked. I had to fight the urge to pull it away from him and use it to shove my hair back. "If I want him to hear what I need to tell him, I have to tell him myself."

Walther frowned. "I don't like this."

"I don't expect you to. When do you think you can have results on that cup?"

"I can start testing it while the antitoxin for the Cat's Court is brewing. Will you be careful, at least?" He put the jar down and reached for a scrap of gauze, wrapping it over the dressing Marcia had already taped in place.

"I'll be as careful as I can. It's not my first priority."

"Not being careful doesn't mean you have to be stupid." He turned back to the flasks of chemicals littering the counter, beginning to mix something rapidly together.

"You're right. It doesn't, and I try not to be. What are you doing?"

"Helping." He picked up the result of his efforts: a beaker half-filled with clear liquid. "Rinse your eyes with this."

"What is it?" I asked, taking the beaker from his hand.

"Willow bark, rose oil, and a few other things, mixed together with a hedge charm whammy. It won't counter the poison completely, but it should help a little."

"Right." I tilted my head back, drizzling the liquid into my eyes. "Ow. Stingy."

"But good for you."

I offered a smile instead of the forbidden thanks, blinking the excess liquid from my eyes as I handed the beaker back to him. "Find Tybalt when the antidote is ready. The Court of Cats usually has an anchor in the alley next to the Kabuki Theater outside Golden Gate Park. Failing that, ask Marcia. I'll call when I finish dealing with Sylvester, and I'll try to be careful."

Walther nodded. "Deal. Open roads. If you have an accident, I'll kick your ass."

"Open roads," I echoed. It was time to get moving. Oberon protect us all.

TWENTY

I TOOK THE ROADS BETWEEN BERKELEY and Pleasant Hill at a speed that would've made me public enemy number one in the eyes of most traffic cops, if they'd been able to see through my don't-look-here spell. Walther's little concoction did something right; my headache was almost gone, and performing minor magic was no longer an insurmountable problem.

Walther put a name to what was wrong with me: I'd been poisoned. Fine. I couldn't fix it, but I could understand it, and it fit with Oleander's way of operating. I needed to figure out how she'd been able to get to me during the Ball, but until then, I needed to keep moving and trust Walther to fix things as quickly as possible. I hadn't known him long enough for the trust to come easily.

If I was being honest, I've never trusted *anyone* easily. It wasn't a comfortable feeling, especially considering that Walther wasn't the first: by putting my life in Tybalt's hands, I'd declared my trust for him. That was unsettling. I trusted Tybalt enough to let him decide whether or not I should be allowed to live?

"When the hell did that happen?" I asked, and jumped, startled by the sound of my own voice. I started to laugh, relaxing even more. Did it matter when I started trusting Tybalt? It was too late to change it, and I wasn't sure I wanted to. Either he'd betray me, or he wouldn't. I needed to believe he wouldn't.

I needed that to be enough.

I turned on the radio, scrolling through stations until I found one that promised "all eighties and nineties, all the time." Those stations always play songs written after I disappeared, but I don't mind the way I used to. It's nice to hear bands I recognize, even if the songs are strange. If it weren't for the DJs, with their modern phrasing and to-the-minute slang, I could pretend I was listening to radio transmissions from my own time.

The Paso Nogal parking lot was empty, and the afternoon air was cold, making me draw my jacket a little tighter. It wasn't winter by a long shot, but the air felt colder than it should have, like it was promising worse things to come. The hillside was marshy, the ground softened by recent, unseasonable rain. It still took me less than ten minutes to race through the complicated approach to the knowe. Stress, anger, and mild panic will do that for a girl.

The door didn't open when I knocked. I frowned, knocking again. The door usually swings open on its own if there's not a page close enough to answer it, and even that almost never happens. The Torquills pride themselves on their hospitality. Unless the entire knowe was in mourning, someone should have answered.

The door opened when I knocked for the third time. I stepped through—and stopped dead.

Heavy curtains covered the entry hall windows, giving the room a haunted, funereal air. Flickering candles illuminated the room, their flames sending dancing shadows up and down the walls. I shuddered. Fear of the dark is a human phobia—or so I thought, before I got myself lost in Blind Michael's lands. Now my heart tries to stop every time I see shadows dancing by candlelight.

Blind Michael is dead. I killed him myself. And when the lights are low and the shadows dance, it doesn't matter, because I'll be waiting for him to come back for the rest of my life.

I won't be waiting alone. A small figure was curled in one of the entrance hall chairs, eyes closed, head tucked forward until his chin rested against his chest. I walked over and put a hand on his knee. "Hey. Wake up."

His eyes opened immediately, betraying the shallowness of his slumber. He offered me a small smile that was fueled almost entirely by relief. "Toby."

"In the too, too solid flesh." I stepped away. "Come on. Let's go see how Sylvester's doing."

"Okay." Quentin scrambled out of the chair, sticking close to me as we started down the hall. He wasn't looking at the candles either.

I glanced at him. "They're bugging you, too?"

"They give me the creeps. It's like . . ."

"I know." Admitting it seemed to help. "Can you take me to Sylvester?"

Quentin nodded. "He's in the Duchess' chambers. I can take you there."

"Good. Has there been any change?"

"Rayseline's been ranting a lot. It's impressive. She seems to think she's in charge because her parents aren't coming out of their rooms. And we had to cancel the post-Beltane Court," Quentin said. "I'm scared. What's going to happen if Luna dies?"

"I don't know. I wish I did." I sighed, raking my hair away from my face. "It depends on whether Sylvester steps down, and whether Rayseline inherits, first off. If she becomes Duchess, things are going to change. How long are you fostered for?"

"I'm sworn to Shadowed Hills until I turn twenty-five or my liege finds me a suitable knight." He glanced away. "I'll probably still be here. Most of the knights I know are sworn to Shadowed Hills. But there's a chance my oaths will be transferred when he finds someone appropriate."

I blinked. That was a long term of service. Daoine Sidhe are considered immature until they reach their early hundreds, but fostering normally ends when they reach physical adulthood. Given the rate he was maturing, Quentin should have been released when he turned eighteen, or thereabouts. "Well, I guess we'd better hope Raysel doesn't inherit." I shoved my hands into my pockets, trying to ignore the dull throbbing in my fingers.

"Yeah, I guess." He paused. "What did you do to your hands, again?"

"I didn't say," I said. He gave me a wounded look. I shrugged. "I had a fight with a hawthorn bush. The hawthorn won."

Quentin eyed me for a moment before he sighed, shaking his head, and offered me his arm. "Okay, I give up. You hurt yourself in the *weirdest* ways."

"It's a talent." I took his arm, letting him lead me deeper into the knowe. We made it halfway down the hall in companionable silence before the footsteps started behind us.

Quentin tensed. "Toby—"

"Shhh." I counted to ten, listening. I knew who it was before I reached five. I stopped walking. Quentin did the same, every inch of him vibrating with stress. Neither of us turned. "Hello, Etienne."

"You came back," said Etienne. There was a hint of reproach in his voice.

"Not expecting me?" I looked over my shoulder. He was carrying a spear. That worried me; the guards at Shadowed Hills don't normally go around the knowe armed with more than ceremonial swords.

"I thought you had more sense than that." He leveled a narrow-eyed gaze on Quentin's back.

"Don't blame Quentin for my being here; he didn't do it. I have news, and I have proof, and that means I need to see the Duke."

"You know that isn't a good idea."

"Lily's dead."

Quentin made a small sound of protest. I hadn't told him. Damn.

Etienne's eyes went wide. "What?"

"Lily, the Lady of the Tea Gardens, has stopped her dancing," I said, tension adding a clipped cadence to the traditional announcement of a pureblood's death. I kept my eyes locked on Etienne's. "She dissolved in my *hands*, Etienne. Now, are you going to let me tell Sylvester what I've learned before the same thing happens to Luna, or are you going to keep standing there?"

"Oberon's balls, October, you—" He hesitated, stepping closer and dropping his voice before he said, "It's not safe here. You, of all people, should know that."

I raked one bandaged hand through my hair. "She's gunning for me?" He nodded marginally. "How badly?"

"Badly enough to make this a terrible idea." He sighed. "Don't even think about trying to slip me. Rayseline will take it as an excuse to have you arrested, and I won't be able to stop her."

"Believe me, I won't."

"Fine. This way."

Shadowed Hills was living up to the "shadow" part of its name; the halls were dim, and most of the windows were covered. A heavy silence hung over the place, forming a shroud that didn't want to be disturbed. It was like the knowe was in mourning. Goldengreen was like that after Evening died: bitter, cold, and empty.

I paused. Goldengreen was mine to use as I saw fit. It wasn't a small knowe. Evening only used a percentage of its space, and she hadn't been using the grounds on the Summerland side at all. Lily's people needed a place to go, and thanks to the Queen, they just might have one.

None of the people we passed would meet my eyes; it seemed that Raysel's opinion of me was more popular within the Duchy than I'd hoped. It made sense—no matter how many times I saved their asses, I was still the misfit changeling daughter of a crazy woman—but I won't pretend I was happy about it.

Something was wrong with the rooms around us. I frowned, trying to figure out what it was. We passed through a hall whose floors were being polished; the windows were open to let air circulate, and I glanced up instinctively. The wrongness became suddenly clear, and suddenly terrifying. "Oh, oak and ash," I breathed.

There were no roses around the windows. There were no roses anywhere.

Every Duchy has something that makes them unique. Golden Gate excels at political intrigue, Wild Strawberries produces amazing chefs, Dreamer's Glass threatens to invade the neighbors, and so on. They're proud of their distinctions, and they take every chance they get to show them off. Shadowed Hills grew roses, and now those roses were gone.

We stopped at a marble arch. "Wait here, and don't wander off," said Etienne.

"Check," I said, leaning against the wall. "I'm not going anywhere."

Etienne nodded and vanished through the arch. Quentin glowered after him. I put a restraining hand on his arm.

"Don't. He knows me well enough to know that I'd go chasing shadows right now if I thought it would help, and that would just get us in more trouble."

Quentin gave me a plaintive look. "He should trust you."

"He does." I nodded toward the nearest window. "When did all the roses die?"

"The night of the Ball," Quentin said. Then he frowned. "How did you know the roses died?"

"This is the only time I've been in this knowe and not seen live flowers." It felt like there was something I wasn't seeing that would make everything make sense. Something about Luna and the roses . . .

Raysel stepped around the corner and froze. She was wearing a black dress, her hair in artful disarray; she looked every inch the grieving daughter, except for the part where she didn't look sad. Angry, yes, and faintly smug, but not a drop of sorrow.

The three of us stared at one another for a frozen moment, no one quite sure what the appropriate reaction would be. "Hello, Rayseline," I said, finally.

She frowned. "What are you doing here?" She didn't sound angry; just irritated, like I'd been downgraded to "minor annoyance." Interesting.

"Lily's dead."

"I'm aware." She shot a murderous glare at Quentin. "I'm not sure what that has to do with your being here."

I silently resolved to get Quentin out of there sooner than later. Having a man on the inside wasn't worth the risk of having Raysel truly angry with him. "I'm just here to see your father."

"Why should I let you anywhere near my parents?" She jerked her chin toward Quentin. "He can't help you. He's just a page here."

"I know that. But I have news, and I need to speak with my liege."

"You can give your news to me. My father will listen to you, even if your message comes from my lips." The venom in her voice was unmistakable.

The words escaped before I could stop them. "Why do you hate me so much?"

"Don't pretend you don't know. I won't let you."

"Raysel, I'm not pretending. I don't—"

She cut me off, demanding, "Do you have *any* idea where I grew up?"

I stared at her, not sure how I was supposed to answer. Quentin's expression was as blank as mine. "No, I don't," I said, lacking anything else to say.

"I grew up in nothing," she said. Her eyes narrowed, and for a moment she achieved a look I'd seen on her father's face a hundred times: pure and righteous anger. "It was dark and cold, and it hurt to breathe, and it never ended. They threw us food, sometimes, and water, sometimes, but never enough, and I was always hungry. I almost forgot what light was until the day the binding fell away, and then I thought the sun had come to kill us, and I was *glad*."

"Root and branch," I breathed. "Raysel . . ."

"Don't you dare say you're sorry. Do you know what my mother said to me every day—every hour—of my childhood? *Do you?!*"

"No," I said. Watching Raysel's anger was like watching a train wreck. It was horrifying, but I couldn't look away. Somehow, I couldn't shake the small, terrible feeling that she was right; this was my fault.

"'Your father's coming,'" she said, in mocking parody of Luna's measured tones. "'He'll save us. He won't let us die here.'" She shook her head, voice returning to normal. "But he didn't come. So she told me about his allies. She told me everything."

I winced. It was obvious I'd been included in those "allies." I was starting to understand why she hated me, and I didn't want to.

Raysel ignored my distress, continuing, "'Evening will find us, and your father will raise an army, and Toby—'" She faltered, looking confused and a little lost. That was the first time I saw her truly unguarded. "Toby will come. That's what she does. When we need her, she comes."

"Raysel . . ."

She glared. The moment was over. "You weren't there. You didn't see my mother go crazy calling for my father, calling for *you*. She never lost faith in either of you. She *believed* in you. And you never came. So you can make all the excuses you want, and Father will believe them, because he wants to. He wants to think you're perfect, but you're not. You're just a stupid changeling, and you have no business here."

"I tried to find you." The words sounded feeble. I'm supposed to be a hero. So why didn't I save them?

"You failed," she said. "You died for us, but you didn't have the decency to stay dead. You wonder why I hate you? Because you came back. You abandoned us, and then you came back and took everything away from me! My husband, my parents, everyone in this Duchy wishes I were you. What did I do to deserve that?"

She was right. Her father didn't know her, and her mother didn't understand her, but they knew me. They loved me. "It isn't my fault."

"Do you think I care? Besides, it doesn't matter now. You won't be my problem much longer."

"What are you talking about?"

"Do you really think I believe you poisoned my mother?" She giggled. "You're the family dog. You couldn't hurt her if you wanted to. That doesn't matter, because when she dies, my finger points to you. The Duchy has its justice, and I have my peace."

"You'll never convince the Queen," said Quentin.

She smiled sweetly. "I think you'll be surprised, little boy. You're a foster here, and your word will never stack up against mine. You have no power, no authority, and no reason to be trusted."

"You'll let the real killer go?" I asked, aghast. I understood revenge, but this wasn't revenge. This was insanity.

"Oh, no. We'll realize our mistake once you're dead, and whoever did this will be caught and punished." Her smile was thin and triumphant. "All's well that ends well. Now, if you'll excuse me, I need to fetch something." She turned and stalked away, clearly intent on having the last word.

Quentin started to go after her. I grabbed his sleeve, holding him back. "No, Quentin. She's not worth it."

"But she—"

"Can you prove it?"

He stopped. "What?"

"Can you prove she did anything? Can you even prove we had this conversation? You and I have a past. We've worked together. I could have convinced you to take my side." I sighed. "We can't prove a damn thing." Raysel was clever. Telling Quentin didn't endanger her; it just gave her a chance to discredit him if he tried to come forward. We were stuck.

He stared at me for a moment, and then sagged. "This *sucks*."

"Yes," I agreed. "It does."

TWENTY-ONE

ETIENNE LOOKED MORE DISTRESSED THAN ever when he returned. "His Grace didn't answer when I knocked. I've called for Jin, but it may take some time."

"That's okay." I raked my hair back, grimacing as the movement tugged on my bandages. "I could use a moment to catch my breath."

"If you don't mind my saying so, you don't look well," said Etienne, hesitating before adding, "I've never seen you maintain a human persona inside the knowe."

"What?" I felt the rounded edge of my ear, resisting the urge to laugh. "Oak and ash, Etienne, I didn't even realize I was still wearing the damn thing." I hesitated before adding, "I'm not sure I could put it up again if I took it down right now. I'm not exactly at my best."

"You could try."

"That seems too much like work."

Etienne smiled a little, looking relieved to have me back on what he viewed as familiar ground. "Still lazy, I see. I'll never know how you survived your training."

"The Puck looks out for the lazy and suicidal?" I suggested.

"Possibly the only explanation," he agreed.

I was trying to figure out how to say "by the way, I've been poisoned" without freaking either Etienne or Quentin out when a door opened in the wall across from us, cutting off any further conversation. We turned, almost in unison, to see Dugan—the Queen's messenger—step through. He was closely followed by Rayseline, Manuel, and five men in the Queen's livery. All of them stopped when Dugan did.

I straightened, wishing I'd thought to drop my human disguise when I came in.

"My lady—" Etienne began.

Raysel cut him off with a sharp gesture of her hand. There was a strange, bright triumph in her eyes. "I told you she was here," she said. "Do your duty."

"With pleasure," said Dugan, stepping forward. "October Daye, you stand accused of murder and attempted murder. Will you come quietly?"

"Don't I even get a title when I'm being arrested?" I asked wearily.

"His Grace—" began Quentin.

"This isn't his concern," said Dugan.

"Yes, it is," I said. "He's my liege. He has a right to be here."

"No, he's not," said Raysel, the triumph in her eyes bleeding into her voice. "You may be my father's knight, Daye, but you're the Queen's Countess."

I froze. "You're kidding."

"No, she's not," said Dugan. "When you took that title, your fealty changed."

I wanted to protest. I couldn't. Fealty is a tricky thing; it's a debt, of a sort, one you pay with loyalty, duty, and action. Goldengreen was in the Queen's own lands. Oberon help me, but I was hers.

"Will you come quietly?"

"Tell me what I'm accused of," I countered. "You owe me that much."

"We owe you nothing," Raysel said sharply.

Too sharply; Etienne's eyes narrowed. "My lady, she is sworn to your father. You overstep your authority."

"Fine," said Raysel. "Dugan, read the charges."

Dugan looked at her sharply, clearly displeased by her casual orders. Then he cleared his throat, and said, "You stand accused of the murder of the Lady of the Tea Gardens and the attempted murder of the Duchess of Shadowed Hills."

"What makes you accuse me?" I asked, fighting to keep my temper in check. Getting mad wouldn't do me any good. Etienne looked like he was fighting the same battle; he was glaring daggers at Raysel. "It could have been anyone."

"I saw you run out to the terrace just before the Duchess collapsed," said Manuel, with unconcealed malice. "You went out and spoke with her, and then she fell."

"You know I'd never hurt Luna."

"Like you didn't hurt my sister?" he hissed.

"You were a captive in the Tea Gardens, and now their Lady is dead." Raysel ignored Manuel's outburst. "You became a captive because of my mother, and now she's dying. An interesting coincidence, don't you think?"

"That isn't all we have against you," said Dugan. "Manuel?"

Manuel pulled a leather pouch from his pocket, handing it to Dugan. Dugan held it toward me, asking, "Do you recognize this?"

"No. What is it?"

"Open it and see."

I took the pouch, feeling the weight of it. My heart sank, and kept sinking as I untied the strings and looked inside, seeing the contents for the first time.

Lily's pearl looked like some strange, half-rotten fruit. It was the size of my fist, and glossy white, except for the black streaks marring its lower half. I reached into the pouch and scooped the pearl into my hand, turning it until the blackness was all that showed. Gouges scored the enamel at the center of the decay.

"That was found at the edge of the Tea Gardens," said Dugan, taking the pearl from my unresisting hand. "An uncorked vial was driven into the mud a few inches away. It was empty when we found it, but had it held poison—"

"—the current would have carried it over the pearl and into the scrapes. Oh, root and branch, how could we have been so *stupid?*" Of course Walther's samples tested pure. The poison was so diffuse by the time it reached the main water system that it registered as normal contamination of the groundwater. "When was this found?"

"Yesterday morning. The Undine guard such treasures fiercely. How many people knew that fiefdom well enough to know its location?"

"You found this before Lily died?" Fury rose hot in the back of my throat. I tamped it down, demanding, "Why didn't you *save* her? Why didn't you *try?* The Queen—"

"Has no jurisdiction in the park," said Dugan.

"So why is she trying to prosecute me for a crime committed outside her jurisdiction?" I snapped.

"It was in her Kingdom. She could not prevent, but she can punish. Now will you come quietly?"

"I don't think she has to," said Etienne.

"Stay out of this," snapped Raysel. "It's not your concern."

"Actually, it is. She's your father's knight, Rayseline, just as I am. Would you turn me over so easily?" Etienne shook his head. "This isn't right. The Duke must be told before we allow them to take her."

Dugan was opening his mouth to answer when a tired, familiar voice said, "The Duke must be told what?" We all turned, even the Queen's men, to watch Sylvester step into the room. "Have I missed something, Rayseline?" he asked. "Hello, October."

"Hello, Your Grace." I bowed. The Queen's men hastened to do the same. "These nice men were just arresting me."

Rayseline shot me a look dripping with hatred. "They're taking Countess Daye for questioning, Father. They think she might help them answer some questions about Mother's illness."

"Is that so? Interesting. Are you here on the Queen's orders?" His question sounded almost aimless. I knew better. Sylvester's at his most dangerous when he sounds like he doesn't care.

"Your daughter requested our presence, Your Grace," Dugan replied.

"As I expected. She's a good girl, but sometimes she rushes things." Sylvester smiled, looking no less exhausted. "You'll have to speak to the Queen before I let you remove my knight from my fiefdom. I'm sure you understand."

"She's a danger!" Raysel snapped.

"You're not in charge yet, Rayseline," he said, tone sharpening. "I appreciate your initiative. Now get your friends out of my knowe before I get angry."

She stared at him before she whirled and stormed past me, the Queen's men following in her wake. My fealty might belong to the Queen, but Sylvester was right; without either a direct order from her or his consent, they couldn't take me.

"This isn't over," Manuel hissed as he left.

I held myself stiff as I watched him go. So this was the way they wanted it? Fine. At least we all understood where we were coming from.

It was only a few moments before Sylvester, Etienne,

Quentin, and I were the only ones in the room. Sylvester sagged. "Toby, I'm sorry. I didn't know she would . . ."

"It's okay," I said. "You *didn't* know, and she hates me. She always has."

"I expected more from her."

"I'm sorry." What else was I supposed to say? Raysel was his only child, and his wife was dying. He wasn't going to get another chance unless I somehow solved this.

"I know." He shook his head. "Did you come here for a reason? Etienne seemed quite set that you should see me."

"Yes, I did," I said. "I think I know who's behind this." I tensed, waiting for him to fly off the handle again.

He just looked at me dully, and asked, "Oleander?" I nodded. Sighing, he said, "I assumed you'd try telling me as much. I've had Jin prepare a calming tonic to keep me . . . reasonable while this is going on. Is there proof?"

"More all the time. Someone poisoned the meat Tybalt feeds to his Court with pure extract of oleander flowers; several Cait Sidhe are already dead. The Queen's men have Lily's pearl. They found it next to an empty vial."

"Poison?" asked Etienne.

"I think so. And . . . I went to see a Tylwyth Teg named Walther, who used to work for Lily. He ran some tests on my blood. I've been poisoned, too. Low-grade—it's intended to confuse me, not kill me—but it's still poison."

Sylvester's mouth thinned into an angry line. "You say these things and then expect me to let you go charging back into danger."

I sighed. "Because I know you will. It may be Luna's only chance."

"You're right," he said, softly. "Toby, you can't come here again. I'll send Quentin or Etienne if I need you, but I can't stop the Queen if you've been accused."

"I understand. Go back to Luna; stay with her. If I can fix this, I will."

"If you can't fix this, she'll die."

"And so will I."

"I know." He turned away. I started to reach for him, but stopped myself, shaking my head. There was nothing left to say.

Etienne stepped up beside me, offering his arm, and I took it without hesitating. Shadowed Hills was no sanctuary for me anymore. In the end, there's never a sanctuary. You run until there's nowhere left to run to, and then you fight, and then you die, and then it's over. That's how the world works, and if there's a way to change that, I hope someone's eventually planning to let me know.

TWENTY-TWO

I WAITED UNTIL QUENTIN AND I were halfway down the hill outside the knowe before saying quietly, "Try to stay out of Raysel's way. If she's gunning for me, she may start gunning for you, too—out of spite, if nothing else."

"Yeah." He sounded subdued. The poor kid was practically worn through. If we survived this, I was going to take him to Great America and make him ride roller coasters until one of us threw up. Never doubt the restorative powers of a good amusement park. "I think she's probably going to try."

"If she accuses you of anything, run for my mother's tower. It will know you from Jan's funeral, but nobody else who's not family will make it past the gate." The dream I'd shared with Karen was still vivid in my mind. I needed to call her. Even if she didn't know why she sent the dream, she might remember details I'd forgotten.

Quentin cast a sidelong look in my direction. "I still can't come with you?"

"She'd add kidnapping to the list of charges, and I

need you here so you can get Connor out, too. I don't trust her not to hurt him." He didn't love her. With the way she was acting, that might be enough of an insult to let her justify punishing him for his insolence.

"You're probably right," Quentin said glumly. "What are you going to do?"

"It's too soon to go back to the university—having me show up asking Walther for results will just distract him." He hadn't had time to get used to the way things speed up when people start trying to kill me. Hopefully, he'd live long enough to learn. "I guess I'll head for Golden Gate Park, bring Tybalt up to speed on what's been going on. After that—"

Quentin's pocket started ringing.

He shot me an apologetic look as he pulled out his phone and flipped it open. "Hello?" He stiffened. "Oh." Lowering the phone, he turned to me. "It's for you."

"What?" I plucked the tiny plastic oblong from his hand, bringing it to my ear. "Toby here."

"Toby, you have to come home. You have to come home *right now*."

May sounded panicked enough that it took a moment for me to recognize her voice. It felt like my heart froze solid. Putting a hand on Quentin's shoulder—as much to keep me upright as to reassure him—I asked, carefully, "What's wrong?"

"It's Spike. It won't wake up."

The frozen feeling in my heart just grew at that statement. With Tybalt's Court in chaos and Luna still in a comalike state, the last thing I needed was for the poisoning to start following me home. "I'll be right there."

"Toby—"

"Call the Luidaeg if it gets worse before I can get home." She wasn't willing to help before, but she wouldn't turn down my Fetch, not when it was Spike. She knew how much the rose goblin meant to me.

I could almost hear May swallow her first response before she said, softly, "Get here fast." The line went dead.

I took my hand off Quentin's shoulder, practically shoving the phone back at him. "I have to go. Get inside, and see if you can get Connor somewhere private. Tell him there's something wrong with Spike. If anything changes—*anything*, no matter how small it seems—call the apartment and get the hell out of the Duchy. Okay?"

"Promise," said Quentin, eyes wide. He gave me a quick hug before turning to run back up the hill, beginning the series of gymnastics that would let him into the knowe. I didn't take the time to watch him. I was already racing toward the parking lot.

I was too stressed and worn down to throw any sort of illusions over the car, but I still drove like no one could see me, risking traffic accidents and speeding tickets as I raced across the Bay and back into San Francisco. All told, I probably set some sort of record. I wasn't really thinking about that. I parked the car and jumped out without taking time to lock the doors, running up the concrete path to the front door.

The wards were unset but unbroken—May hadn't had any unexpected company. I was fumbling for my keys when the doorknob turned under my hand and May tugged the door open. Her newly-long hair was skinned back into an untidy ponytail, and Spike was cradled against her chest. Its eyes were closed. It didn't look like it was breathing.

My own breath caught. "Is it—"

"It's alive," she said. Taking my wrist, she tugged me inside, kicking the door closed behind me. "The cats woke me up just before I called you. They wanted to be fed." A brief, all-too-bleak smile crossed her lips. "No matter how bad the world gets, you still have to feed the cats. I filled all three dishes. Spike didn't come."

"Oh, sweet Titania." I scooped the rose goblin from her arms. It never weighed much, but this was like picking up a dried branch; Spike's narrow body seemed to weigh nothing at all. "When was the last time you saw Spike awake?"

"I don't know." The admission seemed to pain her. "It's the middle of the goddamn day. We're lucky I was awake enough to notice at all. I fed it when you dropped us off, but then my hair grew and I got distracted . . ."

Spike had been sleeping on the couch the last few times I'd seen it. That was longer than I liked to consider. "Well, was it okay when you got home from the Ball?"

"It was quiet. It didn't eat much—" She stopped in mid-sentence, staring at me. I stared back, realizing what she was about to say. It was so *obvious*, once you considered all the factors. "Toby—"

"Spike was fine before the Ball, but it wasn't fine afterward," I said. "It was listless. Tired."

"Wilting," she said, in a small voice.

"Oh, oak and ash." I pulled Spike back against my chest. "I'm an idiot."

Luna Torquill was Blodynbryd, a Dryad of the roses. The rose goblins are her children, created before she changed her face. Their health was probably somehow connected to hers; Faerie likes that sort of small, vicious irony. As for Luna . . .

Luna was connected to the roses in her fiefdom. The signs were there all along, if I'd just been paying *attention*. Spike's listlessness, the way the roses in the knowe died when she got sick—everyone must have assumed that her health was affecting them, but what said the health of the roses couldn't affect *her*?

"You're not an idiot, you didn't know," said May. The reassurance rang hollow. I should have stopped to think, not gone haring off after half-leads and possible answers.

My head was throbbing. "It doesn't matter now. Come on."

"What?"

"I have to get back to Shadowed Hills, and you're coming with me." I shoved Spike into her arms. It chirped softly. "Someone needs to be with Spike."

"Why can't I stay *here* with Spike?" May asked, cradling the rose goblin.

"Because Sylvester should see it, and it might be stronger on home ground." Spike's roots ran through Shadowed Hills, just like Luna's. I wasn't going to count on anything saving it at this point, but I had to hope.

May sighed. "I should stay with you anyway." She didn't need to say why. She was my Fetch. She'd be with me when the end came, whether she wanted to or not.

"You're right," I said, touching her shoulder. "You should." Then I turned away, crossing to the phone as I rummaged through the pocket of my jeans.

"What are you doing?"

"Calling for help." I balanced the phone between my cheek and shoulder, dialing the number off Walther's business card with my free hand.

Jack answered. "Professor Davies' office, Jack Redpath speaking, how can I help you?"

"Jack, hi. This is Toby Daye. Is Walther—I mean, Professor Davies—in?"

"Oh, hi!" He sounded positively gleeful. "He's in the lab working on that project you gave him. Hang on, I'll go get him."

"No problem." May was staring at me. I put my hand over the receiver, saying, "Walther's Tylwyth Teg. He's doing some toxicology work for me."

"You have weird friends."

"I know."

There was a clatter from the phone, and Walther said, "Toby? Are you there?"

"I'm right here, Walther. How are those antitoxins coming?"

"I've finished the serum for the Cat's Court. It needs to mature for about an hour, and then it should be ready. Yours is more complex. I need more time."

"That's fine." I doubted he'd have time to cure me before the end. That didn't really matter. Rubbing my temple with one hand, I asked, "Did you test the cup?"

"I did. There's no poison. I found a lot of Phenobarbital—a sedative that probably helped with the whole 'passing out' thing—and some salt, but nothing that should have made her seriously ill."

"Would it make the drink taste bitter?"

"That much Phenobarbital would make sugar taste bitter."

"Can the antidote for the Cat's Court travel?"

"There's no reason why not."

"Good. I want you to bring it with you, and come meet me at Shadowed Hills."

"What?" He sounded taken aback; apparently, random women didn't usually call his lab and ask him to drive to Pleasant Hill. Well, he'd learn.

"I may have some leads on Luna Torquill. Listen." I outlined the situation with Luna and the roses, giving a quick explanation of Luna's heritage. This was too important to confuse with polite falsehoods. The only thing I left out was my encounter with the Queen's guards—there was nothing he could do about it, and he'd find out about my pending arrest soon enough.

Walther was silent when I finished. I paused before asking, "Well? Will you help me?"

"What are we going to do? Why do you need a chemist? They're not going to let me take blood samples from the Duchess."

"I don't want you to take blood samples." I'd been trying to approach things too linearly; that was my problem the whole time. Faerie *isn't* linear. "We're taking soil samples."

"Why would we—oh. I see. Yes, that makes sense."

"Do you know how to get to Paso Nogal Park?"

"Yes."

"Good; meet us there, in the parking lot. We're not going into the knowe. Bring whatever you'll need to get a quick answer on what's in the dirt."

"All right. See you soon."

"Count on it." I hung up briefly before dialing again. This time, the phone only rang once.

"Hi, Auntie Birdie," said Karen, skipping the unnecessary "hello." "I don't know anything else. I'm sorry. I've been trying. I even tried dreaming for the mean girl, to see what she knew, but . . ." Her voice faltered. "I don't like her dreams."

The mean girl? She had to mean Rayseline. "What did she dream about?"

"Only the dark."

I winced. Definitely Rayseline. "Okay. If you think of anything else, no matter how small, call May, okay? She's going to be with me."

"I will . . . but you need to be careful. Something's coming. Someone's dreaming you a new dream, and whoever it is, I can't quite see them." On that encouraging note, she hung up.

"Great," I muttered, hanging up the phone. "Okay. Come on. Walther's starting from Berkeley. We need to get moving if we want to beat him to Shadowed Hills."

"Who's Walther again?" asked May.

"Tell you in the car." We crossed the living room together. The sky outside was that ludicrously cheerful blue that seems to haunt California summers. It should have been raining. Considering everything that was going on, the sunshine seemed unfair.

I locked the door, pressing my hand against the wood and reciting, "Ring around the rosies, a pocket full of posies; ashes, ashes, we all fall down." The wards flared and writhed, becoming a web of thin red lines as the smell of cut grass and copper rose around us. If anyone broke into the apartment, we'd know. A bolt of pain lanced through my temples, making my lingering headache worse. The poison was gaining on me. "Damn," I muttered.

"What is it?"

So May wasn't getting my headaches in real-time. That was good to know. "Just the headache. Can I get you to throw a don't-look-here on the car? We don't have time to deal with a speeding ticket."

"Sure." She gave me a sidelong look. "You've been using a lot of magic while you're driving lately."

"I've been in a hurry," I said, brushing past her on my way to the parking area.

May followed, silent as I performed my usual check of the backseat and unlocked the doors. She climbed into the passenger seat, shifting Spike into her lap. "I didn't say I wouldn't do it. I'm just concerned."

"Don't be. It's not like my chronic migraine is going to kill us."

"Right." She closed her eyes and pressed her hands against the dashboard, reciting, "There's a man who lives a life of danger. To everyone he meets, he stays a stranger. With every move he makes, another chance he takes." The smell of cotton candy and ashes filled the car.

"'Secret Agent Man'?" I asked, amused.

May slumped back in her seat. "Not everyone shares your lousy taste in music." She wrinkled her nose. "Ugh. Now I have your headache *and* my own."

May was pureblooded. If she was starting to get magic-burn, her condition was even more synchronized with mine than I'd thought. That wasn't good.

"You relax," I said. "I'll drive."

May nodded, slumping in her seat as I started the car.

We drove in silence. It was close enough to rush hour that traffic was picking up; once we were on the freeway, most of my attention was taken with avoiding an accident. We made good time, but there were a few points—especially at the freeway interchange on the Oakland side of the Bay Bridge—where I was forced to drop to a crawl or pay the consequences. Going through the Caldecott Tunnel when none of the other drivers could see me is one of the most harrowing things I've ever done of my own free will.

There was only one other car in the parking lot when we arrived at Paso Nogal: a battered but serviceable silver Toyota that looked familiar enough to have been made before I wound up in the pond. Walther was standing next to it, attention on the small glass vial in his hand.

I pulled up beside him and killed the engine. He didn't look up. I glanced to May. "Okay. That's a good spell."

Even May looked impressed. "I didn't realize it was *that* good."

"Well, drop it. We need to talk to him."

"Right." She clapped her hands, bobbing her head a la Barbara Eden. The spell burst like a soap bubble, leaving us visible to anyone who was looking.

Like Walther. He jumped, nearly dropping the vial as he whipped around to face us. "Toby!"

"It's me," I said, sliding out of the car. May followed. I gestured between them, saying, "May, Walther Davies. Walther, May Daye, my—"

"Your roommate. You said. A pleasure to meet you, Ms. Daye." May looked surprised but pleased as Walther tucked the vial into his pocket, turning his attention back to me. "I only got here a few minutes ago. Did you drive the whole way invisible?"

"Yeah, we did. It's faster. Sort of." I took Spike from May, holding it toward Walther. "This is Spike."

"The rose goblin? Marcia mentioned things might get odd around you." I gave him a quizzical look. He shrugged. "I asked her to fill me in on what to expect when I started working with you." Quickly, he added, "You were right; it doesn't look healthy."

I decided to let Walther's digging into my background slide. I would have done the same thing in his shoes. "It was fine until Luna got sick."

"May I . . . ?" He reached for the goblin.

"Be my guest." I passed Spike to him, wincing as I saw how shallowly it was breathing. I wasn't sure it actually needed to breathe—it was as much plant as animal—but that didn't mean good things would happen if it stopped. May settled beside me, shifting her weight uneasily from foot to foot. I put a hand on her shoulder, and waited.

Walther cradled Spike against his chest, listening to its breathing before putting a finger on its throat to test its pulse. Finally, he said, "This is a very sick goblin."

"We know. That's why I want you to take soil samples here."

"Because of the connection between the Duchess and the goblins?"

I nodded.

To my surprise, he chuckled grimly as he passed Spike to May. "Faerie never fails to stay interesting, does it?"

"Like a Chinese curse," I said. "Let's go find some roses."

We didn't have to look for long. The bush was half-dead, its few surviving flowers liberally mottled with brown. I stopped. "Here's one."

"Got it." Walther pulled a spoon out of his pocket and knelt to dig around the roots of the bush. He stopped after only a few seconds, frowning. "That's not right."

"What isn't?" May asked.

"The texture of this soil is all wrong." He pulled a small jar from his coat pocket, dumping a spoonful of dirt inside. Then he uncapped the vial he'd been studying when we arrived, pouring its pale red contents into the jar. The resulting mixture fizzed and turned clear. Walther's frown deepened.

"I don't like that look," I said. "What's wrong?"

"There's no poison here. Something's still not right." Walther waved his hand over the jar, muttering in Welsh. The liquid turned gold and started fizzing again.

"He's weird," said May. "If he pulls out a Bunsen burner, we're leaving."

I bit back a smile. If she was feeling well enough to be snide, we were doing better than I'd thought. "He's Tylwyth Teg," I said, like that explained everything.

Apparently it did, because May looked satisfied with that answer. Walther kept chanting as the liquid changed colors, finally settling on a glittering white.

"Ah," said Walther, and stood.

I raised an eyebrow. "Talk to me. What's going on?"

"Salt." He held up the jar for my inspection.

"What do you mean, 'salt'?" I squinted at the jar like I expected his words to start making sense. "Isn't there always salt in dirt?"

"A little bit, but plants die if they get too much. This dirt has too much salt. Think of it as dosing a person with a little bit of arsenic at a time. It's essentially slow murder." He shook his head. "The only way to get rid of it is to leech it out, and the plant still might die if there's enough damage."

"Leech it? How?" I demanded. The implications were sinking in. The damned drink was a red herring; the salt was our real culprit. There could be another poison involved, something to knock her out once she'd been weakened, but poisoning the roses would be enough to incapacitate her.

"The soil needs to be flushed with water and treated with gypsum. Uh, that's a mineral that pulls salt out of the ground."

"How fast can we do that?"

"This isn't something you can just snap your fingers and do. It takes time for the soil to recover, and that doesn't take into account how long it'll take the plant to get better." He shook his head. "I might be able to speed things up, but it won't be instantaneous. I'm a chemist, not a horticulturist."

I shrugged. "You're all we have."

Walther paused. Then he held his hands out to May. "Give me the goblin."

She glanced to me. I nodded consent, and she reluctantly handed Spike over. Walther pulled it to his chest, cradling it as he reached into his pocket for another vial.

"If this doesn't work, there's nothing else I can do," he said, not looking up.

"I understand," I said.

Prying Spike's jaws open, Walther uncapped the vial and poured its smoky purple contents down the rose goblin's throat. Spike went limp, and Walther began chanting in rapid Welsh.

May grabbed my arm, hissing, "What's he *doing?*"

"Trying to save us." I put my hand over hers. The air crackled with the scent of yarrow and the cold, bitter tang of ice as Walther's human disguise started to waver, flickering around him like a bad special effect. That wasn't a good sign. Everyone has their limits, and I didn't know where Walther's were.

I stepped forward, putting my free hand on his shoulder to steady him as his chanting took on a more frantic pace. He flashed me a grateful look, finishing his chant with a string of repeated syllables. The magic shattered, and Walther sagged into my arms.

Spike opened its eyes, making a small, bemused sound.

"Spike!" cried May, rushing to embrace the rose goblin. It chirped and scrambled onto her shoulder, holding itself in place with three paws as it started grooming the fourth.

I was occupied with keeping Walther from knocking us both over. He wasn't a small man, and he was heavier than he looked. I wound up locking one knee and shoving, supporting him against my shoulder. "You okay in there?"

"I'm fine," he managed, trying to stand. "Ow. My head."

"Magic-burn. It's not pleasant, but you get used to it." I glanced at Spike. It looked perfectly normal. "What did you do?"

"Something I shouldn't have?" he said, rubbing his forehead as he managed to get his feet back underneath him. "I'd rather not get used to this, if it's all the same to you."

"Seriously, what did you do?" If he'd cured Spike, he might be able to cure Luna.

He must have guessed what I was thinking, because he shook his head, expression grave. "I pulled the salt out of its—sap, blood, whatever—and replaced it with gypsum."

"So you couldn't do that for Luna," I said, letting go of my fragile hope. Even I know that mammals need salt, and even if Luna was part-plant, she was still a mammal.

"It would kill her," he said. "As it is, I don't know how long this 'fix' will last. The salt's still in the soil. Your goblin's probably going to get sick again."

"If we don't fix this, you mean," I said.

"If you don't fix this, a sick rose goblin is going to be the least of your problems."

"True enough." Something rustled in the bushes, and two more thorny heads poked through the leaves. One had electric pink eyes; the other's eyes were a mossy green. Rose goblins. I smiled. "Looks like your spell was more effective than you thought."

"That explains my headache," he said, wincing again.

"Toby gets those all the time," said May, reaching up to pry a thorn out of her shoulder. Spike chirped, annoyed. "Usually after she does something stupid."

"I'm not normally this dumb," he said wryly.

May flashed a smile. "Toby inspires stupidity."

"Hey!" I protested, not really minding. Walther got dragged into things by Lily's death, and May was involved as long as I was; if they could relax, even a little, more power to them. "I do not. Walther, are you safe to drive?"

"I should be. I have some aspirin in the car."

"Good. I want you to head for Golden Gate Park. Find Tybalt; give him the antitoxin and tell him what to do with it. Get things started."

"Right." He gave me a sidelong look. "And you?"

"I'm going to send a message to Sylvester. I'll meet you at the Tea Gardens in a little while." Assuming I got out of Shadowed Hills alive.

"Your wish is my command," he said, and smiled, a trace of impish humor showing in the set of his jaw.

"Good. Let's get moving." Spike rode on May's shoulder as we walked back to the parking lot, watching with interest as our train of rose goblins increased. There were more than a dozen of them following us by the time we reached Walther's car.

"There's something you don't see every day," I commented.

Walther laughed. "Maybe you would if you gardened more." He opened the car door. I suppressed the urge to tell him to check the backseat. "See you soon?"

"Count on it." He waved to May, then climbed into the car and drove away.

"He's nice," May said, lifting Spike from her shoulder and putting it on the top of my car. "Weird, but nice. And what he did for Spike, I mean, that was really cool."

"What he did for Luna, too," I said. "This is the best lead we've had in a while." I glanced toward the top of the hill and frowned.

May followed my gaze, asking, "Is it safe to go in?"

"No, probably not." I looked away. "I should call. See if I can get Quentin to come out. I just wish . . ."

"I know." May put her hand on my shoulder.

The payphone at the edge of the parking lot rang. I jumped.

May laughed, starting toward it. "It's just a phone. Relax."

"May—"

"It's just a *phone*." She picked up the receiver, still half-laughing. "May Daye here." Then she paused, going quiet.

"May?" I called. "May, are you okay?"

She turned and held the phone toward me, expression uncertain. "It's for you."

TWENTY-THREE

THE SCENE WAS STARTING TO ACQUIRE A strange, dreamlike quality, like it wasn't really happening. *I must have been poisoned again,* I thought, as I walked over and took the phone. *I wonder when that happened.* "Hello?"

"I see you found the salt," said Oleander. "I have to admit, you've impressed me. I heard about your little game with Blind Michael, but I thought it must have been dumb luck. When did you learn how to think?"

I dug the nails of my free hand into my bandaged palm. The pain was almost reassuring. "I'm not going to let you get to me. And you're not getting near Luna ever again."

"How were you planning to stop me? It's brave of you to rattle your spears in my direction, but you don't know where I am. You don't even know whether you're really talking to me. I could just be a dial tone."

"May heard you."

"Who'd believe the word of a Fetch? She'll see you dead, you know."

"You poisoned me."

"So I did; three times now. You check your car so carefully, but you never wipe the handles on your door." She sounded amused. "Did your little Tylwyth Teg tell you about my work? Meddler. He won't be helping you anymore."

"What did you do to Walther?" May's eyes widened. I waved her back. "I swear, if you've touched any more of my friends—"

"You'll what, whine me to death? 'Oh, poor me, I'm poisoned, my friends are dying, I'm a fish, oh, I should *die*.'" Her voice dropped, becoming predatory. "Don't worry about the last part. It's going to be arranged."

"Oleander—"

"Is it already time for the empty threats of violence? I thought you'd go slow with me. After all, I'm going slow with you."

"Leave us alone!" I shouted, my pent-up anger boiling to the surface. Spike yowled, thorns rattling.

Oleander laughed. "Not likely; I have unfinished business with your 'friends'—and with *you*." The venom in her voice answered a question I'd almost forgotten: whatever she had against me was bigger than I could have earned on my own. What Karen showed me—the dream she sent me—really happened. It was the only explanation. "You're taking the fall for this one."

"You're not getting away with this." It was a cliché, but I couldn't think of anything else to say.

"I already have. Checked on Luna recently? I understand she's about to take a turn for the worse." The phone went dead. Spike was still yowling, and the other rose goblins were picking up the cry, creating a chorus of chirps and snarls.

"Toby? What's going on?"

I dropped the phone. "Oleander's coming," I said numbly. "We're too late."

"What are you—" May began, but I was already running for the hill. Answering her didn't matter. What mattered was getting to Luna before Oleander did; what mattered was finding a way to haul this situation around to a happy ending before it ended all on its own. There was no time to think.

There was only time to run.

Spike raced ahead of me. It was all I could do to keep it in sight, scrabbling for balance whenever the loose dirt of the hillside rolled beneath my feet. I fell twice, catching myself on hands that felt more and more like ground hamburger. We were skipping the normal leisurely assault of the summit; this was a full-on siege, and for all I knew, we were already too late.

Spike keened, and more rose goblins flashed out of the trees, joining my escort. They covered the hill in a flood of thorny bodies, yowling as they charted the fastest path to the summit. It always helps to have native guides. We halved my best previous time, taking small paths and hidden shortcuts I'd never seen before. I was scratched and dirty when we reached the top, and blood was seeping through the bandages on my hands, but we were there. The rose goblins flashed through the pattern to unlock the knowe, darting over, under, around and through as they forced their way inside.

I wrenched the door in the oak open as soon as it appeared, racing inside with the rose goblins at my heels. The hall was still deserted. I skidded to a stop, looking down at the goblins that thronged around me. I'd never seen so many rose goblins before. "Find Luna," I said, gasping for breath. "Find Luna, Spike."

My goblin rattled its thorns and turned, taking off into the depths of the knowe. Its family followed, and I ran after them, struggling to keep up. My sneakers were coated in mud, and they found no purchase on the marble, slowing me down. The rose goblins stayed in front of me, keening their distress and doubling back when I fell too far behind. They knew that something was wrong.

I knew Shadowed Hills, but they knew it better, and

they knew where Luna was. I followed, and prayed we weren't already too late.

The rose goblins stopped at a filigreed silver gate set against what looked like a solid wall. I knew that gate; it was one of the gates people didn't try to pass without an engraved invitation and possibly a formal escort. There were very few restricted areas in Shadowed Hills, and that meant it was best to respect the ones that existed. The enchantments used to lock the doors didn't hurt, since they made it practically impossible to violate the restrictions by accident.

I've always done my best to serve Shadowed Hills, and I've always believed the knowe could understand that. It was time to test that theory. I kept running.

The brick dissolved just before I would have slammed into it, allowing me to stumble into the private quarters of the royal family of Shadowed Hills. I stopped to catch my breath, looking frantically around. The room I'd broken into was actually a small, carefully tended garden ringed with marble benches. Cobblestone paths circled a decorative fountain before branching out to mark the way to two smaller, freestanding versions of the silver gate. The sky overhead was pristine gold, studded with two small green moons—a Summerlands sky.

Connor was seated on the edge of the fountain with his head in his hands, letting the spray wash over him. "Connor!" I shouted.

His head jerked up, eyes widening. I'll give him this: he didn't waste time. I'd just burst into a place I wasn't supposed to be, panting and trailed by a dozen or more rose goblins. He didn't bat an eye as he stood, asking, "Toby? What's wrong?"

"Where's Luna?"

He must have seen something in my eyes that didn't allow for debate. He pointed to the gate on the left, saying, "In her room with Sylvester and Jin. Are you okay? How did you get in?"

"It doesn't matter." I started down the path. I was suddenly, unspeakably tired, and I wanted nothing more than to call a five minute time-out and huddle in his arms. Sadly, not an option. "I have to go save your mother-in-law's life."

"What?" He stood, falling in behind me.

"Oleander's on her way."

Connor made a choked noise somewhere between a gasp and a seal's startled bark. "That isn't possible."

"There isn't time to explain," I said, and froze as the leaves in the hedge behind him began rustling. The rose goblins keened a high, warning tone, alerting me to the danger I'd already spotted.

Sometimes speed is all that saves us. The world comes down to action and reaction, physical science becoming all-too-physical reality. I was braced to run before the archer behind Connor finished standing. It was a man I didn't recognize, tall, thin, and scarred, with ears like a bat's. He was one of Faerie's shock troops, nothing more, and it didn't matter, because he was also the one holding the crossbow.

My knives were strapped to my waist; I'd never reach them before he had time to shoot. Fighting wasn't an option, and with Connor standing between us, neither was running away. He'd try to save the day if I gave him the chance, and he'd fail. He wasn't made to be a hero.

I was. "Connor, look out!" I dove forward and slammed my shoulder into his chest, forcing him to the ground. He made a small, startled sound as he fell, reminding me of the last time I tackled him, just a few years and the better part of a lifetime ago, in the darkness of Goldengreen.

The momentum of my leap dragged me down with him. I'd moved fast; Connor was down before he really realized what was going on. I didn't move fast enough.

The first bolt hit my left shoulder, penetrating just below the scar tissue left by a long-dead assassin's bullet.

The arrowhead wedged against my collarbone, seemingly without encountering any resistance from my flesh. The second bolt hit lower, sinking even deeper before hitting bone. There was barely time to turn my head, see the shafts protruding from my shoulder, and realize I'd been hit. Then the world exploded in pain, like acid flowing into my blood.

I was on fire, I was being eaten alive, and it would never end. I'd never felt that kind of pain before, but I knew what it was: there's only one thing in Faerie that hurts like that. And I finally knew how I was going to die.

Oberon wouldn't stand for killing in his Kingdoms. Find another way or answer to me, he said. Pain without death became the way to fight—as much pain as you could manage without causing lasting harm. They were clever and cruel, those Firstborn, especially when they were waging war on each other. They set out to make something that could hurt without killing, and they succeeded. They created elf-shot, a weapon that caused crippling pain followed by a sleep so deep it could last for a hundred years. Sleeping Beauty didn't prick her finger on a spinning wheel; she was shot by an angry sister who refused to live another day in her shadow. Elf-shot hurt the purebloods before it put them to sleep for a long, long time. As for changelings . . .

Humans were still something to hunt for sport when elf-shot was created, and Oberon's law didn't say anything about their lives. By the time anyone realized elf-shot was deadly to changelings, it was too late; the weapons had been made.

Devin was the one who warned me about elf-shot. It isn't used much anymore—there are fewer compunctions about killing these days, with Oberon and the Queens showing no signs of coming back—but he told me what it looked like, what it would feel like, and that if I ever saw it, I should run. I was too close to human. I'd never wake up.

Connor pushed himself out from beneath me, eyes wide. He'd seen the arrows hit me. Even if they hadn't been elf-shot, I would have been in trouble. As it was . . .

"Toby, are you all right?" He pulled me into a sitting position, leaning me against his chest. "Don't die, please, don't die. Guards! I need some guards over here!"

The pain was fading. It hit too hard to last for long; it was burning itself out, and it was taking me with it. Devin never told me that. He never told me that when sleep comes, the pain stops.

I tried to force a smile, looking at Connor through increasingly unfocused eyes. I'd just been elf-shot, and he was yelling for the guards? He'd have been better off yelling for someone to open the windows and let the night-haunts in. "I loved you, you know," I murmured.

"I know. I always . . . Toby, please." He moaned, but I couldn't see his face; he was gone, faded into black as my eyes stopped working. That was too bad. I would've liked to look at him while I was dying, to take that sight with me into the dark.

The footsteps of the guards echoed like thunder as they ran toward us, and past us, without slowing down. Past us . . . what was wrong with that? Part of my mind was screaming, trying to break through the peaceful mist that was wiping out the pain. That part of me demanded action, motion, resistance from a body that wasn't paying attention anymore. Why were they running past us? Why didn't they stay? Connor called the guards because I was hurt. They should have stayed with us, not run toward Luna's . . .

Luna.

Oh.

I went limp, turning toward the choked sound of Connor's breathing. I could feel my human disguise burn away like fog in the sun as my magic deserted me. It didn't matter. Not if the guards ran past us to the Duchess' chambers. Not if I'd failed.

The darkness was almost complete. Part of me was still able to look at it analytically and say, "I'm going to die." The rest of me just wanted to beat its fists against the walls and scream. For myself, for May and Luna, and for Sylvester, because damn me forever, I'd failed him again.

"Connor . . ." I whispered. "Connor, the Duch . . ." And then my body, which had seen me through fire, iron, and Firstborn, finally betrayed me. I could still hear Connor crying, and the keening of the rose goblins, but even that faded, and there was nothing but the black. And then even that was gone, and I was gone with it, and I was glad.

TWENTY-FOUR

THE MOON WAS A CRESCENT in the midnight sky, the kind of moon my father used to call a "smile without a cat." Cheshire cat moon. I stared up through the window, barely daring to breathe. I knew that moon. Not the phase, not the general shape; that exact moon. Time runs differently in the Summerlands, but the memory of that moon followed me for years, through days when the sun never rose and the stars never set. That was the moon that watched my father read me my last bedtime story, tuck me in for the last time, and give me my last kiss good night.

The fae came for me the next day, interrupting my tea party to offer me the only choice that was fully mine to make. Human or changeling-child? Was I theirs, with their pointed ears and illusions, or was I my father's, with his easy smile and human concerns? I only got one opportunity to make my choice. In all the years that followed that night, I never knew whether I chose correctly, and I never forgot that moon.

I was tucked into bed. I pushed back the covers and sat up, unsurprised to realize that I was apparently a child of seven. My hair, which stayed baby-fine and impossibly easy to tangle until I was twelve, was braided to keep it from getting hopelessly snarled in the night. The lace cuffs of a flannel nightgown too new to be yet worn soft bit into my wrists. I knew where I was. This was what I left behind, once upon a time.

"Karen?" I called. "I appreciate the impulse to make the whole 'dying' thing easier, but this isn't funny, kiddo." There was no reply.

I climbed out of the bed, noticing as I did that my favorite doll—a felt Peter Pan made by my mortal grandmother—was on the pillow. Moving in a body I'd outgrown so long ago was strange, but my memory would have known the way even if the Luidaeg hadn't forced me into a literal second childhood not long ago. Best of all, there was no pain. Blessedly, wonderfully, there was no pain.

The room was small and cheery, filled with familiar toys my mind insisted on viewing as old-fashioned; the trappings of my childhood. The walls were painted yellow, and braided rag rugs softened the floor. It took me a long time to realize what I gave up when I left that room behind me, but I cried for my toys from the day I lost them. They were the only mortal things I had the sense to miss.

"Hello, October," said a voice from behind me.

I sighed. Not Karen; nothing as merciful as a niece trying to ease the pain. "Hello, Mother," I said, and turned to face her.

She was standing next to the bed, just like she used to before everything went wrong, back in the days when she'd tell me stories, kiss my forehead, and tell me to sleep tight. This was the Amandine I knew before the Summerlands: perfectly coiffed white-gold hair, makeup done just so, jewelry chosen with a care that implied she might be graded later. She looked like my mother when she still *was* my mother, not just a lady I happened to be related to, one who tolerated my living in her house.

She wasn't wearing a human disguise—she usually didn't when we were alone—and her impossible beauty was entirely out-of-place against her blue cotton dress and sensible shoes. Offering a small smile, she said, "Hello, my darling girl."

"Quick question before you start with the crazy— are you real, or a really lousy dream?" I couldn't decide whether I wanted to hug her or hit her. Amandine has a gift for making me feel that way.

"I'm afraid that's up to you."

"Of course it is." I sighed. "Where are we?"

"We're . . . waiting." She looked at me sadly. "I tried to spare you when I could, but I wasn't fast enough."

"What are you talking about?"

"It's time to make a choice, October. More importantly, it's time for *you* to choose. I won't force you one way or the other." Her lips drew down in a small grimace. "No one can. Not anymore."

"You'd think I might hallucinate something more pleasant than a lecture from you, you know," I said. "Tybalt in those leather pants would be a nice start."

"What makes you think you're hallucinating?"

She had me there. "I got hit with elf-shot. Pretty sure that's fatal, and since you're not Karen, pretty sure this isn't real."

"Reality aside, do you want it to be fatal? Are you ready to go?"

It was sort of funny. I've spent a lot of time thinking about death—it's hard not to when you spend so much time either running toward or away from it—but I'd never considered whether I'd be ready when it came. "Not really. But I don't think I have much of a choice."

Amandine shook her head. The air around her seemed to freeze, catching the beams of the Cheshire cat moon and holding them suspended in a sphere of slowly expanding unreality. "This *is* the choice. You've made it at least three times, even when I tried to stop you, but the only time you admit to is the one that happened the day after you saw this moon for the first time. Remember?"

"I don't understand." I folded my arms. "You know, I don't appreciate being ignored for years and then having you show up in my hallucinations."

She didn't answer. She just sighed, expression growing even sadder as she walked to the windowsill and rested her hands against it.

"Mother?" No reply. "Mom. This isn't funny." Still no reply. I walked over to stand next to her. I had to rise up onto my tiptoes in order to peer out the window. "What are you looking at?"

"The moon. See?" A smile ghosted over her lips. "Do you remember what your father called the moon when it looked like that?"

I nodded. "Cheshire cat moon."

"A smile without a cat."

"Curiouser and curiouser," I said. "Mom, please. Can you just talk straight for once in your life? I'm not in the mood for riddles."

"Is it down the rabbit hole again, darling, or will you be a good girl this time and stay where you can be found for marmalade and tea?" Amandine's voice was sad and distant; her eyes stayed on the moon. "It's up to you. It's always been up to you, even when I thought it could be up to me. But you're choosing for keeps this time; you're choosing to stop deceiving yourself. Out of the tower now, no more protection for Daddy's precious princesses."

"What—"

"No." Her voice was like a whip cracking through the air. "Choose. No more arguments. No more letting me lie to you. Choose."

"I don't understand."

"You didn't understand the first time either, and you chose then."

I dropped back to the soles of my feet, looking around the room. The shadows had deepened, twisting my toys into strange new shapes. This wasn't my childhood reality anymore. This was something new, sea-changed and wild, like a mirror reflection of what had really been. "What's going on? What are you doing?"

"You have to choose." There was no pity in her voice, no mercy; just a strange echo, like distant bells. My reflection in the window changed, growing taller, melting into my adult self before the lines of my flesh thinned and refined themselves, becoming something altogether different.

The face in the glass was familiar and unfamiliar at the same time. It was too delicate, with sharply pointed ears and eyes that were even more colorless than before. Even my hair looked bleached, going from brown to a silvery ash-blonde. It was who I would have been if I'd been born a pureblood, immortal, bred to the faerie rides and the dark at the bottom of the garden path.

I'd never realized how much I look like my mother.

"It's not too late," she said. The bells were stronger now, layered with moonlight and madness. "This is your choice to make, and there are always other roads. Look." Amandine gestured to the window. The glass cleared, reflection fading. I looked.

A second window had replaced the Cheshire cat moon, separated from ours by a few feet of empty space. It framed a second me, a frightened little girl in a too-new nightgown, standing next to her own version of Amandine. But this little girl and her mother were human, without fae strangeness or illusions.

"What is this?" I pressed my palm against the window. The other me did the same.

"This is the choice you can't take back." Amandine's voice came from above and slightly behind me. The other Amandine's lips moved in perfect time with the words. "If you take it, nothing you do will change the road you're on."

Swallowing hard, I asked, "What am I choosing?"

"Me or her, October. Humanity or fae." There was a pause before she added, much more quietly, "Freedom or the crossroads burden."

"The Changeling's Choice?" I twisted around to face her, my hand still pressed against the glass. "I already made that choice."

"Now you have to make it again."

A second chance? "What happens if I pick the human road this time?" I asked. "What happens if I say I want to stay here?"

"If you choose that road, I'll tuck you into bed, kiss you good night, and walk away. You'll sleep, you'll dream, and you'll die. I don't know whether it'll hurt. I've never died of elf-shot." She shook her head. "It probably won't, if that helps your decision at all. You'll just sleep until your heart stops."

"What if I choose the road I took last time? Does that mean I'll live?"

"Maybe. Nothing's certain." She looked away. "This has only happened a few times."

"Great. Even my hallucinations aren't normal." I shook my head. "Go away. I'm not choosing anything."

"October—"

"I'm not!" I pressed my hands over my ears. "I'm dying. You can't change it, you can't stop it, and you're nothing but a bad dream! Now *go away*!"

"Toby?" This voice was different.

I lifted my head, uncovering my ears. The dreamlike twisting of the room was gone. I was back in the bed; the lights were on, and most importantly of all, my father was standing in the doorway, one hand still on the light switch.

"Bad dream, baby?" he asked.

For a moment, it felt like I'd forgotten how to breathe. Swallowing, I managed to whisper, "Daddy?"

My mother didn't bring any pictures of my father when we left the mortal world, and I was too young to understand how much I'd want them someday. I didn't take my teddy bear, much less the family photo album. No one told me I'd never see my father again; I wouldn't have believed them if they had.

I barely remembered what he looked like until I had him standing right in front of me. He was tall, with broad shoulders, a thick waist, and pale Irish skin speckled with a lifetime of freckles. I got my rotten knees from his side of the family, even though I didn't inherit his height or bright blue eyes. I always looked like a changeling next to him, even before I knew how true that really was.

"Yeah, baby, it's me," he said, smiling as he walked over and sat on the edge of the bed. He smiled at me. I found the strength to smile back. I had my father's smile. Mother never told me that. Mother never told me a lot of things. "Can't sleep?"

"Not really." I couldn't take my eyes off him. Maybe I was hallucinating while the elf-shot shut my body down, but I hadn't seen my father in a long time. I wanted to look at him as much as I could. "I'm sorry I yelled."

"It's all right. I was up." Daddy was a tax attorney. He brought a lot of work home during the week and worked on it after I'd gone to bed, leaving his weekends and afternoons free. I never forgot that, even though I'd forgotten the way the skin around his eyes crinkled when he smiled. "Just don't wake your mother."

"I won't," I said earnestly. Amandine went away when I told her to; I didn't want her coming back.

He ruffled my hair, asking, "Everything okay in there?"

"Sort of. Daddy?"

"Yes?"

"Is it wrong to walk away from a choice you're supposed to make? If you're supposed to pick something, is it bad not to pick anything at all?"

"I guess it depends on what you're choosing," he said, with his usual careful deliberation. "If you were deciding whether to take your teddy bear to bed with you, I guess you could take a different dolly and never make up your mind about the bear. But if you were deciding whether you'd do something that needs doing—like cleaning your room—I guess it would be bad to never decide."

"What if it was something more important than cleaning your room?"

"How much more important?"

"As important as going away or not going away."

He stiffened before nodding, saying, "With something like that, it would be bad not to choose. You planning on running away from home?"

"No. But if I had to decide whether to stay or go, wouldn't it be better to just not decide? To stay without choosing?"

"Not really." He reached out again, putting his hand over mine. "You have to decide what matters to you, baby, and follow that decision. I'd be sad if you left, but I know you'd only do it for something that mattered so much you felt you had to."

Oh, Daddy, I thought, *you were more than sad when I left.* "So you want me to choose?"

"You have to make your own choices in life. If you don't, what's the point?"

"You're right." I managed to smile again, blinking back tears. "I love you."

"I love you, too, baby." He leaned over and kissed my forehead before standing and walking to the door. "Get some sleep, and think about it, okay?"

"Okay, Daddy."

"Good night, Toby." He turned off the light, closing the door as he left.

I wasn't afraid of the dark when I was a kid, but for a moment, I wished my childhood room had come with the usual night-light. It would've been nice if those shadows had been just a little shallower as I climbed out of the bed and walked to the window. The Cheshire cat moon grinned down on me like a beacon.

I fumbled with the latch until it came loose, and then pushed the window open, leaning out on my elbows until my face was in the wind. "I don't want to do this again," I said. "It's not right, and it's not fair, and I don't want to. You shouldn't be allowed to make me do this again."

The moon didn't answer. I didn't expect it to. "I'm a hero. That's what Faerie made me, and I think my father would be proud. I don't want to make this choice again, because there's no right choice for me. But there *is* a choice that's right for the people who count on me to be there when they need me."

"Does that mean you're going to decide?" Amandine asked, behind me.

"I don't think 'none of the above' is an option."

"No, it isn't," she said. "What do you want? What's your choice?"

"I choose the evil I know." I turned to face her. "I can't be a hero with no one to save, and I can't run out on them just because I'm scared. I already walked away from this world once. I don't get to go back."

"So you choose Faerie?" she asked. The blood-and-roses smell of her magic was rising around us. This was my last chance to back out. But what would I be backing out on? You can't rewind reality. Choosing to stay human wouldn't change history; it wouldn't unmake anything I'd ever done, or seen, or been, and I wouldn't want it to. Faerie may not always have been the kindest place to live, but it was still my home. I owed it to Gillian, to May, to Dare, and Tybalt and January and all the others not to say that my life had been a mistake. Not when it had been so intertwined with theirs.

"Yes," I said. "I choose Faerie. Take me home."

Amandine's smile was ripe with sorrow. "This may sting," she cautioned, and kissed my forehead. There was a moment of stillness, of perfect rightness and serenity.

Then the pain came.

I screamed, dropping to my knees. This wasn't elf-shot pain; this was something new, something even worse because it was so intrusive. I screamed again, and my voice echoed like it was the only sound in the world. The pain kept increasing, building to a fevered pitch that shook me all the way down to my bones. It was worse than dying; dying ends, but this pain seemed to be settling in to stay forever. The room was dissolving around me in streaks of watercolor black and gray. The dream landscape couldn't survive this much turmoil.

Dream. That was the answer; that was the way out of this. I had to wake up. My eyes were already open, but that didn't matter. Not in a dream.

Concentrating as hard as I could through the pain, I ordered myself to wake up.

And I opened my eyes.

TWENTY-FIVE

THE PAIN FADED BY INCHES, leaving me numb. I tried to flex my fingers, moving carefully in case the pain decided to come back. They obeyed. I lifted a hand, shielding my eyes as I cracked them cautiously open. The light burned at first, but the glare faded quickly, leaving me squinting up at a pale purple sky.

I gradually realized that I was leaning against something soft. Hand still shielding my face—just in case—I tilted my head back until I saw what was supporting me: Connor. His eyes were wide and grave, making him look like a little kid whose Christmas prayers had been suddenly, impossibly answered.

"Is . . ." I rasped. I licked my lips to wet them and tried again: "Is Luna okay?" Connor nodded. "Thank Maeve. Did anybody get the number of that truck?"

Connor didn't smile. He just kept staring at me.

I frowned and lowered my hand. The world danced a drunken reel around me, spinning to an irregular beat. I've never been a fan of motion sickness. "Dammit," I muttered, sitting up a little. "Luidaeg?"

"Why . . . Toby, why are you calling for *her?*" asked Connor.

"Isn't that how you fixed me?" It was the only thing that made sense. The Luidaeg brought me back from the edge of death once before, after I'd been shot with iron bullets. If anyone could deal with elf-shot, it was her.

The thought seemed to be a signal for the pain to come surging back. This was a new sort of hurt, dull and throbbing, like an all-over bruise. It felt like I'd just finished running a marathon. I groaned, slumping against Connor.

"It wasn't the Luidaeg," said Sylvester. I squinted as I turned toward the sound of his voice. He was standing a few feet to my left, his fingers clenched white-knuckled around May's upper arm. May didn't seem to mind how tightly he was holding her; she was just staring at me, eyes gone as wide as Connor's.

"It wasn't the Luidaeg," Sylvester repeated. "I would have sent for her, if there'd been time. But there was no time."

I used Connor's shoulder for balance as I levered myself into a sitting position. Every move awoke another cascade of aches. My head hurt, my legs hurt—pretty much everything that *could* hurt, hurt. Pain does nasty things to my patience. "Does somebody want to tell me what the hell's going on? Starting with, I don't know why I'm not *dead?*" Purebloods sleep. Humans and changelings die. It's in the rules.

Sometimes life seems to take an obscene pleasure in throwing me curve balls.

"You have to understand, there just . . . there was no time." Sylvester was almost pleading. "I didn't know she'd come. Once she did, I couldn't refuse her."

"You died, Toby," said May. Her voice was matter-of-fact, entirely out of synch with her shell-shocked expression. "Your heart stopped, and you died."

I stared at her before twisting to face to Connor and demanding, "Tell me what they're not saying."

"The rose goblins ran away when you fell, and they came back with Amandine." His eyes searched my face, looking for a sign that I understood. "Sylvester and I were . . . you were having some sort of seizure, and we were holding you down. She pushed us out of the way when your heart stopped."

"I was fading," said May. "But she told me to stop, and I *did*. She just said 'stop,' and I was here again. She yelled at you to choose. She yelled until you started breathing again, and now, you're . . ." Her voice faltered. Barely above a whisper, she added, "I'm not your Fetch anymore. I can't feel you."

I raised my hand. She stopped talking.

If I thought about it—really *focused*—I could almost remember hands holding me down, and shouting, all of it filtered through dream images of a little girl's room and a second Changeling's Choice. I dropped the hand I'd used to signal May to silence and wiped my lips. My fingers came away smeared with blood. I looked at them without any real surprise. I didn't bother tasting the blood; I already knew which of my memories it held. Nothing but a little girl's bedroom, and a choice she was only supposed to be offered once.

"It's always blood and roses with you, isn't it, Mother?" I murmured. I was starting to understand. It fit with too many things, going back too far, to be ignored. I just didn't want to believe it. The balance of your blood is the one thing that shouldn't change . . . but if that's true, why did Oberon make the hope chests?

The hope chests were made to turn changelings all the way fae. At that moment, they represented a final chance to reduce the magnitude of the lies my mother told me. I seized the possibility for all that it was worth. "Did she have a hope chest?" I asked.

"You know she didn't," said Sylvester. The resignation in his voice was almost impossible to bear. "It was the only way to save you. She didn't ask for consent, and I didn't stop her. I'm sorry, Toby. I couldn't let you go."

May's hair grew to match mine overnight, like the sudden growth of a thorn briar around a castle meant to sleep for a hundred years. Would it grow again if she cut it now? Somehow, I didn't think so.

"Connor, help me up."

He nodded, wrapping an arm around my shoulders and guiding me gently—almost tenderly—to my feet. It took several minutes of teetering before I was stable. Connor held me the whole time, and didn't let go even after I could have stood on my own. I was quietly relieved. I had the feeling I was going to need the support.

"Toby—" Sylvester began.

"Give me a minute." Amandine offered me a second chance to make my first decision. It shouldn't have been possible, but it was my mother, and I was starting to realize that "shouldn't" didn't apply. "No more letting me lie to you," she said.

Someone had been lying to me, all right. More than one someone. I held on to Connor with one hand as I raised the other and pushed my hair back, feeling my ear. The planes and edges I knew were gone, replaced by a sharper angle, rising to a more tapered point. My breath caught. So. I was right. Now what was I going to do about it?

"I want a mirror." I wasn't sure whether I was overreacting, underreacting, or doing both at once. Part of me wanted to blame the poison in my blood, but the answer was probably simpler. I came close to dying—hell, I actually *died*—and I was panicking. Isn't stress fun?

Sylvester sighed. "Please don't strain yourself before I get back," he said, and turned, walking through a nearby doorway.

I gave the garden a slow once-over once he was gone. My eyes were still adjusting to the light, but the glare was becoming less painful. I was unsurprised to see the body of the assassin on the path not far away, arrows sticking out of his back. They were fletched in the colors of Shadowed Hills. "He hit anybody else?"

"Sir Archibald," Connor reported. "He's asleep in his quarters."

"Shit. I hope they remember to dust him." There were rose goblins on every surface, watching us with bright, unblinking eyes. "They're worse than cats," I muttered.

"What?" said May.

"Nothing." Sylvester came back through the door, carrying a long, cloth-draped mirror. I forced myself to meet his eyes. "Where's my mother?"

"She left," he said, as he moved to prop the mirror against the fountain.

"Of course she did." That was just like Amandine. She'd show up when I was dying, but she couldn't stay to see me live. "How long did you know? Don't say you didn't. All that 'Amandine this' and 'Amandine that'— you *knew*. And you didn't tell me."

"Know what?" asked Connor. "I still don't understand what's going on."

"Well, Sylvester? You want to answer the man?"

He looked away.

"Right," I snarled, pulling myself out of Connor's hands and wobbling over to the fountain. I yanked the fabric off the mirror, throwing it unceremoniously to the side.

And then I stopped, unable to make myself move. Even knowing what I was going to see did nothing to prepare me for actually *seeing* it. "Oh," I said, finally. "Tybalt was right."

Almost a year ago, Tybalt followed me to the County of Tamed Lightning, where he helped me find a killer and saw me raise the dead. He got strange after that, and avoided me for months while he went looking for something. We returned to what passed for our normal relationship once he found what he'd been looking for. He wouldn't tell me what it was. He said I had to find it for myself, because I wouldn't believe it coming from him.

He was right. Maybe I'm weird, but if he'd said, "By the way, you're not Daoine Sidhe, because Daoine Sidhe don't work the way you do," I would have laughed him out of the room.

Well, I wasn't laughing now. And I wasn't Daoine Sidhe.

The woman in the mirror was pale with exhaustion, and her eyes were a gray almost pale enough to be white. Her stick-straight hair was ashy brown shot through with streaks of gold. Even her features were finer than I expected. I could still see my father in the cant of her chin, but he was blurred and half-hidden. She'd been— *I'd* been—tilted further from human. What Amandine did changed everything. I knew that, even as I closed my eyes and gathered my magic around me, reaching inward as I tried to do something I never felt the need to do before, and measured my own heritage.

The smell of copper rose hot as I asked my blood, *What am I?* Its answer was incomprehensible, the taste/ sound/feeling of a race I didn't recognize and had never encountered before. Whatever Amandine and I were, we didn't even share a Firstborn with the Daoine Sidhe. I dug deeper, looking for a clearer picture, and my eyes snapped open, meeting the shocked stare of my reflection.

There were subtle watermarks scattered all through me, marks I somehow knew showed the places where the balance of my blood had changed. I'd never been able to see them before. Now, they were all too visible. The freshest was less than an hour old; the one before it matched the night I touched the hope chest. There were other marks before those; all short, brusque changes that read almost like a tug-of-war.

Amandine stopped voluntarily touching me after I

made my Changeling's Choice. I used to think it was because she blamed me for taking her away from my father. That was never the reason. She just couldn't risk it around people who'd see what she was doing to me. I looked at the watermarks in my blood and suddenly being the weak daughter of the most powerful bloodworker in Faerie actually started making sense.

May was behind me when I opened my eyes. She had no human blood—as a Fetch, she mimicked my changeling traits without sharing them—but her reflection looked more human than mine did. She put a hand on my shoulder. "Amandine saved you," she said. "She came out of that fog she lives in and saved you. Please don't hate her for doing it."

I ignored her, watching my lips in the mirror as I asked, "Sylvester? How long?" I wanted to kick and scream and throw things, but I knew that wouldn't achieve anything. So I waited for his answer, and I watched my reflection speak.

"Always." Sylvester laughed bitterly. "I'm Daoine Sidhe, remember?"

I turned to face him. "And I'm not."

Connor gaped at me. Sylvester just shook his head. "No, you're not. You're what everyone's always told you that you were." His smile was strained. "You're Amandine's daughter."

"I'm still a changeling. I can feel my mortality. It's thinner, but it's there." I kept my eyes on Sylvester's, challenging him to look away. "Why didn't you tell me?"

"Because your mother asked me not to, and I couldn't deny her." His smile died. "I never dreamed that it would take her this long."

"Yeah, well." I glared at him. It didn't help. I'd never felt so betrayed. Not by Devin, not by Amandine, not by anyone. Sylvester was the father I'd never been allowed to have. He was the one man who wasn't supposed to lie to me. "That's Amandine for you. Always taking the long way around."

"She came when you needed her," said May. "Doesn't that count for something? She loves you." Her tone was wistful. She had my memories; she remembered being Amandine's daughter, but she was still a Fetch. She'd never had a mother.

My mother loved me. It was an interesting notion, and almost enough to take my mind off what she'd done. It was nowhere near enough to blunt the sting of what *Sylvester* had done. "Did she say anything else?" I asked.

"She said beware the Lady of the Lake, because she's never forgiven you your story, but to be more afraid by far of Morgane," said Connor. I gave him a quizzical look. He shrugged. "I don't know what that means. Amandine's a little weird, even when she's being sane. Are you really not Daoine Sidhe?"

"Guess not." I raked my hair back again, wincing as my hand hit my ear. This was going to take some getting used to.

May's sudden smile was vibrant enough to make me feel selfish for my panic. "I'm not your Fetch anymore, and I'm still here."

I matched her smile with a more subdued smile of my own. "I'm so glad."

Connor cleared his throat. "Now can you stop dying on us?"

"I'll do my best. No promises." I glanced at Sylvester. "I'm not done being angry with you, but this isn't the time. Did May tell you what we found?"

"I got a little distracted, boss," May said, sounding sheepish.

Sylvester looked between us. "What's going on?"

"We were here because we had some ideas about what happened to Luna," I said. "We were at the bottom of the hill when Oleander called to taunt me."

"May told us that much," he said, nodding. "But Luna?"

"She wasn't poisoned; that's why Jin can't find anything wrong with her. It's the roses that are sick. Someone's been salting the earth around them."

Sylvester's eyes narrowed. "And as the roses die . . ."

"So does she. Have you noticed the rose goblins acting strangely?"

"I haven't noticed much," he admitted, glancing at the goblins clustered around his feet. "I've been a little preoccupied."

"I have," said Connor. "They got sick the same time Luna did. Some of the smaller ones have died. I thought it was because she was sick."

"So did I, but we were coming at things from the wrong direction. If we cure the roses, we cure her. Walther cured the goblins by turning the salt in their blood into gypsum. He may be able to help with the soil, once he's had a little more time."

"I see," said Sylvester. His smile was less vibrant than May's, but just as alive, and twice as relieved. I felt a pang of guilt over taking time to panic before getting down to business; they needed me to be sane, and I hadn't been doing it.

Then again, I just came back from the dead, and learned that the one person I'd trusted more than anyone had been lying to me for my entire life. Maybe I needed to cut myself a little slack. "We can save her," I said.

"I hope so," said Sylvester. "And—"

I never learned what he was going to say next. The gate connecting the Ducal chambers to the rest of the knowe banged open, and Dugan strode into the garden at the head of a troop of guards in the Queen's colors. Raysel and Manuel were right behind. Raysel looked gleeful; Manuel looked smug. Neither expression was very comforting.

May whirled to face her, eyes wide and angry. Sylvester's turn was slower, and more dangerous; there was a cold fury in the way he was holding himself, and I knew that his fuse wouldn't burn for long.

Dugan focused on May, ignoring me completely. "October Daye, you have been charged—"

Oh, oak and ash. I looked like a stranger to anyone who wasn't there when Amandine shifted the balance of my blood, while May looked like, well, me. I moved to put myself between her and the guards, ignoring Connor's attempt to grab my wrist and stop me. "I think you've got the wrong girl," I said, projecting as much false bravado as I could manage. "Unless you came here to harass my Fetch?"

Dugan hesitated. "October Daye?"

"The same."

He hesitated a moment more. Then, slowly, he smiled. "October Daye, you have been charged with the murder of the Undine known as Lily, and the attempted murder of Luna Torquill, Duchess of Shadowed Hills. You are under arrest by direct order of the Queen of the Mists. I suggest you come quietly."

"This is madness!" snapped Sylvester. "Sir Daye has been injured. I won't allow—"

"Don't." I put my hand on his arm. "It won't do any good. You know what to do. Call Walther—May knows where he is—and he'll help you."

"Are you *quite* done?" Raysel asked. "You're being arrested, not taking a tour."

I looked at her coldly. "Raysel, you told me yourself that your father wasn't my liege anymore. I don't have to obey his wishes, spoken or unspoken, and so I can finally say this: go drown yourself, you self-righteous little bitch."

She stared at me, cheeks reddening, before turning on her heels and storming out of the room. Manuel gave me a venomous look and followed.

I turned back to Dugan. "Well? Weren't you going to arrest me now?"

He motioned two of the guards forward. One grabbed my hands and yanked them behind me. The other snapped iron manacles around my wrists, making my skin crawl. "This isn't necessary," I said. "I'm not fighting you."

"For once in your life, be silent," said Dugan, with no real rancor in his tone.

I looked at him blandly, trying to pretend the iron wasn't already starting to burn. The second guard removed my knives from around my waist. "What's your full name?"

"Dugan Harrow of Deep Mists," he said. The answer was automatic; like it or not, changeling or not, I outranked him. Eyes narrowing, he asked, "Why?"

"Because, Dugan Harrow of Deep Mists, I'm going to remember you. I'm going to remember this. And you're going to be sorry." One of the guards shoved me between the shoulders, catching me squarely on one of the punctures left by the elf-shot. I staggered, biting my lip to keep from crying out, and let them push me toward the gate.

I only glanced back once as they forced me out of the room. Connor was rigid with anger as he stared after us, hands balled into useless fists. May was sobbing, slumped against Sylvester, who watching us go with a bleak, calculating anger in his eyes. If Luna lived and I didn't, the Queen might find herself facing insurrection from a quarter she never bargained for.

The gate closed behind us, and the guards led me away.

TWENTY-SIX

HAVING MY HANDS MANACLED BEHIND ME added a new, nerve-racking dimension to the trip along the beach leading to the Queen's knowe. The guards yanked me upright every time I started to fall, pulling so hard they wrenched my arms and rattled my teeth. For some reason, I wasn't particularly grateful. The iron in the manacles disrupted and dissolved my magic, leaving me dizzy and making it impossible for me to spin an illusion. I threw up twice before we even reached the beach. Amandine saved my life, but she also made me more vulnerable to the touch of iron. Nice trade, Mom.

The don't-look-here Dugan had thrown over our group was itchy and foreign-feeling, but it hid us from the mortal world, and that was what mattered. There'd be no tourist providing a last-minute save for me. Not this time.

We somehow made it over the rocks without anyone toppling into the Pacific. I tried to stop long enough to catch my breath, and one of the guards shoved me forward. The third stone in as many minutes turned under my foot, nearly sending me tumbling. "Be a little more careful, asshole," I snapped. I was already soaked to the knees. I didn't want to get any wetter.

Dugan laughed, pushing me into the cave ahead of us. The iron had me too dizzy to catch myself. I dropped to my knees before pitching face-first into the icy water.

"I'm not that worried about you remembering me," he said. More loudly, he added, "Get her up. We're late as it is."

Hands grabbed my shoulders, hauling me to my feet. The effects of the iron were getting worse. I wasn't sure how much longer I could go on, but I wasn't going to give Dugan the satisfaction of knowing that. I shivered, asking, "Could you calm down? The Queen's going to be pissed if you kill me."

"Why should she care, *murderess?* You've broken Oberon's law one time too many. You're finally going to burn for it." He shoved me again. This time I didn't even hit my knees before falling straight into the water. I rolled to my side, barely managing to lift my face from the water before I drowned. The guards pulled me up. I hung limply in their hands, choking and gasping as they half-shoved, half-supported me the rest of the way down the tunnel.

Dugan was right. I broke Oberon's law when I killed Blind Michael, and the Queen could sentence me for that even if I'd done nothing else wrong. The Queen cleared her debt to me by giving me Goldengreen, technically claiming my fealty at the same time. That meant she could take me from Sylvester's lands without his consent. I'm not a conspiracy theorist—there's usually a nice, normal, supernatural explanation for whatever's going on—but that didn't mean I hadn't been set up. The only question was just how high up the conspiracy actually went.

Dugan gave me a final shove as the guards released

me, pushing me through the cave wall and into the Queen's knowe. I staggered to a stop, barely managing to stay upright as my waterlogged shoes slipped on the marble floor of the audience chamber. Shaking my hair out of my eyes, I gaped at the crowd. It looked like everyone in the Kingdom who wasn't at Shadowed Hills when I was arrested had come to see this farce of a trial.

Mitch and Stacy stood at the edge of the crowd, hands clasped tightly together. I was relieved to see that they'd left the kids at home. Tybalt wasn't far from them. He looked absolutely livid. His eyes narrowed as we entered the room, gaze swinging around to focus on the center of Dugan's don't-look-here. He might not see us perfectly, but he knew where we were.

Dugan planted his hands on my shoulders, shoving me forward and ripping away the don't-look-here at the same time. A gasp ran through the crowd. I could understand the reasons: I was wet, muddy, and bloodstained. Not the sort of thing one normally sees at Court, even at a murder trial.

Stacy clapped a hand over her mouth, eyes going wide. Even Tybalt was staring at me—Tybalt, who's seen me in much worse shape. I met his eyes, bewildered. He mouthed a single word: "When?"

I winced, two hot tears escaping as realization hit me. Everyone who knew me knew that I was a half-blood. The changes Amandine made to save me were too strange to be natural, and unnatural enough to be scary. They sure as hell scared *me*, and I'd had the time to start getting used to them.

The guards nudged me into the open space in front of the Queen's empty throne. Dugan pointed to the floor. "Kneel."

I looked at him. I looked at the room. I made my choice. "No."

"Kneel. You won't like what happens if you don't."

He was starting to look uneasy. I guess he expected a less mixed crowd when he brought me to "justice."

Looking at his handsome, weasely face, all I felt was tired. "I won't kneel for you." My tone was light, even reasonable, if you ignored who I was talking to.

"In that case, you can kneel for me," said the Queen. I looked up.

She was seated on her throne, regal and calm, like she'd been there for hours. She smiled as our eyes met, expression filled with hot satisfaction. Her appearance had changed again, moving from "punk" to "perfection." Her black-and-white hair was styled in an elegant bob and crowned with a circlet of braided platinum; her fishnets and miniskirt were gone, replaced by a gown made of silver mist. She looked like the pinnacle of glamour, while I looked like something just shy of a natural disaster. I doubted that was an accident, either.

"Your Highness." I inclined my head. "Good to see you again."

"Is that so?" She pursed her lips. "My man told you to kneel, Countess Daye. Now *kneel*."

The power of the Queen's Banshee blood made the command impossible to resist. I hit the marble on my knees before I could even try to resist. The compulsion kept pushing until I bowed my head, supplicating myself before her.

"That's better," she murmured. Raising her voice, she said, "We are gathered to witness the trial and sentencing of October Daye, regarding the deaths of Katai Suiyou of the Tea Gardens and Blind Michael, Firstborn son of Oberon and Maeve. She is also charged with the poisoning of Duchess Luna Torquill of Shadowed Hills, with the understanding this crime will only bear sentence of death if the injured dies. October Daye, how do you plead?"

"Wait—that was really her name?" I lifted my head, electrified. I'd only heard Lily's real name once before . . . and now I knew, beyond all question, that I couldn't have been talking to myself. "Highness, you're making a mistake. Oleander told me—"

The Queen smiled. That was all: just smiled. "How do you plead?" she repeated.

"You're not listening to me, and that's not a fair question." Putting Blind Michael on the list forced me to plead guilty. Not to everything—but pleading guilty to anything could condemn me.

"That isn't what I asked," she said. "How do you plead?"

"Innocent! Highness, you have to listen to me. Oleander—"

"How can you be innocent when you admit to killing Blind Michael?" One of the guards stepped onto the dais, handing her my belt. She held it up, displaying the scabbards holding my knives to the assemblage. "Tell me, I beg."

"Blind Michael's death was self-defense," I objected. "Ask the parents of the children he stole whether he deserved to die."

"Airs and arrogance aside, you remain a changeling. Your blood is impure. You don't decide who lives or dies." She dropped my scabbard. It landed with a clatter. "That's a job for your betters, not for you."

"I didn't hurt Lily or Luna. Ask the subjects of the Tea Gardens. Ask Sylvester Torquill, or any of his knights! This isn't fair. This isn't—"

She cut me off again. "We have testimony telling us that you've taken advantage of his affection for you, convincing him of your innocence."

I froze. "Testimony? Whose?"

"Mine." Raysel stepped from behind the throne, smiling. "I've seen you talk my father in circles. He could watch you pour the poison and still call you innocent."

"One voice isn't enough to convict," said the Queen. "Is there another?"

There was a pause almost long enough to let me breathe before Manuel stepped out to join Raysel. "Her lies killed my baby sister. She's the one who poisoned the Duchess." The hitch in his voice was slight, but it was there.

I closed my eyes. Manuel was willing to lie in front of the Queen? I knew he hated me. I'd just never realized how far he was willing to let his hatred take him.

If Manuel was willing to lie, the Queen was willing to let him. "Two accuse you, and you've already lied in your own defense. None will stand for you."

In a voice loud enough to rebound off the walls, Tybalt demanded, "How *dare* you?" I opened my eyes, turning as far as the Queen's command allowed to see Tybalt striding forward. His shoulders were locked, showing how much effort he was putting into staying even that calm. "Call for her defense! Don't assume we won't appear!"

Seeing him made me realize that neither Dugan nor the Queen had mentioned the deaths at the Cat's Court. I was willing to bet she didn't even know. Tybalt's people lived in her Kingdom, and she was so busy trying to entrap me that she didn't even realize they were dying.

The Queen snapped her fingers, jerking my attention back to her. "You overreach yourself, King of Cats," she said, voice gone honey-sweet. "You have no right to stand defense of her. Or have you forgotten the arrangement made when your people chose to claim a Court outside Oberon's own?"

There was a dangerous pause before he said, much more smoothly, "You misunderstand me. There are debts between us. I owe her."

"So be grateful I do not intend to claim them as my own upon her death."

"You can't—"

"Do not presume to dictate my Kingdom as you do yours." Her tone was still sweet, but it carried a barely veiled warning. Tybalt's footsteps stopped. "Go, now. This trial is none of your concern."

There was another long pause before Tybalt said, "My promises stand. All of them." There was a soft in-rush of air, accompanied by the pennyroyal and musk signature of his magic. Claws clicked on the marble, and he was gone.

"Does anyone else wish to speak out of turn?" asked the Queen.

Hesitantly, Stacy called, "Your Highness, might we . . . ?"

"Say your piece," said the Queen. "This is meant to be a fair trial."

I barely kept from laughing. My exhaustion helped. The iron manacles binding my wrists helped even more.

"Your Highness, October has always been a good and valiant friend. If she says she's trying to solve these murders, I believe her." Stacy sounded frightened but sincere. I didn't try fighting the Queen's compulsion this time. I didn't want to see Stacy's face.

"Be that as it may, your friend is a changeling. I hardly need remind you how many changelings have changed as their blood drove them mad. Alas, madness is known to run in her bloodline." The Queen paused as a murmur ran through the Court. "We can't assume that who this woman *was* has any bearing on who—on *what*—she has become."

"That's not fair!" cried Stacy, startled into forgetting protocol. "How can you ignore her services to this Kingdom? She saved my children! How can you not *care?*"

"Changeling madness is always a danger, and it seems clear that October has succumbed. A tragedy, but not an unexpected one." The Queen smiled benignly. "Your objection is dismissed in the face of existing evidence. Will anyone else speak in this woman's defense?"

"How about I speak up to call you a crazy bitch?" bellowed a familiar voice.

I winced. "Danny . . ."

Sometimes Danny is an absolute idiot. He strode into my field of view, every inch of his massive frame vibrating with fury. "Look, lady, I don't know what you're pulling, but you've got the wrong girl."

The Queen looked at him with obvious amusement. "My, such gallant saviors you have. Perhaps I should embrace a life of crime. It might net me men such as these." Her fingers flicked toward Danny. He froze in mid-step, face going blank.

I stiffened.

Catching the motion, the Queen offered me the smallest of smiles. "Your mother's wicked ways of enticement and deceit live again in you. I'll be gentle on him, in consideration of that. Now." She looked back to the crowd, a challenge in her expression. "Will there be anyone else?"

I listened to the silence. It wasn't as bad as it could have been. Tybalt would protect the Tea Gardens. May would live. Walther would cure the subjects of the Cat's Court, and if Sylvester went to him, Luna might have a chance. Oleander was out there somewhere, but I'd done everything I could to save the people I loved; at this point it was up to them, because I didn't think my mother could bring me back from the dead more than once. There are limits to everything, and I'd finally found mine.

"Very well," said the Queen. "October Daye, rise."

My trial—such as it was—was over. The Queen's binding dissolved, letting me stagger back to my feet. I stole a quick glance around the room. More than half the crowd looked stunned, even frightened; good. They saw the Queen's madness as clearly as I did. Let her do whatever she wanted to me. She wouldn't hold her throne if she stayed that careless.

The Queen didn't seem to notice the mood of the crowd. "October Daye, you have been found guilty of breaking Oberon's law. Do you have any last words before your sentence is pronounced?"

I looked back to her. "I've served those who held my fealty as well as I could, and I've never willingly broken Faerie's laws. I didn't do what you accuse me of, but you're my liege, and your word is law. Tell me what guilt is mine to bear."

Her smile faltered. This was what would be remembered, and she knew it: I was condemned in innocence, and I went bravely, according to the law. When the revolution came, this moment was part of what would be used to take her down.

Pulling herself straight, she asked, "You understand your fate is mine to choose?"

"I understand I can't change your mind. I just hope you'll choose justice over whatever lies you've been offered." Raysel was standing at the edge of the crowd; I saw her tense, but she didn't speak. Clever girl.

"What is true and what is false is mine to decide," said the Queen.

"My apologies." I squared my aching shoulders. "I'm done. The rest is silence."

"Very well. October Daye, Countess of Goldengreen, Knight of Shadowed Hills, daughter of Amandine, I declare you guilty of violating Oberon's law. In three days' time, you will be taken to the crossroads where the Iron Tree grows, where you will be bound, blinded, tied to the tree, as have been so many criminals before you . . . and burned. This is your sentence. This is what will be."

I stared at her, barely able to believe her words. That wasn't just death; it was torture of the worst kind. And there was nothing I could do to stop it.

"Take her away." The guards grabbed my arms, and she shouted, "See how justice is served?"

There was a long pause—too long—before the crowd started clapping. Even then, the applause was timid and broken, like they couldn't believe what they were seeing. The Queen glared and the applause swelled to more acceptable levels as the guards half-walked, half-dragged me out of the room.

The sound of it followed us down the hall until the doors slammed shut, blocking the rest of the world away.

TWENTY-SEVEN

THE GUARDS DRAGGED ME DOWN THREE
halls and a dozen flights of stairs, not pausing to let
me rest or recover my breath; my comfort ceased to be a
concern when the Queen ordered my arrest.

I was barely staying upright by the time we reached
the iron-barred dungeon door. Gremlin and Coblynau
charms were etched into the wood, warding the rest of
the knowe from the iron, but that wasn't enough to wash
the taint from the air. The closer we got to the door, the
harder it got to breathe. The guards were all in better
shape than I was, and they still flinched and paled when
we got close to the dungeon door. I found it oddly hard
to feel sorry for them. None of *them* were wearing iron
manacles, and I was willing to bet they hadn't started the
day by coming back from the dead, either.

The door's handle was rowan wood. It has a dampen-
ing effect on iron, making it easier for purebloods to tol-
erate the stuff. Dugan still pulled a length of silk out of
his pocket, wrapping it around his hand three times before he touched the latch. The lucky bastard had prob-

ably never known the touch of iron in his life, much less been bound or shot with it.

Stepping aside, he signaled the guards to pull me forward. I glared, and he smirked, offering a mocking bow as they hauled me past him. He followed us down the increasingly narrow stairs, the pressure from the iron growing heavier with every step we took into the dark.

The guards were visibly anxious by the time we reached the base of the stairs, and I was starting to wonder which would turn and run first. We came to a second door, this one barred even more thickly with iron, and banded with yarrow. Yarrow wood dampens the magic of those rare races who aren't bothered by iron. A Gremlin will saunter through an iron seal, but yarrow stops them cold.

Dugan pressed his hand against a panel at the center of the door, avoiding the iron as carefully as he could, and whispered something. The strips of yarrow flared yellow as the door swung open to reveal a square of pure darkness. "Can you walk?" I stared into the dark, shaking my head. "Fine. You don't have to. Take her."

Three of the guards lifted me off the ground and carried me down the last flight of stairs. Down into the dark.

The hall at the bottom of the stairs was claustrophobically narrow, and the smoky rowan-and-yarrow torches lining the walls didn't help. Their flickering light was close enough to candlelight to bring me to the edge of panic. We passed half a dozen iron-and-yarrow doors before Dugan waved the guards to a stop. "Here," he said.

One of the guards stepped forward, grimacing with disgust as he opened the nearest door, revealing a small, totally dark cell. I could feel the iron permeating it, and I went cold, the enormity of what they were about to do driving itself home. They were going to put me in that room and leave me, alone with the iron.

By the time they came back for me, burning would be a mercy.

I panicked, struggling with a strength I didn't know I still had. One of the guards laughed, smacking me across the back of the head. The world erupted into blinding pain. That was the end of my resistance. I went limp, staying that way as they shoved me into the cell, slamming and locking the door behind me. I landed hard in the dank, half-rotten straw covering the floor.

The pain faded, replaced by more dizziness. I lifted my head, squinting as I tried vainly to make out any features of the room. It was dark enough that I couldn't even tell whether my eyes were open, and with my hands manacled and the iron confusing my senses, it was impossible to be sure. Even purebloods can't see in total darkness. Sitting required leaning back on the palms of my hands to keep my weight distributed enough that I wouldn't fall. It took four tries. The manacles made balance almost impossible, but I didn't dare touch the walls; I could already feel the iron in the stone threatening to overwhelm me.

My catalog of impossible pain was growing daily. Before Amandine changed my blood, I would have called being hit by elf-shot the worst thing in the world. Before the elf-shot, I would have given that honor to forced physical transformation. Now severe iron poisoning was threatening to put all the other kinds of pain out of the running—and believe me when I say that wasn't a race I'd ever wanted a winner for.

I held my position until I was sure I was stable before trying to stand, tucking one knee under my body as I braced myself against the floor. I had to stop twice and wait for the dizziness to pass before I managed to get to my feet.

Once I was upright, I couldn't remember why I wanted to get up in the first place. I was still standing there, trying to decide what came next, when I heard footsteps outside the door. Hope surged forward, threatening to overwhelm me. The Queen changed her mind. She realized she was making a mistake, and she changed her mind; she was going to let me go. "Oh, thank Oberon," I whispered.

Relief died as the Queen's voice came slithering into the room. Her Siren blood meant she only had to whisper to make herself heard. "Not Oberon," she corrected. "Flattering as the comparison is. Are you comfortable, October?"

"Your Highness." I swallowed. "Now that we're alone, maybe . . . maybe we can talk. I need to explain."

"No. You really don't. You see, I don't care whether you killed the Lady of the Tea Gardens, or attacked the Duchess Torquill. Your failure is in thinking I would."

"I . . . what?"

"We were peaceful while you were gone. Your mother ceased her meddling, and my Kingdom was untroubled. But you had to come back, didn't you? And murder and madness and chaos followed in your wake, as it always had to, daughter of Amandine. Well, I'm through with your games. You killed Blind Michael. That's more than enough to bring you here. You'll burn, October. And like the Harvest Queen, who burns to bring plenty to the land, your death will bring peace back to my Kingdom."

"Highness—" I began, and stopped. There was no point to it. The rustling had stopped; the oily presence of her voice had faded. She was already gone.

The Queen's words echoed in my head as I started pacing. Had things really been that much better while I was gone? I didn't want to believe it. Considering the world I'd come back to, I wasn't sure I should. Just how out of touch—just how insane—was she?

The room was about eight by eight feet square. The air near the walls was so saturated with iron that it hurt to breathe there. Only the center of the room was at all clean, leaving less than four square feet where the iron wasn't pressing in on me.

I was on my third circuit when my foot hit a slippery patch in the straw. I toppled, unable to catch myself. My cheek hit the iron-laced stone wall, and I screamed. Jerking away, I staggered back until I hit the wall on the opposite side of the room. Even my leather jacket couldn't offer protection from the iron. I screamed again as it hit the wounds in my back. I crumpled forward into the straw, forehead cracking against the stone floor beneath it, and the blackness took me.

I woke up some unknowable time later, dizzier and more disoriented than ever. "Oh, no," I muttered, trying to sit up. The straw slipped beneath me, making it impossible. "No, no, no." I've had iron poisoning before; I knew the symptoms. I was dizzy, aching, and unable to focus. The room was warm, probably to keep the walls radiating poison, but I felt like I was freezing.

I curled into a ball and buried my face in the straw, using it as a sort of primitive air filter. It smelled like mold, urine, and decay, but it was better than the alternative. I was holding on as tightly as I could, for all the good that it was going to do me. There was no way out, and with the iron manacles burning against my wrists, even breathing through the straw wasn't going to help for long.

Iron has a physical presence for the fae. Give it enough time and it starts making a sound, like fingernails on a blackboard inside your head. If you leave a fae prisoner in an iron cell for a few days, you won't have to worry about them anymore; the iron prevents them from using magic to escape and breaks them at the same time. It's practical cruelty. When you drive your prisoners catatonic, you don't have worry about them escaping and coming back for revenge.

The length of imprisonment before execution varies depending on the severity of the crime; the worse you were, the longer they keep you locked up before they let you die. I was starting to understand why. After three days of this, I'd welcome death with open arms. Part of me realized dying would mean Oleander and Rayseline won, but the rest of me didn't give a damn. It just wanted the hurting to stop.

Time slipped away as I drifted in and out of fitful, iron-soaked sleep. I rose and fumblingly relieved myself at the edge of the safe zone at least once, kicking the soiled straw against the wall. No one brought me food or water. That didn't matter. I wasn't hungry. During my increasingly rare moments of lucidity, I tried to figure out a way to escape with my hands chained and my strength fading. There wasn't one.

At first, I thought the knocking on my cell door was just another symptom of iron poisoning. I groaned, burying my face in the straw. The knocking continued, getting louder. Lifting my head, I shouted, "Go away!"

The knocking stopped. I sighed, content in the knowledge that I'd vanquished my hallucinations. I wasn't completely crazy yet.

And then I heard Quentin whisper, "This one! She's in here!"

My eyes snapped open. "Quentin?" At least I was hallucinating people I liked. That was a nice change.

"It's okay," he said. "We're getting you out of here."

A hallucination wouldn't say that. A hallucination would bring me a blanket and offer to hold my hair while I threw up. "You're real."

"Um, yeah." He sounded unsure. "Are you . . . Toby, are you okay?"

"You can't be here." I slumped back to the floor. "It's death to be here."

"Just relax, okay?" A barred window scraped open in my door, letting a dim glow into the room. Quentin's face appeared in the opening. "Guys, she doesn't look so good . . ."

"Move aside," said Tybalt, stepping into view. The light brightened as he approached. I flinched away, closing my eyes. I'd been in the dark too long.

"Turn it down," I whispered.

"I'm sorry," said Tybalt, earnestly. The light receded. "Can you stand?"

"I can barely breathe." I opened my eyes. "Are you real?"

"Real as I've ever been. Connor, we've found her."

"Thank Maeve." Connor's face appeared next to Tybalt's, looking as pale and worried as the rest. Some of the worry vanished when he saw me, replaced by relief. "Hang on, Toby. We'll have you out in a second." He ducked out of sight. A steady scraping noise began. "I told you teaching me how to pick locks wasn't a waste of time."

"Don't touch the door!" I protested. "It's iron!"

"I know," he said, unperturbed. The scraping noises continued.

"Connor left his skin in my Court," said Tybalt.

"What?" A skinshifter without his skin was essentially human. Connor wouldn't even be able to see large portions of Faerie without the aid of faerie ointment. "Why—"

"Got it." Connor stood, coming back into view. This time I was looking closely enough to see the faerie ointment ringing his eye. "Get back as far as you can."

I had just enough time to roll to the edge of the clean zone before the door swung open, banging against the wall. The sound sent sympathetic vibrations through the iron in my blood, and I whimpered. Tybalt stepped into the room, letting out his breath in a low, angry hiss as he got his first good look at me.

"She's chained," he said, deceptively calm, "I can't move her with iron on her."

"Coming." Connor pushed past him, ignoring the iron

in the doorframe. Mortality has its advantages. Then he stopped, eyes widening. "Oh, *Toby* . . ."

"I look like hell," I mumbled, closing my eyes. "Point taken, move on."

"I'm sorry," he said. I heard him kneel, and he gripped my wrists. I whimpered. He stroked my hair one-handed, saying, "Relax. I'll have these off in a second."

"Be fast," said Quentin. "The guards are gonna be coming down here to check on her any minute."

"What did you guys *do*?" I asked.

"A minor diversion," said Tybalt.

"There are seventy rose goblins enchanted to look like three hundred rampaging through the Court," said Connor.

There was a snap as the lock on the manacles gave way. I opened my eyes and pulled my hands around, staring at them. My head was already starting to clear. The pain and the low, chattering hum of iron were still there, but I could think again. "You have to get out of here," I said.

"What?" Quentin stuck his head into the room. He was wearing leather gloves thick enough to let him knock without hurting himself. "What do you mean?"

"Get out," I repeated, pushing myself up onto one elbow. "Leave me and get the hell out before the guards show up and give you cells of your own."

"No," said Tybalt.

I glared at him. "Just listen to me for once. I'm not worth this. Get out and save the others. Stop Oleander."

"Not without you," said Connor. I turned toward him again, distracted enough to miss Tybalt moving into position behind me until he was scooping me off the floor.

"Hey!" I yelped.

"Hey, yourself," he said, walking toward the door. "Connor, leave the shackles."

"You don't have to tell me twice," he said, following.

"This is suicide," I said.

"If it's suicide, it's our choice," said Quentin. "You can't stop us."

"I'm getting that," I said, letting my head drop and closing my eyes. The rolling motion of Tybalt's steps was almost enough to lull me back to sleep—an honest sleep this time, brought on by exhaustion, not hopelessness and terror.

We were halfway up the last flight of stairs when Tybalt spoke again. "Did you think I could walk away and let you die?" I didn't answer. He shook me, demanding, "*Did* you?"

"Easy, Tybalt!" said Connor. "She's sick."

Tybalt subsided. I could still hear him growling in the back of his throat. "She'll recover."

"Not if you break her first."

"I won't," said Tybalt. He took another step. "October, are you awake?"

I considered lying, but cleared my throat and whispered, "Barely."

"We're going to take the Shadow Roads."

"What?" I opened my eyes, staring up at him. His face was only a foot away, but it was blurry and hard to focus on. "Tybalt, I can't—"

"You have to," he said, gently. "There's no other way out of here."

"I'll suffocate." Not long before, I'd been waiting to die; now, I wanted to avoid it if I could. It's amazing how quickly things can change.

"You won't. Not if you trust me and hold your breath. Can you do that?"

"I . . ." I realized that he'd try to take the overland route if I said I couldn't handle the Shadow Roads. Quentin and Connor couldn't move through the shadows without him, and all three would die or be imprisoned for the crime of trying to save me. I wasn't worth their lives; if they'd made it this far, I wouldn't stop them from making it the rest of the way. "Do what you need to."

He kissed my forehead, whispering, "Hold your breath." Quentin gave him a sidelong look. Tybalt quelled it with a look of his own. Then he tensed and took a great leap forward, throwing himself into a running start. Quentin and Connor grabbed his belt, straining to keep up. I took a deep breath and closed my eyes, and Tybalt dragged us all into the shadows.

The world turned to ice, making me feel like going to sleep would be not just comforting, but final. I screwed my eyes more tightly closed, hands seeking Tybalt's arm and clinging. I'd been through these shadows before. I could make it out the other side, if I could just hold on . . .

Sometimes I think Tybalt times our little runs to match the absolute limit of what I can take. I was about to breathe in when we broke through into warmth and light once more, Quentin and Connor coughing and wheezing behind us. It was too much light; even with my eyes closed, it burned. I whimpered, burying my face against Tybalt's chest. He covered my head with one hand, barking an order, and the lights dimmed until I could look up and slowly open my eyes.

We were in an alley. The streetlights were swathed in fabric; that explained how Tybalt could have them dimmed. Cait Sidhe in feline and human forms watched from every flat surface. What I could see of the skyline reflected Berkeley by night, with the familiar form of the University clock tower rising above everything else. We were outside San Francisco. I was as safe as I could get without leaving the Kingdom entirely.

That was all the encouragement I needed. "Tybalt?"

"Yes?"

"Are we safe now?"

"Fairly, yes." He sounded amused. I lifted my head to face him, and frowned at the undiluted relief in his eyes.

Looking at him, you'd think saving me was some sort of miracle. "The Queen's guards can't enter my Court without my consent."

"Good," I said, closing my eyes on the strange satisfaction in his expression. There was too much iron in my blood, and I was too tired; I couldn't cope. "Wake me when the world ends."

"Your wish is my command," he said.

I would normally have called him on that. I'm not normally exhausted and trying to shake off a bad case of iron poisoning after an unexpected run down the Shadow Roads. I went limp against his chest, trusting him to hold me up, and slipped into a deep, dreamless sleep.

TWENTY-EIGHT

"**O**CTOBER."

The voice was distant enough to be of no concern; if people wanted to talk to me from a million miles away, that was their problem, not mine. The iron singing in my blood was doing its best to drown out everything else. It was almost like being back in Blind Michael's mists—that horrible place where there was nothing but suffering and songs I never quite understood—except for one crucial difference: when I was in Blind Michael's mists, I didn't hurt. Sure, I was the captive of a mad First-born who planned to make me his unwilling bride, but I wasn't in pain when he wasn't actually beating me.

Now that I had the cold gray fog of iron-song burning through me, I was starting to wonder whether that hadn't been the better deal.

"October, please."

The voice hovered on the very the edge of the category I'd internally dubbed "almost worth bothering to pay attention to." I wanted to tell whoever it was to shut up, go away, and let me fall back into pain-free oblivion, but I couldn't get my body to obey me. It was vexing as hell.

"I know you can hear me."

Did he? Something in the tone made me realize I knew the speaker: Tybalt. Oh, well. If anyone had the right to bother me while I was trying to figure out whether I was going to die, it was probably him.

"Please listen." He paused. The nuances of his tone were becoming clearer. I couldn't move—Oberon's balls, I couldn't even tell him he was right about my being able to hear him—but I could at least try to figure out what he was talking about.

The pause lengthened, stretching out until I thought he might have changed his mind and gone away. Then, much closer, like he was whispering in my ear: "What she did, what your mother did, you've done it before. Your scent was different when you left the pond. That's why I followed you so closely those first few months. I was trying to decide whether you were you, or something else, trying to trick us all. The changes were subtler, but they were there. You did it to yourself to break the bastard's spell."

There was real hatred in his tone when he mentioned Simon. That might have been a surprise, if I hadn't been preoccupied with the dual stresses of pain and paying attention. I filed the surprise away for later.

"I don't know whose child your mother is, which of the Three made her, but it's time to stop letting her lies define you. She's Firstborn, October, and you're the only child of her line I've ever known. You can change your blood if you have reason enough. And Toby . . . humans don't die of iron. They die of time, but not of iron."

His breath was hot on my cheek. I realized, with a dim lack of surprise, that this wasn't the first time he'd tried to talk me back from the edge of dying: I really *did* hear him begging me to live on that long-gone day

when Devin's hired lackey shot me and sent me staggering into the Tea Gardens to bleed to death.

"Shift yourself the other way. Be as human as you
can, and survive." He paused. Something touched the
side of my face, too faint to be identified as anything but
contact—kiss or slap, my iron-riddled body couldn't tell
the difference. And then, quieter still: "Don't leave me
again. Please."

And he was gone, leaving me alone in the darkness
where the iron sang songs of suffering and eternity. With
a sigh that felt a thousand times too large for my aching
body, I surrendered and let myself topple back into the
black. Tybalt's words had been a nice dream, but they
were silent now.

Only the iron remained.

Another voice, some untold time later; this one was
tired, and sounded almost disinterested as it asked, "Is
passing out your hobby or something? Because if I
were you, I'd get a better one. Like, I don't know, bank
robbery."

"What?" The fact that I could answer surprised me
into opening my eyes. I found myself looking at an
oaken ceiling covered in a coat of dust thick enough to
give Hobs heart failure. I didn't recognize it. I searched
for words, settling for: "Where am I?"

"Like you don't know? Welcome back to the Court of
Cats." The speaker coughed. "What's left of it, anyway."

I grudgingly turned my head, eyes widening as I saw
the tiger-striped changeling sprawled on a pallet of
crumpled rags to my left. "Julie?"

"Currently. Check back in a few hours and you may
get a different answer." Sweat matted her hair into
cherry-red spirals, and her voice was raspy and strained.
That's probably why it took me so long to realize who
she was. "Forgive me for not getting up and killing you,
but I hurt too much to move."

The iron in my blood still ached, but it had faded while I was floating in the black; it wasn't singing any more, and it barely even burned. "What's wrong?"

"Where do I start?" She closed her eyes. "First I think I'm going to die, and then Tybalt puts you in the room where I'm trying to get better. This keeps getting less and less like fun."

"At least you're not dead." I tested my limits by ordering one unwilling arm to move. It lifted with a minimum of protest. Emboldened by success, I sat up. When this didn't make me black out or vomit, I pushed myself to my feet, ready to grab the nearest wall if the world started spinning. It didn't seem inclined to. Bit by careful bit, I relaxed. "Right now, that's about the only positive thing I can see about the situation."

"True. You're finally a felon, or whatever it's called when the Queen wants you dead." She opened her eyes, giving me an interested look. "Do you think they'll torture you when they catch you? Before the execution, I mean. Which should be televised."

"Good to see that you're as upbeat as ever. How long have I been here?"

"Long enough for Tybalt to freak out twice because you didn't look right, four times because he was sure the royal guard had been beating you, and six times because you weren't waking up. It's been a big circus of psychodrama. Thanks for that." Julie shifted on her pallet. "It's no fun around here when our lord and master isn't slamming people into walls for breathing too loudly in your presence."

"Uh-huh," I said, looking around.

We were in what looked like an abandoned hunting lodge; dust and debris covered every surface, save for the spots that had been swept clean to make room for more pallets. Each held one or more Cait Sidhe, all as worn and sick as Julie. A fire blazed in a vast fireplace that took up most of the far wall. It was obviously sustained by magic—real fires don't burn that high for long without getting out of control.

Cat-form Cait Sidhe covered the hearth, furry bodies obscuring the stone. The room must not have been as dark as I thought at first. My eyes adjusted quickly, picking out surprisingly clear details, like the pattern on a dozing calico.

"You going to stand there all day?" Julie asked. "I bet the King would appreciate knowing you're not planning to play Sleeping Beauty."

"I don't even know where I am," I said, keeping a careful distance from her. She said she was too sick to attack me, but I wasn't taking any chances. "I mean, besides the Cat's Court."

"You shouldn't know." She shook her head, and winced. "Ow."

"It still hurts?"

The look she shot me was pure hostility. "I bet there's some of that poison left, if you want to try it for yourself. Get a firsthand idea of what this feels like."

"I'll pass. I've been abused enough this week." I pushed my hair back, noting that my hands were entirely healed. That was something. "Still planning to kill me?"

"As soon as I get the chance."

"Why?"

She paused. "What do you mean, 'why'?"

Maybe this wasn't the time to try convincing her to drop her vendetta—the Queen had her own vendetta, and I doubted Tybalt could stop her by bouncing her off the walls the way he did Julie—but it was worth a shot. I needed this to be over. I missed my friend, and I didn't need the extra enemies.

"I mean exactly what I said. Why are you still trying to kill me?"

Bitterly, she spat, "You killed Ross." Ross was Julie's lover, and he died when an assassin sent to kill me didn't judge his aim quite the right way. Devin's assassin. I was starting to feel like I'd be spending the rest of my life cleaning up that man's messes.

"I didn't kill him." I forced myself to keep looking at her. I started this confrontation; I was going to deal with it. "I blame myself for a lot of deaths—it feels like more all the time—but I didn't kill him."

"He got shot by a man who was aiming for you. What do you call that?"

"Bad timing. Neither Lily nor I knew the assassin was there. If we'd known . . ." I shook my head. "If I'd had any idea, I wouldn't have taken you down that hill. I didn't mean to let anyone get hurt. I'm sorry. But I didn't kill him."

She glared for a moment longer before the expression faded, replaced by confusion. "You mean that."

"By oak and ash and thorn, I mean it."

"So he died for nothing?"

That stopped me. Ross's death was a tragedy . . . and in the end, it changed nothing but my relationship with Julie. "Julie—"

Her eyes narrowed. "Did he die for nothing?"

Reluctantly, I answered, "Yes."

"Yeah." She slumped, turning away. "He wasn't going to live forever, but he should have lived longer than he did."

"I'm sorry."

"You keep saying that."

"I mean it."

"That makes it worse." She waved a hand, shooing me away. "I hurt too much to kill you, and I can't forgive you if I can't choose not to kill you. Go find my damn King before he breaks something, okay?"

"Right," I said, heart sinking, and turned to walk away.

"Toby?"

"Yeah?" I looked over my shoulder. Julie was watching me, eyes narrowed.

"Don't get killed. I know you got that guy to fix things, and . . . and we won't know who to pay our debts to if you die."

I smiled. That was the closest she was going to come to telling me to be careful. "I'll try."

"Good." She put her head down again. I turned, heading for the door.

Crossing the room was like walking through a living jigsaw puzzle. Most of the Cait Sidhe were unconscious or asleep; the others moved sluggishly, winding up underfoot at the worst possible moment. I wasn't dizzy, but that didn't mean I was running at full speed. I had to stop and brace myself several times while I got my breath back, waiting for the equally miserable-looking cats to move out of the way.

They all seemed to be breathing; that was a small blessing, at least. If Walther's antidote worked, Tybalt wouldn't lose any more of his people.

The hall on the other side of the door obviously belonged to another building, with ivy-patterned carpet and gilded chandeliers loaded with mismatched candles. I kept a hand against the stained wallpaper as I walked, doing my best not to look up. The third time I stopped to rest I realized I was clean, and that I wasn't wearing the clothes I was locked up in; they'd been replaced by a floor-length velvet robe that smelled like pennyroyal and fabric softener. My hair was loose and brushed smooth. I was hungry, but not excessively so; they'd been keeping me fed, somehow. Weak, yes; starving, no.

"I hope they didn't lose my jacket," I muttered, and started walking again.

It took me almost twenty minutes to reach the end of the hall—some showing for the big, bad knight. I was leaning against the wall, panting, when a door swung open and Raj stepped through, carrying a glass bottle full of something fizzy and fire truck red. He froze when he saw me, faintly feline ears flicking briefly back.

"Hi," I said, waving weakly.

Raj tried to speak, and failed. Licking his lips, he tried again: "Toby?"

"Yeah, it's me. Look, I'm kind of lo—" That's as far as I got before he dropped the bottle, leaping for me. He might have gotten himself smacked aside if I'd been feeling better; as it was, he threw his arms around my neck before I could decide whether to dodge. The bottle hit the ground with a soft clunk, rolling to rest against the wall.

And I realized he was crying.

"Hey, it's okay." I patted him awkwardly on the back. "I'm here."

The words made him cling more tightly. His tears were silent; instead of sobbing, he was purring. Cait Sidhe don't purr much in public, and most of them don't like to have it pointed out. I kept patting.

"I'm tired and in pain, but I'm going to be fine," I said. "My head doesn't even hurt much."

"We were sure—I mean, Uncle Tybalt was sure—" His voice faltered as he pulled away, wiping his eyes with the back of one hand. "You went to sleep, and you wouldn't wake up, and you still look so *strange*. We thought you were gonna die."

"Well, I didn't. I'm real, and I'm me. Promise."

"You really promise?"

"I really do. Life's been weird, but I'm still me."

He smiled brilliantly, giving me another hug. This time I returned it, tightening my arms around him before he pulled away. "I was scared," he admitted.

"So was I," I said, and pointed to the bottle. "You dropped that."

"Oh!" He went red and hurried to retrieve it. "This is yours."

I took the bottle when he offered it to me, and frowned. The liquid was even brighter when I looked at it closely. "What is it?"

"Walther made it. We've been giving it to you every three hours for the last two days. It's supposed to make the iron in your blood stop hurting you and let your body wash it out faster."

I paused. "Two *days?*"

He nodded. "That's how long you've been asleep."

"Wow." I gave him a third hug, this time one-armed. He nestled against my side, resuming his purring as I uncapped the bottle and sniffed the contents. "It smells like mulberries."

"Sometimes it smells like bananas or artichokes," said Raj.

"Right," I said, and chugged it. I was immediately glad I'd taken that approach—it tasted like pickles and peanut butter, but I'd swallowed most of it before I started gagging. Coughing, I handed the empty bottle back to Raj. "I slept through *that?*"

"For two days," he confirmed.

"I must have really been out of it." I shuddered, shoving my hair back with both hands. I didn't even flinch when my thumb hit the still-unfamiliar edge of my ear. "Think your uncle might want to see me?"

"I think he'll kill me if I don't take you to him."

"That would be bad. Lead the way."

He walked back through the door he'd emerged from, slow enough for me keep up. I accepted the courtesy without comment, keeping a hand on his shoulder, as much for balance as to comfort him. We passed through half a dozen rooms, taking twice as many rest breaks, before we stepped through what looked like a plain brick wall and into an open alley.

The setup was familiar: mattresses at the end of the alley, crates blocking the entrance, tattered tapestries draped over the trash cans. The silence, on the other hand, was strange. There were no cats there, no lounging Cait Sidhe in either human or feline form. It felt like we were walking into a hospital waiting room.

A small knot of people was gathered near the alley's mouth, some standing, some sitting, none quite looking at the others. They just continued the impression of walking into a hospital; the family of the terminal patient, waiting to hear whether it was time for grief or elation.

Quentin saw us first. He'd been leaning against the wall with his hands in his pockets and his chin canted down, a light morning wind teasing his darkening hair into knots. My robe rustled as we emerged, and Quentin turned toward us. "Hey, Raj," he began. "How is—" His eyes widened, and he took off running, shouting, "Toby! *Toby!*"

The others turned when Quentin started shouting. Connor was the first on his feet, a disbelieving grin spreading across his face. Tybalt was on his feet half a beat behind, wide-eyed and suddenly pale. He looked like a man who wasn't sure whether to cry or start looking for the catch.

I was too focused on Quentin to comment on anyone else's reaction. "Careful!" I said, holding out my hands to stop him. "You have to be gentle. I'm still sore."

He skidded to a stop a few feet away, beaming. "I knew you'd come back."

"I didn't go anywhere," I said, smiling back. It felt good to be outside, even with the buildings blocking most of the light. For the first time in days, it felt good to be alive.

"Yes, you did."

I didn't have time to argue. Tybalt's approach was as swift as Quentin's, if more decorous and substantially quieter. I didn't see him make his way down the alley; he was just suddenly there, stopping behind Quentin and looking at me like he wasn't sure it was safe to come any closer.

"October?" he whispered.

My smile didn't waver as I turned it on him. "Hey."

"I ... hello." He sounded hopeful and scared at once, like admitting hope would cause me to collapse into dust. Quentin stepped aside, leaving Tybalt and I facing one another. "I assume this means you're feeling better?"

"A little bit." My smile softened, until I was certain I had to look like a total idiot. Somehow, I couldn't find it in myself to care. I stepped forward, narrowing the gap Quentin left behind. "Sorry I didn't listen to you before. I think I was too out of it. I probably would have hurt myself if I'd tried."

He blinked, pupils narrowing. "You heard me?"

"Every word."

"Ah." He raised a hand to cup my cheek. We stood that way, frozen in a moment I couldn't quite name, but never wanted to have end.

Everything ends. Connor stepped up next to me, touching my arm like he didn't believe I was real. Tybalt stepped away, and I turned to face Connor, offering him the same smile. "You jerk," he whispered, and pulled me into a tight embrace. "You had us all scared out of our minds."

"I'm not that easy to break." I let my head rest against his shoulder.

"We weren't so sure of that," said Tybalt. I pulled away from Connor as I turned to face him. Connor let go with obvious reluctance, and so I took a small step backward, letting my shoulder blades graze his chest. The solidity of him was a comfort beyond measure. Voice even, Tybalt continued, "That was the worst case of iron poisoning I've ever seen. You had us all seeing visions of the night-haunts. How many times do you have to die before you stay buried?"

"How long was I in the cell?" I asked.

"A little over two days," said Quentin.

"Two *days?*" I squeaked, leaning on Connor to steady myself. Two days in that cell explained why I still felt shaky: iron can be fatal in less time than that.

"Sylvester kept trying to argue or find a way to get you out of it, but the Queen blocked everything. You were going to be executed in the morning," said Connor. "That's why I was willing to leave my skin here if it meant getting you out."

"Oh, root and branch," I breathed, shuddering. Connor put a hand on my shoulder, bracing me. "I . . ."

"It's okay," said Connor. "We know."

"All three of you could have died."

"We didn't," said Tybalt, implacably.

"You could have."

"And you *would* have. Don't argue with me, Toby, we'll both lose. Did Raj give you your medicine?" The look Tybalt shot at Raj made it clear that a "no" wouldn't bode well for the young prince.

"It's disgusting," I said flatly. "He said Walther made it. I assume that means he knows you got me out?"

"Unfortunately, yes. You'd have died of iron poisoning if it weren't for him." Tybalt reached over to brush my hair back, fingers lingering against the tip of my ear. I could practically feel Connor glaring. "Are you adjusting?"

"Not sure yet." I sighed. "I think the Luidaeg and I need to have a little question and answer session when this is all over." So many of the things she'd said to me were starting to make sense. I'd been missing the context I needed to understand them.

"May told us what Amandine did," Quentin said. "It seems . . ." His voice trailed off. He didn't have the vocabulary to express what she'd done to me. That was all right. Neither did I.

"Bizarre? Tell me about it." I looked to Tybalt again. "Did the antidote work?"

"Yes." He smiled. "My people are recovering."

"And Luna?"

The smile faded. "The Duchess isn't well."

"We've treated the roses, but she's getting worse," said Connor.

"That's not acceptable." I looked around the group. "I have to find Oleander."

"You're not leaving here," said Tybalt.

"You're right," I said. Before the looks of relief on the people around me could get too entrenched, I added, "Not until after I've put on some real clothes, had a real meal, and drunk about a pot of coffee. Is there coffee?"

"October—" started Connor.

I pulled away. "We can't hide here forever; either I find Oleander, or I get executed the first time I go home. You *know* Tybalt would get sick of us."

"Perhaps some of you," said Tybalt, sounding grudgingly amused.

I looked from face to face. All these people were such vital parts of my life, and I was asking them to let me go again. The trouble was, they knew me well enough to understand why I didn't have a choice.

"So." I turned my attention back on Tybalt, and smiled. "Breakfast?"

TWENTY-NINE

"NO. ABSOLUTELY NOT."

I glanced up from the vital business of trying to construct a sandwich from French toast, rubbery fried eggs, bacon, and strawberry jam. "What's this objection to?"

"You are not leaving here without me."

"Ah. Yeah, I am. Sorry about that." I used a liberal amount of syrup to compensate for the sandwich's lack of structural integrity and took several messy, wonderful bites before continuing, "I wish I could take you. I really do. But the Queen has to suspect you were involved in breaking me out, if she doesn't already know. Your subjects need you too much for me to let you put yourself in danger for me again."

Tybalt glared but didn't argue. I offered an apologetic smile in return.

"Bet you're sorry you fed me, huh?"

"There are many things I'm sorry to have done."

Half an hour ago, I was barely staying upright under my own power. It's amazing what a difference a solid meal makes. Even better, Tybalt had returned my clothes, including my jacket; freshly cleaned and smelling as strongly of pennyroyal as it did when he first gave it to me. I suspected he'd been wearing it while I was knocked out. Somehow, I couldn't find it in me to mind.

I've always been a fast healer, but this bordered on ridiculous. One more side effect of Amandine's little parlor trick, and one more thing to discuss with the Luidaeg. Silly me, I always assumed accelerated healing was a Daoine Sidhe thing that just didn't come up often in company that didn't make a habit of brawling.

"You can't go alone," said Connor, in a carefully non-offensive, "Toby isn't thinking things through again" tone. "Assuming you're in your right mind—which you might not be after the last week—running in alone is begging for trouble."

"I don't even know why you think you're going to find Oleander," said Quentin. "Won't she be hiding?"

"She's cocky, and she wants me to think I'm going crazy," I said. "She won't be able to resist showing herself if I come looking." It was so much easier to think without iron and poison clouding my mind, and with half a pot of coffee in my belly. I wasn't sure what diner Tybalt had arranged to have raided, or whether they'd been paid, but the coffee was strong, and everything else was at least edible. That was all I cared about. "Besides, who said I was going alone?"

Connor frowned. "You said—"

"I said Tybalt couldn't come, and I have good reason for that," I said, trying not to let myself notice the hurt look on his face. He might see my logic. That wouldn't make him like it. "Raj, you're out, too. The Court of Cats is already too involved in this, and the last thing I want to do is give the Queen an excuse to start trouble."

"She can try," said Tybalt icily.

"I'll go," said Quentin.

"No, you won't," I said. Quentin added his own

wounded look to the one Raj was already giving me. I finished my coffee before saying, "I need you here. The Queen might not connect a random foster with my escape, but Raysel will. Until we know whether she's reported your disappearance to the Queen, we can't risk it."

"My parents will be *so* proud if I get kicked out of the Kingdom of the Mists," deadpanned Quentin.

"Who, then?" asked Tybalt. His tone was quiet, and still cold. He knew what I was going to say, and I knew from the look on his face that he wasn't happy about it.

I took a deep breath. "I'm taking Connor." Connor looked startled, then pleased. "Even if everyone at Shadowed Hills is watching for the escaped felon, they're not going to be watching for *him*. He knows the knowe as well as I do, if not better by this point, and most importantly, all the locks are keyed to him."

"And if someone assumes his absence has been unwilling, rather than because he was a part of your rescue?" Tybalt narrowed his eyes, all but glaring at Connor. "There are those who will be happy to say he was forced, and use that as justification for harming you."

"Yeah, but I'm not one of them," said Connor. "People know Toby and I were close in the past. The courtiers in the Duchy also know that my wife's been a little bit unhinged lately. They're going to assume I ran to Roan Rathad after Toby was arrested, and Sylvester will support that."

The two men glared at each other. Unexpectedly, Tybalt was the first to look away. "I don't like this," he muttered.

"You don't have to." I wiped my syrupy hands on a napkin and stood. "Connor, how did you get here?"

"I took the bus." He grimaced as he rose to follow. "Not so helpful, huh?"

"Not unless we want to be the cavalry of public transportation." I sighed. "There's another option. Is there a phone around here?"

Quentin pulled a cellular phone from his pocket and offered it to me. "I don't like this either," he said, "but here."

I took the phone, relaxing slightly as I saw the crest of Tamed Lightning etched into the plastic. Countess April O'Leary of Tamed Lightning is an ally, and more, she's a techno-Dryad—something that may be completely unique in Faerie, and was only possible because of her adopted mother's particular mix of Daoine Sidhe and Tylwyth Teg heritage. Her skill at adapting modern electronics to work in the Summerlands makes her the envy of every Gremlin in the Kingdom. If this was one of April's phones, it was secure.

"Cool," I said, flipping the phone open and dialing.

Danny picked up on the second ring. "McReady's Taxi."

"Danny? It's me."

"Toby!" His voice boomed through the phone loudly enough for everyone to hear. "Fuck's sake, girly, I thought you were—" He cut himself off. "Never mind what I thought. You safe? You need me? Where are you—no, wait. Don't tell me where you are if it's not safe. When they said you'd escaped, I thought—"

"Danny!" I hated to interrupt, but I didn't have time for him to calm down on his own. "Connor and I need a ride to Shadowed Hills. Are you available?"

"You, ah, sure that's a good idea? What with the Queen and the sentence of death and everything? Not saying I won't do it—pretty sure she's gunning for me already, after the way I mouthed off at your trial—just it might not be the safest thing you could do."

"I have to."

"In that case, I'm yours. Just say where."

"Great." I cupped a hand over the receiver. "Tybalt? Where are we?"

He sighed, muttering, "I shouldn't tell you," before adding, in a normal tone, "The exit will place you at the corner of Derby and Telegraph."

"Okay." To the phone, I said, "Berkeley. Derby and Telegraph."

"Be there in ten," said Danny, and hung up.

I tossed Quentin his phone. "Come on, Connor. He'll be here in ten minutes. You guys . . . just be safe. I'll be back as soon as I can." I spread my fingers, filling them with shadows, and almost lost hold again as my magic rose eagerly to answer. It was too fast; I didn't know how to control it. Forcing myself to keep breathing, I wove the cut grass and copper strands into a human disguise, throwing it over myself and letting my hands unclench. It was easy; too easy.

"Your magic smells funny," said Raj, bemused.

He was right. The copper was too sharp, like fresh-minted pennies. There'd be time to think about that later. Not letting myself hesitate, I turned, gesturing for Connor to follow. We almost made it before Tybalt caught up with us, grabbing my arm and spinning me to face him. I raised my eyes to his, barely aware of holding my breath.

"Come back to me," he said. Then he let go, shoving me away as he turned and stalked back to the table. Quentin had his head down and his shoulders locked as he pretended to focus on his breakfast. Raj was staring after us, looking heartbroken. I looked at them. Then I shook my head, mouthed, "I'm sorry," and kept going.

The transition between the Court of Cats and the Berkeley street was smooth, depositing us outside in the cool of evening. I breathed deeply, realizing as I did that this was the first time I'd been allowed to breathe mortal air since my trial. I didn't have to look back to know that the entrance to the Court of Cats would be gone; Tybalt was too smart to leave it open, no matter how much he didn't want us to leave.

"Hey." Connor touched my elbow lightly.

"Hey." I slanted a smile in his direction. "Like the new look?"

He laughed unsteadily, dropping his hand away from my elbow and threading his fingers through mine. I didn't pull away, but stepped closer, resting my head against his shoulder and letting the heat coming off his skin warm me through. "To be honest, I don't know. But you're not dead, and that's good enough for me."

There didn't seem to be anything I could say to that. We stayed that way, waiting, until a battered green taxi-cab roared around the corner and screeched to a stop in front of us. It had barely stopped when Danny launched himself out of the driver's-side door, charging around the car and sweeping me into a massive hug. My feet left the ground, and I found myself faced with an interesting predicament: kick my ride to Shadowed Hills in the knee, or suffocate?

Connor solved the issue by tapping Danny on the arm—as high as he could reach—and saying apologetically, "I don't think she can breathe."

"Aw, hell!" Danny put me down, grinning ear-to-ear as he clapped his hands down on my shoulders. "You're alive!"

"I am. But we need to get moving. Can I fill you in on the way?"

"Yeah, yeah. Here." He opened the passenger door for me, waving me to get in. "Seal-boy, you're in back. Not that I don't like you, but it's a chivalry thing."

"I understand," said Connor. He started toward the car, only to stop dead as two of Danny's Barghests stuck their heads out the window. They were panting, venomous fangs retracted and tongues lolling.

"What?" demanded Danny. I pointed to the Barghests, fighting to keep myself from laughing. Understanding dawned. Danny grinned. "That's Iggy and Lou. Don't worry; they don't bite unless you poke 'em. They may drool a little, but it ain't acid or nothin'. That's a myth."

"They're . . . Barghests," said Connor carefully, in case we hadn't noticed.

"Yeah." Tone turning crafty, Danny asked, "You want one?"

It was too much. I burst out laughing, managing to say, "No, Danny, Connor doesn't want a Barghest." Then, because Danny looked so hurt by the idea that Connor wouldn't want one of his pets, I added, "It wouldn't get along with the rose goblins."

"True enough," said Danny, mollified. "Well, get on in."

Connor shot me a frantic look. I shrugged, gesturing to the backseat as I climbed into the front. A little Barghest drool wasn't going to kill him.

One of the Barghests stuck its head up between the seats. I scratched it behind the ears while we waited for Connor to get over his monster issues. "Which one's this?"

"Lou," said Danny. "She's my good girl, aren't you, Lou?" The Barghest commenced to licking his face with enthusiasm. "I tell you, even if I can find homes for the rest, these two are staying."

"Good to know," I said. The back door shut as Connor finally got in, and I was saved from making any more small talk about Danny's literal "pet" project as the Bridge Troll hit the gas and sent us rocketing into traffic.

"Now," he said. "Talk."

So I talked. Starting with what I'd been doing at Shadowed Hills when I was arrested, and jumping from there to the trial. Describing the cell where I'd been held was more upsetting than I'd expected; by the time I finished, I was staring fixedly at my hands to keep myself from seeing the looks on their faces.

Silence held in the car for several minutes, broken only by the sound of traffic and the panting of the Barghests. Finally, Danny said, "Yeah, but ... how in the hell'd you get run through the pencil sharpener?" I glanced up. Mistaking my surprise for confusion, he mimed a point over his own disguised ear. "Word on the street is you've got a hope chest you didn't turn in to the authorities."

That startled me into a sharp, barking laugh. "Are you kidding? People think I did this to *myself?*"

"People talk when they don't got the truth," he said implacably.

"I gave the only hope chest I've ever seen to the Queen," I said. "My mother did this to me."

"Your ma has a hope chest?"

"No, Danny. She did it to me on her own."

"Oh." Danny paused to mull this over. Finally, he said, "So your ma, she's not Daoine Sidhe, then."

"No."

"Oh. Well." He paused again before shrugging. "That makes a lot of sense."

I stared at him. "Glad it makes sense to one of us."

"C'mon, kiddo, you thought what? That Daoine Sidhe were made of rubber or something? Half the shit you do shoulda killed you *years* ago."

"He's right," said Connor, abruptly. "I don't know why we didn't see it."

"Because we didn't want to." I slumped in my seat. "If we saw it, we'd have to deal with it, and with everybody saying she was Daoine Sidhe, and me being too weak to worry about, it got to stay invisible."

"A lot of things make more sense now," said Connor.

"Yeah," I agreed. "They do."

We were approaching the Caldecott Tunnel. Tunnels represent an essential difference between humans and fae. When the population of Berkeley and Oakland filled the available space and needed to expand, mankind found a way to run the road right through the mountain. The fae would have picked the mountain up and put it down someplace less inconvenient. The idea of driving a permanent road through the middle would have never occurred to us.

When did that turn into an "us"? When did I stop thinking of myself as human?

"Uh, Toby? Not to distract you while you're brooding and all, but we may have a problem." Danny's voice was level. Too level. Anyone who sounds that calm and isn't actually sedated is upset about something.

I tensed. "What is it?"

"Look in the mirror."

Connor leaned over the back of the seat as I craned my neck to see the rearview mirror, both of us studying the same view of the road behind us. Three of the visible cars were surrounded by an odd yellow haze, like someone had smeared honey on the glass. "What the hell is that?" I asked, twisting around to look directly at the road.

The three cars weren't there—instead, there were three holes in traffic that could be easily blamed on cars with strong don't-look-here charms on them, if I wanted to be that paranoid . . . and after the past week, I couldn't afford not to be.

"That's a don't-look-here," Danny grunted, putting a hand on my shoulder and pushing me back into my seat. "Mirror's Gremlin work. Same place as does my speed charms. You may wanna check your seat belt."

I wear a seat belt as a matter of habit. That didn't stop me from double-checking the clasp. I could hear Connor doing the same thing. "What are you going to do?"

"Just watch the mirror," he muttered, gunning the engine and cutting off several startled drivers as we plunged into the tunnel. He was accelerating rapidly toward the tunnel's main curve. There's no following visibility around that turn—you have to go with it and trust you're going slowly enough not to slam into anyone. Given that the taxi was rapidly cresting toward ninety miles an hour, "slowly" wasn't a factor. "Second you can't see them anymore, you throw down a hide-and-seek."

"But I can't—"

"*Do it!*"

A hide-and-seek spell is like a don't-look-here in the sense that both keep people from noticing you. The hide-and-seek is just a little more, well, advanced, which makes them a lot harder to cast. Anyone who's looking when the hide-and-seek goes up won't lose sight of you right away—although they will if, say, you go around a curve or otherwise break their line of sight. That makes hide-and-seek spells safer to cast in traffic, since they don't lead to immediate accidents. It also makes them harder to follow.

I'd never cast a successful hide-and-seek spell in my life, and this seemed like one hell of a time to start trying.

Our car slid around the sheltering curve of the tunnel, blocking the following traffic from view. "*Now!*" Danny roared.

There was no time to argue; they'd be around the curve in a second. I slammed my hands against the ceiling, chanting, "Go make thyself like a nymph o' the sea: be subject to no sight but thine and mine, invisible to every eyeball else!" The smell of grass and new-penny copper filled the car. I dropped my human disguise, grabbing the freed magic and feeding it into the casting I was fighting against. "*The Tempest*, act one, scene two!"

The spell gathered and burst as Danny turned us hard to the right, swerving around a minivan as we blasted into the daylight outside the tunnel. I slumped in my seat, panting and rubbing my forehead.

". . . I think it worked," said Connor, sounding awed.

I risked a glance at the rearview mirror. The yellow-ringed cars were still there, but they'd stopped actively following us, and were weaving in a search pattern. "Oak and holy mother-fucking ash," I breathed, and paused, realizing that my head didn't actually hurt. That was . . . wrong. I should have been groaning and digging for the Tylenol. More quietly, I muttered, "Just how much of my humanity did she *take?*"

"Worry about that later," rumbled Danny. I glanced toward him. His expression was grim. "They've spotted us again. Bitch must've given them tracker charms."

I looked to the mirror. The car at the front of the pack was arrowing after us, and two more flanked it. The fourth car hung back, probably waiting to see what we'd do.

Danny hit the gas, swerving around drivers who didn't see us and didn't react to being cut off. "I didn't want to do this," he announced. "Seal-boy, hang onto the kids, will ya? I don't want them getting banged around. Toby, hang onto the dashboard." After a pause he added, "Also, praying to the sacred ash and all that shit might be good." The engine screamed as he shifted gears. We couldn't maintain this speed for long.

I pressed my hands against the dashboard to brace myself. From the backseat, Connor demanded, "What didn't you want to do? What are you doing?"

"Hopefully proving my mechanic is as good as she says she is." Danny turned toward the barrier in the middle of the upcoming freeway split, driving for the thickest part of the concrete. "Toby, watch the mirror."

"Danny, are you sure this is a—on the right!" One of the cars in the mirror was swerving toward us.

Danny jerked the car to the left. Not fast enough; something I couldn't see slammed into us from behind, knocking me forward with enough force that I nearly hit my forehead on the windshield. Connor made a squawking sound, and the Barghests started to make a noise midway between a bark and a trash compactor. Danny hit the gas, adjusting our trajectory so that we were once again aiming straight for the wall.

It was just a few yards away when we were hit again from behind. Danny shifted gears, and a strange whining noise began vibrating the car. "Trust me!" he shouted, above the sound of the engine, the mechanical keening, and the Barghests.

Then he stomped on the gas, and we plowed into the concrete.

THIRTY

THE WALL FLOWED AROUND US LIKE MIST. I was too busy screaming to notice the moment when it changed from concrete gray to foggy white. Connor was doing the same thing, while the Barghests rattled madly around the backseat, howling their heads off. Danny swore steadily but calmly as he navigated the taxi through the paling gray.

We still hadn't splattered against the retaining wall. I stopped screaming, waving Connor to do the same as I cast a narrow-eyed look in Danny's direction. "What is this?"

"Remember when I said I had an awesome mechanic?" Danny's grin revealed craggy teeth. The car continued to barrel forward. The Barghests and Connor were still making enough noise to constitute a public nuisance—if we'd been someplace with a public, that is. "Turns out I was right." He hit the brake, bringing the car neatly to a halt.

The last of the gray cleared away, revealing the marble birdbath directly in front of us. It was choked with clematis vines and climbing roses, much like the rest of the overgrown garden surrounding us. More roses did their best to block the pathway to the tall stone tower that rose against the skyline ahead of us. I blinked, barely noticing that Connor had stopped screaming. The pathway to my *mother's* tall stone tower.

"Danny?" I said.

"Yeah?"

"Did you just drive your taxi into the Summerlands and park it in the middle of my mother's garden?"

"Pretty much." Danny unfastened his seat belt. "Good thing it worked, huh?"

The implications of that statement were a bit more than I cared to think about just then. I twisted in my seat to face the back, asking, "Connor? You okay?"

"I think I'm going to be sick," he replied faintly. Danny opened the door and the Barghests went rocketing out, making as much noise as they possibly could as they began racing around the garden. Connor winced at the racket before asking, "Are we dead?"

"Not yet. If you're going to barf, don't do it in Mom's birdbath." I undid my own belt and climbed out of the car, stretching to cover the fact that my legs were shaking. "Root and branch, we can *walk* to Shadowed Hills from here."

"You're gonna have to."

I looked toward Danny as Connor got out of the backseat and moved to stand behind me. "No roads?" I ventured.

"That's most of it. The rest is that Connie warned me when she set up the doohickey that it'd leave a trail a mile wide." Danny shook his head, expression going grim. "The Queen's got folks who can open doors to the Summerlands. It won't take them long to track us."

"So we start walking. Come on."

"No. You're going to need something to distract the

folks that chased us in here, and I'm in the mood to punch something. Me and the kids are staying. You just tell your summer home over there," he flapped a hand in the direction of the tower, "to let us in when we ask. We'll hold off the guards till we can't, and then we'll go inside, shut the door, and have a nice nap."

"Danny—"

"Don't argue. It'll just waste time, and they already know I was with you." Danny shrugged. "We're not exactly inconspicuous. Your ma have cable?"

"Not last time I checked." I walked around the car, hugging as much of him as my arms would allow. "This was good."

"Just squaring up for my sister's tab," he said, patting me on the head with one massive hand. "Now get out of here, both of you." He pushed me away. I went.

"Connor, come on." I started for the gate leading to the woods between my mother's land and Sylvester's. He followed. I paused at the garden wall, tapping the stone and whispering, "These three are with me. Let them in, and no one else." Nothing happened—nothing visible—but I knew the tower heard me. When the time came, it would do its best to offer sanctuary to Danny and the Barghests.

The image of what they'd do to Mom's furniture was enough to bring a brief but sincere smile to my face.

"This is definitely turning into one of my more interesting nights," said Connor, following me into the woods outside the garden wall. "What's next?"

"Hopefully, nothing this exciting." The trees around us were citrines, with orange-veined leaves and paper bark. The ground was relatively smooth; citrine trees have deep, narrow roots. "Get in, find Sylvester, and tell him what's going on. Find Oleander. Don't die."

"Got it," he said.

We kept walking. The citrines were replaced by delicate ferns with pearl-white-and-rose fronds that stood taller than our heads. Connor took my hand without saying a word. I squeezed his fingers and kept going as the ferns thinned, replaced by trees with dark green leaves and delicate thorns covering their branches.

"Almost there," said Connor.

"Yeah." The thorny trees gave way to towering ornamental hedges as the Great Hall of Shadowed Hills came into view.

The term "Shadowed Hills" describes a lot of things. It's the Duchy. It's the knowe. It's the Great Hall that houses the Torquill family. In the mortal world, it's just a hill. But in the Summerlands, Shadowed Hills is a manor house spread over three acres of land, saved from castle-hood only by its lack of turrets and a moat. And Sylvester may eventually have those added.

"Something's wrong." Connor tugged me to a halt. "I don't know what it is, but something's wrong."

I frowned, studying the outline of the Great Hall as I tried to find the missing piece of the picture. Then I saw it, and went cold. "Luna's coat of arms is gone." Sylvester's arms were still there, as were the Duchy's, but they were flying at half-mast.

"Do you think she . . . ?"

I didn't even want to dream the words, much less hear them spoken out loud. "Come on," I said, briskly, and started moving again.

There are almost a dozen ways into Shadowed Hills from the Summerlands-side. Connor and I followed the line of hedges past the main door, heading for the nearest servants' entrance. Stacy, Julie, and I used to sneak in that way when we were kids; Kerry's mother worked here, and she'd feed us in exchange for taking Kerry off her hands. I just hoped the door was where I remembered it. Things at Shadowed Hills tend to move around, but that doesn't usually include the servants' quarters—Luna's passion for interior decoration has never extended to pots, pans, and the kitchen help.

Footsteps approached along a path to the left.
ducked behind the hedge, pulling Connor against m
as four knights in the livery of Shadowed Hills walke
by. I knew them. I'd fought with them, practiced wit
them, and gotten roaring drunk with them. They weren'
friends, but they were people I respected, and if the
saw me, they'd turn me in. It was their duty. Not eve
Sylvester could protect me from the Queen unless h
wanted to declare war on the rest of the Kingdom.

My heel scuffed the gravel. The knights paused, an
I flinched, aware of how exposed we were. If they fo
lowed the sound they'd find us, and that would be th
end. There was nowhere left to run.

Connor and I held our breath, clinging to each othe
as the seconds ticked by. Finally, the guards shook thei
heads and continued on their way. I waited for the foo
steps to fade before I started breathing again, and I sti
counted to a hundred before I stood and bolted for th
hall, Connor racing to keep up. We crossed the remain
ing distance in a matter of minutes, my heart hammerin
against my ribs as we ducked behind the narrow bit c
stonework that concealed the kitchen door when I wa
a kid.

Luck was on our side; the door was still there. "Com
on," I whispered. Connor nodded, and followed m
inside.

Nothing at Shadowed Hills is small. The main kitche
is a vast room filled with ovens, stoves, counters, and th
sweet smell of baking bread. The ceiling is low so tha
pots, pans, and dried herbs can be hung from the rafter
that keeps the sheer size of the place from being daun
ing, but only barely. I held the door long enough to pee
out and be sure no one was following before easing
shut and turning to face the room.

Despite the sheer size of the kitchen, there was onl
one person in sight: a small, wizened man with a lon
white beard, contentedly washing dishes in the large

of the three sinks. Six Hobs—even halfbloods—can do the work of three dozen humans, and they get cranky when you shove too many of them into one place. I gestured for Connor to follow as I began creeping toward the door on the far wall.

We were halfway across the room when the man said, "Afternoon, Miss Toby, Master Connor. Wouldn't go out there, were I you. There's a ruckus on."

I winced as I turned to face him. Connor moved to stand next to me, taking my hand again. It was a show of support, and I appreciated it more than words could possibly have said. "Yeah, we know about the ruckus, um ..."

"Ormond, dear. You knew me when you were younger, but it's been a bit, hasn't it? Haven't seen you in the kitchens since, oh, year before young Meriel got herself sacked for malingering. That's a good three decades, I'd say."

"It's probably been longer." I raked my hair back with my free hand. "I know it's rude of me to ask, but could you—"

"We'll keep quiet; we know the Duke doesn't want you found. He'll be glad you've gone to ground here, it's what he hoped for." He winked at Connor, grinning broadly. "I see you're the cause of the young Master's absence. Good for both of you."

"Er." I exchanged a glance with Connor. He was blushing madly. Judging by the heat in my cheeks, I wasn't much better.

Ormond kept talking, ignoring our dismay. Hobs are like that. They'd play matchmaker in the middle of a nuclear strike if the opportunity presented itself. "Why don't the two of you stop in the pantry? There's apples and such." He indicated a door near the spice racks. "You'll both feel better for having eaten, and I'll call Melly. She'll gladly put you up in the servants' quarters while I fetch His Grace."

This was all getting a little out of control. "Look, we really don't want to get you in any trouble. We can find him on our own."

"There's no trouble here." Ormond's expression turned grim. "We saw you all over these kitchens when you were just a pup, and maybe it's been a bit since you came belowstairs, but we remember you. Amandine's girl, and the Duke's girl, and there's never been a rotten bone in your body. Whatever that washed-out 'Queen' says, you didn't hurt anyone. Especially not our Duchess." He glowered, daring us to argue.

I gaped at him. Connor took a half step forward, clearing his throat. "That's very kind. Can you tell Melly we'd be honored if she found a place for us to rest while we figure out what to do next?"

"It's my pleasure." Ormond hopped down from the stool he'd been using to reach the sink. Like most Hobs, he was small, barely reaching my waist. "Get yourselves some food before everyone thinks I'm abusing you, and I'll let Melly know she's to make a room for two fugitives. She'll be delighted. She hasn't had nearly enough in the way of blood and grass stains to wash out of the linens since the Duke gave up questing."

"Right," I said faintly, as I watched him turn and walk away. Once he was out of earshot, I said, "Connor?"

"Yeah?"

"Did we just let Ormond walk away thinking we ran off to have an affair?"

"That depends."

"On what?" I asked, turning to face him.

Instead of answering aloud, Connor quirked a smile, put his hands on either side of my face, and kissed me.

I was basically a kid the first time I kissed Connor. He was attached to Shadowed Hills as the diplomatic representative from Roan Rathad, and he was as baffled by the land fae as I was by purebloods in general. Kissing me was something he understood, and my changeling heritage didn't bother him—Selkies are born mortal, after all, and they only become fae if they're lucky enough to receive a skin. After Devin—after the men Devin hired me out to—Connor's salt-sweet kisses and careful hands were a revelation.

It didn't last. We'd barely progressed past stolen kisses and casual groping when the folks back home put their collective foot down. Selkies only get involved with other Selkies, or with pure humans. No changelings. No mixed-breeds. Not ever. I got involved with a human man. By the time that ended, Connor was caught in a marriage of political convenience that conveniently ignored the "rules" his family used to kill our brief-lived relationship. Not the sort of thing that inspires renewal of past passions.

His lips still tasted like sweetened saltwater. I kissed him back without realizing I was going to do it, and once that was done, there was nothing to do but step closer, still kissing him. The webbing between his fingers was cool in comparison to his hands; the rest of his body was hot, pressing against me like he thought our clothes might conveniently disappear.

No such luck. Connor reluctantly broke the kiss, stepping just far enough back to see my face as he said, "Maybe we did." He left his hands against my face.

"They'll be thrilled," I said, trying to sound dry and mostly succeeding in sounding dazed. The Shadowed Hills house-Hobs would be thrilled if Connor and I ran away together. I was a much saner match for him than Rayseline, and they all knew how much I meant to Sylvester. Most of the staff had been with the Torquill family for generations.

I froze. Connor must have taken my expression for rejection, because he dropped his hands, a hurt look flashing over his face. "I'm sorry," he said. "I just thought—"

"Ormond mentioned Meriel's dismissal like it was

a big deal." I grabbed Connor's hands before he could step back. "Was it?"

"What? I don't know. I wasn't here then." Connor's expression turned confused. "Who's Meriel?"

"One of the house-Hobs." Sick realization was washing over me. Hobs don't get fired from Shadowed Hills very often. They leave on their own even more rarely. House-Hobs are territorial enough that they don't like to create unnecessary jobs even for their own children, which meant *someone* had to leave to make an opening for Nerium. Why didn't Ormond mention that departure? It would have been a lot more recent. "Has anyone been fired recently? Or left? Or gone on vacation?"

Still confused, Connor said, "I have no idea."

Nerium, who was at the Ball. Nerium, who knew me. I left my wine unguarded when I danced with Sylvester, and Nerium knew where I'd been standing. Sure, I didn't *drink* the wine when I came back to it . . . but Oleander bragged about putting contact poison on the door handles of my car.

It was always possible that I was being paranoid. Something about this situation still didn't add up. "So who the hell is Nerium?" I muttered.

"That's not a person," said Connor, sounding relieved to be sure of something. "That's a plant."

"What?"

"Nerium oleander. That's the scientific name of the oleander." I stared at him. He shrugged. "I heard Walther explaining his antitoxins to Tybalt. Six times. Dude was a little tense, what with all the poison and dying and you not waking up."

"Connor?"

"What?"

I swallowed hard, letting go of his hands. "I know how Oleander got into the knowe." His expression turned perplexed again. I raked my hair back from my face. "I think we're in serious trouble."

"Yes," said a voice from the kitchen door. We turned, and found ourselves looking at Etienne. His sword was drawn, pointing at us. Eyes narrowed, he continued, "I think you are."

Swell.

THIRTY-ONE

I TOOK A DEEP BREATH. "This isn't what it looks like—"

"Really," he said, in a voice like ice. "Because what it looks like is an escaped prisoner in my liege's fiefdom, endangering us all even more than she already has." He turned his narrow-eyed gaze toward Connor. "As for you . . ."

"Don't start on him, Etienne," I said. "He didn't do anything wrong. I was set up, and you know it."

"No, October, I don't." Etienne's attention swung toward me. "What I know is that you didn't fight the guards or ask your liege for help. His Grace was petitioning King Sollys for your release when we heard you'd escaped. The Queen's guard is ripping the Kingdom apart looking for you. How can you even *think* of coming here? And why are you attempting to disguise yourself as your mother?"

One thing stood out from what he'd said. "He was petitioning the *High King*?" I demanded, leaving the topic of my changed appearance alone, at least for the moment.

Sword still raised, Etienne nodded.

The Queen of the Mists is a regional power. Her Kingdom makes up all of Northern California, but her influence ends at her borders. Even a feudal government needs some sort of "highest authority," unless you want to be at war all the time. In the Westlands—North and South America—that power is the Sollys family. King Aethlin and Queen Maida reign from the royal seat in Toronto, and with Oberon and the Queens gone, they're as far up the political food chain as most people can go. If King Sollys was involved, there was a chance the Queen would be punished for my "trial."

Not that I could count on being alive to see it. "I didn't escape; I was rescued. I don't think anyone involved knew that Sylvester had gone to the High King."

Etienne glanced at Connor. Connor looked away. If there'd been any question of whether he was involved with my rescue that answered it. Eyes narrowed, Etienne looked back to me. "Why are you here?"

"Because I believe Oleander may still be here."

"No one else has seen her."

"She's too clever for that. The poisons Walther found—"

"Convenient, that. You're accused of poisoning people, and you suddenly have an alchemist of your very own to clear your name."

"She's working with Raysel. She has a way in."

"Raysceline has been under close observation since the beginning of this tragedy. She's done nothing but grieve."

"And turn me in!"

"Yes, well. It seems that may have been warranted." Etienne glared at me. I blinked back.

"You were willing to believe me before," I said. "What changed?"

"You fled the Queen's justice," said Etienne. "Your

oaths as a knight forbid such acts of cowardice, however much you may disagree with the decisions of your liege."

"Oak and *ash*, Etienne," I swore. "I'm sorry your sensibilities are offended by the fact that I'm not dead, but since I'm trying to keep our mutual fucking liege from ending up that way, you'd think you could give me the benefit of the doubt! You *trained* me! Doesn't that count for anything?"

"I wouldn't have helped get her out if I didn't think it was the right thing to do," said Connor.

"I'm *quite* sure it was your *mind* that ordered that action," snapped Etienne. Connor turned red, and stopped talking.

The three of us were still standing there, glaring, when Ormond came back into the kitchen. A plump female Hob with curly brown hair and a wide smile trailed along behind him. She brightened when she saw me, spreading her arms in greeting.

"Toby, darlin'! Ormy said it was you, but I wanted to see for m'self. Master Connor, Sir Etienne." She bobbed quick curtsies to each of them before turning back to me. "You're a sight and a half for sore eyes."

"Hi, Melly," said Connor.

"Right," muttered Etienne, and turned to stalk away. Ormond reached up and grabbed his arm, bringing the startled Tuatha to a halt.

"Wasn't expecting to see you here," he said, conversationally.

Etienne tried to pull away, scowling when he realized he couldn't. Hobs are stronger than they look. "His Grace must be informed," he said.

"His Grace, and none other, you hear?" said Ormond. "She and the young master are here on Duchy's business, and that seems a thing as should be judged proper before people run and carry tales."

Etienne cast a glare in my direction. I looked at him pleadingly. We held that position for several seconds before he sighed, relenting. "The Duke, and no one else. Let him decide what's to be done."

"Good man," said Ormond, and released him.

"Come on, let's get the pair of you out of sight," said Melly, starting to bustle us out of the kitchen. Etienne held his position next to Ormond, watching us go without another word. Melly was more than willing to fill the silence. "We've a guest room, it's not much, but it'll do. Have you seen Kerry recently? How's she doing with that new gentleman of hers?"

"Not too well," I said. Connor reached for my hand. I let him take it.

"Oh, she never gets on well, does she?" Melly asked. Kerry gets a lot of her gregariousness from her mother. Melly's just better at keeping it from becoming annoying. "Well, she's young yet. I was four hundred before I met her father, dear man that he was, and him the only one meant for me. Just give her time."

"That's what we all need," I agreed. Clearing my throat, I asked, "Does the name 'Nerium' mean anything to you?"

"Can't say as it does, dear. Is that a friend of yours?"

My fingers clenched on Connor's, causing him to shoot me a wounded look. "Not quite," I murmured, forcing myself to loosen my grasp.

Connor and I walked the rest of the way in silence, letting Melly's constant chatter wash over us like rain. The guest room she led us to was small and spotless, with a single round window looking out over one of the knowe's many gardens. A narrow bed was against the wall across from the window, and there was a dresser next to the door.

Melly crossed the room quickly, twitching the curtains shut. "No one should bother you here," she said.

I exchanged a glance with Connor before saying, "This is great."

"It's good of you to say, dear," said Melly, beaming.

Looking from me to Connor, she added, "I'll just let you two have some privacy while you wait," and slipped out of the room before either of us could protest.

I pinched the bridge of my nose. "So now I'm wanted for murder, I'm pretty sure Oleander's in the knowe masquerading as a member of the staff, and the house-Hobs are convinced we're sleeping together. This is good. I was worried I'd get bored."

Connor barked a laugh. "Things stay interesting when you're around."

"Since I'm always around myself, I don't find that at *all* reassuring." I lowered my hand. "So what, we're supposed to just wait here?"

"Etienne'll bring Sylvester, so yeah." Connor walked over and dropped himself onto the bed, tucking his hands behind his head. He looked perfectly at ease, calling up memories of hot summer nights spent sitting on the beach, mapping one another with our hands. He shot me an encouraging look, kindling a low fire in my stomach. Maybe I wasn't the only one remembering those nights. "At least nobody's trying to kill us."

"If only Danny and the Barghests could say the same." I started toward the bed, pausing as I heard a faint scraping sound from the wall behind me. Someone was moving a hidden panel. I stiffened, motioning for Connor to hush as I kept walking. It wasn't Melly or Ormond—they'd have announced their presence—and it wasn't Etienne. He trained me. He's not dumb enough to sneak up on me.

Great. A mystery attacker was *just* what the day needed, and unless I moved, Connor couldn't see whoever was approaching. I make a better door than a window. If I *did* move, he might get some bright idea about "defending" me. I had to hold my ground.

Still motioning an increasingly alarmed-looking Connor to silence, I pulled the pillow from beneath his head and clutched it to my chest, trying not to let my tension show. From behind, it would have looked like we were getting ready to get physical. I was—just not in the expected way.

Soft footsteps to my left marked the position of our "guest" as he or she crept up behind me. Whoever it was didn't sneak up on people very often, or they'd have known to remove their shoes before coming in. They also didn't have a ranged weapon, or I'd have already been shot in the back. That gave me a chance, especially if they didn't realize they'd been heard. The footsteps came closer.

"Okay, darling," I said sweetly, stooping forward like I was leaning in to deliver a kiss. Then I whirled, slamming the pillow at what I estimated to be chest height.

I was wrong; the person behind me was shorter than I'd expected, and I caught him full in the face. That was a good thing, because I also caught the knife he'd been about to slide between my ribs. The shock of the impact caused him to drop his personal invisibility spell, and I glimpsed golden hair behind the flurry of motion and freed feathers. Manuel.

The blade drove deep into the pillow. I heard Connor scrambling to his feet as I twisted hard to the side, yanking the knife away. Manuel gaped, giving me time to jerk the knife out of the pillow and into my own hand. His eyes widened and he lunged—a gesture I interrupted by hitting him again with the pillow. I dropped the pillow while he was dazed and slid my arm around his neck, holding the knife an inch from his throat. He froze.

The whole thing had taken less than thirty seconds. "Hi!" I chirped. "Nice of you to visit. Are you going to bring us a new pillow?"

Manuel swallowed before whispering, "Be careful with that." His voice was a child's, frightened and alone.

"Don't you want a closer shave?" I brushed the flat of the blade against his skin. "They can't execute me twice. Now tell me why I shouldn't hurt you."

"Careful!" he squawked. "It's poisoned."

"Is it?" I said, without surprise. "Gee, Connor, did you hear that? I love getting poisoned presents. You're such a great friend, Manuel. What are you doing here?"

"I was here to . . . to . . ."

"To kill me?" He nodded wordlessly. "To kill us both?" Again the nod; I heard Connor gasp. "Why am I not surprised? Who sent you?"

Manuel licked his lips. "If I tell you, will you let me go?"

"I'll consider it." I brought the knife carefully closer. "Talk."

"It was Oleander. She gave me the knife."

"Oleander." I sighed, letting go of him and stepping back toward Connor. "You idiot. I suppose she offered you wealth? Power?"

Manuel jumped away, turning to glare at us when he was halfway across the room. "Revenge," he spat. "The power was for Rayseline. I just wanted you to pay for what you did to my sister."

"You idiot," I said, resisting the urge to check on Connor. He didn't make a sound when Manuel spoke his wife's name. He always knew she was crazy. Getting proof still had to hurt. "You let Raysel use you so you could hurt me for something I didn't do."

"You didn't save her!"

"Neither did you." I looked at him levelly. "Devin would never have let us go, not *any* of us. He was going to kill me and make you into a murderer. Do you think he would've let Dare live if she kept challenging him? I don't. I think he would have made you pull the trigger when he ordered her death. He was using you, Manuel, the way he used everyone else. We're both responsible for her death, but we didn't kill her."

Manuel started to cry. "I . . . you . . . I . . ."

"I know." I put the knife on the dresser before sliding my arms around Manuel again—embracing, not restraining. He hugged me back, sobbing against my shoulder. I didn't stop him. I had a feeling he hadn't let himself cry for a long time.

He let go and stepped away several minutes later, wiping his eyes with the back of his hand. Connor moved up behind me, putting his hand on my shoulder. I covered it with my own, asking, "Feel better?" Even I couldn't have said which I was talking to.

Manuel sniffled, nodding. "A little bit. I . . ."

"I know." I laced my fingers with Connor's. "Did Oleander salt the roses?"

"What?" Manuel blinked, obviously thrown, before stammering, "No."

It was Connor who asked the next question in a voice gone dead and dull with resignation, like he already knew the answer: "So who did?"

Manuel glanced between us, and said, "Rayseline."

"Crap," I said, looking quickly toward Connor. He'd turned his face away, staring at the wall. "Connor—"

"Don't." A pause. "Please."

"What's wrong?" asked Manuel, sounding baffled. "The salt's not going to do any permanent damage. It was just to keep the Duchess out of the way while we . . . while they . . . took care of things."

"No, Manuel," I said wearily, biting back the urge to slap his oblivious little face. "Salt kills plants. If the soil doesn't get cleansed, Luna's going to die."

"But Rayseline said—"

"She lied to you." Connor yanked his hand from mine, turning to face Manuel. I'd never seen him look that angry. "Don't you get that? She's trying to kill her mother."

Manuel looked as stricken as if I actually *had* slapped him. "Kill?"

"That was probably the goal all along." I glanced at Connor. He was glaring at Manuel like he thought looks alone could kill. "Oleander likes to cause as much damage as she can. Using Luna's daughter as the murder weapon is the sort of thing she'd love."

"But . . ." Manuel bit his lip. "Raysel was going to go sit with her mother while I took care of you. For an alibi, she said."

I stared at him. "Raysel's alone with Luna? And you're just telling us now?"

"She's not alone! She took one of the serving girls."

My head snapped up. "Which one?" Manuel must have seen something in my face that he liked even less than Connor's glare; he took a step backward. "Which one?!" I demanded again.

"The new one—Nerium. I—"

He didn't get a chance to finish. I grabbed his arm, leaning back to snatch the poisoned knife from the dresser. "Connor, come on!" I shouted, and dragged Manuel behind me as I took off through the panel he'd opened in the wall.

The concealed door led into the maze of hidden hallways and servants' corridors winding through the knowe. Like the kitchens, those corridors don't move much—they need to stay consistent for the sake of the household staff. I ran as fast as I could, taking the turns half on instinct, praying I wasn't already too late. Luck wasn't on my side; I knew that. Neither was time.

Manuel followed without fighting, letting me lead the way. He didn't understand yet, but he would, and one way or another, he'd find that understanding over a corpse. It might be mine, and it might be Oleander's; I just wanted to make sure it wasn't Luna's.

There was nothing I could do but hope, and so I hoped. And I ran.

THIRTY-TWO

ONE ROOM BLENDED INTO THE NEXT, the rooms blurring around us until even I was forced to admit that I was lost. "Connor!" I looked back without slowing down. "Where are we?"

"Not a clue," he wheezed. He was clearly having trouble keeping up, although he was doing his best. Selkies aren't built to be endurance runners.

Manuel grabbed my elbow and dug his heels into the floor, jerking me to a halt. Connor slammed into us from behind, knocking Manuel and me both forward a step. "Look!" said Manuel, pointing to a heraldic rose carved at the top of the nearest wall. "We're three halls over from the solarium."

"You can tell your way around the knowe by the *roses?*" I said, feeling suddenly stupid. The look on Connor's face told me he was feeling something similar. The staff always appeared where they were needed, like magic. I should have remembered that sometimes magic is just a convenient excuse for not looking any deeper. It's no replacement for common sense.

"Well, yeah," said Manuel, like it was self-evident.

"It's a heraldic rose, so we're on the northern side of the hall, and it has five petals, so we're in the eastern part of the north side. The rest is in the notches on the petals and the way the rose is tilted. I'm not as good as the Hobs, but I'm learning."

Connor leaned against the wall, struggling to get his breath back. I cast him a sympathetic look before asking, "So which way is it to Luna's room?"

"From here?" Manuel turned in a slow circle. I flexed my hands, resisting the urge to shake him until he answered. I'd already rushed off half-cocked once; I wasn't going to do it again. He stopped and pointed down a side hall. "That way, right, left, and two more rights. We'll come out in the library next to the Ducal quarters."

"Then let's go."

We started off again, jogging until Connor was breathing better, and then breaking into a run. The knife I'd taken from Manuel was my only weapon, and if I used it, it would be to kill, not wound; Oleander's poisons were too well-made for me to assume they'd leave people alive. If I struck out, even to defend myself, I really would be breaking Oberon's law.

I'd worry about that when the time came . . . and *after* I knew that Luna was safe.

We ran for about ten minutes. Manuel took the lead, calling out the turns as we came to them. I wasn't tired. I should've been, just like the hide-and-seek spell should've left me reeling from magic-burn. This wasn't like the Luidaeg's transformations; this wasn't going to wear off. Tybalt seemed to think I could undo it myself— but that wouldn't make me Daoine Sidhe. Whatever I was, it was something I was going to have to learn to live with. Of course, that was assuming I survived to live with anything at all.

"Here." Manuel waved us to a stop.

I reached for the door he indicated. "If this is a trick . . ."

"I never wanted Luna to die." He looked from me to Connor. Streaks of pixie-sweat were drying on his cheeks and forehead, making him look as young as Dare was when she died. "I just wanted to avenge my sister."

"I believe you. Don't make me regret it."

"I won't."

"Okay," I said, and opened the door.

Light flooded the hall, filling my vision with bright spots. I blinked them away and saw that we were exactly where Manuel said we'd be: the library next to the Ducal quarters. Connor followed me, and Manuel brought up the rear, tapping the door behind himself. It slid closed, becoming a simple decorative panel.

Manuel offered the ghost of a smile when he caught my expression. "A lot of the servants' entrances are hidden. It's so we won't disturb people."

"Right," I said. Kerry showed me the servants' halls when we were kids, but I forgot about them once I grew up. Oleander wouldn't have been that careless, and if she knew about the secret doors, she could have come and gone with ease. Shadowed Hills mostly employs Hobs; the knights and pages aren't technically "servants." All she had to do was pay attention and she could avoid them all.

Manuel kept smiling, almost desperately. He still wanted me to approve of him. Hell, after everything he'd been through, he probably didn't care *who* approved of him, as long as someone did. Dare had been his only living relative, and Devin never taught his kids how to grow up. No wonder Oleander and Raysel were able to convince him to go along with their plan. They just had to give him their attention.

"It's cool," I said. His smile brightened, losing its anxious quality. "Now come on. We have to get to the Duchess." I took Connor's hand, pulling him along at a fast trot as we followed Manuel out of the library and down the hall to the filigreed silver gate leading to the Ducal quarters.

Manuel stopped, looking dismayed. "It's closed. We can't get in."

"Let me," said Connor. He released my hand and reached for the door handle, turning it—or trying to, anyway. It remained firmly shut. Connor scowled. "That's weird. It's supposed to open for family."

I put a hand on his arm. "Connor, with everything that's happened . . . do you really think Raysel would leave the locks open?"

"I guess not."

"Let me try." I stepped forward, ignoring Manuel's startled stare as I rested my forehead against the door. "Me again," I murmured. "Sorry, but I need another favor."

Manuel snorted. "Quiet," I said, sharply, before turning my attention back to the knowe. "Sorry about the interruption. Your Duchess is in danger. I know I've been asking a lot lately. But please, let us in." I stepped back.

"Was that a spell?" asked Manuel. "I didn't feel any magic—"

"Hush," I said. Then I repeated: "Please."

The door swung open, revealing the garden on the other side.

I cast a smile at the ceiling before grabbing Connor's hand and running through the open door. Manuel followed us, demanding, "How did you—"

"Just run!" I said, passing the fountain. There were two smaller, freestanding gates on the other side. One would take us to Luna's room, and the other would take us somewhere else in the Ducal quarters. I just didn't know which was which. "Connor?"

"This way." He pulled me forward, taking the lead as we passed through the gateway on the left and into a small, round room filled with lights.

The vast bed where Luna slept still dominated the room, but the rose goblins covering every surface were new. They were on the bed, the floor, even twining their way between the lamps and candles. Spike was curled in the middle of Luna's chest. It raised its head as we entered, chirping a greeting.

I smiled. "Hey, guy. Good to see you."

Manuel stopped next to me, and frowned. "Toby, where's Luna?"

"She's right here." I stepped closer to the bed, a strange mixture of love and regret catching in my throat. I could see her breathe when I stood this close. She wasn't dead yet.

"No, it's not," objected Manuel.

"Yes. It is." I leaned down to touch her cheek. She wasn't burning up anymore, but she was still warmer than she should have been. I understood Manuel's confusion, because the woman in the bed looked nothing like the Duchess of Shadowed Hills. She looked like Luna, Blodynbryd daughter of Acacia and Blind Michael.

She was taller than the Duchess we knew, thinner, and more fragile-looking. Her skin was the alien white of new marble, and her hair was a long tangle of pink and red. The fox ears and tails she'd worn so proudly were gone, her second, stolen heritage burned away by the resurgence of her first. We might save her life, but we couldn't save the skin she'd worn.

"I don't understand," said Manuel.

"You don't need to," said Connor. "Where's Rayseline?"

"I don't know. She said she was coming here."

I straightened, turning to face him. "What did she say, exactly?"

"That she was going to see her parents. To get to the root of things."

"The root of things?" I stared. Connor had gone milk-pale. "Oh, oak and ash. Come on!" I ran back out the door, almost stumbling as my feet hit the cobblestone path, and charged straight through the other gate.

Connor was close at my heels, and Manuel wasn't far behind.

Every child in Faerie learns the sacred symbols of our world. It's the fae equivalent of Sunday school, packed with useless knowledge and bits of history that humans take for fairy tales. We're taught to swear by the sacred woods, by Titania's rose, and Maeve's tree, and by the root and the branch—Oberon and his children. Oberon is the root of Faerie. By that same archaic, undeniable interpretation, Sylvester is the root of Shadowed Hills.

The gate led to a terraced hall, laid out like the walkway of a Spanish villa. Arches branched off to the left and right, but I kept running, following the curve of the main hall. Connor was gasping. He was close to the end of his endurance, but we couldn't afford the risk of slowing down.

Manuel shouted, "Wait! Where are you going?"

"To Sylvester!" We were chasing blind again, but there was no other option. These were the Duke's private apartments; Connor and Manuel didn't know them any better than I did. Quieter, I muttered, "Come on, come on. We need the Duke." If Shadowed Hills had ever been my friend—if a hollow hill *could* have friends . . .

A door opened to the left. I spun and dove through it, moving so fast I nearly fell before I'd finished taking in the scene in front of me.

The walls were adobe with deep insets every five feet filled with plumed gray-and-purple ferns, turning the room into an indoor garden. Wicker chairs irregularly placed around the floor created an effective barrier to swift movement; trying to run through them would mean tripping over them. Sylvester sat in one of those chairs, hands tucked between his knees, talking earnestly to Raysel. Raysel reclined in her own chair, nodding in time with his words, looking every inch the dutiful daughter.

Raysel wasn't the real problem. That honor was reserved for the woman standing between them, honey-gold hair falling over her shoulders in careful disarray, holding a tray out toward Sylvester. He smiled, murmuring something, and reached for a cup.

"*No!*" I shouted, and charged forward, shoving chairs out of the way.

"Toby?" Sylvester's head lifted. "What are you doing here?" He sounded surprised and delighted at the same time, joy clearing the exhaustion from his voice. Raysel snarled soundlessly, the action going unseen behind his back. I didn't miss it. I was never turning my back on her again.

Nerium's expression was more frightening than Raysel's. The amiable servitude slid out of her eyes like a knife sliding out of a sheath, leaving her expressionless and cold. Standing her ground, she flung the tray toward me. It didn't fly well, but it did fly, spraying liquid in all directions.

"Hey!" I yelped, dodging. I was too slow: a goblet caught me on the shoulder, splashing my jacket and the side of my neck in viscous green. The liquid burned when it touched my skin. Behind me, I heard Connor bark in pained surprise. I didn't stop. There wasn't time.

"What is the *meaning* of this?" shouted Sylvester. I looked up. He was facing Raysel, his back toward the door, and Oleander was between them with a knife in her hand. The blade glistened in the light. She still wore a Hob's face, but she wasn't making any attempt to look like anyone but herself. The masks were coming off.

"Sylvester, get back!" Manuel flashed past me, still running. "*Manuel!*"

He heard me. I know he heard me, and I know he knew his former compatriots well enough to know what would happen if he didn't stop. He didn't even pause. He just kept running.

I was ten feet away and gaining speed when Manuel shoved Sylvester aside; his expression was frighteningly like the one his sister wore when she threw herself at death to save my life. Oleander lunged forward, burying her knife between Manuel's ribs. He fell, taking the knife with him, and she found herself staring down the blade of Sylvester's sword.

"Explain yourself," he snarled.

She turned and ran.

Sylvester looked toward his daughter. She stared back at him, golden eyes wide and frightened. Rayseline was no innocent, but she'd been used, just like Manuel. The only difference was that she'd known what she was getting into.

"Raysel—" I began.

She whirled and ran after Oleander, moving with desperate speed. Sylvester watched her go, sword still naked in his hand. "Rayseline?" he repeated, like he'd never heard the name before.

I pushed past Sylvester and dropped to my knees, trying to roll Manuel onto his back. He was heavier than he looked—most teenage boys are—but I managed to hook my hands under his shoulders and flip him over. "Manuel?"

His eyes were open and glazed; he wasn't looking at me. "Yes?"

"Are you all right?" It was a stupid question: the answer was sticking out of his chest. There wasn't much blood. The knife formed an almost perfect seal against his skin, keeping his life locked inside. My own skin was burning from the liquid that splashed me, but I ignored the pain. Manuel's danger was a lot more immediate.

"I'm fine." He smiled. His eyes were getting more and more distant. "I'm really, really good."

"Toby, is he—" began Sylvester.

"Get help!" I snapped, resting Manuel's head on my knee. "Don't talk. We're going to get Jin, and it's going to be okay. Just breathe until she gets here." Connor came puffing up behind Sylvester, one hand clapped over his left shoulder. The fabric of his shirt was wet there; he'd clearly taken the brunt of Oleander's attack.

Manuel closed his eyes. "Was that the Duke?" he asked.

Sylvester was still standing there, seemingly rooted in the spot. "Yeah," I said.

"Is he hurt?" Manuel's voice was fading.

"He's fine. You saved him." I looked back down, biting my lip as I saw how pale he'd become. "We're gonna get you some help. You'll be fine."

"Liar," he said, and smiled again.

"Just hold on. Sylvester, why are you still here? Why aren't you getting Jin?" I sniffled. "Please, hurry . . ."

Sylvester knelt beside me. "Look at him, Toby."

I glanced at the knife again and winced. Thick, near-black blood was starting to leak out around the blade. Blood isn't supposed to be that color. "What's happening?"

"Was that Oleander?" Biting my lip, I nodded. Sylvester sighed deeply, putting his hand on Manuel's shoulder. "Manuel, can you hear me?"

"Of course, my liege." Manuel opened his eyes, forcing another frail smile. "Can I be of service?" His voice was fading in and out, becoming weaker.

"No, son, you're fine; rest," said Sylvester. "I have something for you."

"We need to help him."

Sylvester raised his eyes, looking at me. "There's no help for him now, October. You know that."

"There must be *something!*" Connor put his hand on my shoulder. I fumbled to take it, clinging.

"Oleander does her work too well. Let go." Sylvester looked at Connor's hand and said nothing, turning back to Manuel. "You're going to die, Manuel. I'm sorry."

Manuel licked his lips, whispering, "I betrayed you."

"I know," said Sylvester. "I knew as soon as I saw Raysel's face."

"She betrayed you, too."

"I know. Hush, now." He closed his eyes. "By the root and the branch, the rose and the tree, by oak, ash, yarrow, and thorn, I say you've served me well; by the moon and stars, by ice and fire, by willow, rowan, elm, and pine, I name you a knight of my service, bound to Shadowed Hills until Faerie is no more. What say you of this?"

For a moment, I thought Manuel had already slipped past answering. Then, in a voice that was barely a whisper, he asked, "Really, Your Grace?"

"Yes, Manuel. What do you say?"

"Of course. Thank you, Your . . ." He closed his eyes, sighing. I waited for him to take another breath and finish the sentence.

He never did.

THIRTY-THREE

SYLVESTER OFFERED ME HIS HAND as he stood. I laced my fingers through his, letting him pull me to my feet. Then I pulled away, stepping back to lean against Connor. The fae don't age: purebloods stop when they hit adulthood, holding onto the illusion of youth forever. Despite all that, at that moment, Sylvester looked very old.

"I didn't know he'd run ahead," I said, barely above a whisper.

"Yes, you did." Sylvester smiled sadly. "He's been waiting for that sort of cavalry charge ever since his sister died."

"I guess so." I glanced at Manuel. He looked more asleep than dead, if you ignored the knife sticking out of his chest. "The night-haunts . . ."

"They'll come." He bent to pull the knife free, not flinching at the gush of black blood that came with it. "Follow me, both of you. We need to be away from here before the guards arrive."

"The guards?" I asked numbly. Manuel was dead. Paradoxically, I wanted to wait for the night-haunts. I wanted to see Dare again; wanted to apologize for sending her brother to join her so soon.

"Yes. Rayseline knows you're here. She must have called the guards by now, and told them you kidnapped Connor and attacked me—Connor, it's good to see that you're well. I was concerned."

"Sir," said Connor, sounding pained. I glanced back. He was still clutching his shoulder. "Sorry I didn't call. I was busy."

"I can see that," said Sylvester. He touched the wall. A door swung open, revealing a narrow hall. "Raysel is doubtless going to say October killed Manuel and possibly kidnapped you, Connor. She'll claim I don't know my own mind."

I stared at him. "Sylvester, she's your daughter. How can you—"

"Simon was my brother. How can I not?"

I bit my lip before I could say anything more and followed Sylvester into the wall.

Sylvester closed the door once Connor was through. "They won't find us here," he said, dropping the poisoned knife. "Raysel thinks she knows my halls better than I do. Half the plans were drawn with me watching over the architect's shoulders, and yet she thinks she can sneak around without my knowing. Can I have the other knife?"

"What—oh." I offered the knife I'd taken from Manuel. He took it delicately, dropping it beside the first. Then he turned and pulled me into a tight hug, pressing my face to his chest.

"Stop *dying* on me," he whispered fiercely.

"I don't do it on purpose." His betrayal still stung. I hugged him back anyway. Angry as I was, I'd loved him for too long to let that come between us. There'd be time to yell at him for lying to me later, when we weren't all in danger.

"I know you don't. It's still becoming a habit." He

pushed me out to arm's length, studying my face. "Are you hurt?"

"A little scorched, but okay. None of the poison got in my mouth. Connor is—"

"Connor is fine," said Connor firmly. "Just go on."

"Right." I sighed. "I'm sorry, Sylvester. I didn't know—"

"I know." He reached out to tuck my hair behind one pointed ear, and sighed. "You look so much like your mother. I'm sorry. Now come on." He stepped back and started down the hall.

I followed him, shivering slightly; Connor followed me. When the silence got to be too much, I said, "I wasn't sure Raysel was involved."

"Of course she was." Sylvester sighed. "I hoped you'd find it was someone outside the knowe, even someone outside my fiefdom altogether, because if it was someone on the inside, Raysel was involved. It's that simple."

"But how did you—"

"I didn't; not until Connor vanished, and she took it as calmly as if a vase had been broken. If I'd known for sure—if I'd known *anything* for sure—I'd have stopped her." There was ice in his voice. "Being my daughter wouldn't have protected her."

I glanced at Connor. He was looking steadily forward, face an expressionless mask. Hearing that your wife didn't care when you vanished had to hurt, even if the marriage was strictly political. There was nothing I could say to make it better, and so I turned my attention to Sylvester. "We left the knives."

"We can't carry them with us."

"Why not?"

Sylvester looked at me blandly. "Do you really want to wander the knowe with a poisoned knife when my daughter's telling people you're trying to kill me?"

Sometimes it's impossible to argue with him. "No," I

admitted, "but that doesn't make me happy about being unarmed."

"Unarmed?" He laughed. "Toby, the day you're unarmed, I'm giving you the Duchy."

"That's not fair."

"Yeah, but it's accurate," said Connor. I wrinkled my nose at him, and he smiled. It was a small smile. It still made me feel better about how he was taking things, and how badly he might have been hurt in Oleander's attack. If he was being snotty, he was going to be okay.

Sylvester stopped, opening a small door. I looked at him curiously. He motioned for Connor and me to go through. When Sylvester gives a direct order, it's best to follow.

The room on the other side of the door was large but seemed small, since it was jammed past capacity with swords, spears, and other instruments for making people die. I stopped, staring. Connor did the same. Sylvester knocked him into me as he came through the door, nearly sending us both sprawling.

"We're in the *armory?*" I said. "You just said I shouldn't be armed!"

"No: I said you shouldn't carry Oleander's knives. I didn't say anything about being unarmed." Sylvester turned to select a sword from the wall. It was a delicate thing, with a hard, gleaming edge that promised sharpness. A trail of brambles and wild roses was etched near the hilt—the sort of ornamental touch Faerie has never been able to resist. The purebloods would carve pretty pictures in the sky if they could find a ladder long enough. "This should do. Not too heavy, but you have enough muscle in your shoulders that I don't want to give you something too light, either."

"I don't know how to use a sword," I protested.

Connor snorted, taking down a bow for himself. "If you can use it to break something, you'll figure it out." I shot him a look. He grinned.

"You did well enough with Blind Michael, and it's time you learned," Sylvester said implacably, pressing the hilt into my hand. "Hang on. I'll find you a scabbard."

I studied the sword, feeling the weight of it as Sylvester moved away. I've watched people fight with swords for most of my life, but I never got past the "swing it like a baseball bat and hope for the best" stage. Etienne gave me lessons. Three of them. Then he said I was a menace and refused to teach me anything more for fear that I'd slice his head off. Still, if Sylvester said it was my sword, it was my sword.

Sylvester returned, offering a scabbard and belt. "This should do until we can get something fitted to your hips," he said.

"I'll refrain from taking offense," I said dryly, and held out my hand.

Etienne opened the armory door.

The four of us stared at each other. I had time to say, "Etienne, this isn't—" before he rushed forward, knocking the sword out of my hand and driving me to the floor. For once, I landed on my ass rather than either my abused back or shoulders. That was the only positive side of the fall. The armory floor was hard as hell, especially when I was being slammed into it by two hundred pounds of testosterone-charged Tuatha de Dannan. As often as men slam me into things, you'd think I'd get laid more.

The impact knocked the air out of my lungs. Etienne yanked my head back, slamming it against the floor, and I winced, although not too hard. I was too busy trying to figure out when the knife wound up in his hand. Connor was trying to pull him off me, but wasn't having much luck—Etienne outweighed him by a good thirty pounds, and a whole lot of angry.

"How *dare* you attack our liege?" Etienne snarled. Wisely, I refrained from trying to defend myself. It wasn't like I had enough air to talk, anyway. "I trusted you! I believed you when you said you were trying to help! How *dare* you?"

Mildly, Sylvester said, "Please don't kill her. She'd be difficult to replace."

Etienne looked over his shoulder. That was the opening I needed. Balling my right hand into a fist, I punched him in the jaw. It's not easy to swing a good punch when you're flat on your back and fighting to breathe, but it was enough to throw him off-balance. Using both hands, I shoved him away and scrambled to my feet. Connor immediately grabbed his arms, pinning them behind his back.

Etienne glared. I glared back. "Your Grace, she was holding a sword on you!"

"No, she was simply holding a sword. It was nowhere near me. I should know, as I was the one who handed it to her. It would've been rude of her to drop it. Toby, please stop punching Etienne in the head. It's not helping."

"He started it," I said.

"That's nice. It's finished now." Sylvester bent to retrieve my sword from the floor. "Is either of you hurt?"

"She hit me!" said Etienne.

"You body-slammed me," I countered.

"You were holding a sword on the Duke!"

"He *gave* it to me!"

"Do I need to send you to your rooms?" Sylvester stepped between us. "Etienne, Toby wasn't attacking me. We're here because I'd rather we weren't wandering around without weapons when Oleander de Merelands is loose in the knowe. Toby, Etienne was trying to defend me. Please refrain from treating his head like a punching bag. Connor, you may release my knight now."

"Gotcha," I said.

"Yes, sir," Connor said, and let go of Etienne.

Etienne was too busy staring at Sylvester to move. "Oleander?"

"Yes. October was right." Sylvester sighed. "Rayseline is working with her."

"Truly? But we watched her. She gave no sign." Etienne looked almost painfully amazed. The Tuatha don't deal well with the idea of treachery; that's why the Daoine Sidhe rule most of Faerie, while the Tuatha support the throne. They're not sneaky enough to stage a coup.

"Yeah, Raysel," I said, rubbing my sore hip with one hand. "Next time you knock me over, make sure I land on something soft. Like your head."

"Toby—" Sylvester said, in a cautioning tone.

"Sorry. It's been a long day."

"I believe it's likely to get longer."

"Raysel's working with Oleander?" Etienne said, not moving past that point.

"It's a big whirligig of fun," I muttered, taking the scabbard Sylvester was offering and belting it around my waist.

"Yes," said Connor. Etienne gaped at him, while Sylvester wordlessly handed me the sword. If there was going to be any explaining, it looked like I was going to do it.

Lucky me. "Oleander convinced Raysel and Manuel to help her poison the Duchess." I slid the sword into the scabbard. "They salted the earth around the roses."

"I knew that," he said impatiently. "That's why we've had that man from the Tea Gardens here all week."

"His *name* is Walther," I said. "Has her condition improved?"

"Yes," Sylvester said. "But she's reverted to her original form, and it seems . . . unlikely . . . that she'll be able to change back, given the nature of her original transformation. A thing, once broken, is difficult to restore."

"Damn." Shaking my head, I said, "I think Oleander targeted Lily partially to frame me, and partially because she and Simon failed to kill me in the Tea Gardens."

"If October and Connor hadn't arrived when they did, I doubt we'd be having this conversation," added Sylvester. At Etienne's look, he explained, "I was about to be poisoned when Toby broke in. Her timing saved my life."

"Didn't do much for Manuel," I said, looking away.

"Manuel?" said Etienne. "What about him?"

Sylvester answered before I could: "He was working with Oleander and Rayseline. They said they could get him revenge for his sister's death. Unfortunately, he was a very angry young man, and he believed them."

"He wasn't working for them at the end," I said.

Etienne paled. "Does that mean . . . ?"

"Manuel Lorimer died a Knight of the Shadowed Hills," said Sylvester, tone leaving no room for argument. "My daughter may not have held the knife, but she's as responsible for this as Oleander was. They'll both pay for what's been done."

"We're wasting time," I said. "Etienne, we're afraid Rayseline will try to convince the guards that I'm trying to kill the Duke."

"She already has," he said grimly. "Grianne has her Merry Dancers scouring the gardens, and Garm has gone to the mortal side of the park to check the entrances."

It's a sign of my respect for Sylvester that I didn't deck Etienne again. "*What?*"

"She was persuasive, October. I tried to argue, but you'd already run from the Queen's justice, and it seemed you'd slipped Ormond's hospitality . . ." He had the good grace to look embarrassed. That was the only thing that prevented me from kicking him in the shins. "They sent me to the armory because we needed weapons to hunt you with."

"Oh, for Maeve's sake." I put a hand over my face. "Sylvester—"

"Don't get huffy at me," said the Duke, taking several knives off the wall and tucking them into his doublet. "I warned you she was going to do that."

"Yes, but . . ." I stopped, sighing. "How bad is it?"

"There are two search parties combing the knowe for

you, in addition to Garm's group." Etienne recovered his composure enough to take a knife off the wall for himself. "I'm supposed to lead the third."

"Goody," I said.

"This is still manageable," said Sylvester. "Etienne, do you know the way to the Garden of Glass Roses?"

"Yes, if it hasn't been moved recently."

"It hasn't."

I nodded, getting the gist of where he was going. "Meet folks there and explain?"

"Exactly." Sylvester slid another knife into his sleeve. I'd be surprised if he didn't clatter when he walked. "We'll simply explain, and they'll side with me."

Etienne and I exchanged a glance. "How can you be sure?" he asked.

"This is my Duchy, Etienne. I hold the fealty of everyone here, and unlike my daughter, I'm not presently insane." Sylvester's expression hardened. "I love Rayseline, but she hurt Luna on purpose, and that's the one thing I can never forgive. Anything else, she might have been able to get away with—I'm sorry, Toby, but she might even have escaped the punishment for killing you—"

"Forgiven," I said. Connor didn't say anything; he didn't need to. The fury in his expression was enough.

"I thought it might be," Sylvester said, and smiled a sad, short-lived smile. "She could have gotten away with anything but what she did. This isn't forgivable. One way or another, she's going to pay."

"You heard the man." I looked to Etienne. "Get the others and meet us in the garden as soon as you can."

"What are we going to do?" he asked.

"We're going to fix this."

"But what are we going to *do*?"

I sighed. "Whatever it takes." I just had to hope we'd all survive the experience.

THIRTY-FOUR

EXPLAINING THE SITUATION TO SYLVESTER'S knights took almost fifteen minutes. It would probably have taken longer if I hadn't had the presence of mind to slap an illusion over myself before we went to the Garden of Glass Roses. Not a human disguise: a disguise to make me look the way I did before Amandine twisted the balance of my blood.

It took eight tries and active coaching from Connor for me to spin a convincing version of my own face. It wasn't something I'd ever needed to do before, and even as I shaped the spell, my instincts were insisting that looking like myself meant dropping the disguises, not constructing new ones. Unfortunately, we needed people to listen, not ask questions I didn't want to answer, and that meant keeping the focus on the situation.

Even with my masks up and Connor struggling to mediate, it seemed everyone had a question or a comment to make before they were willing to pay attention. Herding the fae really is a lot like herding cats, only pointier and less rewarding. Normally, Sylvester would have cut the discussion short and ordered them all to start looking for Oleander ... but this wasn't a normal situation, and sending them off before they really understood what we were up against would be a good way to get a lot of people killed.

Tavis cracked his knuckles, drawing himself up to his full height. Many breeds of fae trend toward "tall," but Bridge Trolls are tall *and* built like linebackers; when Tavis stood all the way up, it was like watching a wall decide to get involved. "When do I get to hit someone?" he demanded.

"You can hit Oleander if you find her, but you might want to use a net instead," I said. "She's enough of a snake that I wouldn't be surprised if she spits poison."

"Assuming she's there at all," muttered Garm. That was enough to set the room shouting again. Only Grianne stayed silent. Her Merry Dancers were expressive enough to make up for it. They'd been spinning wildly when we started, flashing a variety of garish colors that telegraphed her doubts. Now they were bobbing in the air on either side of her, glowing a steady green. That was reassuring. If we could convince Grianne, we could convince anybody ... or at least, Sylvester and Connor could.

Sylvester made inspiring pleas for cooperation. Connor provided support and a second voice arguing for my innocence. I just stood there trying to look harmless—whatever that meant. I was mostly fighting not to squirm. Disguises make my ears itch. After the third iteration of things I already knew, I backed away, moving to sit on one of the nearby benches. I was close enough to be visible, but maybe taking me out of the conversation would finally make it end. I could hope, anyway.

The light in the garden slanted through the roses around the bench, casting tiny prisms around me. I leaned on my hands, letting my attention drift. I've always loved the Garden of Glass Roses. It's soothing, and sometimes, I need to be soothed.

The argument had moved on to how Sylvester's guards were supposed to find a killer in a space the size of Shadowed Hills. Tavis was pointing out—with increasing volume—that if we didn't start looking soon, it wouldn't matter. The Queen would send someone to collect me, and we'd be done discussing.

The shouting was loud enough that I didn't hear Etienne coming until he sat beside me, folding his hands in his lap. I kept my attention on the roses. Neither of us spoke for several minutes, until finally, quietly, Etienne said, "I'm sorry."

I didn't look at him. "Don't worry about it. You didn't know."

"I saw the sword, and I thought—"

"Like I said, don't worry about it." I glanced back to the group. Sylvester seemed to be getting the crowd under control. "Poor guy."

Etienne followed my gaze. "The Duke?"

"Raysel's in this to her eyebrows. Being willing to admit that, and to deal with it . . . imagine having to sacrifice your own daughter."

Etienne stood, giving me a sidelong look. "What do you think he did when he stood by and let the Queen's guard have you?" he asked, before walking back to the others without waiting for an answer. I stared after him, speechless.

Sylvester's not my father. He's the man who pulled me out of the mortal world, and who kept Mom's secret for decades, watching me struggle to be Daoine Sidhe when he knew damn well that I wasn't.

He's also the man who took care of me when Mom wandered off on her little "expeditions." The man who watched me grow up, got me knighted, and made sure I would always have a place. He was "Uncle Sylvester" long before I understood that we weren't related. In all the ways that mattered, he'd been my father for a long time. It wasn't like his real daughter had set the bar particularly high. "At least I'm not planning to murder my mom," I muttered.

"October?" I looked up. Sylvester was gesturing me back. A consensus had apparently been reached, because the crowd dispersed as I stood, breaking into smaller groups and moving toward the door. Some offered me nods or fleeting smiles as they went, but none paused to say good-bye.

After less than a minute, only a few of us remained: Sylvester and Etienne, with matching grim expressions on their faces; Garm, looking quietly terrified; and Connor, who looked simply and deeply weary. Only Grianne had no expression to speak of, sitting frozen as a statue while her Merry Dancers flickered around her like strobe lights.

I turned to Sylvester, raising an eyebrow. "Well?"

"The others have gone to begin the search," said Sylvester. He sounded as worn-out as I felt. "They'll call if they see Rayseline or Oleander."

"Do they know what Oleander looks like?" Oleander and Nerium looked nothing alike. It wouldn't do us any good if they were so busy looking for a Hob that they walked right past the Peri, or vice versa.

"They know she may be disguised, and have descriptions of both of her known faces. She may have more; there's nothing we can do for that."

"It's a start." I glanced at the others. "So what are we going to do?"

"You're going to close your eyes and allow Garm to make sure that if Rayseline has called the Queen's guard, they don't take you away again," said Sylvester.

I blinked. "What?"

"Illusions," said Grianne. All of us turned to look at her. She shrugged. "They work against us. They can work for us, too."

Sylvester raised a hand, cutting me off before I could object. "Think about it."

I didn't like to admit it, but he was right: it wasn't safe for me to be seen wearing my own face with the Queen's guard, Raysel, and Oleander all out looking for me. Still . . . "Why can't I cast my own illusions?"

"Garm's Gwragen," said Connor, like that explained everything.

Sadly, it did. "Fine," I muttered, feeling balky and sullen. I hate having other people enchant me. It makes me itch even more than my own illusions do.

"Close your eyes," said Garm. I did as I was told. His hands pressed against my cheeks as the air filled with the taste of moss and swampy water. My cheeks and ears began to tingle and itch. I didn't move. Squirming too much could make him lose the spell, and I didn't want to make him start over.

The smell faded, taking the tingle with it, although the itch remained. Garm pulled his hands away. "It's done."

"Whee," I deadpanned, unsurprised when my voice came out higher than usual. The Gwragen are some of the best illusionists in Faerie. When they disguise something, they do it *right*. Opening my eyes, I blinked up at Connor, who was suddenly about six inches taller than me. I looked at my hands. They were slightly darker than I was used to, with long, slim fingers. I raised them to feel my face. My ears were even sharper than I expected, and my hair was a short, sleek bob. "Tuatha de Dannan?"

Etienne nodded. "There are enough of us in the knighthood that you shouldn't stand out."

"Right." Garm's illusion had traded my clothes for the livery of Shadowed Hills. I ran my fingers over the embroidered daffodil at my breast. It felt real. I'm not normally that paranoid, but after what Amandine did . . . "You're sure this is an illusion?"

"Of course," said Garm, sounding amused. "It's just a good one."

"Right." I was starting to sound like a broken record. "Let's get going."

"I won't be coming with you," said Sylvester.

That stopped the rest of us. "What?" I demanded, as Connor asked, "Why not?"

"I attract attention. Garm's illusions are good; they aren't flawless. I'd rather not subject them to any additional scrutiny."

I sighed before leaning over to hug him. "Open roads, Sylvester."

"Good luck." He hugged me back before letting go and walking deeper into the garden. If there was a way to get from there to where Luna slept, he'd know it.

The rest of us exchanged a glance. Etienne voiced what we were all thinking: "His Grace didn't tell us to stay together."

"You're right. He didn't." I looked at him. "Are you suggesting we split up?"

"We'd cover more ground that way."

"And you don't want me behind you and armed."

"Well . . . no," he said. "I truly believe your innocence. I'm still not comfortable with the idea that you're a fugitive from the Queen's justice."

"I'll stick with Toby," said Connor.

"As will I," said Grianne implacably. One of her Merry Dancers swung out to spin a lazy circle around my head. "It will be educational."

From the looks on Garm and Etienne's faces, she couldn't have surprised them more by announcing her intention to leave the knighthood and become a professional streetlamp. "Are you . . . sure?" asked Etienne, cautiously.

"Do you wish to debate?" There was a cold challenge in Grianne's tone. If they wanted to fight her on this, she'd fight. And she'd probably win.

"As you like." Etienne offered a shallow bow. "Garm and I will go left. The three of you may go right."

"Scream if there's trouble," I said. "I'm sure someone will hear you."

"I'm sure someone will." Etienne paused
"October . . ."

"Get out of here. We have a murderess to catch."
started down the hall, Connor pacing next to me, and
Grianne bringing up the rear like a silent shadow with
its own mood lighting. Etienne and Garm didn't call us
back. I didn't really expect them to.

We could hear the other knights calling to each other
as we walked through the knowe. They had their voices
pitched low, but in a space as enormous and quiet as
Shadowed Hills, even whispers carry. It was like walking through a world filled with ghosts. It didn't help that
Grianne's Merry Dancers were burning a steady, spec-
tral green, making the shadows jump and dance.

Periodically someone would cross our paths, nod
and keep going, even though none of them could have
recognized the face I was wearing. I was accompanied
by Connor and Grianne; that was all the permission
needed. I was starting to understand how Oleander in-
filtrated the knowe. If the other knights didn't look at
me closely when I was wearing their livery, with a known
killer loose in the knowe, how closely would they look at
a new member of the household staff?

Sylvester and I were going to have a talk about secu-
rity when this was over.

Shadowed Hills is massive on a good day. On a bad
day, it's like walking through a museum. Corridors lead
to nowhere, rooms follow rooms, and you find yourself
taking turns that make no linear sense. I've wanted a
map—or at least location signs on the corners—for a
long time. "You are here" doesn't seem as cheesy when
you've managed to stumble into the eighth library in as
many minutes. I tried to take note of the roses carved on
the walls, looking for the hidden patterns that Manuel
talked about, but they eluded me; I needed them explained before I could start following them.

I let my hand rest on the pommel of the sword I didn't

know how to use as we entered the long hall that led to the receiving room. Sometimes luck is all you have. Mine hadn't been treating me very well lately; maybe that meant I was due for a break. Connor stepped forward to open the receiving room door. He held it as Grianne and I walked through, finally slipping in behind us.

The receiving room lights were low enough to interfere with even my improved eyesight. Grianne made a complex gesture and the Merry Dancers soared upward, hanging in midair and brightening until they cast a strong enough glow for us to see by.

I glanced at her as we walked toward the dais. "Handy."

Her expression was as bland as ever as she nodded, but her Merry Dancers shifted color, turning a warm yellow. Maybe she wasn't as cold as everyone thought. Maybe we just read her wrong.

I waved Grianne to circle the dais to the left, and Connor to circle to the right, while I mounted the two shallow steps to the Ducal thrones by myself. They looked perfectly normal, like they were just waiting for their owners to return, but something about the scene was bothering me. Something that wasn't right—

A glint of light from one of the Merry Dancers reflected silver off the cushion on Raysel's throne. I leaned closer, until I was near enough to see the circle of needles embedded in the velvet cushion. Their tips protruded maybe half an inch, no more; just enough to break the skin. With Oleander, that was all they'd need. Each of those needles probably had enough poison on it to kill a Manticore. They would have been easy to overlook. I'd almost missed them, and I'd been looking for something out of place.

I almost had to admire Oleander's thoroughness. Use Raysel to kill Luna, and then kill Raysel: no loose ends, no untidiness, just a lot of dead bodies. From Oleander's screwed-up point of view, it was probably the ultimate in "cleaning up after yourself." When you're done playing with your toys, throw them away.

"We need gloves," I said, straightening up. "Gloves, and maybe some pliers."

"Why?" asked Connor, stepping onto the dais and moving to join me.

I gestured to the throne. Connor bent forward to squint at the cushion, and I grabbed his shoulder, keeping him from getting too close. Grianne stepped up on my other side, narrowing her eyes as she saw where we were looking. "Poison," she said.

"Exactly. Now come on." I started to step off the dais, and froze, sniffing the air.

I smelled blood.

I was raised Daoine Sidhe. That particular lie worked mostly because Daoine Sidhe know blood, and so do my mother and I. Blood has spoken to me since the day I was born, and with the changes Mother made in me, I could almost hear it screaming. I turned, walking toward the "sound" of the blood. My breath was tight in my chest, and my ears were ringing. Oak and ash, how was I supposed to live like this?

And then it didn't matter, because three red drops stained the dais next to Luna's throne. Blood. Fresh blood, or fresh enough, anyway.

"Toby?" said Connor, uncertainly. "What is it?"

"Blood." I knelt. "Can't you see it?"

"No."

"Nor I," added Grianne.

I ignored them, running a finger through the largest drop. The blood was still warm, fresh enough to come up in a slick red smear. It smelled like copper and fear, with a sharp floral undertone I couldn't quite identify. I took a deeper sniff and sneezed, my nose protesting against whatever that underlying flavor was.

"It's either Oleander's or one of her victims," I said, standing and wiping my hand against my pants. Connor nodded. Grianne, who was watching me with a mixture of wariness and amazement, did the same.

"Ah," said Grianne softly.

"I think it's poisoned; I can't ride it safely." It would have been wonderful to know who'd been hurt, but with Oleander loose, anything that smelled of flowers was likely to be poisoned. Even as little poison as could be in those three drops of blood might be enough to kill me. "On the bright side, whoever did the bleeding may be dead already."

It's never a good sign when I'm hoping to find a corpse. Connor grimaced, while Grianne cracked a brief smile, apparently seeing the irony. I echoed it back to her as I started scanning the area around us for more traces of blood.

The floor was checkered white and black. Even with the Merry Dancers floating overhead, the light was diffuse enough to make the blood all but invisible on the black squares. That didn't seem to matter, because once I started looking, the blood was practically glowing, seeming like the only source of color in a monochrome world. It didn't just stand out: it screamed for attention, proclaiming itself in the hopes that I would notice it. The drops in the next square over were smaller, like whoever it was had managed to staunch the bleeding.

"Well?" asked Grianne.

"Regular chatterbox tonight, aren't you?" I indicated the blood trail. "It picks up here." Whoever was doing the bleeding was at least trying to conceal it. After that first, probably accidental, series of drops on the white marble, all the blood was on the black. If I were anyone besides my mother's daughter, I might have missed it altogether.

"Do we follow?" asked Connor.

"You and I do. Grianne—"

"I will find the Duke," she said solemnly. Her Merry Dancers darted downward, spinning around her, and all three were gone, leaving Connor and me in darkness.

"Gosh, I love teleporters," I deadpanned. At least I didn't need the light anymore. The blood still stood out like spots of neon in the darkness. I started to follow the trail across the room, with Connor in my wake.

The blood led to the wall and stopped, save for a smear on the wainscoting. I touched the stain, and the wood slid down under my fingers, revealing another hidden passage in the service halls. More splashes of blood were on the floor there, getting sparser as they vanished into the darkness.

Connor followed me through, and the door swung shut behind us.

THIRTY-FIVE

THE SERVICE HALL WAS EVEN DARKER than the ballroom, but that didn't matter; I didn't need light to see that the trail was getting fresher. I took Connor's hand, guiding him. My other hand rested on the pommel of my borrowed sword. Sylvester wanted me to stop dying on him, so what did I do? I followed a trail of blood from an unknown source into a dark, enclosed area. *There's* a way to increase your life span. All I needed was a hungry dragon to walk behind me and I'd have all the "get dead faster" bases covered.

At least I wasn't doing it alone. If someone was hurt, we needed to find and help them if we could. It might be one of the other knights. It might even be one of the Hobs. Of course, most people don't take refuge in dark corners when they've been hurt. The Hobs might, since they spent most of their time in those halls, but I doubted it. Whoever was hiding back here probably wasn't wounded defending the honor of Shadowed Hills.

The hall bent to the left before coming to a dead end. I stopped, frowning at the walls. They looked solid, but I'd stopped believing anything in the place was as solid as it seemed. The doors might be hidden, but they were there, and they didn't seem to want to be found. "Connor? Which way?"

"Like I'd know?"

"Great," I muttered, dropping Connor's hand and leaning forward to touch the wall in front of me. It was dry. So was the left-hand wall. The wall to the right was damp, and my fingers came away sticky. I sniffed them Blood and flowers. The traces were getting stronger because I recognized them now: foxgloves, yarrow, and oleander.

How egotistical was it of Oleander to keep killing people with the flower she was named after? "Somebody didn't get hugged enough as a kid," I said.

"If we get out of here alive, you can have all the hugs you want."

"Noted." I pushed the wall, opening the hidden panel and stepping through into one of the knowe's many libraries.

The trail of blood picked up right outside the door standing out starkly against the gray carpet. It was so fresh that the smell was almost cloying; we were moving faster than the person we were following. We followed the blood out of the library and paused in near-unison as we realized that we were standing in front of the door to the Garden of Glass Roses. We'd followed the blood trail all the way through the knowe.

It didn't make sense unless the person we were following was actively trying to avoid Sylvester's guards If they were, the best place to be was somewhere the thought was already clear. The blood trail didn't enter the garden, streaking down the hall away from u instead. I sped up, grabbing Connor's wrist to tug him along and around the corner.

The trail ended at another door. This one was mahogany, with a narrow sword carved in place of an eyehole. recognized it more from rote memorization than actua familiarity; it led to the practice grounds, where members of the Court went for duels or sword-fighting lessons. I hadn't been there in decades, not since Etienne declared that my training was over. I opened the door and stepped out onto the packed earth of the grounds, Connor close behind me.

I'm not sure what I expected to see: I'd followed the blood trail through the knowe without knowing who I was running to ground. I had a few ideas, but they were all vague, half-formed things . . . and as it turned out, none of them was even close to right.

Oleander and Rayseline circled each other at the center of the field, each of them holding a knife. Oleander had a hand clamped against her side, shivering with something that looked like it ran deeper and closer to the bone than simple cold as she glared at Raysel. A flask was shattered on the ground between them, its golden contents sinking into the dirt. Oleander came like a snake, bearing her own venomous gifts, and it looked like she'd also been the one to receive them. The illusion that masked her as Nerium was gone, burned away by pain or maybe just released when it wasn't useful anymore.

Raysel glanced toward us as the door slammed shut. Oleander seized the opportunity, raising her knife and going into a lunge.

"Raysel! Look out!" shouted Connor.

Raysel whipped around, grabbing Oleander's wrist and stopping the knife in mid-descent. She brought her own knife up at the same time, burying it in Oleander's stomach. Oleander choked. Rayseline grinned, suddenly looking like the perfect predator—suddenly looking like Blind Michael's granddaughter.

"Connor, get behind me," I hissed, wishing desperately that I had my knives, or my baseball bat, or any sort of weapon that I actually knew how to *use*. A sword was impressive and all, but I was as likely to hurt myself as anybody else.

Raysel took a step back, yanking her knife free and watching with evident satisfaction as Oleander sank slowly to the ground. "Thanks for everything, Auntie," she purred. Turning, she blew a kiss at Connor. "Thank you, too, lover-boy. Go ahead and fuck your slut for now. Just don't get too attached. I'll be back."

She pulled a vial from inside her bodice, yanking the cork out with her teeth and spitting it at Oleander before downing the vial's ice blue contents. The dust-and-cobwebs scent of borrowed magic rose around her in an instant, carried on a bitterly cold wind. The air seemed to thicken, almost frosting over . . . and then she was gone, leaving the air to rush into the space she'd left behind.

"Did she just . . . ?" whispered Connor.

"She did." I stared at the empty air. "Someone loaned her that spell. Someone—root and fucking *branch*, who the hell loaned that crazy bitch a teleport spell?"

Oleander raised her head. "Wouldn't you like to know?" Blood had matted her hair to her forehead, and her dark eyes were narrowed, filled with fury.

"Yes," I said, not moving. If we were going to save her, it needed to be now. But Oleander was like a snake in more ways than one. She might strike if either of us came into range, just because she could, and there was no way to take her knife away.

"It's good to want things. Don't worry, it's safe; you can laugh all you want," she hissed. "I brewed the poison on her blade myself, and this wound might have been fatal even without it. I trained her well. I shape my tools in more than just bottles."

I motioned for Connor to stay where he was and stepped forward, keeping my hand on the pommel of my sword. I didn't care *how* wounded she was; if she moved, I'd kill her. "Do you want us to call for help?" I asked.

"No. No, I don't think so." She laughed, unwinding

her arms from around her middle. The skin of her hands and forearms was dark and slippery with blood. "Look."

There was a deep slash across the front of her tunic, lower than the wound we'd seen Raysel deliver. The edges parted as she moved, revealing a wound too long and deep to be anything but mortal. The last time I saw anyone cut that deeply it was January, Countess of Tamed Lightning, and she was already dead. Oleander's black clothing kept the blood from showing until it hit the ground, but that didn't matter. I could smell it.

"It could be healed if it were just a wound," she said. "With the poison, all that's left for me is dying. I'm good at what I do. Or I was. They'll never forget my name. In a thousand years, they'll still be whispering about me. The lives I took. The kingdoms I felled. I'm immortal." And she smiled.

"Look out!" shouted Connor.

It was pure instinct—instinct, and long years spent walking the line between "impulsive" and "embalmed"— that caused me to respond to his cry by ducking, whirling around, and drawing my sword, holding it in front of my face the way I would normally hold my baseball bat. The real Oleander's dagger glinted off the pommel, sending a spray of sparks into the air between us. She'd swapped herself for an illusion while we were distracted by Raysel's disappearance. If her decoy had held my attention for just a few seconds longer . . .

Oleander pressed down, putting as much weight as she could onto the blade of her knife. "You're coming with me," she snarled. "I'm not leaving here without one last kill." She pushed down a little harder with each word. Her eyes were glassy, the pupils huge. She was in shock and falling deeper as her body raced to see what would kill her: blood loss or the poison burning in the blood that remained. Only her age and the strength of her magic were still allowing her to throw illusions, and Maeve only knew how long that would last.

She was weak, and she was making one major, unavoidable mistake: she was applying the amount of
pressure she'd need to knock down someone six inches
shorter than I actually was. I gathered myself, tensing,
and shoved her away as hard as I could. She staggered
back about four feet, eyes widening with surprise, and
disappeared.

"Oh, great," I muttered, as I straightened and moved
the sword into a defensive position. "It's time for crazy
bitch illusionary hide-and-go-seek." The smell of her
blood was still heavy in the air.

The smell of her blood. I closed my eyes, trying to
relax. With as much as she was bleeding, she had to be
the strongest blood marker in the area. Let her disappear. I'd still find her—there. I whirled, raising my sword
back, and heard, again, the clank of metal on metal. She
withdrew as quickly as she'd come, leaving me tense and
waiting.

We repeated that pattern twice more—turn, parry,
retreat. The fourth time, she came at me too fast for a
simple block to stop. She'd been fighting for centuries,
and I barely knew one end of a sword from the other. I
didn't know how else to stop her, and so I swung at the
air as hard as I could, putting all my weight behind the
blade.

It hit resistance. I opened my eyes.

Oleander was visible again, staring in wide-eyed
amazement at the sword driven deep into her side, almost bisecting the older of her wounds. Her knife toppled from her fingers as she raised her head to stare at
me, and she dropped to her knees on the hard-packed
dirt, hands starting to scrabble uselessly against the hilt.

Connor stepped up behind her, the bow he'd taken
from the armory in his hands. He had an arrow notched
and ready to fire. Placing the tip against the back of her
neck, he said, pleasantly, "Make one wrong move, and I
swear to Maeve, I'll shoot you."

"There's no more damage to be done," she said, in a faint, almost thoughtful voice. "No more damage, no salvation. One more of Faerie's glorious monsters lost."

"If you'd left us alone—" I began.

"You'd have sent some hero after me, given time enough. I killed, I die. At least I killed like a monster kills, instead of with iron, and dying by inches. That's Titania's way, the Queen who stands in darkness and screams about her light. My poisons are kinder." Oleander touched the sword's pommel gently. "This is how it should end. They won't remember the way I died, but they'll remember how I lived, forever. I was the monster under your bed, wasn't I? I'll be the monster waiting for your children."

"Be still," I said. "Sylvester will be here soon."

"I suppose you want me to think you told him where you were going?" Her laughter was harsh, punctuated by gasps. "I know better."

"Why did you do this?" Grianne would have found the others by now, and she'd left us recently enough that her Merry Dancers would be able to lead her straight back to us. The cavalry was coming. That might not matter, because Oleander was fading fast.

"There's only one person I'd tell, and neither of you is her." She shuddered, her hand dropping away from the sword. "This ends here."

"Who are you waiting for?" I asked. "The Duke?"

"That dandy fool? No." She laughed again, bitterly. "I've finished my business with that one. I'm waiting for the one who got away."

The one who . . . I froze. "You're waiting for October."

"Yes," she said. "Bring her, and maybe I'll tell you. Bring me Amandine's heir."

They always ask for the one thing you don't want to give. "I'm here," I said.

She opened her eyes and frowned, looking at me. "I'm dying. I'm not stupid."

Scratch that idea. "I'm under an illusion spell."

"So drop it."

"I can't. It's Gwragen crafting."

Her frown remained. "Liar."

"I'm not lying! I just—"

"It's her," said Connor, quietly. "On my skin, it's her."

"Don't make oaths for her sake, Connor," I snapped. "She doesn't deserve it."

Oleander suddenly smiled. It was the kindest expression I'd ever seen on her face. "You *are* Amandine's daughter. Only her children ever manage that sort of self-righteous disgust."

"Children?" I echoed. "What are you talking about? Why are you here?"

"The Duke's little daughter invited me." Her smile didn't waver. "Oh, I hurt her once, and it seems she held more of a grudge than I knew, but she still invited me because I had something she wanted. I had the power to make the ones who failed her suffer. I may have helped to break her, but you, October, you and your kind . . . you're the ones who let me do it."

"It wasn't like that."

"Of course *you* can say that. You're sane." Oleander sighed. "Sometimes I wonder how that marshmallow of a man spawned someone so beautifully insane. But I really made her, didn't I? Sylvester's flesh, my heart. A fair return for what your mother stole from my Simon— what she stole from *me*." Her voice was weakening. It wasn't going to be much longer. Musingly, she added, "I should be grateful. Without her theft, without her desertion, he'd never have been mine to break."

I knelt, careful to stay out of reach. "I'd kill you if you weren't already dying."

"A rich sentiment from a woman who drove a sword through my gut, Amandine's daughter. At least my death is my own." The fierce lucidity was fading from her voice, leaving it cracked and broken. "You don't even know how much you've lost, do you?"

"Fourteen years, a husband, and a daughter. I have a pretty good idea."

"Like that matters? Mortality ends. We did you a favor." Oleander's laugh tapered into a bubbling cough. "We should have killed you then."

"You tried."

"We almost succeeded. It was a game." She sighed. "A wonderful game. I wasn't ready to stop playing."

"Well, you just lost." I didn't feel sorry for her anymore. She'd admitted to kidnapping Raysel; not in so many words, but still an admission. Whatever she was getting, she'd earned it.

"The game is just beginning. I was only a piece on the board." She sighed again, slumping backward. "Not even the strongest piece, although I tried so hard to take her."

"October?" Sylvester strode onto the practice grounds, with Garm and Etienne close behind him. All three of them stopped, Sylvester's eyes going wide. "You really found her."

Oleander didn't acknowledge their arrival. "You don't know how much you paid. Silly little bitch. You should've stayed in the pond. You should . . ." She coughed, blood foaming on her lips. "You should have taken the death I offered; at least it was yours alone. You could have ended the verses, then and there. How many times before your traitor's blood gets it right?"

I stood. Sylvester put a hand on my shoulder, stopping me from stepping forward. "No," he said. "Don't let her goad you."

"It's not like I was planning to *help* her," I muttered.

Oleander snorted. "I wouldn't take aid from you if you offered it. Never from you, daughter of Amandine, last and latest child of the great betrayal. You'll see the end of us all, and you won't be content until you know the gates are locked and sealed; your own death will refuse you. You'll destroy your beginnings and forsake your heart's desire, and there will be nothing for you but what's already been turned aside ..." Her voice trailed off. She sighed one last time before falling to one side, suddenly still.

We stood in that tableau for several minutes, staring at the body. It was almost like coming in at the middle of the movie; none of us knew what to say or how we were supposed to react.

Finally, I asked, "Is it over?"

Sylvester's hand tightened on my shoulder, and he nodded. "I hope so."

"Good." I paused. "Am I still going to be executed?"

He smiled before answering, "That's a good question."

Connor lowered his bow and moved to stand beside me, sliding his hand into mine. Sylvester nodded, seeming to accept this gesture as being the right thing to do. Grianne's Merry Dancers zipped through the open door, circling around us as we turned and walked back into the hall. I listened the whole time for the sound of the night-haunts' wings. I've heard them often enough that the sound is familiar. Soothing, even, in its messed-up way.

They were just beginning to beat when the door closed behind us, sealing the sound—and Oleander, one of Faerie's most glorious monsters—away.

THIRTY-SIX

I STOOD ON THE LUIDAEG'S DOORSTEP with one hand raised to knock, unable to force myself to finish the motion. Oleander had been dead for ten days, and the only person who could give me the answers I needed was on the other side of that door. I just wasn't sure they were answers I could live with.

The door opened before I was done arguing with myself. The Luidaeg's familiar, sun-weathered face poked out. "Well?" she demanded. "Are you coming in or not?"

"I'm coming," I said. She moved out of the way, motioning me impatiently forward, and I stepped inside.

The Luidaeg isn't one of the world's great housekeepers. She seems to enjoy living in squalor, allowing mold to grow on her walls and trash to build up on her floor. Still, there's usually at least a pretense of organization to the place—decaying pillows on the couch, soda cans and dishes in the kitchen. Not this time. Most fae celebrate Beltane with spring cleaning. The Luidaeg appeared to have celebrated with spring destruction.

"What—"

She cut me off with a gesture. "Don't." I looked at her

blankly. She shook her head. "This isn't a social visit; we both know that. That means you don't get an unlimited supply of questions, so let's not fuck around. Got me?' I nodded mutely. "Good. Now drop the masks. I need to see how far she took it."

Taking a deep breath, I did as she requested.

If the Luidaeg was surprised by the way I looked she did an admirable job of not showing it. Her eyes narrowed slightly, but that was all. That tiny gesture could have meant almost anything. "How's your magic been?"

"Good. Things seem to be coming a little easier."

"That's about what I figured. Congrats, kiddo, you're finally back to where you started. Why'd it take you so long to come and see me? I expected you the minute heard what happened."

"How did you—" I stopped myself. Knowing how the Luidaeg heard about my blood being rebalanced didn' matter as much as some of my other questions. Curios ity and necessity don't always match. "I crashed as soon as things calmed down. I slept for six days." You'd think my body would be used to my doing horrible things to it but when the adrenaline faded, I faded with it.

"Yeah, well, you put yourself through a hell of a lot That takes care of six days. What about the other four?

"I had to find a safe way to get here. The Queen's stil a little annoyed."

The Luidaeg snorted. "Right. So you got here by . . . ?

"Waiting for Acacia to show up and then asking he to open a Rose Road." That wasn't my first choice. M first choice was the Shadow Roads, preferably with Ty balt as my escort; we needed to talk. Unfortunately, th Cat's Court was still in chaos, and now that I wasn't i danger of dying, I wasn't a priority. Tybalt and I neede to have that talk. We were just going to have it later tha I liked.

The rose goblins went for Acacia as soon as Luna was recovered enough to open a gate for them, and Acacia did more for her daughter in a few hours than anyone else had managed in days. The Firstborn are handy that way. I just wish we'd been able to reach her sooner.

"Good call." The Luidaeg tipped her chin down, studying me. "Three questions, and then you have to go. Don't waste a question asking why it works that way. It just does."

"Faerie and her traditions, fucking up my life since time immemorial." I sighed. "All right, Luidaeg. I know I'm not Daoine Sidhe. What does that make me?"

"It makes you my sister's daughter."

I gaped at her. "I . . . you . . . what?"

She ignored my second question, continuing, "My father named your race before he left; he called you the Dóchas Sidhe. You're blood-workers. You must have figured that part out. Beyond that? What you're for, why Faerie needed you? I can't say."

"Can't say, or don't know?"

"Ah." The Luidaeg glanced away, but I saw her smile. "I bet you asked that without counting questions, didn't you? Congrats. Your impulsiveness isn't wasted for a change. I can't say. I'm not allowed, just like I'm not allowed to answer more than three questions today. Don't ask who made the rules. You'll find out soon enough."

"I hate riddles," I said, still staggered by her statement. Amandine was Firstborn. I wasn't just "not Daoine Sidhe," I was the daughter of one of the Firstborn.

That explained a lot, actually.

"Sorry," said the Luidaeg, unapologetically.

I took a deep breath, and asked the one thing I really needed to know: "Luidaeg, why did my mother lie to me?"

"Fuck, Toby, you just can't ask the easy ones, can

you?" The question had the bitter lilt of the rhetorical; she didn't expect an answer, and I didn't give one. Sighing, the Luidaeg said, "She lied because she was trying to save you."

"From what?" I asked, before I could stop myself.

Offering a small, warning shake of her head, she continued, "There are things in Faerie that don't like your mother much, and they don't like you either, because you're the last one left to play heir for her. Sorry. She tried to spare you. First by changing your blood to make you mortal before anyone knew you existed, and then by lying about your heritage. You'd always be weak if you considered yourself Daoine Sidhe. Your race doesn't have any of Titania's blood, and she's the mother of illusions. But if you knew yourself, if you knew what you could do . . ."

"So she lied to me?" This time, I was the one asking the rhetorical question.

"She thought she was doing the right thing," said the Luidaeg, tone off-handed enough to make it plain that she wasn't answering me; just making an observation. "Amandine was never the most stable of my siblings, and that's saying a lot. Faerie wasn't kind to her. She thought getting you out was the best thing she could do for you."

"I . . ." I paused. I would have agreed wholeheartedly with Amandine's decision to turn me human not that long ago. Maybe not after Evening died—I gave back the hope chest, I'd like to think I would've been together enough to tell my mother "no"—but before that? Before the pond? I would have told Sylvester thanks but no thanks for a place in his service, told Devin I had a way out, and gone off to live happily ever after in the mortal world.

If I'd done that . . . Rayseline would still have lost her mind. Evening would still have died. Blind Michael's

Ride would still have taken the children. And I wouldn't have been there to do anything about any of it.

The Luidaeg sighed at my expression. "She did the best she could. It was fucked-up and wrong for you, but it was still the best she could do. Don't get me wrong," she raised a hand, palm turned toward me, "I'm not a fan of Amandine's. She and I have some old issues. But mothers are allowed to make mistakes."

If I'd been human, I wouldn't have left my own daughter behind. Mothers make mistakes. "Luidaeg—"

She shook her head. "No. You've had three questions, and as much wiggle room as I can give you. Now's the time where you get the fuck out of here. Besides, you still look like hammered shit. Go get some sleep. You're staying at Shadowed Hills?"

"I am." I dug a hand into my pocket, coming up with a fistful of red-black rose petals that glowed with their own interior light. "Acacia gave me a ticket back for when we were finished here."

"How sweet of her. I have a detour for you to make before you go back."

I eyed her warily as I tucked the petals back in my pocket. "Define 'detour.'"

"Detour. A word meaning 'I'm Firstborn, and I could kick your ass without thinking about it, so how about you just go along with me and nobody gets hurt.'" A corner of the Luidaeg's mouth tipped upward in the semblance of a smile. "If all my nieces and nephews were as stubborn as you, Faerie would have a much larger under-population problem, because I would never have let them live to breed."

"You say the sweetest things," I said blandly. "All right. Where am I going?"

"Through here." She turned and opened the door to her kitchen closet, displaying rotting mops and ancient canned goods. I raised an eyebrow. She glanced into the closet, said, "Whoops," and closed the door, pausing a moment before opening it again.

The closet was gone. The doorway opened on the familiar greens of Lily's knowe. I could see figures in the distance, clustered around one of the pavilions that seemed to crop up there like mushrooms after the rain. I looked at the Luidaeg. She nodded.

"Right," I said, and offered a wan smile. "So I'll see you later."

"After you've dealt with the Queen, you come and see me again. Just make sure it's not for at least a week. I've got shit to do."

"Luidaeg . . ." I hesitated. "Is everything all right?"

The whites of her eyes darkened for a moment, almost vanishing against the ordinary brown of her irises. She blinked and her eyes were normal again; normal, and sad. "Nothing in this world is ever all the way right, October," she said quietly. "Now get out of here. There are people you need to be looking after."

"Right," I repeated, and stepped through the door.

There was no real moment of transition, no distortion or disorientation. It was as easy as stepping through a normal doorway, if you discount the fact that walking through a normal doorway doesn't usually result in quite that extreme a change in temperature. The Luidaeg's apartment was warm and dry. Lily's knowe was moist, and cold enough to border on clammy. I stopped where I was, taking an uneasy breath as I realized what the change in temperature meant.

Lily was gone. And with her out of the picture, the knowe—which had always been sustained almost entirely by her unique sort of magic—was dying.

Marcia spotted me before I trudged more than halfway across the mossy expanse between my point of arrival and the pavilion. She came racing down the pavilion steps, looking small and frazzled in her oversized obviously secondhand sweater. "Toby! You're alive!"

"Hey, Marcia," I said. "Yeah, I'm alive. I've just been in hiding. Still am, sort of. I'm not quite ready to cope with the Queen yet. How's everybody here?"

"Cold," said Walther, exiting the pavilion at a more sedate pace and walking out to join us. "Hello, October. How are you?"

"I think we've already established 'alive' as the important thing. How far has the temperature dropped?"

"Far enough. Some of the outlying ponds have already blended back into nothing. It won't be long now."

Marcia looked between the two of us, expression openly perplexed. Poor kid. My education was acquired in drips and drabs, either spoon-fed to me by Devin to prepare me for a job or offered up by Sylvester when he realized there was something I needed to know. That was still probably a lot more education than Marcia ever got.

Shadowed Hills was built. Hands shaped it out of the stone and earth of the Summerlands; spells were cast to shore up the walls and define the grounds. Undine don't build their knowes that way. Undine tie themselves to springs in the mortal realm, and become springs in the fae realm, channeling not water, but the fabric of their personal homes. Without Lily to channel the magic that made her knowe real, it was fading.

"What's going on?" she asked. "What are you talking about?"

There were a lot of things I could have said. I considered them all, and decided on the hardest thing of all: the truth. "Lily's gone," I said. "The knowe's dying."

Marcia's eyes widened, the color going out of her cheeks. In the end, she didn't cry. She just nodded, shoulders slumping. "I was afraid you'd say something like that," she said. "Isn't there . . . isn't there anything you can do?"

A choice needed to be made. I could tell her "no." I could tell her I'd done everything I could to take care

of them, I had problems of my own, I had the Queen o
the Mists gunning for me and a possible death sentenc
hanging over my head. I could tell her Lily couldn't pos
sibly have thought I could really save them.

"Yeah," I said, looking from her to Walther. He wa
smiling like the sun. "Has either of you ever been t
Goldengreen?"

THIRTY-SEVEN

"WILL OCTOBER DAYE, COUNTESS of Golden-green, knight errant of Shadowed Hills, please stand forth?"

The herald's voice was cold. I swallowed as I rose and approached the throne, trying to chase the dryness from my throat. My shoes pinched my feet, making me stumble. It could've been worse. I could've been wearing heels.

It had been almost three weeks since we ran Oleander to ground: three weeks of sleepless days and anxious nights spent waiting to see what was coming next. Oleander was Simon's constant companion. If she was here, he should've been there, too. But the days passed, and Simon never appeared.

There was no sign of Rayseline. Sylvester looked, but his heart wasn't really in it—he didn't want to fight his own daughter, and I couldn't blame him. It was a fight I was happy to delay, because I was sure that if we found her, we'd find Simon; snakes den together. I wondered if he knew what he'd created when he set out to break his niece. Oleander certainly hadn't. She'd been surprised

as she died, amazed that something she'd helped to cra
could really be that unreservedly, killingly cruel.

That's the thing about children: they pay attentic
and they learn. Raysel learned coldness, cruelty, a
how to kill. Teaching her those lessons may have be
the most foolish thing Oleander ever did, and more th
ever, I was glad she'd paid for what she'd done. Sylvest
and Luna didn't deserve this.

Neither did Rayseline. She was an innocent when O
ander took her, and she'd never had a chance to cor
all the way home. Now she never would. It wasn't rea
a surprise when Saltmist sent a herald to announce t
formal dissolution of the diplomatic marriage betwe
Rayseline and Connor. Marrying one of your dignitari
to a madwoman was one thing; marrying him to a m
deress was something else entirely.

The Queen has never been a patient woman, and t
wolves were at Sylvester's door long before I made n
visit to the Luidaeg or moved Lily's subjects into t
deserted front hall of Goldengreen. Sylvester did h
best to shield me from the trouble she was causing hi
I heard, instead, that Connor was going to be resumi
his diplomatic post within the Duchy, that Luna's hea
was improving steadily, and that May and Quentin h
broken six vases and a crystal ball trying to play hock
in the solarium.

And then one day, I heard that Luna was out of be
Jin called Walther a godsend. He was a chemist, no
healer, but his understanding of plants and poisons ma
it possible for her to take proper care of Luna until A
cia could get there. He told Jin what Luna needed, a
Jin made it happen, pulling Luna back from the ec
of whatever abyss she'd been facing. Her stolen Kitsu
skin was gone, but she would recover. Somehow, wate
ing Sylvester cry as he folded her back into his arm
thought her recovery was the only thing that mattere

Sylvester found me in the Garden of Glass Roses t

ays after Luna woke up. I was plucking the petals from
frosted pink rose and dropping them to the path, lis-
ening to the crystalline chimes they made when they
anded. He sat beside me, tucking his hands between his
nees in an almost guilty posture.

"Hey," I said, putting the flower down.

"The Queen's guard was here today," he said. "She
nows you're here, Toby. She's not . . . the Queen is not
stupid woman, and she knows we're hiding you." He
aused. "She's known for a while."

"I'd be more surprised if she didn't." I wasn't fright-
ned anymore—just numb. Everything ends. Lily's peo-
le were safe in Goldengreen. I'd done what I needed to
o. "Are they still here? I can go with them."

"No. We sent them away."

"What, then?" I leaned back on my hands. I hadn't
xpected him to let me go quietly, but I didn't see much
lse he could do. She was the Queen of the Mists, and he,
or all that he'd been a hero, was just a Duke. She'd take
ne eventually, unless—a thought hit me, and I froze,
yes widening. "You're not planning to go to war, are
ou?"

Sylvester shook his head. "Not quite. We've admitted
at you're here. She's not willing to lay siege to Shad-
wed Hills; we're too well-defended, and she knows
ost of the Kingdom would come to my aid, not hers."

"The man who would be King?" I said lightly.

"I should hope not."

"So what are we going to do?"

"We're going to wait." He smiled, but his jaw was set
the hard line that I'd long since come to recognize as
sign that he wouldn't budge. "And then we're going to
o to her and find out how far she's willing to push this
tle game."

"I don't understand."

"You don't have to." He stood, kissing my forehead
fore turning and walking away. I watched him go. He

was a hero once, and it's the nature of heroes to thro
themselves headlong into impossible odds, believir
that somehow they'll come through them alive. Th
problem is that it's also in the nature of heroes to di
and I had no way of being sure that Sylvester didn't pla
to do exactly that. I should know how heroes are. Som
where along the way, I became one.

I was still mad at him. I still loved him. I didn't kno
what to do about that. So I didn't do anything, and e
ery day, Karen came to me and kept me dreaming fe
as long as she could, guiding me through fanciful lan
scapes and showing me her siblings' dreams. There
something to be said for having an oneiromancer in th
family. Her visits, intangible as they were, helped n
feel like I wasn't quite as trapped as I actually was. The
probably reassured Mitch and Stacy, too. That was a ni
bonus.

May came to my rooms eight days after I sat wi
Sylvester in the garden. She was carrying an armloa
of clothes I recognized from our apartment. Her sele
tions confused me. Normally my Fetch—former Fetc
these days, even if neither of us is sure exactly what sh
is now—goes out of her way to dress me in bright colo
and fabrics. These were simple, bordering on sedate:
knee-length black cotton skirt, the matching blazer, ar
a burgundy silk shirt. There were even nylons. She mu
have stopped at a store before coming to the knowe, b
cause I knew I didn't have those at home.

I looked at the clothes, then at her. "What's all this'

"Clothing." She held up a pair of black dress fla
with the price tag still attached.

"I got that far," I said. "Why do I need these clothes

"Because it's time to go to Court."

It took a moment to realize she meant the Quee
Court, not the Court at Shadowed Hills. It was time,
other words, to face the music and deal with everythi
that had happened. There was still a death senten

anging over my head. I'd have to face it sometime, and sometime" was apparently "now."

The night was cold when we drove into San Francisco. Mist hung heavy all the way around the coast, blurring the shape of the land. The narrow beam of a lighthouse lamp swept through the distance, trying to warn any ships stupid enough to be out sailing that they were about to have a final, fatal encounter with the shore. It wasn't the sort of night you want to be outside on, no matter what species you are.

We parked in the shadow of a crumbling tenement that miraculously had a parking lot large enough for all seven of our cars. Magic comes in handy for a lot of things, not the least of which is finding parking on a Saturday night in San Francisco. It was a short walk from here to the beach. Sylvester and May paced on either side of me, prodding me whenever I slowed down. I was as anxious to get this over with as they were, but that didn't make it easier to walk to my own execution.

"I think I'd welcome a sea serpent right about now."

May glanced at me, eyes glittering in the moonlight. "What?"

"Nothing."

The rest of the Court of Shadowed Hills walked right behind us, clad in the cold sparkle of their human disguises; Luna was still at the knowe, having pled exhaustion. I was the only one wearing formal clothes visible to mortal eyes. If the Queen stripped my illusions away, I wouldn't be marching to the Iron Tree in jeans and a dirty sweater.

Sometimes I hate the morbid turns my mind can take. I could almost see the tree and the rope they'd use to tie me to the trunk before they lit the fire—

I shook my head, brushing the image away. "I don't like this."

"You don't have to like it," said May, prodding me forward again. "You just have to keep walking."

"That's good, because I *don't* like this." We we
climbing over the rocks now. My dress shoes provide
surprisingly good traction. Sylvester caught me ar
smiled every time I stumbled. He'd been smiling sine
we left Shadowed Hills. I would've felt better if I
known exactly why.

"Shut up and keep walking," May said. I glared at h
and did as I was told.

Our footsteps sounded like an approaching arn
as we waded through the shallow water pooled at t
mouth of the cave entrance to the knowe. We were a
most halfway to the door before I realized that my fe
weren't getting wet. I blinked, looking down.

"Warding spell," said Sylvester. "Tybalt uses it to st
dry. He taught it to me."

"Right," I said, and kept walking as I considered t
improbability of Sylvester and Tybalt spending enou
time together to teach each other spells. We were almc
there, pushing against the intangible barrier betwe
the fae and mortal worlds ...

... and we were through. The Queen's kno
opened in front of us like a mountain appearing throu
the mist, marble floors and pillars unfolding as the ca
walls and the sharp smell of the sea dropped away. I e
pected that.

It was the size of the crowd that brought me stagg
ing to a stop.

I thought the group that assembled for my first tr
was vast. I was wrong. This one was twice that size. Mit
and Stacy were there again; Tybalt was missing, but F
and Helen were there, holding hands. Walther, Marc
Kerry—even April O'Leary, the cyber-Dryad Count
of Tamed Lightning, and her seneschal, Elliot. I sto
there, stunned and staring until Sylvester made the m
ter moot, pushing me into the open space between t
crowd and the dais.

The Queen's throne was empty, waiting for her d

matic entrance. The crowd washed me up in front of it like a wave washes driftwood onto the beach; the driftwood can't fight, and neither could I. Sylvester squeezed my shoulder as he stepped away, whispering, "It will be all right."

Then he was gone, and the herald called for me to step forward.

"Here," I said. My voice broke. I paused, closing my eyes, and repeated, "Here," in a deeper, calmer tone. If I was going to die, I was going to do it with dignity.

"Finally," said the Queen from behind me. I couldn't help myself; I whirled to find myself looking directly into her eyes. "I wondered when you'd come see me again."

My knees dipped in a curtsy without consulting the rest of me, letting me rip my eyes away from her half-mad, black-rimmed gaze. "Highness," I said, still looking down. I couldn't forget the things she'd said to me while I was her captive, and suddenly, she scared me more than ever.

"You missed our last appointment," she said, the heels of her shoes clacking on the marble floor as she walked past me. "I came to see you to your—shall we call it a reward for services rendered, do you think?— and found that you'd left us far too early."

Even now, she wouldn't say "death." Purebloods almost never will. "I'm sorry, Highness," I said, rising and turning, eyes still downcast, to face the dais.

"No cries of innocence or pretty words geared toward your own defense? You disappoint me." I heard, rather than saw, her settling onto the throne.

"The Duchess of Shadowed Hills was in danger." It was true: if Tybalt and the others hadn't broken me out of jail, Luna would have died.

"So you placed the value of one woman above the Queen's own justice?" she asked, seemingly oblivious to the murmur that ran through the already whispering crowd. The Torquills have always been well-loved in San

Francisco, and from the sound of things, I had more support in the crowd than the Queen thought.

"Yes, I did," I said, raising my head. "I was half-dead from iron poisoning when I was pulled out of your jail, and I could barely stand, but yes, I chose not to return. I placed the lives of Luna Torquill and the subjects of Shadowed Hills above your justice. And if I had it to do over again, I *still* wouldn't come back to be lit like some sort of birthday candle." I shook my head. "You say I placed Luna's life over your justice; I say you're wrong, because whatever sentenced me to die here, it wasn't justice."

She stared. I looked back as calmly as I could, daring her to speak. For a long moment, all was silent. Then she leaned back, crossing one leg over the other, and said, "Very well. For your crimes against this Kingdom, again I sentence you, October Daye, to burn—"

"Excuse me?" Sylvester's voice was mild and almost unobtrusive.

The Queen's head snapped up, eyes narrowing. "It isn't your turn to speak, Torquill. Your trial is next."

"I believe," he said, still mild, "that as a subject of this kingdom, I have the right to ask why this charming young lady—a friend of my fiefdom, and a knight in my service—is going to be burned. It seems rather a waste of a good knight, if you ask me."

"I don't believe anyone did," she said, between gritted teeth.

"Even so, I'd like to hear the charges, since I believe it's been established that she killed neither the Lady of the Tea Gardens nor my charming—and quite living—wife."

The Queen's eyes swept the crowd, finding no support. Sharply, she said, "She stands accused of the murder of Blind Michael, Firstborn of Oberon and Maeve." She couldn't accuse me of Oleander's death. No one who wasn't there to see what happened knew the truth about how Oleander de Merelands met her end.

"Oh, yes! Yes, she killed my father-in-law. There's just one problem, Highness."

"What's that?" she asked, voice dropping to a dangerously low register.

"She's been pardoned for the crime." Sylvester snapped his fingers. Quentin stepped out of the crowd, a scroll in his hands. If that kid's grin had been any bigger, it would've split his face in two. "Permission for my page to approach the throne?"

"Granted," hissed the Queen. Quentin crossed the space between Sylvester and the Queen in about eight steps, pressing the scroll into her hands before he bowed and stepped away. She looked at him suspiciously, breaking the wax seal on the parchment.

A deep, melodic voice filled the room. "By the order of King Aethlin Sollys and Queen Maida Sollys, rulers of the Western Lands, Countess October Christine Daye, daughter of Amandine, is granted full pardon for her role in the death of the Firstborn known as Blind Michael. We have examined the events leading to his death and determined that what fault exists is upon Blind Michael himself. We thank the Countess Daye for acting as our executioner in this matter. By our hands, King Aethlin and Queen Maida Sollys of the Western Lands."

The crowd erupted into cheers as the proclamation finished. Not everyone was cheering—some were silent out of shock, I was sure, and some because they'd wanted to see me burn. Sylvester was quiet, watching the Queen with the mild expression I recognized as a sign of intense concentration. He wanted to see how she reacted.

So did I. My first trial wasn't a trial; it was an excuse to condemn me. This one would have been the same, but Sylvester changed the rules. He and I were going to have words about that pardon later. I knew it was genuine. He wasn't dumb enough to forge a message from the King of the Westlands. She didn't have an excuse to send me to my death this time. She couldn't even prosecute me for the jailbreak, because the King had made the crime she imprisoned me for irrelevant. So what was she going to do?

The cheering faded, and the crowd waited to hear what she'd say. The Queen stared at the scroll with narrowed eyes, like she could will the words to change. Then she lifted her head, looking at me.

"A pardon," she said, as lightly as if she were requesting a cup of tea.

"Apparently so, Highness," Sylvester said.

"From King Sollys, no less. Fascinating. I didn't know he kept such close tabs on what goes on in our little Kingdom." This time her gaze was for Sylvester, moonmad eyes filled with suspicion. He met that look without flinching. Maybe he cheated by requesting that pardon his look said, but she'd cheated first by requiring it.

"Apparently so, Highness," he said again.

Her eyes came back to me, and I could see the hatred there. I just kept screwing up her plans. "Fine," she said, throwing the pardon aside. It hit the floor and rolled closed, the wax seal turning deep blue as it melted back together. "It seems we have no crimes to charge you with. Oleander de Merelands killed Lily and was killed in turn by Rayseline Torquill; you've been pardoned for the death of Blind Michael. Your luck has held."

"Does that mean I'm free to go, Your Highness?"

She glared at me even as she nodded. "Yes, you are."

I paused. It probably wasn't worth it, but . . . "Your Highness?"

"What is it?" she snapped. Great. Trust me to push my luck with an angry, half-crazy queen.

"My knives, Your Highness."

She stared at me, then clapped her hands and disappeared. My scabbard appeared in front of me, hitting the floor before I had a chance to catch it. I stooped to pick it up, checking to see that both knives were where they belonged. They were. I could feel the iron knife, even through the leather of the scabbard. That was going to be a problem.

And then May and Quentin were there, swinging me into an embrace that was half joy, half relief. Quentin was laughing, and May was grinning through her tears. I barked a laugh that was almost a sob and hugged them back.

Sylvester walked over, moving at the head of a slightly more sedate wave of people. He nodded to me. "I told you not to worry, didn't I?"

I stepped away from Quentin and May. "You could've warned me."

"And had you mouth off to the Queen more than you already were?"

He had a point. I do tend to get cocky. "It was still sneaky."

"Agreed." I leaned over to hug him, ignoring the way my scabbard dug into my belly. That seemed to be some sort of cue, because Stacy, Cassandra, and Raj hit us from the left, while Walther, Mitch, and Connor came from the right. Someone in the middle of that massive, relieved embrace was laughing; after a moment, I realized it was me.

We weren't finished. Raysel was missing, and Simon, wherever he was, wasn't going to be happy about Oleander's death. The Queen of the Mists hated me, and Goldengreen was full of Lily's former subjects. Luna was recovering, but weak. And for the moment, none of that mattered. We were here, we were alive, and somehow, things were going to work out. I was sure of it. Things have to work out in the end, even if it takes throwing yourself at them until something gives way. Most of the time it's you, but sometimes, when you get lucky, it's the world.

"Satisfied now?" asked Sylvester, shouting to be heard over the crowd.

I grinned, shaking my head. "You *bastard*."

"And?"

"And nothing." We weren't done yet—the world probably still needed to be saved. The world almost always needs to be saved.

The world could wait.

Closing my eyes, I leaned forward and hugged Sylvester more tightly, letting the laughter of the people around me chase away the fears of the last few months. It would be all right, because we would *make* it that way. We had to. Wait and see.

Coming in September 2011
the fifth October Daye novel from

SEANAN MCGUIRE

ONE SALT SEA

Read on for a sneak preview.

THE DINER WAS SMALL ENOUGH TO BE claustrophobic, and the state of the floors and windows told me the owners weren't particularly worried about the Health Department. The smell of hot grease and fried fish hung in the air, so thick that breathing it was probably enough to clog the average man's arteries. Pixies hovered above the counter, occasionally diving to seize chunks of deep-fried *something* from a platter that seemed to have been set out for that express purpose.

The man working the grill was portly, balding, and blue-skinned, with fringed gills set deep into his neck. This had to be a purely fae establishment, like Home used to be—a business on the borderline between worlds, owned and operated without mortal intervention.

I glanced at Connor. "Could I find this place without you?"

Connor grinned. "Not unless Bill wanted you to." He raised a hand in greeting to the man behind the counter. "Hey, Bill."

Bill looked up, jerking a thumb toward the door at the back of the diner. "She's waitin' for you."

"Got it," said Connor. "Toby, come on."

"Private room?" I asked, following. Quentin was only a step behind me, although his attention was diverted by the fish on the counter. Daoine Sidhe and knight-in training or not, he's still a teenage boy. "Do they serve food back there?"

Quentin shot me a grateful look. Connor nodded.

"Sure." Looking back over his shoulder, he called "Bill! Three seafood stews and a fish and chips platter to the back." He glanced at Quentin and added, "And a chocolate milkshake."

"Large," said Quentin.

"Got it," rumbled Bill. "Herself has already been here for a while. I'd move it if I were you."

"We're moving," said Connor. He pushed open the door to the back, shooting me a pleading look before stepping inside. I'd have had to be blind to miss the "please behave" in his expression.

I rolled my eyes, following him into the room, and stopped dead. "Holy . . ."

We could have been standing in the main dining room of a five-star restaurant, the sort that tourists would sell kidneys to get reservations at. The opposite wall consisted of three sets of massive sliding glass doors, leading out to a balcony that might, on a warmer night, have been a pleasant place to nurse a cocktail or two. They were open, letting a fresh breeze blow through and circulate the air. The walls were varnished redwood, and the tables were elegant and expensive-looking, made from deep gray slate shot through with veins of white. An appetizer plate in a place like this would cost me a month's rent. Maybe two.

Dianda Lorden sat alone at the room's sole occupied table. A half-empty plate of seafood linguine was pushed to one side, and she was sipping from a wineglass of cloudy liquid. Whatever she was drinking was probably heavily laced with salt. Merrow shunt salt almost as

ast as they take it in—that's how they can survive in salt
water without getting poisoned. Normally, just breath-
ng underwater would replenish her body's supply. Up
here, she needed to find other ways to take it in.

The other local Duchess of my acquaintance, Luna
Torquill, nearly died from salt poisoning not that long
ago. The irony didn't escape me.

At first glance, I thought Dianda was wearing a long
blue dress and sitting in a low chair. Then I realized it
was actually a short blue blouse, and she was sitting in a
wheelchair, which would let her retain a certain amount
of mobility on land without the strain of being bipedal.
Where her legs had been, she now had a classic mermaid's tail, scaled in jewel-toned blue, green, and purple.
Her flukes trailed to brush the floor, flipping upward
every few seconds in what looked like an involuntary
motion. She couldn't have been mistaken for human,
or even for Daoine Sidhe . . . but oak and ash, she was
beautiful.

She looked up, gaze going from me to Quentin, and
finally to Connor, before she raised her eyebrows in silent question.

If anyone was going to justify Quentin's presence,
it was me. "He's my squire, Your Grace." On land, any
invitation issued to knights automatically includes their
squires. I didn't know if things worked differently in
the Undersea, but Connor hadn't said anything, and I
trusted him to keep me from sticking my foot too far
into my mouth.

Dianda's attention swung to me. "Countess Daye,"
she said, raising her wineglass for another sip. "Patrick
couldn't join us. He was afraid you'd decide to knock
him over again." A slight quirk of her lips told me she
was joking. Possibly.

"I could have decided not to, Your Grace, but then
he'd probably be out cold until sometime next century."
Elf-shot won't kill a pureblood, but it'll put a major

crimp in their social life. "I appreciate your seeing m
on such short notice."

"When the Luidaeg asks me to do something, I tr
to oblige her." She set her glass aside. "Besides, I kno
you. You're Sylvester's changeling knight, or you wer
until they decided to give you the Winterrose's Count
You're the one who killed Blind Michael. The Underse
owes you a debt of gratitude for that. He took from u
too." She paused before adding, more quietly, "You'r
Amandine's daughter."

"All true," I admitted, walking over to her table. "Ma
we sit?"

Dianda looked at me appraisingly before turning t
Connor. "Take the kid to the front and feed him. Fee
yourself, too. Those landers let you get way too thin."

"Quentin, go with Connor," I said, still facing Diand
"But—"

"You'll be between us and the door. Now go eat yo
fish. We'll be out in a minute."

"Come on," said Connor. Quentin doubtless wante
to stay and argue more, but his training won out; arguin
with me in front of a Duchess would have been inappr
priate. Two sets of footsteps moved away.

Dianda's flukes slapped the floor as the sound of th
closing door echoed through the room. "Now you ma
sit."

"Good." I took the chair across from her. "Nice, u
fins."

"Legs are tiring when the water is distant. I need
save my strength."

"Right, about that . . . I want to find your sons. I nee
your help for that."

"Why don't you try asking your Queen?" she aske
mildly.

"Because I don't think she has them." I shrugge
"Everyone knows the Queen of the Mists hates me. Sl
wouldn't let me anywhere near this investigation if sl

ad your sons, because she knows that if I find them, ou'll get them back. Not her, not anyone else, *you*. They von't be bargaining chips."

Dianda reached for her wineglass, picking it up and urning it slowly. She seemed to reach a decision, be- ause, without looking up, she said, "Their names are Dean and Peter. Dean's older—he's almost eighteen— nd he's less willing to trust strangers. He lost his best riend to a fishing boat a few years back, and it's made im cautious."

"There's no way he'd have gone willingly?"

"Not unless it was someone he knew, and my de- nesne has been searched. We deal with conspiracies uickly and permanently in the Undersea. If it were one f my people, the boys would be home by now."

"What's Peter like?"

"Innocent. Sweet. He's twelve." Dianda's expression as pained. "He likes the sun. Says it's pretty. He takes nore after my side of the family."

"Takes after..." Dianda was Merrow, but Patrick as Daoine Sidhe. Daoine Sidhe can't breathe water. How do you keep Dean alive?"

Her wince told me I'd guessed right. "The Court lchemist brews a special potion for him and for his ather."

"How often does the dosage need to be refreshed?"

"Once a day."

If Dean was being held underwater, he was either ead already or would be soon. The son of a mermaid, rowning. There was a sort of horrible poetry to the lea. "So we don't have much time. Do you know any- ing that might help me find them?"

She paused, studying me as she put her wineglass own again. "You mean it, don't you? This isn't some azy attempt to stall for time. You're serious."

"Even if you said that proving the innocence of the nd Courts wouldn't make you call off the attack, I'd

look for your kids." I shook my head. "Children aren
pawns. They deserve better than this."

She smiled hesitantly, offering her hand across th
table. "That's what I needed you to say."

"Good." I took the offered hand. Her skin was chill
almost cold. I let go. "I'd like your permission to vis
Saltmist. I need to see the place the boys were take
from."

Dianda nodded. "How, exactly, were you planning
manage that?"

"I'd say 'scuba gear,' but I have something a litt
better." I opened my jacket, showing her the pin. "Th
Luidaeg made this for me; she says it should let me vi
your land safely. Well. Assuming we count 'capable
surviving' as safety. I guess you could still have me sh
on sight."

"The Luidaeg gave you that?" said Dianda. Her e
pression was torn, half-dubious, half-hopeful.

"More like made it for me, but yeah. She used n
blood, her blood, the blood of the local King of Cats .
it was a production. Things with her generally are."

"I . . . she said I should meet with you. She didr
mention that." Her flukes slapped the floor again b
fore she nodded. "All right. You are welcome in n
waters."

It was a ritual phrase, and that meant it carried t
weight of law. I nodded the thanks I couldn't give h
"Good. Now, I was wondering if—" I paused, eyeing t
glass doors with sudden suspicion. The fog outside r
duced visibility to mere feet. I was getting real sick
fog. "Did you hear that?"

"Hear what?"

"I'm taking that as a 'no.' " I rose, starting for the wi
"Stay where you are."

"Why?" She pushed herself back from the table.

"No, really, I—" She was already wheeling herself
my direction. I sighed. "Suit yourself."

I stepped cautiously onto the balcony, noting the gate nd three broad steps connecting it to the sidewalk be-)w. The wood had been treated with some sort of var- ish that kept it dry despite the fog, and made it easier)r me to keep my footing. There are advantages to be- ig in an establishment owned by the Undersea. Noth- ig gets wet unless they want it to.

The angle was all wrong, and the surrounding build- igs were unfamiliar. It took me a moment to realize why; was facing away from the direction my internal compass)ld me I should be facing. Somehow, the balcony was riented entirely in opposition to the rest of the build- ig. If I squinted, I could make out the word "Leaven- 'orth" on the nearest street sign. I shot a glance back t Dianda. "Leavenworth? That's a mile from where we ame in. And on the other side of the street."

She shrugged. "We like our privacy."

A lot of people like their privacy. Few like it enough) put the front and back rooms of a diner several streets)art. I was considering the geography when I heard the)und again, more clearly this time: a short, crisp snap, ke a branch breaking . . . or a crossbow bolt being slot- ∙d into place.

"Your Grace?" I took a step back. "Do you have any uards here?"

Dianda stiffened, expression registering mild alarm. Just Bill and Connor. I was trying to be subtle."

Bill and Connor were up front, which meant—issues f geography aside—they were probably distracted by uentin, the appetite that walks like a squire. "You man- ¿ed it," I said, smothering my irritation. The fog was ∙tting thicker. "Can you please stay where you are?" his time, she did as I asked. That was a small mercy . . . ∙ maybe it was just that she was starting to pick up on .e growing air of something not quite right.

My only warning before the shot was fired was an ldy in the fog to my left, a swirl of motion that could

have been natural if not for the light glinting off som
thing at its center. I hit the deck—literally—as the a
row whizzed through the space where my head ha
been a moment before, burying itself in the wall. Diane
gasped. I lunged to my feet and ran back to her, sca
ning the room.

The corners were full of fog, too thick to be natura
There were three more small snaps from the room b
hind us, as more bolts were slotted into place.

"Right," I said, and leaned over to grip the handl
of Dianda's chair. "Your Grace, I just want you to kno
that I'm really, really sorry about this."

"What?" she asked. Another snap sounded behind u
There wasn't time to explain. I started to run.

Dianda was shouting for me to let go and stop acti
like a crazy woman when we hit the balcony. I turne
the chair to face the room while I fumbled for the lat
on the gate, and her shouting got even louder, turni
frantic. I glanced up to see what she was yelling abou
and swore, redoubling my efforts to find the latch as fo
Goblins stepped out of the fog. They weren't wearii
the colors of any fiefdom I knew, but that mattered le
to me than the loaded crossbows in their hands.

The damn latch wasn't there. I kicked the gate as on
of the Goblins opened fire. Dianda shrieked and duck
to the side of her chair, letting the bolt embed itse
harmlessly in the padding. I boosted myself up and I
the gate with both feet as hard as I could. Somethi
popped inside my left knee. The gate swung open.

"Brace yourself!" I shouted, and stepped off the ed;
Going down a short flight of stairs is easy. Doing
while pulling a wheelchair full of agitated mermaid
a little harder. We thumped hard down to street-lev
and I danced rapidly backward to keep Dianda fro
overbalancing. She was clinging to the arms for dear li
barely keeping her head from knocking against the ba
of the chair.

Shouts from the balcony told me we didn't have long. I backpedaled into the middle of the street. Dianda twisted around to stare at me, face white, eyes wide.

"Hold on," I said, and grabbed the handles on her chair.

She must have realized what I was doing, because she shouted, "Are you insane?!" as I started to run, pushing her along in front of me.

Like many major streets in San Francisco, Leavenworth runs up one side of a hill and down the other. It's at an angle sharp enough to discourage all but the most dedicated walkers, and joggers regard it as one of the lesser circles of Hell. Even hampered by my knee, we picked up speed at an impressive pace. The sound of feet behind us told me our lead was getting narrower, despite momentum and gravity combining to keep us moving ever faster.

The marina stretched out at the bottom of the hill, sparkling dimly in the darkness. I only saw one way we were going to reach the water alive. I just had to hope Dianda would forgive me for the indignity. Still clinging to the right handle of the chair, I stepped to one side and sped up until I was running alongside it.

Dianda stared at me, demanding, "What are you doing? This thing doesn't have any brakes!"

I didn't have the breath left to shout. Leaning over her, I grabbed the left arm and hoisted myself onto her lap. Freed from the drag of my feet, the wheelchair started to accelerate, plunging straight down Leavenworth. Crossbow bolts zinged past. I folded my arms over Dianda's head, keeping her down, and ducked my own head as low as it would go. If we could avoid getting shot until we reached the bottom of the hill . . .

This entire escapade was breaking several rules of life in the mortal world, chief among them the injunction to never, ever go out in public without wearing a human disguise. I was still wearing my illusions. Dianda and the Goblins, on the other hand, were totally exposed. There wasn't time to worry about it. Hopefully, anyone who saw a woman riding a screaming mermaid in a wheelchair down Leavenworth at fifteen minutes to five o'clock in the morning would just think they'd had too much to drink.

We were still accelerating. Gasping, I managed to ask, "Is this a good time for that visit?" Dianda stared at me, eyes widening in understanding, before she nodded.

We were almost to the bottom of the hill when I fumbled the scale out of my pocket and shoved it into my mouth. It dissolved like spun sugar, leaving my tongue coated in a gummy-tasting film. A taxi blared by, horn blazing as we hit the dock, shooting forward. Dianda screamed again, the sound magnified by proximity to my ears, and I heard a crossbow bolt whiz by as I yanked the pin from the lining of my jacket and jammed it into the meaty part of my right thigh with all the force I could muster.

Then we hit the water, and everything went black.

Seanan McGuire

The *October Daye* Novels

"...will surely appeal to readers who enjoy my books, or those of Patrica Briggs." —*Charluine Harris*

"Well researched, sharply told, highly atmospheric and as brutal as any pulp detective tale, this promising start to a new urban fantasy series is sure to appeal to fans of Jim Butcher or Kim Harrison."—*Publishers Weekly*

ROSEMARY AND RUE
978-0-7564-0571-7
A LOCAL HABITATION
978-0-7564-0596-0
AN ARTIFICIAL NIGHT
978-0-7564-0626-4
LATE ECLIPSES
978-0-7564-0666-0

To Order Call: 1-800-788-6262
www.dawbooks.com

P.R. Frost
The Tess Noncoiré Adventures

"Frost's fantasy debut series introduces a charming protagonist, both strong and vulnerable, and her cheeky companion. An intriguing plot and a well-developed warrior sisterhood make this a good choice for fans of the urban fantasy of Tanya Huff, Jim Butcher, and Charles deLint."
—*Library Journal*

HOUNDING THE MOON
978-0-7564-0425-3
MOON IN THE MIRROR
978-0-7564-0486-4

and new in paperback:
FAERY MOON
978-0-7564-0606-6

To Order Call: 1-800-788-6262
www.dawbooks.com

Gini Koch

The Alien *Novels*

"This delightful romp has many interesting twists and turns as it glances at racism, politics, and religion en route. Darned amusing." —*Booklist* (starred review)

"Kitty's evolution from marketing manager to member of a secret government unit is amusing and interesting ...a hilarious romp in the vein of 'Men in Black' or 'Ghostbusters'." —*Voya*

ALIEN TANGO
978-0-7564-0632-5

TOUCHED BY AN ALIEN
978-0-7564-0600-4

To Order Call: 1-800-788-6262
www.dawbooks.com

Laura Resnick

The Esther Diamond Novels

"Resnick introduces a colorful cast of gangsters and their associates as she spins a witty, fast-paced mystery around her convincingly self-absorbed chorus-girl heroine. Sexy interludes raise the tension as she juggles magical assailants, her perennially distracted agent, her meddling mother, and wiseguys both friendly and threatening in a well-crafted, rollicking mystery." —*Publishers Weekly*

"Esther Diamond is the Stephanie Plum of urban fantasy! Unplug the phone and settle down for a fast and funny read!" —Mary Jo Putney

DOPPLEGANGSTER
978-0-7564-0595-3

UNSYMPATHETIC MAGIC
978-0-7564-0635-6

To Order Call: 1-800-788-6262
www.dawbooks.com

Once upon a time...

Cinderella, whose real name is Danielle
Whiteshore, did marry Prince Armand.
And their wedding was a dream come true.

But not long after the "happily ever after,"
Danielle is attacked by her stepsister Charlotte,
who suddenly has all sorts of magic to call upon.
And though Talia the martial arts master—
otherwise known as Sleeping Beauty—
comes to the rescue, Charlotte gets away.

That's when Danielle discovers a number of disturbing facts: Armand has been kidnapped; Danielle is
pregnant; and the Queen has her own Secret Service
that consists of Talia and Snow (White, of course).
Snow is an expert at mirror magic and heavy-duty
flirting. Can the princesses track down Armand and
rescue him from the clutches of some of
Fantasyland's most nefarious villains?

The Stepsister Scheme
by Jim C. Hines
978-0-7564-0532-8

"Do we look like we need to be rescued?"

DAW 130

Sherwood Smith
Inda

"A powerful beginning to a very promising series by a writer who is making her bid to be a major fantasist. By the time I finished, I was so captured by this book that it lingered for days afterward. I had lived inside these characters, inside this world, and I was unwilling to let go of it. That, I think, is the mark of a major work of fiction…you owe it to yourself to read *Inda*." —Orson Scott Card

INDA
978-0-7564-0422-2

THE FOX
978-0-7564-0483-3

KING'S SHIELD
978-0-7564-0500-7

TREASON'S SHORE
978-0-7564-0573-1 (hardcover)
978-0-7564-0634-9
(paperback)

To Order Call: 1-800-788-6262
www.dawbooks.com